Praise for Denis Hamill and *Fork in the Road*

"When you follow the career of Denis Hamill in his journalism and novels, you see the development of a powerful talent. But this is a big surprise. I expected another tough thriller. I expected another tour through the underbelly of New York. I didn't expect a love story, and I certainly didn't expect to be left wide-eyed at Denis Hamill's grasp of backstreet Dublin street talk. When you read FORK IN THE ROAD, make sure your chair is comfortable because Denis Hamill hooks you and keeps you to the end."

—Frank McCourt

"Denis Hamill writes with the observant touch of a Gaelic Ian Fleming giving an American's vivid unexpurgated look into a dramatically changed modern Ireland."

—J. P. Donleavy, author of *The Ginger Man* and *A Singular Man*

"Equal parts hilarity and heartbreak. With this unique novel, Denis Hamill has very nearly invented a new genre, the slapstick tragedy. Its astonishing heroine, Gina Furey, is as indelible as a tattoo. You may never get over her."

—Susan Dodd, author of *The Mourner's Bench* and *Mamaw*

Also by Denis Hamill

Stomping Ground
Machine
House on Fire
3 Quarters
Throwing 7's

Fork in the Road

a novel

Denis Hamill

WASHINGTON SQUARE PRESS
PUBLISHED BY POCKET BOOKS

New York   London   Toronto   Sydney   Singapore

A Washington Square Press Publication of
POCKET BOOKS, a division of Simon & Schuster, Inc.
1230 Avenue of the Americas, New York, NY 10020

Library of Congress Cataloging-in-Publication Data

Hamill, Denis.
     Fork in the road : a novel / Denis Hamill.
        p.   cm.
     ISBN 0-671-01674-1
       1. Journalists—United States—Fiction. 2. Irish Americans—
Fiction. 3. Tinkers—Fiction. 4. Dublin (Ireland)—Fiction.
I. Title.

PS3558.A4217 F67 2000
813'.54—dc21   99-059315

First Washington Square Press trade paperback printing March 2001

10 9 8 7 6 5 4 3 2 1

WASHINGTON SQUARE PRESS and colophon are registered trademarks of Simon & Schuster, Inc.

Cover design and imaging by Honi Werner from a photo by Andrea Pistolesi/TIB

Printed in the U.S.A.

*To the loving memory of my parents,
Billy Hamill and Annie Devlin, who gave
me the great gifts of Ireland and America*

*And to their grandson, Liam John Hamill,
who continues their journey*

Fork
in the
Road

EIGHTEEN MONTHS BEFORE THE BEGINNING

Fade in, thinks Colin Coyne.

INTERIOR. HOSPITAL ROOM. DAY.

My mother's death-bed scene. The room is lit in golden celestial hues from a setting sun that pours through the windows of the hospital near Little Neck Bay in Queens.

Flowers. Get-well cards. Sad-faced silent nurses checking final vitals. My father and two brothers in the hall, the old man trying to remain strong, but failing miserably, his face a crumbling mosaic.

My big brother, Jack, twenty-eight, who has an opinion on everything—speechless. My little brother, Eddie, twenty-two, trapped between being the baby in our family and the father of three babies who will never remember Granny—you can see the dry ache in his throat as he tries to swallow.

Now it's my turn alone in the room with Mom, Colin thinks. *My last turn. I close the door.*

If this were the movie of my life, this would be the pre-credit sequence, Colin thinks, in a vain attempt to turn his emotions into "art."

Before all the rest of the shit happened: before Gina, Brianna, and Seamus. Before the Oscars and the house. Before half the tinkers in

1

Ireland wagon-wheeled into my life. Before that fateful Fourth of July, there was Mom, lying in this sun-gilded room, in that bed, talking to me about my life for the last time before she died.

Mom waves me closer. At fifty-seven, her skin is remarkably wrinkle-free. Pretty. Strong. Colin imagines the cancer eating her innards like a bubbling acid spill. Her dark eyes still clear. Focused. Intelligent. She still has the safe, protective, warm life smell as she did when she used to give me baths, when she helped me with my arithmetic home-work, read me bedtime stories. Clean scents of honest toil, strong soap, home cooking, our family. Probably smelled it first when I was feeding from her breast. Now Colin notices that the life smell is mixed with the dying smell, like spoiling lamb. The smell of old people who live alone.

You can never get smells into a movie, he thinks, unless someone mentions one, or physically reacts to it. In a novel you can get the smell of baking bread and fresh fish and frying bacon. But how could I ever convey the smell of my dying mother up there on the screen?

He sees Mom wave to him.

MOM: Colin. C'mere, son.

The Irish lilt still rolling from her white dying tongue.

COLIN: Hey, Mom.

Colin realizes that if he cries she might not live long enough to see him stop. He doesn't want his mother to exit seeing him that way. So he imagines there's a camera rolling and the script specifically calls for no tears.

Stick to the script, he thinks. For this scene there's only one take. Get it right or it's wrong forever. There are no rehearsals for the death of your mother—no reshoots, no way to fix it in postproduc-tion. Be strong. Like her. No fucking way she is gonna die crying. Not Mom.

MOM: Sit on the bed where I can talk to you.

He does.

COLIN: You look good, Mom.

MOM: That's a lie and a bad one at that. Like a big piece of my life.

COLIN: You were always the truth times ten, Mom. Even when it hurt.

MOM: What's that expression you always use? Cut to the chase? Colin, love, I must tell you something I never told anyone else. You have another brother, a brother you don't even know about.

Colin is startled.

This isn't in the script. It was supposed to be a thanks-for-everything, you-were-the-greatest, see-you-at-the-pearlys, I-love-you-Mom good-bye. Colin says nothing, stares in a long silent beat.

MOM: The baby's father was a soldier. A British soldier. It was a two-week schoolgirl's silly dreamy lark when I was in Bournemouth on holiday. I was sixteen, seventeen when he was born—and not a schoolgirl anymore. I named the baby Thomas but I'm sure he was renamed, after. He would be thirty-nine, almost forty now.

COLIN: I have a forty-year-old brother? Where?

MOM: No clue. His father went off to the Congo after I learned I was pregnant. He said he would marry me when he returned. He sent me the silver bells a month after he left.

COLIN: The bells over the front door at home?

MOM: Aye. First came those lovely bells and then he came home in a box three months after that. The baby came five months later. Back in Dublin, my family was mortified that I had a baby by a dead British soldier. My father, whose people were from The North, said the only good part of the equation was that he was a dead British soldier.

Mom laughs. Coughs. Sweat breaks on her brow like a line of mismatched buttons.

COLIN: Mom, you okay?

MOM: No, I'm dying for chrissakes. Just let me finish. Back in Dublin, my mother and my aunts convinced me that I should put the wee fella up for adoption. It crushed my heart, but I surrendered. I turned my back on my instincts; I abandoned my own baby. I started dying that terrible sad day. The rest of me dies today.

She coughs again, her whole body rattling and gasping for air.

COLIN: I'll get the nurse.

MOM: Bollocks on the nurse, God forgive my language. I put my baby up and he was snatched up right away. I tried everything to find him over the years, but never saw him again. I stopped looking on his eighteenth birthday. By then he'd have been too old to ever forgive me so . . .

Another phlegmy coughing fit. Colin is silent. The death smell grows stronger than the life smell with each desperate breath. Colin reacts visibly, recoiling, as if for the camera. Anger passes over his face, anger toward his dying mother.

COLIN: How the hell could you have done it, Mom?

MOM: I'm glad you're cross. So you should be. I want you to be angry because I want you to make me two promises, so.

The sadness returns as he's reminded that she is talking to him for the very last time.

COLIN: Anything, you know that.

MOM: I know you like the ladies and the ladies sure like you and why wouldn't they, so?

He smiles, embarrassed.

COLIN: Yeah, but no marriage for me, Mom. It'd get in the way of the career. What promises, Mom?

MOM: Never walk away from a child that's yours like I did. It will kill you in installments every day of your life.

COLIN: I'm pretty careful, Mom, if you know what I mean . . .

MOM: Promise me.

COLIN: Okay, sure. I promise I'll never abandon a child of mine. What's the other one?

MOM: I knew early on you had special talent, were creative. The wee movies you used to make. The scripts you used to write in your copy books at school when you were supposed to be doing maths. The way you watched a movie and took it apart line by line, scene by scene, figure it out like a magician's trick. No, you were never meant for the civil service, the toolbox, or the suit and tie. So, no matter what happens, promise you won't abandon your talent, son. Make your movies, keep at it; you'll get your break, Colin. We had that dream together, so, promise me you won't give it up.

Colin nods, flashing back to images of Mom signing for loans she never told the old man about, to pay the tuition for NYU film school, to pay for cameras, raw film stock, film lab bills, mixing studios, lenses, lights.

She was like my producer, he thinks, *imagining it now as a voice-over. I always promised I'd dedicate my first Oscar to her. Like Spielberg did for his mother.*

COLIN: Promise, Mom.

MOM: I stashed away some money for you inside the statue of the Infant of Prague in my bedroom at home. Make the wee movie we talked about. Maybe it'll get you the big break.

He could feel the tears forming, building, the pressure of holding them back pounding at his temples.

COLIN: Now I know why you always loved the Infant of Prague— because of the baby.

More coughing, deep, rattling, the room filled with the putrefying death smell. Then silence.

COLIN: Mom?

She closes her eyes, takes two short breaths.

MOM: I'm scared. The prayers don't help. I'll miss you, Colin, so.

He leans closer.

COLIN: It's okay to let go, Mom.

The script is getting harder to follow, he thinks. *My mother is about to die and I want to cry my fucking eyes out. She takes my hand, grips it. The golden light begins to fade, the room crowding with shadows.*

COLIN: I'm here, Mom.

She doesn't answer. The grip tightens, then goes limp.

COLIN: *Mom?*

Silence. The last of the life smell begins to dissipate.

Now I can throw away the script and have myself a good fucking cry, he thinks.

Crash cut to the wake in Lloyd's on Thirty-ninth Avenue in Bayside, Queens. Dissolve to the funeral. As the coffin is lowered into Pine Lawn Cemetery, fade to black as Colin Coyne vows he'll keep the promises he made to his dying mother.

Part I

Dublin, Ireland

one

December 20

Someone is picking my pocket, he thought.

For Colin Coyne, the beginning, those first days in Dublin were indelibly suspended in time, always as immediate and vivid as a movie.

Maybe it wasn't a pickpocket, Colin thought, standing at the two-deep bar of the Shelbourne hotel, gagging down a pint of Guinness. *Maybe it was just an accident, a bump in the crowd.* He clutched the mug in his big right fist, hungover and jet-lagged after his first night on the town in Dublin.

Then he felt it again. *Right cheek of my ass,* he thought. *Under my fucking wallet.* His buttocks were sensitive from flying coach, sitting in a middle seat, sandwiched between a fat nun who'd mumbled the rosary all the way across the Atlantic and a snoring old farmer with hairy ears, who smelled like unwashed feet. Colin had squirmed for a position of comfort and wound up pinching a sciatic nerve in his right ham muscle, which now made him very sensitive to someone touching him back there.

He waited for a second touch. It didn't come. Colin shrugged, took another sip of his stout. This was Holy Hour, that terribly thirsty time in the Dublin afternoon when the regular pubs shut for an hour in supposed deference to the Angelus that peals from every

9

church spire in the city. The hotel bars were exempt from the Holy Hour rule so the afternoon barroom of the elegant four-star Shelbourne was packed. Smoky. Loud. Cross-pollinated conversations, a jumble of American, British, Irish, French, German voices, simultaneously gabbing about the always fragile peace in the long troubled North, the booming Irish economy, starvation in Africa, and the latest White House scandal.

Colin was in Ireland to research a movie he wanted to direct about a young Irish-American filmmaker from Queens, New York, who has failed miserably in every relationship with American women, and so travels to the land of his parents to find and marry a girl-just-like-the-girl-who-married-dear-old-Dad—or some half-formed horse-shit idea like that.

And while he was there, Colin was hoping his life might imitate art, maybe meet a beautiful Irish chick, a young Colleen who would jump at the chance to do the town with a promising twenty-five-year-old film director who had won all the NYU film school awards and whose most recent film short, *First Love, Last Love,* won awards at the Seattle, New York, and Hamptons film festivals. Who might even be nominated for an Oscar. Who already had an agent, and who just sold a $15,000 option on his first feature-length screenplay, *Death Dunes,* a big-budget murder mystery set in the Hamptons. Unfortunately, the studio wouldn't let Colin direct that one but he was using the option money to finance this trip to Dublin.

On the flight over, while ambling up and down the aisle to relieve his aching ass, he'd even hounded a pretty Aer Lingus flight attendant for a phone number. Finally, after the plane landed, she slipped him a phone number on a piece of paper torn from the edge of *The Irish Times.* When he called the number later in the afternoon he discovered he'd reached an animal rescue shelter. *Great sense of humor, these mickettes,* he thought. *Have to get that into my movie.*

Now he felt the hand on his ass again. Fingers deftly positioned under the bottom of his wallet. Tapping it upward. *Pickpocket,* he thought. *Aha. Drama. Let it play . . .*

Colin was determined to use the option money from his first script to finance the development of his "Irish roots" script. Maybe he'd direct this one himself. According to his agent, two independent film companies were interested in having him direct a very low-budget feature film if they liked the script. So he was in Dublin to fill his notebook with locations, customs, textures, images, anecdotes, idioms, dialogue, stories, songs, and history that could bring his embryonic idea kicking to cinematic life. . . .

There it goes again, he thought.

Now he felt his wallet moving up a half inch from the back pocket of his snug jeans. Half amused, Colin took a big gulp of his tepid stout, the black beer bucking down like medicine. *There!* A third tap on his wallet. Still he didn't react because his money was in his front pants pocket. And he wasn't sure he wanted the confrontation, a bar brawl in a foreign city: cops, jail, lawyers with white wigs, calls to the embassy. Plus he was interested in seeing how the whole incident turned out. *Maybe I'll use it in the script,* he thought.

Colin was sweaty under the heavy Irish wool sweater and Irish tweed jacket that he'd bought earlier across from Trinity College. Now the hand on his ass made another tap on the bottom of his wallet. Then another. Inch by larcenous inch, Colin felt his wallet climbing along his sensitive butt.

Finally, his amusement turned to anger. He'd shot documentaries in the slums of Brownsville, student movies in Alphabet City, transported Arriflex cameras from Washington Heights home to Queens on the subway and the Long Island Railroad at three in the morning and never once was robbed. So *I'll be fucked if I came to the land of my parents to get pickpocketed during Christmas week,* he thought. *I'll lay this asshole right out on the fuckin' floor.*

He gently placed the glass on the bar, leaving both hands free. As his wallet slowly left his pocket, Colin, without turning, quickly reached behind him and clutched the wrist of the pickpocket. A thin wrist, soft and covered in jangling bracelets and bangles, jerked abruptly in Colin's strong grip. He spun to confront the thief, fist cocked. And found himself looking down into two huge brown

eyes, adorned with long dark lashes, set into a small, lethally beautiful face. He felt himself instantly aroused.

He saw her in flashes. Jump cuts. Angles. Bright curly blond hair.
Floppy brown felt hat. A choker of pearls. Long thin neck. Tiny pearl
stud earrings. Flawless olive-tinted skin. *Cheekbones like the Jersey
Palisades,* he thought. Full lips twisted into a wet red snarl. White
gleaming teeth gnashing. *A fucking man-eating plant,* he thought.
More Mediterranean than Irish. More young Brigitte Bardot in . . .
And God Created Woman *than Maureen O'Hara in* The Quiet Man.
Sexy as mortal sin.

His wallet dropped from her right hand. Colin bent at the knees
to pick it up, still clutching the stunning young woman by the wrist,
never breaking contact with her big angry eyes. He waved the wallet
in her face, cleared his throat, smiled.

"Buy you a drink?" he whispered.

"Fuck off, Yank!" she shouted in a voice twice her size, which
was no more than five foot three, bringing the entire barroom to a
gawking hush. "If yeh touch me bum again I'll have yeh charged, I
will! All yous Yanks is the same. But in Ireland there's laws about
touching up a woman's privates in public. The cheek of yeh, yeh
pig's melt, offering me money for a durty visit to yeh room."

Colin panned the room, saw dozens of eyes on him as he
gripped the small beautiful woman by the wrist and his wallet in his
other hand, realizing he looked like a propositioning john.

"Jesus, you're gorgeous," Colin said, smiling.

"And you're a right swine, you are," she said. "Good Irish women
don't need your durty Yank dollars."

She wrenched free of his firm grip, the recoil sending her reeling
backward and crashing into a small round cocktail table, which
overturned, spilling pints of Guinness, glasses of whiskey, club
sodas, and smoldering ashtrays onto the laps of the five incredulous
customers who sat on the tiny stools around it. In the commotion,
Colin noticed a thick buff-colored envelope drop from the pickpocket's coat. Colin stepped on it with his cowboy boot. As the
customers gasped and cursed, Colin bent to help the pickpocket
to her feet. Her hat had fallen off and now Colin could see more

of her fiercely attractive face and the full mane of blond ringlets.

"Go way outta dat, you moldy eejit!" she shouted, slapping away Colin's hand and pushing herself to her feet.

The hotel manager, a thin man in an oversized suit with purple spider veins crisscrossing his bony cheeks, wedged his way through the transfixed crowd. Customers murmured to him as he passed.

"Yank was propositioning the young wan, sir," said the barman.

"Very sorry, madame . . . shall I call a guard?" the manager asked, glaring at Colin, the veins in his face darkening with anger.

"I can handle one lousy wanker Yank meself," the pickpocket boasted, brushing ashes from her long wool coat and adjusting the floppy hat back onto her head. She proudly made her way through the crowd, bumping into people as she strode. Colin closely watched her hands as she moved, saw them darting in and out of coat pockets like ferrets into holes until she located at least one billfold, which disappeared professionally up the sleeve of her coat as if on a spring. She turned once to look at Colin, a devilish glare in her eyes, and then she hurried away in a confident flourish, her floppy hat bouncing across the crowded lobby.

"Hey!" Colin shouted.

She raised the index and middle finger of her right hand in a V and made upward thrusts as she pranced on.

Colin picked up the buff-colored envelope from under his boot.

"I'm afraid we're going to have to ask you to leave, sir," the manager said as Colin slid the envelope into his jacket pocket.

"I'm a guest here, pal," Colin said, looking at the floppy hat bobbing for the street exit.

"And we'd like you to check out altogether."

"Fine, then ring up my fucking bill," Colin said.

Colin hurried through the afternoon crowd, trying to catch up with the pickpocket. He rushed out to the street facing the wide winter-bare park called St. Stephen's Green and looked to his left down Baggot Street toward the black-and-white sign of O'Donoghue's pub, where he'd drunk himself sick the night before listening to traditional Irish folk music. Then he looked to his right, up St. Stephen's

Green North toward the top of Grafton Street, one of the city's busiest shopping hubs. He didn't see her anywhere. *Gotta find her,* he thought, as he felt himself growing aroused. *Makes no sense, but I gotta find this one. She's perfect fucking casting. Like Selznick finding the real Scarlett O'Hara, except this time she found ME!*

Then he saw her, across the street. She was bouncing up the steps of a moving double-decker bus crammed with wool- and tweed-wrapped bodies. She came into view in the rear window as the crowded bus groaned away from the curb and sped along the side of the park. Colin fiddled with his cock as it grew along his thigh, straightening it. When the bus stopped for a red light, Colin bolted through the moving traffic. He looked right. Brakes slammed from his left. Tires screeched. Horns honked madly at him. "Feckin' eejit," someone shouted. Colin sprinted after the departing bus along the park side—his erection slowing him down—waving the buff-colored envelope the lady pickpocket dropped in the bar. He glimpsed her momentarily in the steamy window of the bus. *Is she looking at me? Please, look at me, babe.* He paused, arms akimbo. *Look what you're doing to me.* The lady pickpocket fiddled with her golden hair in her own reflection in the windowpane. She didn't notice Colin. He was a panting flailing twenty yards from the rear of the idling bus when the light changed green. *No! Shiiiit!* The bus turned wickedly left, rattling off into the labyrinthine city.

Colin stood in the middle of the busy street, gulping big breaths, horns blaring at him, adjusting himself as he looked down at the envelope in his hand.

"Arsehole," shouted the driver of an *Irish Independent* delivery truck that swerved madly around him.

You're right, pal, Colin thought. *I must be an asshole. Fuck logic and common sense. Something tells me that crazy broad is meant for me, for my movie. I gotta find her. She found me; now I gotta find her. As they say in Hollywood, she was born for the part.*

two
___

Colin snapped his American Express card on top of the Shelbourne hotel bill. Both of his credit cards were "second cards" his older brother, Jack, got for him. Colin's credit was still a mess from overdue student loans and financing student films.

A line of people were waiting to check in. The smoldering manager with the veiny face stood watching the transaction as the clerk ran the bill through the credit-card machine. The clerk presented the bill for Colin to sign, which he did with an exaggerated Ed Norton flourish.

"Thanks, pal," Colin said, loud enough for the arriving guests to hear. "But you really should do something about the *rats* in the rooms. They woke me up rattling all over my room-service dishes this morning. One of them was chewing on a rasher."

"Don't mind him," the agitated manager said to the startled guests as Colin walked past him.

The guidebook recommended the Temple Bar Hotel in the newly bohemianized section of the city, just ten minutes away.

"Fuck the Shelbourne anyway," the cabby said on the ride across town. "Temple Bar is the liveliest part of town for a young fella like yerself. At night the streets is only black with young wans, university girls, and tourists, droppin' their knickers like tarts but for feckin' free. I was born forty year too soon, me. In my day, getting' a bit a hole was like feckin' safecrackin'. Today it's like pickin' daisies."

Colin checked into the Temple Bar Hotel and unpacked quickly in his modern room, which was equipped with a fax machine, direct-dial phone, color TV, and VCR. Pulling on a pair of gray sweats and Air Jordans, he loaded a fresh ninety-minute microcassette into a three-by-two-inch tape recorder that clipped onto his waistband. Then he hit the hotel gym and bench-pressed 220 pounds on the Nautilus for four invigorating, sweaty sets of twelve. Then he curled with sixty-pound dumbbells, his arms jumping to life, groaned through four sets of fifty on the abdominal crunch machine, and pedaled the stationary bike at level seven for thirty minutes, paging through *The Irish Times*. He read a story about the lingering poverty that festered in the belly of the healthy economy called the Celtic Tiger. Unemployment in Dublin, which had been at about twenty percent in the early 1990s, was down to eight percent. But in neighborhoods like Ballymun, Ballytara, the Docklands, where illiteracy in this computer age of the new century had made unemployment rates climb to forty percent, the rate in some pockets was as high as ninety percent, with work-minded people subsisting on the dole for several years.

He lifted the tape recorder to his mouth, hitting record.

"Poverty always looks great on film," he mumbled into the small microphone, his breathing fast and hard. "Whether it's De Sica's *Bicycle Thief* or Singleton's *Boyz N the Hood*. The camera loves poverty. Especially juxtaposed with wealth. Like this new money in Ireland. Maybe make the pickpocket a chick from the slums who robs from rich tourists in the four-star hotels and the guy character falls in love with her. That's a start. Call the guy character, what? Kieran? Maybe. Yeah, *Kieran*. What Dad wanted to call me before Mom insisted on Colin. Kieran the naive Yank falls in love with the mickette who picks his pocket. But who the fuck is she? What's her name? What's her back story?"

Colin realized that the faster he pedaled, the louder he spoke. He clipped the recorder back on his waistband, looking around the gym. Suety businessmen working off bacon and eggs, butter and bread, cheese and beef. One attractive woman in her thirties, dressed in spandex, with the thong of her leotard up the crack of her ass, drilled her lean body in an aerobic seizure. Colin caught her eye. They exchanged polite smiles. *Nah,* he thought. *Gotta find the pickpocket chick.*

Putting the recorder in his locker, Colin ended the workout with a steam and sauna and shower, same routine he did four times a week in the neighborhood gym back home in Queens. But nothing could get the girl with the floppy hat out of his mind.

That night, he pub-crawled through the section called Temple

Bar, tape recorder and notebook and pen in his right jacket pocket. In his left-hand pocket, he carried a three-inch compact Olympus Stylus Zoom 140 35-millimeter camera, fully loaded, equipped with zoom lens. He moved down the cold cobbled streets, reminiscent of Greenwich Village in the 1960s and 1970s, stopping occasionally to peer through the viewfinder of the camera, then walking slowly with it at his eye, simulating a wide dolly shot. He shot stills with available light. Frosted pub windows. Shadowy doorways. A wary cop on patrol. A biker roaring down a side alley.

The packed pubs had names like Bad Bob's, the Garage Bar, the Bad Ass Cafe. Shivering young men stood in tight knots in old doorways holding pints of Guinness, smoking cigarettes and clumsily rolled joints of weed, chatting up pretty young women dressed in the best suggestive fashions of Paris and London.

Colin entered Bad Bob's, blinking, noticing the change in light from the moon- and neon-lit street to the incandescent fog of the crowded smoky pub. He envisioned the claustrophobic barroom in a medium shot, then a two-shot. As he struck up an idle conversation with a patron, he tried to get the attention of the overworked publican. Although he didn't smoke, Colin took out a pack of Marlboros he'd bought duty-free in JFK. He'd been told the smokes would be a good icebreaker in Dublin pubs, and they were.

"Always this crowded?" he asked a full-bearded guy near the bar, offering a cigarette.

"Only when it's feckin' opened," the patron said, taking the smoke.

"What're you drinkin'?" Colin asked.

"Anything feckin' damp."

Colin was listening for language, slang, attitudes, idioms of this young, hip, cosmopolitan Dublin he'd heard so much about, this town that had erupted from a quaint provincial backwater into a bubbling European capital. The problems of the big cities all over the world had not escaped Dublin, including a growing drug problem and the psychotic violence that comes with it. He'd read about one British yuppie who'd come to Dublin to have a bachelor party in Temple Bar and wound up beaten to death in a drunken melee. It had nothing to do with his being British, the papers said. It had everything to do with drugs and alcohol. *And, probably, a woman,* Colin thought.

Colin wanted to know all about this part of the new Dublin. He wanted all of that in his movie.

Some of the Dubs—as he quickly learned natives called themselves—found him amusing. A naive young Yank taking pictures and asking asinine questions about a movie he planned to direct about their city. Others were annoyed, even hostile, especially when he asked them to repeat themselves while he recorded or jotted down their barside banter, their slang and colloquialisms.

One surly drunk asked, "Do we look like feckin' citizens of the Planet of the Apes, mate?"

In every smoky pub, Colin scanned the crowd, looking for a golden-haired lady in a floppy brown hat. He watched the front doors, hoping she'd walk in. She didn't.

After shouting "Last call," a Garage Bar barman whom Colin had tipped with a ten-pound note leaned over and suggested that Colin check out a club on Grafton Street called Lillie's Bordello.

"All dem filmmakery and actory poofters hangs out in that kip after hours, with your basic aging rock-star junkies and their young groupie mots, who should be avoided like the feckin' plague because they carry it, with a capital feckin' A," the barman says. "Oh, and by the feckin' way, mind yeh, thanks for the tip. Now here's one from me to you for nothin', righ.' There's no need to tip barmen in Dublin. Only dumb Yanks do that."

Colin thanked him and walked across James Street and up Grafton Street, passing the late-night crowd of buskers and change moochers, newly paired drunken lovers and patrolling guards. He was high, feeling a loose-shouldered boozy buzz. After asking directions twice, he found Lillie's Bordello, but when he tried to get in, a stringy-haired bouncer with teeth like stalactites told him he had to be a member with a special key.

"I make movies in New York," Colin explained.

"Your name wouldn't be Woody bleedin' Allen by any chance, now?" the bouncer asked, giggling with three fellow bouncers.

I could break your fucking nose with one short right hand, Colin thought. But there were four of them so he said nothing.

Colin walked back toward the Temple Bar Hotel, deflated. At the foot of Grafton Street, he passed the statue of Molly Malone, the fishmonger of legend and song. He hummed a few bars, the way his mother used to when she was ironing on rainy days in Queens. The pretty broad Irish face on the statue didn't remotely resemble the chiseled Romanesque beauty of the blond girl in the floppy hat.

Colin entered the hotel bar and sipped two after-hours pints of stout. He chatted with a tall, beautiful, angry blond girl from Amsterdam named Deke who was drinking straight gin shooters like a guy. She was in Dublin on a modeling shoot.

She wore a clinging black minidress with high leather boots. When she asked, he told her why he was there. She said, "Someday I would like very much to be an actress. To show *him.*"

"Him who?"

"Him history," she said, gulping a fourth shot of Cork gin.

"Too bad."

"Are you married?" she asked.

"Nope."

"Lying so you can get laid on the side?"

"Nope."

"Girlfriend?"

"No one steady."

"Are you going to try to fuck me?"

He gagged on his last sip of stout. "You want me to?"

She looked him in the eyes and turned and walked to the ladies' room. He took a sip of beer and she returned within forty-five seconds.

She strode back, her long bare legs, trained on a catwalk, just wobbly enough to make her seem scoreable. She sidled up to him at the bar and reached for his hand, guiding it beneath the bartop. He opened his hand and she placed something soft and silky in his palm. He looked down and saw her royal-blue satin panties in his hand.

"Will you hold these for me until after breakfast?" she asked.

He balled them in his hand, instinctively smelling them. *The three Ps,* he thought. *Perfume, pussy, and permission. This is like already getting laid without getting laid yet.* He slid the panties in his jacket pocket, next to his camera. He loved Deke's Dutch accent and told her she was too beautiful to drink so hard. She defiantly bought Colin a pint and herself a double gin. She took a cell phone from her small purse and dialed a long series of numbers. "Excuse me," she said. She half turned, holding the phone to her ear at the busy bar, which was crowded with guests who were used to later drinking hours than the 11:00 P.M. pub-closing time in Dublin. Finally, she spoke into the phone: "Fuck you both."

A few heads turned to see this statuesque blond, half bombed and angry. They turned away. She folded the phone, downed the gin, and said, "I would like very much to show you my portfolio, Colin."

Colin sensed a World Series vengeance fuck in the works, but all he could think of was the pickpocket who robbed a piece of his imagination. *Thieves and drunks,* he thought. *Where're the red-haired Colleens from the Aer Lingus and Irish Spring commercials?*

"I'm not actually casting or anything," he said.

"Please," she said, flicking a sad smile, taking his hand, and leading him toward the elevators.

In her room, Deke sat close to him on the edge of the bed, drinking from a minibar bottle of gin, the smell of the booze mixing with her expensive perfume. She showed him photos of herself in European ads with her hair piled high, cut short, in bikinis, in lingerie, in tight jeans. *Hot,* he thought. *But smashed. Mixed up. Easy score. But it would be like fucking a retard.*

"The camera loves you," he said.

"My boyfriend tells me the same thing," she said, standing and taking a big gulp of her drink. "He was also telling my roommate the same thing at the same time he was fucking her. Last month, I came home early from a Paris shoot to the apartment in Amsterdam I share with my best friend and the two of them were in the shower together. I got fucked out of a boyfriend and a roommate."

"Sorry to hear about that," Colin said.

She stood, wobbled, then pulled the short black dress over her head in a single audacious flourish. No undies. *Real blonde,* he thought. *Boots, earrings, and perfume. My favorite outfit on a chick.*

"This is me naked," she said, turning and then strutting as if on a runway. *Legs and ass like a giraffe,* he thought. *Small real titties. Flat belly. Two-mile neck. They keep building jails because of broads like this.*

"Fuck me, Colin," she said.

Bombed or not, no fuckin' way I'm saying no to this, he thought as she pushed him on the bed, yanking his belt, unzipping him, her mouth warm.

"I'll do whatever you want," she said, the words like a threat. "Fuck me. Fuck *him!*"

She's using me to fuck her boyfriend, he thought. *A monster vengeance fuck. Double Dutch.*

He went flaccid as quickly as she'd made him erect. He urged her off him, and sat on the edge of the bed, zipping up.

"What's wrong?" she asked, desperate, defeated.

"One too many people in the bed, Deke," he said.

She sobbed, drank more gin. "I'm a loser," she said.

"You're just drunk. You can have any guy. Forget this asshole."

"He's fucking my friend right now," she said, collapsing onto the mattress, pulling a pillow between her legs. Colin kissed the top of her head, sat sipping his Guinness, silently staring at her, the long legs and the bare ass. He imagined the blond pickpocket naked. It began stirring him again. Within five minutes, Deke passed out, the minibar bottle of gin in her hand. He took the little bottle, placed it on the night table, pulled a blanket over her naked body, and went up to his own room.

He picked up the thick sealed envelope the pickpocket dropped at the Shelbourne hotel lounge. Colin felt uneasy about opening it. *Oh, what the hell,* he thought. *This is a chick who tried to rob me. And I want to find her.* He hesitated one last time before opening the envelope, but then finally tore off the edge. He removed an official-looking booklet with a green cardboard cover emblazoned with Gaelic writing and the bureaucratic Harp seal of the Republic of Ireland.

Colin leafed through it, found her name: Gina Furey, age twenty-one. "Gina Furey," he said aloud, his tongue and lips exploring the syllables. *Gi-na Fur-ey.* Her signature was an almost childish, spidery scrawl. There was an address in Ballytara. No phone number. Ballytara was one of the poor neighborhoods *The Irish Times* said had been bypassed by the Celtic Tiger.

He undressed, got under the sheets. As he lay on the pillow, Colin repeated her name.

He serviced himself as he imagined Gina Furey offering him her panties in a crowded pub.

"Gina Furey," he whispered when he was done. "Gina Furey, Gina Furey, Gina Furey."

December 21

In the morning, he glanced at the digital clock radio as he walked naked from the shower—7:17. A dull gray morning brooded behind the chocolate-brown drapes. Rain pecked at the windows. He heard a knock at the door, wrapped a towel around his waist, and let in a young Pakistani room-service waiter. He'd learned that Irish kids won't work for hotel wages anymore. They were all into computers. Or drugs. He took a five-pound note from his wallet on the night table, choked with funny-looking money. The kid nodded and left, silently, as if the tip stunk.

Colin put his wallet down and thought of Gina Furey trying to steal it. His notebook was on the floor beside the bed, with lines of dialogue from various pubs and a sketch of the scene with Deke, written as though it happened with the pickpocket, scribbled into a fat, horny paragraph.

He pulled on a pair of Jockey shorts and looked again at the booklet he'd found in the buff-colored envelope. Gina's address— 378 Whiterock Road, Ballytara.

He found Ballytara on the guidebook map, on the outskirts of the city. Next to a cemetery. There were no sightseeing notations on the map, suggesting it was a part of Dublin the tourist board would rather you didn't see.

Colin was leery of going to Gina's home in case she had a crazy jealous husband. He held the book under the lamp. The English translations under the Irish lettering told him it was a dole book. *A fucking welfare case,* he thought. Furthermore, the chart indicated that Gina Furey was due to sign for her money this very morning, four days before Christmas.

Colin attempted to eat the rashers and eggs, fried tomatoes and buttered toast. But after two pieces of fatty bacon, his stomach was a swamp of grease floating atop a dark pool of sour Guinness. He dropped the fork and dressed in jeans, polished black cowboy boots, a hooded sweatshirt, and leather bomber jacket and hurried out into the cold and rainy Dublin morning. He hailed a blue taxi and took it to the address of the dole office on the corner of a small lane closed to automobile traffic just off Upper O'Connell Street.

The dole office was located on the first floor of a foreboding four-story government building built of gray prison granite. Colin reached into his left jacket pocket for his small Olympus camera, and realized that Deke's panties were still in his pocket. He left them there and fixed the camera viewfinder to his right eye, framing the face of the rain-blotched old building. He clicked a shot. Then he panned and clicked several more shots: *The wet cobblestone street is like a set from a nineteenth-century period movie,* he thought. *Built long before the automobile, two horse asses wide, busy with women pushing prams and umbrella-shielded men in expensive English suits rushing through the morning Dublin downpour.*

Colin found a twelve-table cafe diagonally across the street from the dole office near Parnell Square. As 9:00 A.M. approached, the crowded cafe emptied as if a bomb scare had been phoned in, businessmen and secretaries taking final gulps of tea and coffee and then splashing off to punch the dreaded clock. Colin grabbed a seat in a window booth. A pretty Asian waitress approached, nodded, said nothing. "Mornin'," Colin said and asked for a coffee. She nodded again and brought the coffee with another silent nod. *Cute but probably can't speak much English,* he thought as he sat watching a newly arriving parade of puffy-eyed women pushing prams, most cupping smoldering cigarettes from the rain. They converged from different directions on the drab government building. Most of them were clutching dole books like the one in Colin's hand. Many of these women were not yet out of their teens, some with as many as three kids under the age of five, most of them furiously smoking in the cold wet morning.

The women joined a loose line that snaked around the corner. Colin lifted his camera and slowly panned, zoomed, and clicked on details in the line of women: *cigarettes. Swollen bellies. Apple-cheeked kids with snot-runny noses. Like the soup kitchens and homeless shelters in New York,* he thought. Most of the women were holding umbrellas, some wore hooded jackets, others just let the rain fall on bare heads. Colin zoomed in on three middle-aged women among the young mothers. They clutched infant children and barked at others, some as old as twelve. Even these older women were heavy with the sagging starchy weight of late-life pregnancies. Colin was astonished that in a country with socialized medicine, so many of these women had badly neglected or missing teeth, amazed that in a nation with such a high literacy rate so many still insisted on killing themselves with cigarettes. *Don't they read the papers,* he wondered, *or the cigarette packs? Or listen to doctors? Even fucking witch doctors tell you not to smoke.*

He sipped his coffee, scribbling impressions in his notebook: *well-dressed Christmas shoppers filing into Clery's department store. Big-shouldered cops on pickpocket patrol. Hooky-playing teenagers looking for scams. Salvation Army foot soldiers carrying holiday collection buckets.*

They all passed the frosted, rain-beaded window of the cafe. And then he saw *her.*

"Are yeh havin' another wee bit of coffee, sir?" asked the Asian waitress. Colin looked up, startled, hearing the Dublin accent coming from a smiling Chinese girl. For the first time, he noticed she was dressed in tight jeans and a Chicago Bulls sweatshirt.

"No, thanks," he said.

"No problem," she said. He watched her walk back toward the counter, the lustrous black hair reflecting the overhead lights. She glanced back at him. He nodded.

He lifted his camera and looked back through the rain-streaked window at Gina Furey.

Through the zoom lens, Colin could see that Gina was pushing a hooded stroller that held a red-haired, red-cheeked little girl. The kid was no older than two. Colin's heart sank. *Is that her kid? Is she married?*

With her cheeks rouged with winter cold, expensive gold earrings swaying, rings on every finger, gold bracelets jangling from both wrists, golden chains around her neck, Gina looked more youthful, energetic, and affluent than the rest of the women on line. Her short, shapely body was vacuum-packed into super-tight jeans, her pants legs stuffed into knee-high burgundy leather boots. She clutched at the buckle of a waist-length burgundy leather jacket. Her blond curls fell like a veil down the nape of her neck. Rain beaded on the floppy brim of her brown vinyl hat.

Colin watched her in close-up through the zoom lens, occasionally widening the angle to two-shots and three-shots as she shoved and cracked-wise in dumb show with some of her pals. Colin clicked a series of frames, imagining them as jump cuts: *Gina laughs. Gina lights a smoke. Gina gives a friend the upended double-digit fingers. Another friend admiringly touches one of Gina's earrings. Gina slaps away her hand and balls a bejeweled fist. Her baby drops a pacifier to the wet gutter. Gina picks it up, sucks the nipple clean, jams it back into the baby's mouth, puffs her cigarette.*

She's a regular here, Colin thinks, *a fucking welfare mother wearing $500 boots and a $1,000 jacket. Gold and jewels. Baby carriage probably made by Rolls. Even her perfect little ass is like some priceless stolen art treasure, a Michelangelo marble ass. Belongs locked in a fucking vault. Good living, this pickpocketing racket—nice nonwork if you can find it. So what the fuck am I doing here watching her? This little Chinese waitress is pretty, works hard, sober. She's probably a college student—smart. Chase her. Order another coffee from her, rap to her, ask her to dinner. Instead I'm peep-tomming a welfare thief through my location-scouting camera. Am I losing my fucking marbles?*

He scribbled notes. Then, as the doors to the dole office finally opened at 9:15 A.M. sharp, the line began moving at a steady pace. Through the camera lens, Colin watched: *Gina Furey crushes a smoke under her boot. Gina Furey whispers to a friend. Gina Furey belly laughs. Gina Furey acts out a story.*

It's like an animated ballet, he thought, *as graceful as a performance on a stage. Starring Gina Furey.*

Now Colin realized why he was here, why he found her so intriguing. Beyond the obvious horn-ball pursuit, past her looks—the golden hair, the big brown eyes, the lush red mouth—Gina Furey was a natural-born actress. *Gina Furey is a woman whose life seems to be one long performance,* he thought. *She pretends to be one person while living as another. She dresses in costumes. Her moves are choreographed. Her timing is rehearsed. Her head is crammed with prepared lines like the ones she used to make me look like the bad guy in the Shelbourne hotel bar. She robs from the rich and keeps it. And then goes home to her life as a mother. And probably a wife. And signs for the dole. She's an actress who is also the character she plays. At some point in her life,* Colin imagined, *the woman became the mask she created for herself.*

For Gina Furey, the world really is a stage, he thought. *I'd love to make a movie about her. Have my character, Kieran, fall in love with her in spite of his better judgement. But she belongs to some other guy—the father of the baby, some lazy, rotten-toothed-stringy-haired-unwashed-mick-prick like the wise-mouthed dirty cocksucker of a bouncer last night outside Lillie's Bordello. Some grungy asshole who lies on his stout-farting ass all day while he sends the pretty wife out to rob and steal and sign for the fucking dole before she rushes home to make him dinner and empty his smelly ballbag. Kieran has to find a way to win her heart, to take her away from all of that. There's his crisis, the hurdle, the double arc in the characters. It's perfect.*

Colin took a deep breath, tapping the dole book against the palm of his left hand, and trying to decide if he should approach Gina. Should he walk right across the street, in front of this regiment of down-on-their-luck women? *Why not?* He stood up, gathering his balls for the confrontation.

Suddenly, Gina was engulfed by three women. Colin lifted the camera, zoomed in on the scene. *Obviously they're close friends or relatives,* Colin thought. *Each older than Gina.* The oldest looked about thirty, tall and big-busted, pretty in a careless, neglected way.

The middle one looked to be in her late twenties, with a beautiful, round, pleasant face, but clearly losing the battle with fat, wearing loose clothes as camouflage. The youngest, at least twenty-five, was dressed in gaudy, funky clothes, a lemon-yellow skirt too short and bright for winter, her breasts bulging through a skin-tight blue suede jacket, sporting thick purple lipstick and heavy mascara.

If Gina comes from their world, Colin thought, *she deals with struggle a lot better than they do.*

The women now stood to the side, exchanging kisses, each making a fuss over one another's children. In a tight wedge, they pushed their way to the front of the line and entered the building. None of the others on line dared utter a word of protest.

Colin lowered his camera and signaled to the Chinese waitress for more coffee. She came over and filled his cup.

"Are yeh a spy, a journalist, or a jealous husband?" she asked.

"I'm a filmmaker," he said, hoping she'd be impressed. "Researching a screenplay . . ."

"Och, Jayz, not another one of dem," she said, waving a dismissive hand. "Every chancer and his granny in Dublin dese days is either writin' a fil-im script or makin' a movie. Every barman, butcher, postman, waiter, waitress, and shite-shoveler thinks he's Steven Spielberg."

"Sorry."

She walked off, disappointed. Colin sipped his coffee and scribbled notes. He watched the front door of the dole building, and then, as his coffee cup emptied, in a series of dissolves, he saw the rain slow to a stop. A dull sun pulsed behind the gray clouds.

After thirteen minutes, Gina Furey reappeared, alone. She pushed her pram up the wet cobblestone street under the zinc sky, passing ogling young motorcyclists and middle-aged businessmen who turned to watch her. Colin left three pounds on the table and hurried from the cafe. He donned a pair of dark Ray-Ban sunglasses and yanked up the hood on his sweatshirt. He followed her at a half-block distance, watching her walk in a hypnotic, sexy gait toward the city center, her tight hips swinging and jerking like a teenager's on a dance floor. "She walks like a woman with a song in her head," he whispered into his tape recorder.

Instead of approaching her with her dole book, Colin chose to follow her, to watch her in her element, with his eyes as an imaginary camera. Occasionally, he lowered his sunglasses and lifted the still camera, focusing on her, as if tracking her through the cobblestone side streets of Dublin city, trailing her on her morning rounds. He snapped shots of her along the meandering way in locations he might want to use in the script and movie.

He dogged Gina Furey down Parnell Street, where she entered a modern Bank of Ireland branch, with bulletproof plexiglass teller cages. Through a barred street window, Colin watched with the zoom lens as Gina took her dole check to a special counter, signed it, and grabbed the cash. She hurried out, pushing the pram more aggressively. *A new song in her head,* Colin thought. *Up-tempo.*

Colin followed her into Moore Street, a raucous outdoor Casbah of flowers and fruit and fishmongers, most of them leather-faced women, warming themselves over barrel fires, dressed in grimy overcoats and Wellington rubber boots. He couldn't understand the spiels of the hawkers, but the scores of Irish housewives did, as they shopped for last-minute Christmas provisions.

Gina seemed to know everyone. She haggled amiably over the price of vegetables and bread with a cross-eyed, matted-haired young woman, as if debating over every last penny. She hung the plastic bag of groceries from the handle of her pram, then moved on to the next stall, where she kissed a wizened old woman wearing a head scarf and gloves with the fingers cut out.

Colin stood behind a garbage dumpster piled high with cardboard boxes and wooden crates that stunk of wet, composting produce and rotting flowers. He leaned against a light pole, lowered his sunglasses, and put the camera to his right eye.

With the bustling Moore Street in the background of the composition, Colin focused on Gina as she offered the old woman a cigarette, bit one out of the pack of Dunhills for herself, tore off the filter, and lit both cigarettes with a disposable lighter. The old woman lifted a big silver thermos and poured hot steaming tea—already beige with milk—into two styrofoam cups. She topped each cup with a shot of Jameson Irish whiskey and handed one to Gina. They both sipped the whiskey-tea, smoked, chatted, and laughed as Gina purchased a bag of green apples, polishing one on her jeans and taking a big bite before handing it to the red-haired girl in the pram. As the kid gnawed the apple, the two women studied the leaves at the bottoms of their cups, and the old woman pointed at Gina, pantomiming a swollen pregnant belly and the rocking of a newborn infant. Colin could see Gina recoil in horror and then laugh. She jovially shoved the old woman, and Colin could hear Gina shout above the din of Moore Street, "Feck off outta dat!" Then she stared into her own tea leaves and looked up and shook her jeweled fist at the heavens as the old woman rocked an imaginary infant.

Gina said good-bye and approached a swarthy Pakistani hawker who was using paper towels to dry the rain-spattered luggage and handbags spread in a sidewalk display in front of his narrow storefront. Leather and canvas bags hung on high racks. Colin walked on the opposite side of the street, browsing at the various stalls, the hood of his sweatshirt pulled over his head, sunglasses shielding his eyes. He paused at a stall of used paperback books, thumbing through an illustrated copy of *The Crock of Gold* by James Stevens, watching closely as Gina bought a small change purse from the Pakistani across the street. Then, in a calculated afterthought, Gina pointed to a specific clutch bag mounted on the highest rack of his display. The Pakistani man climbed up on a step stool, turning his back to Gina, and as he did, she gingerly grabbed two large canvas shoulder bags, stuffed one inside the other, and draped the outer one over a handle of her pram. She placed herself in front of the pram to conceal the canvas bag. When the Pakistani came down off the stool to show her the leather clutch bag, Gina examined it, checked the price tag, and Colin heard her fly into a loud rage, in the same piercing voice that she'd used on Colin in the Shelbourne hotel.

"Ten quid!" she bellowed. "Ask me feckin' arse, yeh durty Arab! A chiselin' robber, yeh are."

She tossed the bag onto the wet sidewalk a few feet from the storefront and the furious Pakistani shouted at her as he ran to retrieve the bag, waving his arms. "Go away, crazy lady. Go away!"

Gina stormed off, the canvas bag dangling from her pram.

She rumbled out of Moore Street, Colin following her, then pranced up Henry Street, past the souvenir shops and camera stores, turning the heads of a clump of old white-haired men wearing flat tweed caps waiting to get into a bookie shop, and a publican who was opening the corrugated gate of a touristy pub. Colin trailed her back to the broad frenzied expanse of O'Connell Street. Camera-laden tourists strolled by Gina on the historic street that was now an unsightly, garish plastic-and-neon invasion of arcades and American fast-food joints—McDonald's, Kentucky Fried Chicken, Wendy's, Pizza Hut. She moved down the boulevard, which the guidebook said was the widest street in the world, past the General Post Office, where the legendary 1916 Easter Rising was fought. Colin paused to glance at the bullet holes still visible in the old stone walls as Gina passed the patriotic statues of Charles Stewart Parnell, Father Theobald Mathew, and Daniel O'Connell.

This chick moves past history as though it never happened until she showed up, Colin thought. *What a fuckin' great character for a movie. She knows only one age—her own. She's a twenty-one-year-old twenty-first-century fox. All cocksureness, cunning, and con. A chick who struts across the stage of her life brandishing her woman-hood like a pair of balls. A babe with balls who has swaggered from one century into the next as though she built the fucking doorway. This broad is my movie. A naive Yank named Kieran comes to the land of his parents, the land of poets and saints, and falls in love with a crazy broad when she picks his pocket. This is what I've been looking for.*

Like a tourist, he fixed the camera to his eye and watched men of every age spin on their heels as Gina passed, catching a parting look at her. Christmas music played softly from Clery's, and shoppers scrambled toward the Ilac Center, the Irish Life Center, and Dunne's Stores on the side streets. Tourists lugging plastic bags of gifts waved madly for taxis at the curbsides. A skinny Father Christmas who rang his bell in front of a store called Toyland stopped ringing as Gina passed. He took a deep sigh and said, "Ho-ho-ho-ly shite."

Colin laughed and tagged behind Gina to O'Connell Bridge, which led over the Liffey River toward middle-class Grafton Street.

On the bridge, he watched Gina stop in front of a beggar girl in her late teens, sitting on a dirty wool patchwork quilt, a sobbing ruddy-faced, snot-caked baby in one arm, her black-nailed right hand held out, pleading for alms. Gina suddenly erupted. She smacked the woman on the back of the head, making citizens and tourists back away, a few gasping. Gina then took the beggar girl by the right ear, yanking her to her feet. She lifted the baby from her arms, forcing the beggar girl to collect her blanket and assorted change. Gina grabbed the dirty blanket from the beggar girl and tightly wrapped it around the baby. The respectable Dubliners pretended not to see as Gina Furey took a hankie from her own pocket, moistened it with her tongue, and scoured the baby's face. She tore a piece of bread from a loaf she'd bought on Moore Street and handed it to the baby, who was now wailing with hunger, cold, and fright. The baby jammed the bread into its teething mouth and greedily gnawed it. The wailing instantly ceased. Gina handed the wrapped baby back to the beggar girl and herded her in front of her along the quays of the River Liffey to the busy bus stop at Eden Quay. Colin watched from the bridge entrance as Gina waited with the beggar girl for the desired bus. Gina verbally chastised the beggar girl, waving her finger in her face in dumb show. Finally, the red double-decker bus arrived and Gina handed the beggar girl some pound notes and pushed her and the child on board.

Colin had taken a series of photos and scribbled notes as he watched from down the quay, leaning on the ancient retaining wall overlooking the murky Liffey. Gulls squealed overhead. Traffic horns honked madly. Bells tolled from the church spires. Colin checked his watch: eleven o'clock.

As a damp bone-chilling wind blew down river, Gina Furey marched to the south side of Dublin, turning right along the quays, now flourishing with fancy restaurants and tourist hotels in the timeless, brooding, blue-and-gray stone buildings, where grain warehouses, bawdy pubs, and union halls were once located. At Wellington Quay, Gina forced traffic to a halt as she jaywalked diagonally into busy Temple Bar, pushing the stroller ahead of her like a battering ram to clear away the world.

She stopped in front of a small Catholic church, lifted the pram with both hands, and carried it up the steps, bags swinging from the handles. A young man in a dark shiny polyester business suit coming down the steps offered to help.

"I'm just grand, thanks all the same, sham," Gina said, and bounded up the rest of the steps with the pram. She plunked it down and bent to the little giggling girl. "Dere now, darlin', are yeh righ'?" she said in a singsongy voice. "Time for a wee word with the boss man."

Colin watched her walk through a door on the right side of the church. He stared at the ever-changing Dublin sky, counted one-Mississippi to ten-Mississippi, and then entered through the door on the left side of the church. He took a seat in the very last chilly pew of the gloomy church and watched Gina dip her fingers into a holy-water font and make the sign of the cross on the red-haired child in the stroller. Then she dipped again and blessed herself. *She blessed her kid first,* he thought, scribbling a note for the movie.

Colin knelt and half bowed in prayer, hearing Gina click-clack up the right-hand aisle of the church, the wheels of her pram squealing, her footfalls on the stone floors echoing off the high vaulted ceiling. He looked up and saw Gina genuflect in front of the altar. She knelt in front of a rack of votive candles, at the foot of a looming painted statue of Saint Brendan, the Navigator, known for his legendary travels. Colin looked around to be sure no one was watching him and lifted his camera. He framed Gina in the muted light falling through the stained-glass windows, mixing with the flickering candles, creating a haunted frozen moment in time. *She's beautiful,* he thought. *She's perfect.* She looked up at the statue of Saint Brendan and gave him the thumbs up. She reached into her pocket, took out her folded cash, peeled off a note, carefully creased it, and stuffed it into a collection box. She then lighted two candles, again making the sign of the cross upon her child first, then herself. She hung her head in prayer for a half a minute, mumbling, and then looked over both her shoulders and removed an unlit candle from a jar holder and put it into the same pocket with her cash.

She kissed the feet of the Irish saint, known for his wide and adventurous travels, turned, and pushed the squeaky pram down the center aisle, taking no notice of Colin, who bowed his head as if in prayer, and exited the church.

She even robs Saint Brendan, Colin thought. *Balls.*

Colin continued to trail Gina, watching her duck in and out of various boutiques in Temple Bar. Each time she left a shop, the canvas bag seemed to expand, sagging more heavily from the handle of the pram. *Just three more shoplifting days till Christmas,* Colin thought. *I'll make it a Christmas movie, with her character out looting the tourists and the stores.*

Gina worked in a larcenous loop, circling back toward Dame Street. Colin tailed her to Grafton Street, passing the statue of Molly Malone and several street musicians who strummed guitars, busking for Christmas coins. Gina reached in her pocket and tossed a few coins into two different guitar cases, each time saying, "Fair play to yeh, sham."

In front of Bewley's Oriental Cafe, Gina met up again with the oldest of the three women from outside the dole office—the tall, big-busted one with the attractive but weathered face. Her own toddler was squirming in a pram. The two women had their backs to Colin and were bent over Gina's pram, involved in some sort of transaction. The smell of fresh-roasted coffee coming out of Bewley's was like a tantalizing striptease in the damp winter chill.

Colin was engrossed now, like a gumshoe on a hot case who wouldn't let loose of a scent. *Bogart tailing Elisha Cook in* Maltese Falcon, he thought. *Jack Nicholson tailing Faye Dunaway's car with the busted taillight in* Chinatown. *I've watched a hundred noir movies but I've never been in one myself.*

It gave Colin a sweaty sense of secret power, a privileged advantage, an almost sexually dominating exhilaration. *This must be what excites the Peeping Tom,* he thought. *The juice the stalker gets when he follows a woman. You watch her without her knowing it. No wonder stakeout cops are sick fucks. This shit is getting me chubbed.*

He convinced himself that his growing fixation was simply the labor of an artist at work. *It's just research,* he kept assuring himself, adjusting his stiffening penis in his pants, *like a painter with a nude model. Like a biographer reading old personal love letters.*

The women parted ways again, and Gina entered Green and Timothy's department store, one of the swankier retailers in town. Colin counted five Mississippis and then entered the store after her.

He drifted through the aisles, crowded with Christmas shoppers, most of them women, imagining an elaborate dolly shot, until he spotted her rummaging through the racks of expensive baby clothes, never checking price tags as she held possible outfits up against the red-haired child, who was now fast asleep in the pram with a pacifier in her little mouth. Colin noticed that every time Gina Furey took an outfit down from a rack there were actually two outfits, tightly held together by the hangers to make them look like one. Each time she held an outfit against the child she dropped them, bent down, and stuffed one into the canvas bag and rose with the single one in her hand, which she dutifully hung up on the appointed rack. It took Colin twenty minutes to detect this sleight of hand. *One for Gina,* he thought, *one for the store. Fair's fair.*

With her stylish clothing, confident bearing, assorted bangles, and fine jewelry, Gina Furey hardly looked like a down-and-out shoplifting desperado. *A critic watching this performance on a Broadway stage would say she's a genius at her craft,* Colin thought. *The new Meryl Streep. The fruit of years of schooling, grueling attention to detail, immersing herself in the research for the role. But Gina Furey lives the role for a fucking living. That's why I can't take my eyes off her.*

Colin turned his back on her a moment, lifted his tape recorder to his mouth, and whispered into the microphone, "As Kieran stalks her, he begins to fall in love with her."

Colin followed Gina into the women's lingerie department, where he watched her finger fine lace panties, slips, and bras, before choosing a fishnet teddy from a rack. He put his hand in his jacket pocket and touched Deke's panties. He watched Gina rub the teddy on the soft skin of her face, close her eyes dreamily, and drop it as she had with the baby clothes. Colin now knew the move meant there were two teddies and Gina would probably be wearing one of them to bed at home tonight. *With her nasty-assed man,* he thought, feeling a bizarre little dagger of jealousy jab into him. "Kieran gets jealous thinking she has another man," he whispered into the tape recorder. He imagined what Gina would look like in that fishnet teddy, and it aroused him again. Then he imagined some other man having her as she wears it. *Some undeserving fucking shitbum,* he thought. *Kieran would want to knock his teeth out . . . Hey, wait a fucking minute here. Kieran's developing a teenage crush on this broad. It's absurd. She's a welfare artist, with a little snot-nosed brat, a chick who picked Kieran's god-damned pocket and is now looting every store she passes. But if I cast her right, as close to Gina Furey as the real thing, the audience would swallow it—she's irresistible. She tried to steal his wallet and instead she steals his heart. Like a fucking cowboy song.*

Colin started imagining all the possible dramatic pitfalls. *Intellectually, Kieran knows that the Gina character should be avoided,* Colin thought. *Emotionally, she disarms him. He's in awe of her confidence, her brazen arrogance, her larcenous yet proud command of her own life, which has no rules. He's attracted to her because she moves through her city as if it were her private Eden, picking from any blooming tree, defiantly tasting every forbidden fruit, daring anyone to confront or stop her in her mission. He falls for her the way some women fall for gangsters, killers, and outlaws. Kieran is a good guy who falls in love with a bad girl.*

Colin kept telling himself that his attraction to Gina Furey was purely artistic. She was the perfect model for the woman he wanted to portray in his script and movie. He'd use her as an armature. He would let her show him as much as he could use to give the movie the authenticity and verisimilitude it needed. Then he'd render her with a completely imagined life and fictionalized personality. *Right now,* he thought, *without even knowing it, Gina Furey is also my location scout, giving me a guided tour of the city. I'll follow her for as long as it takes to observe and collect the details, situations, the surprises I need.*

Yes, I'm a voyeur, Colin thought, *but, hell, every movie director, every writer, is a voyeur. Every moviegoer, too. I'm spying on Gina Furey, for Kieran, for the film, for the audience. That's my job.*

He followed Gina out of the lingerie department into the men's department, where she repeated her seasoned drop-and-cop routine, taking two sweaters from a rack, dropping them, shoving one in the black canvas bag, and hanging up the other. Then Colin spotted a middle-aged woman spying on Gina, the same way he was. *Store dick,* he thought. He realized he'd seen the same woman in the baby department and the lingerie department.

The store detective started walking briskly toward Gina, ready to confront her. But before she did, the same big-busted woman Gina had spoken to outside the store appeared.

"Oh, Grace," the woman said, as if she hadn't seen her in ages. "How yeh been, luv?"

"Och, grand, Bridie," Gina said. "State of me and the price of buh'er, wha'? Still, can't complain."

"Ah, Jaysus, look at her," Bridie said, her voice croaking affection as she bent to get a closer look at the little red-haired girl in Gina's pram. "Only the image of yer mammy, yeh are, Brianna, darlin'."

"By Jaysus, that wee Finbar fella of yours is gettin' only *hhh*-uge," Gina said, tearing a crust from her loaf of bread for the boy in Bridie's pram and bending down to give it to him. The baby took the crust, wiped his nose with it, and then began chewing it.

The two women disappeared below the rows of racks and dallied there for several moments, audibly baby-talking to each other's children. Colin watched the store dick craning to see what was going on. Finally, each woman rose, exchanged pleasantries, wished each other happy holidays, and then Bridie wheeled her pram away through the Christmas crowd.

Colin watched Gina push her pram in the opposite direction, toward the exit. As Gina approached the street doors, the lady store detective signaled to a man in a suit and they quickly approached Gina from either side, each grasping an arm.

"Let's have a look in that bag, luv," the female store detective said, a snarl twisting her mouth.

"Get your leper's paws off me, yeh bollockses," Gina shouted.

"I've been watching you for the better part of a half-hour, young lady," the store dick said, grabbing the black canvas bag.

"I dare you to look in the mirror half a minute without vomitin' up your tea," Gina said.

"Quite the greedy little klepto, aren't we?" said the store detective as a crowd gathered and the red-haired girl in the pram began to bawl. "Santy is a little early, isn't he, dear . . ."

"Lady, in India you'd be fuckin' sacred," Gina said.

As the man held Gina by the arms, the woman detective lifted the heavy canvas bag off the pram handles, a gloating smirk on her face, making a show to discourage others from shoplifting.

"You'll be in the courts for Christmas, my dear," said the store dick as the store manager now approached, his starched white collar biting deep purple ravines into his soft, jowly neck.

"I'll call the guards," the manager said. "Woman or no woman, child or no child, an example must be made."

The manager hurried to a cashier counter, lifted a telephone, and punched in a number as the store detective ceremoniously unzipped the canvas bag in front of the crowd, all the while staring into Gina's eyes. She dug her hand into the bag and instantly withdrew it in horror, holding a dirty diaper, her fingers covered in shit.

"A bit o' beauty cream for Missus Frankenstein, wha'?" Gina shouted and began to roar with laughter. "Feckin' gobshite."

The gathered crowd joined her in guffaws as the store detective yelped, shaking the sticky diaper from her finger as if it were a dead animal. The flying diaper hit an astonished well-dressed woman, soiling her beige cashmere coat.

"Jesus wept!" the astonished woman yelled. "My cashmere!"

Colin stood in the back of the crowd, laughing with everyone else as the store detective dumped out the contents of the canvas bag: more shitty diapers, dirty baby clothes, a few cartons of milk. *Kieran loves her even more now,* Colin thought as he boxed his thumb and index finger into a mock camera frame, imagining a wide master shot, like one of Woody Allen's or Spielberg's, filled with lots of visual information. *Gina and the store dick,* he thought, *and the woman in the cashmere coat and the apoplectic manager and the laughing crowd. Complete Marx Brothers mayhem.*

As everyone continued to rock with laughter, Colin saw another figure enter the periphery of his make-believe frame. No one else noticed Bridie wheeling her pram past the commotion out of the store. Colin panned with Bridie, who had an identical, overstuffed black canvas bag hanging from the handle of her pram as she exited.

The old switcheroo routine, Colin thought. He realized that Gina had given Bridie the second pilfered black canvas bag outside of Bewley's Cafe before both of them entered the department store. Then they cleverly switched bags when they bent below the store dick's sight line in the men's department aisle inside the store. The store dick stayed on Gina, going after the decoy bag. *They have it down to a science,* Colin thought. *These chicks could con Houdini.*

The store manager gently cradled the phone, swallowed nervously, his jowls jiggling over the tightly knotted tie and starched white collar. The detective held her one clean hand to her repulsed mouth, as if trying to figure out what to do about her soiled hand. The woman in the ruined cashmere coat peeled it off, letting it drop to the floor, while backing away from it.

"I expect that coat to be replaced," she shouted. "It cost me four hundred pound in this very store only a fortnight ago."

"Of course, madam," the store manager said, dabbing sweat from his neck with a folded hankie.

"And I'd like you to finish calling the guards," Gina snapped. "I want this woman and this other comedian charged with assault. Then I'm going to me solicitor and the newspapers."

The manager approached Gina, holding up his hands in regret.

"Please accept my deepest apologies, madam," he said. "Perhaps we can make some sort of arrangement."

"Now that you mention it," Gina said.

"Would a carte blanche of up to two hundred pound suffice?"

Gina started to walk with him to his office and Colin heard her say, "I was thinking more like five hundred, actually."

"Four, and we have a deal," the manager said.

"Grand, then," Gina said.

Colin watched Gina enter the wood-paneled manager's office, pushing her pram with a cocky authority.

A star performance, Colin thought.

Colin waited out on Grafton Street for a half-hour, watching the shoppers rush both ways on the busy street. His head spun from gaping at the disproportionate number of pretty girls parading the sidewalks of Dublin, most of them dressed in the best fashions of Europe. The men were not nearly as well dressed, most of them wearing shiny jeans and unpolished blocky footwear, wool coats draped over hunched shoulders, cigarettes bobbing from almost every set of adult lips. Everyone talked on cell phones, and a street musician busking for change sang Dylan and Springsteen songs, shoppers tossing coins into his open guitar case. Even he made a phone call between songs. A huge policeman walked by, wearing clown-sized shoes, his face like a cured pink ham with ears. He, too, spoke on a cell phone.

Finally, Colin saw Gina emerge from the department store, wearing a brand new green floppy hat, carrying boxes of merchandise, a smile plastered to her face as she pushed her pram up Grafton Street and through the doors of McDonald's.

Colin peered through the window. Gina sat with Bridie and the other two women from the dole office. All their kids were running around the fast-food restaurant.

Colin noticed right away that this time there was also a man with them, ginger-haired, about the same age as Gina, tall and thin and eerily reserved. He watched the man light one wooden match after another, staring at them burning in a pile in an ashtray.

Then Gina started taking the garments from the boxes and the canvas bag. She presented the man with a double-breasted brown-and-green tweed sport jacket with a belt that fastened in the front. The jacket was unlike any Colin had ever seen before. The man tried it on, a perfect fit, and he gave Gina a tight hug.

Colin painfully watched Gina embrace and kiss the man. *On the lips,* Colin thought, imagining Kieran's heart sinking. *Kieran hates this prick the minute he lays eyes on him. Give Kieran six beers and one wrong word and he'll break the bones in this motherfucker's face . . . Do I want Kieran that nutty? That New York–street primal? Maybe Kieran is a street guy who wound up in a rich kid's school on a scholarship. He wants to become an artist, excel in that world, but he gets sucked back to the gutter whenever anger rises in him. And maybe it's the Gina character's back-alley street smarts and her primal behavior that initially attracts Kieran to Gina. She's the kind of chick he would have chased if he'd stayed on course with his native world of the street instead of following his muse to the world of the arts.*

Colin had finally seen enough.

I've seen some of the city through the eyes of a native and an outlaw, he thought. *Now it's time to get real. And write the fiction. She's OPP—other people's property. Off-limits. Nothing more than a model for your character. Kieran can fall in love with her all he wants. I have to be real.*

He walked back to the Temple Bar Hotel, imagining himself shot from an aerial point of view, a lone dejected figure in a strange city. *I wonder if Deke will take a rain check,* he thought.

three

There was no answer at Deke's room, but Colin didn't leave a message. He ate alone again in the hotel cafe. After lunch, he went into the lounge, took a seat in an empty booth, and ordered a large cognac. He read *The Irish Times,* especially enjoying the highly literate letters to the editor. The biggest and most heated exchange concerned the growing tide of organized crime in Ireland, especially Dublin, which harbored nearly half the nation's population. One letter pointed out that eighty-five percent of Ireland's prison population was from Dublin.

According to the outraged letters, there were drugs, prostitution, and extortion racketeers who drove fancy cars living in multimillion-pound Wicklow estates. There were gangsters so arrogant and brutal that one threatened to rape the young son of a female investigative journalist before eventually murdering her on an open road. They put a guy away for that one. There was also a news story in the front of the paper about the new young gangsters who ran the growing number of illegal after-hours clubs, where cocaine, speed, and Ecstasy were freely peddled. Most were in their late twenties and early thirties, dressed in dark suits and wraparound sunglasses, and were surrounded by armed goons, holding court and making millions, willing to kill and maim to protect their treacherous turf. *These guys must use* Scarface *and* Goodfellas *as training films,* Colin thought. *Crazy fucks. What if some poor unsuspecting tourist, like Kieran, crossed one of these wack jobs? Jesus Christ . . .*

He took out his notebook and jotted down some quick ideas.

Maybe the Gina character is involved with a top Irish hood. And Kieran bangs her. The hood finds out. Kieran and Gina are suddenly being chased across the Irish countryside by insane Irish hoods, an Irish 39 Steps *in the twenty-first century. A little danger mixed into the love story. Some needed tension.*

Colin was surprised that in a city as small and civilized as Dublin, organized crime had gotten such a stranglehold. But the newspapers were reporting that random violence was also on the rise.

The whole country is scamming, he thought. *Ireland is more like John Boorman's* The General, *than John Ford's* The Quiet Man. *There are no more gals just like the gal-that-married-dear-old-Dad. Gina Furey is the new Molly Malone.*

By the time he finished the brandy, a little after 3:00 P.M., the jet lag hit Colin like a crashing wave. Fatigue, sour stomach, sore muscles, heavy eyelids. He went up to his fourth-floor room, took one of two bottles of John Jameson Irish whiskey from the duty-free box, and poured an inch into a water glass.

He threw back a belt of booze and looked around the plain, pleasant hotel room, furnished with two large double beds, a bureau, chair, writing table, and TV. The room was chilly and damp. He turned the radiator temperature-control dial to high, pulled aside the drapes, looked out the window onto the overcast winter afternoon, and shivered. He finished the whiskey, undressed to his underwear, and got under the damp, cold sheets.

Leaning on one elbow, Colin pressed rewind on his small tape recorder. As the tape rewound, he opened a large spiral notebook to a blank page. He referred to the notes he took in the pocket-sized notebook the night before and that morning. He condensed and expanded them in cinematic step-outline form, numbering each scene for later possible dramatization. He tried to remember all the details of Gina Furey's robbing spree, copying specific lines of dialogue, indicating real locations. He described the particular way she dressed, how she walked with a confident, sexy swagger, the brand of cigarettes she smoked, the way she pulled the filters off each butt before lighting it with a disposable lighter. The way she bit the apple, to open the skin, before handing it to the red-haired toddler in the pram. How she blessed her child before she blessed herself in front of Saint Brendan the Navigator. *Need details like these in the first fifteen minutes of the script,* he thought. *To create a spell.*

He had two lead characters: an American visitor and an Irish outlaw, an opening, and a strong way to set the Dublin scene. Now he'd have to make the rest up. In his fictitious screenplay, the woman would be divorced or a widow, a single mother. *Kieran has to bail her out of a tight jam. Maybe her ex—a crazy jealous Irish hood—still loves her,* he thought. *Maybe he chases Kieran and Gina across Ireland. She can't go to the cops because she has pickpocketing warrants out on her. If she goes to jail, they'll take the kid away from her. In the second act, the romance and complications deepen when she flees with Kieran and the kid to America . . .*

The structure was taking shape. The characters were crystallizing. But Colin needed more. *More of Gina Furey,* he thought. He still had her dole book, with the address in Ballytara. But Gina Furey was more than just a prototype for his movie. She was a real-life person with a real-life baby and Colin had seen her kiss a real-life guy who was probably her real-life husband. *Or at least the father of the kid,* he thought. Still, with pen and notebook in hand, thinking inside the skin of his fictional character Kieran, he felt himself oddly and inexplicably missing her. Colin knew a good fictional character thought independently of the author. And Colin figured that Kieran must be working, because now Kieran was illogically and absurdly attracted to Gina. Not just physically turned on. Worse, Kieran felt this dangerous attraction as much in his guts and his head as he did in his loins. He was infatuated, enamored, captivated.

Another fresh twist for the movie, Colin thought, biting the tip of the pen and yawning. *Turn the cliche on its head. Instead of having the proper female character attracted to the outlaw, have the straitlaced male character attracted to the outlaw woman.*

Imagine if I brought this crazy chick home, Colin thought, *with someone else's kid. My brothers would tell me I'm losing my fucking mind. My Bayside friends would spend whole afternoons in Grogan's Tavern on Bell Boulevard laughing at me. My aspiring movie friends in SoHo would think it chic that I was slumming. At first. Then I'd stop being invited to parties when the silverware and jewelry disappeared in Gina's bag. Dad would be happy only that Mom wasn't alive to witness it.*

Colin yawned again. As the heat began to rise in the room, Colin's eyes grew heavy and soon he was fast asleep.

He awakened at 6:11 P.M.

He showered again. Ready for another Dublin night.

He chose black jeans, Timberland boots, a snug beige turtleneck shirt, and a dark, forest-green corduroy sport jacket. He tried Deke's room again. This time a man answered and Colin again hung up without speaking. *Good thing they don't play baseball in this country,* he thought, *or I'd be leading the league in strikeouts.*

By 7:00 P.M. Colin was in Buskers bar of the Temple Bar Hotel, this time switching to a pint of Harp lager beer, which was lighter and easier on his stomach. A soft rock song he didn't understand played from hidden speakers. Through the dense, animated young crowd he spotted Deke at the far end of the bar talking to a handsome young blond guy. Deke saw him, gave him a dazzling smile, and waved for him to join them. Colin carried his beer through the loud thirsty throng.

"Hi," Deke said. "I looked for you at the breakfast this morning but I guess you slept late."

"No," Colin said. "I was out working . . .

"On your film?"

"Sort of," Colin said.

Colin eyed the blond guy with her.

"This is my brother Jan," she said. "We were going to go out for the dinner tonight. Maybe you'd like to come, too?"

Colin shook hands with Jan and introduced himself.

"Hello," Jan said, squeezing Colin's hand harder than necessary. Still, Deke was a very pretty lady, Colin was alone, and he was about to accept the dinner offer, brother or no brother, when he spotted a green floppy hat bobbing in the swelling crowd.

"Excuse me," Colin said, freeing himself from Jan's firm grip. "Be right back." He wedged a few yards into the wall of drinkers, leaned on a support pillar, and watched Gina Furey work the packed room. *She's like a surveyor sizing up a piece of real estate,* he thought.

Gina carried a near-gone glass of Guinness in her left hand while gingerly probing loose jacket pockets and dangling bags in the shoulder-to-shoulder crowd. *Her hand is as silent and swift as an insect's feeler,* he thought. Colin watched her position herself behind a swarthy, heavyset American man who sat on a stool with half of his wide behind hanging over the edge of the seat. His wallet was protruding from a back pocket like an invitation to holiday hell.

Gina was half turned away from the fat American, taking a sip of her stout with her left hand while her right hand gently tapped the bottom of the wallet, pushing it further out of his pants pocket. Gina waited for someone to try to pass her through the crowd and used this opportunity to press herself against the fat American, giving the wallet the final upward nudge and letting it fall gently into the palm of her hand. She then gently placed her drink on the bar. "Pardon me, handsome," she said to the fat American mark, flashing him a dazzling smile.

"No problem, honey," he said, wearing a glassy-eyed victim's grin.

Gina removed her hat with her left hand, switched it to her right hand and neatly folded the wallet under an elastic band inside the hat. She ran her left hand through her golden locks, shook her head to evenly disperse her majestic mane, and placed the hat, with the wallet under it, back on top of her head. She started to make a move for the exit when Colin whispered in her ear from behind.

"Buy you a drink, Gina?"

She froze. When she turned to him, her big brown eyes were momentarily spooked.

"How do you know me name?" she whispered.

"Asked a hotel detective."

"That's a lie."

"Guinness?"

"Glass," she said. "Not ladylike for a woman to drink pints. And me name isn't Gina, either. It's Grainya, which is Irish for Grace, righ'?'"

Colin leaned past the fat American and ordered a half-pint of Guinness for Gina.

"Gina Grainya Grace Furey," Colin said.

"Aye, that's me, the one and only," she said. "Who and what the hell are yeh and what do yeh want with me?"

"I see you're working a new hotel," he said.

"I'm lookin' for a special Yank."

"Like me?"

"You're just a wanker," she said and laughed.

"What's that?"

"Someone who fiddles with himself."

It's like she knows, he thought.

"You're also a pain in me ghee," she said.

"What's a ghee?"

"Me ghee is something you'll never see," she said, doubling over with laughter at her own joke. Deke strolled past with Jan, her face a puzzle of confused insult.

"You are a rude man," Deke said softly.

"I'm sorry," Colin said, abashed. "It's about work."

He watched Deke strut out of the bar, tall and elegant and beautiful, a dozen men turning to watch her go.

"She's dead beautiful, all right," Gina said, watching the model stride haughtily out into the lobby. "Lovely and tall and still not satisfied, wha'? She'd ask for seconds in heaven. That your mot?"

"My what?"

"Mot," she said. "Like what flies into a flame. A mot."

"Oh, a moth," he said. "Like girlfriend?"

"That's the yoke," she said. "Your mot, your bird."

"No," Colin said. "No mot. What about you? You married?"

"Not on yer empty life," she said, then gulped her Guinness.

"Then you're free for dinner?" Colin said, thinking: *research and development.*

"You're asking me out on a feckin' date, like?"

He nodded and she laughed a big loud laugh, causing others in the room to turn their heads.

"Me and a Yank?" she said. "Why would I ever in me worst nightmare want to bore meself at a dinner table with a Yank?"

"So I can spend the money you tried to rob from me on you."

She cocked her head and smiled at him from under the wide brim of her hat, her big confident eyes holding an unblinking stare.

"I rather fancy that answer," she said. "You'll be spending what ought've been mine anyway."

"One catch," he said.

"I bite but I'm not a feckin' fish," she said.

He lifted the hat from her head and removed the fat American's wallet. She didn't flinch, just kept staring at him, even as he tapped the fat, swarthy American on the shoulder.

"Dropped your wallet, pal," Colin said.

The fat American was overwhelmed with gratitude, and offered a fifty-dollar reward.

"No, it's okay," Colin said.

"I'll take it, luv," Gina said, snatching the fifty.

four

Gina picked an expensive French restaurant called Monet's Garden on the quays of the Liffey. They sat at a small table, river view, with candlelight playing on Gina's face as she sipped her chardonnay, which she mixed with Coca-Cola and ice, much to the horror of the French waiter. Colin studied her profile: high cheekbones, straight Roman nose, the ruby wealth of mouth, large dark eyes, and a perfectly pronounced jawline. *Beautiful.*

She turned to him, caught him staring at her, and mugged at him comically: crossed her eyes, smiled, winked, squirmed, fidgeted. *She's nervous,* he thought. *She'd heist the Hope Diamond without missing a heartbeat but a date with a Yank makes her nervous.* Gina tapped an ash from her cigarette into a polished ashtray as a formally dressed waiter placed a sizzling metal dish of escargots in front of her.

"Cross of sufferin' Jaysus, wha's tha'?"

"Escargots," Colin said.

"Ask me granny's arse," she declared, leaning away from the scorching metal dish. She poked the glowing ember of her cigarette close to the meaty horned head of a snail, testing for life signs.

"French delicacy," Colin said.

"You ordered me a load of durty, slimy, garden-path *snails?*"

"You picked the restaurant," Colin said.

"Because I folly all the muckety-mucks here," she said. "And you robbed me money to give back to that fat Eyetalian Yank, you have to make up for tha'. Besides, if I was a Mafia gangster from New York I'd probably come here because the prices is so dear."

"I'm not following."

She signaled for the waiter, dressed in a vest and bow tie, who hurried to the table. "Give us an oul jug of champagne," she said.

"What kind of champagne, Madame?" the waiter asked.

"Expensive," Gina said.

The waiter looked at Colin for approval. He nodded.

"Moet," Colin said.

"Why're yeh askin' him?" Gina asked. "It's for me and me hat. And while you're at it, yeh can feed them smelly snails to yer cat and bring me some egg and chips and a plate of bread and buh'er and a wee pot of tay. And make sure the cup is clean."

The waiter looked at Colin again, as if for help. Colin shrugged, nodded, and smiled. Colin heard Gina mumble to herself, as if speaking a foreign language, *"I'm corribed with the krolus."*

"What did you say?"

"I said, I'm wallfallen," she said. "Kilt with the hunger."

"Oh," Colin said, but he was sure she'd used different words.

"You want the tea with the champagne, madame?" the rattled waiter asked, lifting the metal dish, where her cigarette was extinguished in one of the snail shells.

"I'll mix 'em meself, thanks," Gina said.

The waiter blinked twice, then hurried away, baffled, passing other tables of distinguished Dubliners and tourists, a few of whom glanced over at Gina.

"Bleedin' cheek of him," she said. "Yeh wouldn't get feckin' fat eatin' here, that's for sure."

"Gina . . ."

"Me name isn't Gina," she said. "It's Grainya. Or Grace. Take your pick. Grace Lynch."

Now Colin knew she was a thief *and* a liar. *She lives a deliberate fiction,* he thinks. *Maybe Kieran will fall in love with the character she creates and slowly, as he peels the onion, realize he has become involved with someone else.*

"You live alone?"

"Oh, aye," she said dreamily. "A lovely little cottage in Bray, right on the sea, all cozy and warm with a little back garden where I grow me own vegetables and herbs. Pure beautiful."

Another lie, Colin thought. *The address on the dole book is in Ballytara, a sprawling corporation housing tract somewhere in land-locked southwest Dublin, nowhere near the ocean.*

"All lace curtains with pink trim, bright red-and-blue Persian rugs, and stuffy antique settees and big oul arm chairs," she said, her voice low and dreamy. "There's a cuckoo clock on the wall in the kitchen, right above an old-fashioned black cast-iron cooker. The press is always stuffed with food—six kinds of biscuits and teas from China and India. There's a great big wood-burnin' fireplace in the sittin' room where I burn the driftwood I collect on the seashore."

She paused to take a Dunhill cigarette from a pack, tore off the filter, dropped it in the bread basket, lifted the candle, and lit the shredded end of the smoke.

"Me coal bin is filled twice a week," she said, exhaling the first drag and picking a tobacco fleck off her full lower lip. "And there's a big four-poster bed in the bedroom with lovely patch quilts and down comforters. I lie awake in the mornin' listening to the rain blowin' in off the sea, lashin' at the windas, me by meself, all snuggly and warm and it's only absolutely *gorgeous*."

"You got all that picking pockets?" he asked.

She narrowed her eyes and finished her wine. "Certainly not from your skint few bob," she said. "Good job I likes yeh or I'd give yeh a clatter. And I only do the odd dip as a sorta hobby, to see if I can get away with it. Me parents were proper educated, settled people."

"Settled?" Colin didn't understand the term.

Gina seemed momentarily flustered, gulped some wine and Coke, and then recovered quickly. "Settled in their ways, like, righ'?" she said. "Rich people, if you must know, yeh nosy hole, yeh. But they died in a car accident when I was sixteen. They left me the house and all the lolly I need, righ'? I don't need tuppence from nobody, righ'? Certainly not you, righ'? Or anybody else, mind yeh."

He detected a mounting fury, growing with each sip of wine, and each phrase of every new sentence.

"I didn't mean to insult you," Colin said.

"And I only dips Yanks," she said. "Eyetalian Yanks. I thought yeh was Eyetalian."

The waiter brought the champagne and an ice bucket and a busboy placed a cup, saucer, spoon, milk jug, sugar bowl, and teapot in front of Gina. The waiter stood a fluted champagne glass next to the teapot, poured a sample taste of the bubbly, and waited for approval. Gina looked at the glass and then up at the waiter.

"Something wrong with yeh wrist?"

"Madame?"

"Goldilocks would drink more than tha'," she said.

The waiter looked at Colin and then filled Gina's glass as she simultaneously poured herself a cup of tea and mixed in milk and one sugar. The waiter retreated, as if in surrender.

"It's beautiful here by the Liffey," Colin said, trying to change the subject.

"Beautiful my ghee, that river is so durty it stops clocks."

Colin laughed.

"Don't laugh, they brought in a special clock to count down to the turn of the new century . . ."

"A millennium clock," Colin said.

"Aye, that's the yoke," she said. "They set this amazin' clock up on the Liffey to count down to the limenium and the filth and the shite in the oul river jammed the works in a matter of weeks. Poor Liffey's so durty it lit'rily made time stand feckin' still."

Gina took a bite of a bread stick, waving it for emphasis.

"I'll tell yeh somethin' for nuthin', righ'," she said. "In case yer ever lost in Dublin, remember the Liffey always flows west. If yeh know which way's west yeh can't travel lost. And any bus yeh see that says An Lar on the front means it's going to City Centre. An Lar means the center. There now, yer geography lesson is finished. And yer Irish lesson as well."

The waiter brought three broiled quails served with string beans, carrots, and potato croquettes for Colin. The busboy slid the platter of eggs and fried potatoes in front of Gina, along with a basket of bread and butter.

"You'll have no luck after eatin' those poor craytures," she said, pointing to the quail, served on a silver skewer. "Never eat anything that sings, or your life will be one long sad song."

Colin looked down at the birds on his plate and then at Gina. He stared at the delicious-looking birds, munched a carrot wedge, took a sip of wine, and watched Gina eat. *Now she's stealing my appetite.*

She quickly buttered her bread and dug right into her simple greasy meal, dipping her bread into the plump yolks, sprinkling vinegar and salt on the fries, eating them with her fingers.

"Cholesterol will kill you," he said.

"Never touch the stuff," she said, lifting her glass. "I sticks to the oul devil drink. And a wee cup, a'course."

She guzzled the champagne like a soft drink, using the tea as a chaser. When she finished her first cup of tea, she studied the loose leaves in the bottom.

"I used to make loads of lolly from Yanks reading the leaves," she said. "I was taught by the best readers there is."

"What do you see?"

"Do yeh really want to know?"

"Is it good?"

"Is the truth ever?"

"Tell me."

She squinted at the bottom of her cup. "The leaves say yer going to be successful," she said. "But there's going to be hell to pay. Lots of confusion in yer life. A child."

He laughed. She didn't.

"What?"

"I don't like what I see, I'm in the same cup with yeh."

"Then we're doomed," Colin said.

"When the wrong people are in the same cup, one of them usually suffers a great loss. But not to worry. I wouldn't trust leaves in a French kip, they're notorious liars."

"Unlike you," he said.

"I don't lie," she said. "I just pretend I'm me."

She took two slices of buttered bread and made two fried-potato sandwiches as Colin picked around the quail, nibbling at the vegetables and supplementing his hunger with hunks of crispy French bread. He watched Gina savor the simple breakfast food; she occasionally reached over to his plate to steal a string bean. Looking around, Colin noticed that Gina had captured the attention of several appalled diners.

After finishing her fourth flute of champagne, she took a gulp of tea, and shoved her face out like a turtle in the direction of one middle-aged couple at the next table.

"Is me rent overdue, luv?" she said.

"Pardon?" said the woman, who was dressed in an expensive velour Christmas-colored evening dress.

"Yer after gapin' at me like a feckin' rent collector, face ache," Gina says. "Yeh eats snails but make cartoony faces at someone who eats an oul chips sambo? Yous was raised on too much land."

"Excuse me, but we were minding our own business," the woman said, looking to her embarrassed husband for support. He held a fork aloft as if ready to speak, but Gina didn't give him a chance.

"Yer nothin' but mutton dressed as lamb, ya oul ride, yeh," Gina said to the woman, waving a knife, and then fixed her glare on the husband. "And shut yeh up before yeh open your gob, yeh half an excuse for a man, yeh."

The furious husband wiped his mouth, threw down his napkin, and waved for the waiter. Gina turned and gulped another glass of champagne, mopping up the last of her egg yolk with the end of a chips sandwich.

Colin put down his fork and poured himself a glass of champagne as the maître d' appeared at the next table, where the husband whispered to him.

"Let's get a check and get out of here," Colin said.

"I will in me hole," Gina said. "Actually, I was thinkin' of doing a runner."

"A runner?"

"Just run out on the bill, like," she said. "Och, c'mon, for a bit of a laugh. The crack would be absolutely ninety."

"Crack? You smoke crack?"

"I wouldn't touch drugs if I had gallopin' malaria. The *crack* is what's known as *fun*. Ever heard a that? *Fun?* They have that in America yet? 'The crack is ninety' means the fun is so fast it's goin' ninety feckin' miles an hour. Are you that much of an eejit you never heard of the crack? And you're a picture producer?"

"Director," Colin corrected, realizing that Gina was using the Gaelic word *craic*, which he'd seen in *The Irish Voice* and *Irish Echo* in New York.

The maître d' came over with a stern look on his face.

"Pardon, sir," he said, his back to Gina.

"You're just the dickie bow bloke I was lookin' for," Gina said. "Give us one of them brandies in the big goldfish bowl glass, luv. And tell them people to stop gapin' at us. They're very rude."

The maître d' looked at Colin, his back still to Gina, and softly said, "I'm afraid madame is a little . . . shall we say, *overserved,* monsieur."

"Overserved," Gina said, her voice rising. "I was served a dog's dinner and a wee bit o' piss with bubbles and you call that over-served?"

"Bring me a check," Colin said.

The maître d' signaled and the waiter quickly rushed to the table with the bill. Colin looked at it, roughly calculated the tally into dollars, and counted out the equivalent of two hundred and twenty-five bucks. *It's more money than I planned on spending, but it's R and D,* he thought. Colin got up from the table and coaxed Gina to her feet. She put her lit cigarette in her lips as he helped her on with her coat. She picked up her half-full cup of tea with the clear intention of dumping it on the woman at the next table. Colin quickly caught her arm, and looked her in the eyes.

"Don't," he said softly.

The fury in her face quickly dissipated and she let Colin put the teacup back on the table.

"Yer a quare fella," she said, with a bleary smile. "But yer nice. And good-lookin'. For a Yank."

"I'll get you a taxi," Colin said.

"Yeh will not," she said. "C'mon, I'll take us somewhere we can have a proper gargle and a bit a crack."

She took Colin by the arm and marched him toward the door. As they passed the next table, Gina nonchalantly dropped her lit cigarette into the woman's glass of white wine.

"Good God," is all Colin heard the outraged woman say as Gina led him into the chilly Dublin night.

five

Gina escorted Colin to the Black Armband, one of the dozen loud, crowded, smoky clubs with all-night wine licenses that were crammed into the basements of the handsome Georgian houses on Leeson Street. Taxis idled in a rank at the far end of the street, ready to whisk away the drunks. The bouncers at the Black Armband seemed to know Gina, but didn't call her by her name.

As soon as Colin stepped inside, he felt the eyes of other men undressing Gina, daring him to object. *After-hours joints are the same all over the world,* he thought. Gina took Colin by the hand and led him through the loud, sweaty mass of rummies and druggies to the busy bar. Her hand felt small and warm and exciting in his. He helped her off with her coat, took off his own, and draped both over a stool back. Gina cupped her hands and shouted to the barman above the recorded Corrs music for two double Remy Martins. Colin paid.

They sipped the cognac and then Gina led Colin out onto the dance floor, so crowded it reminded him of rush hour on the IRT. Gina made her own room, dancing in a confident, exaggerated swagger. Colin could dance, but he was no match for Gina, who gyrated around the floor like an unchained spirit. She clicked her high heels on the hard wood floors and did blinding pirouettes and graceful dips, all the while flailing her arms and snapping her fingers. Gina quickly stole the attention of the whole club. Other dancers became intimidated, slowed down, backed away, or sat at tables. The men ogled her while the women glared. Colin quickly became aware of the narrowed eyes of hard-looking Irish men— many dressed in a dark suits with black shirts and white pearl buttons fastened at the neck, sporting wide white suspenders, and wearing ominous wraparound sunglasses, like the new Irish gangsters he'd read about in *The Irish Times. Gina Furey has brought me behind the headlines,* he thought.

The hard men sat at various tables, smoking, staring at Colin, and leering at Gina, who pumped her compact body to the music, all pelvis, hips, and ass, golden hair whipping, gold earrings catching the light from a rotating reflecting ball. She bumped her hips against both of Colin's and circled her arms around his neck, doing a rhythmic, simulated pelvic grind against him, her small firm breasts rubbing against his muscular chest. With her face at belt level, her eyes looked up at him from under the floppy hat, winking at him, blowing him kisses. He felt himself getting hard.

Jesus Christ, Colin suddenly thought. *Maybe one of them is her boyfriend, husband, or the father of her kid. Maybe she's just using me to get him jealous.*

Panic shot through Colin, his sexual arousal fading.

The tune ended, and a sweaty Gina led Colin through the crowd, looking for a table. Colin could feel the hard stares of the men, horny and envious in the desperate, boozy, drug-and-testosterone-fueled after-hours frenzy.

Gina found a table near the rear of the club, against a bare brick wall that was decorated with posters of U2, Sinead O'Connor, The Pogues, Van Morrison, House of Pain, The Corrs, Enya.

"You could earn a living dancing," Colin said as they sat down.

"I likes me life the way I lives it."

A tall, burly man in a black suit, wearing shades, appeared at their table. "Mickey says who's the geezer," the guy said.

"Tell Mickey he's a friend from America," Gina said defiantly, taking a sip of her Remy. "Mafia."

"She's kidding," Colin said.

The big guy ignored Colin and said to Gina, "Mickey says he wants you to dance with him."

"Tell Mickey to go home and dance with his wife," Gina said.

"His wife's in nick," the big guy said. "For assault."

"Who'd she wallop?"

"Him," the big guy said. "Stabbed him in his shoulder."

"He's not usin' mine to cry on, tha's for sure," Gina said.

Colin took a gulp of his cognac.

"She was aiming for his feckin' neck," the big guy said.

"I'd like to give her a few pointers," Gina said. "Tell Mickey if he had any of his namesake between his legs he'd talk to me himself. But since yer here, tell him I says to keep his wet coke nose out of my business, righ'?"

The big guy stared deep into Colin's eyes, then nodded. He walked back to a large round table in a roped-off VIP section, and spoke to a short but lethally handsome man in his early thirties.

"Who's Mickey?" Colin asked.

"Told me he was a bank robber," Gina said. "He also told me he was divorced. Turns out he's married and sells drugs. All I ever did with him was have a few dances and now he thinks he owns me. No one will ever own me, righ'?"

Gina spotted a commotion at the front door and quickly rose from the table. "Excuse me a wee minute, bigfulluh," she said. "Stay put and watch the coats. Don't get involved in this bit a nastiness."

Colin heard women's voices shouting and cursing at the door as Gina quickly pushed her way through the club.

"Who the fuckin' 'ell are you to tell us we can't come in, yeh big poxy cunt, yeh," shouted one very loud woman.

"Get yer filthy fuckin' paws off me," demanded another woman.

"We don't let dirty knackers in this club," a bouncer declared as he pushed the women out of the vestibule toward the stairs.

"Who yeh callin' a knacker, you moldy junkie, yeh," came a third woman's voice.

"No knackers, period," said a second bouncer. "Men or women."

Now Colin could hear Gina's unmistakable voice as she entered the shoving match at the door.

"Let them in, yeh door-thick bollocks, yeh," Gina shouted. "Where does the arse-faced likes of yous get off judgin' other people? You let gear-dealers, junkies, and tuppence-killers in here but keep a few girls out."

The head bouncer looked over at Mickey for guidance and Mickey gave him the hooked thumb of the bum's rush.

"Shut yeh feckin' up, luv," shouted one of the bouncers. "Or someone'll shut yeh up as well."

"Just feckin' try it, righ'?" Gina said. "Those're me cousins yer after callin' knackers, yeh tuppence-ha'penny doorman."

Colin got to his feet and angled toward the commotion.

"G'wan, you big feckin' Nancy, yeh," Gina said, taunting the bouncer. "G'wan and hit me, yeh durty dog's shite, yeh, and I'll live just to see yeh feckin' die, righ'?"

"If yiz was men you'd all be in hospital by now," said the second bouncer.

Colin pried his way through the throng toward the drama at the door. The big man who had approached his table on behalf of the gangster named Mickey blocked his path.

"Mickey'd like to have a wee word witcha," he said.

"I'd like to but Gina is having a problem at the door . . ."

Suddenly, Mickey was in front of him, inches from his face. *A big Sergio Leone close-up,* Colin thought. *His eyes are bubble-wrapped with dark shades.* His tongue was white and gluey. His breath stank like old corn and his teeth were chipped and furry.

"Listen to me, Yank, righ'?" Mickey said as the argument continued at the door. "When she's in here, Grace is *my* bird, righ'? Now, believe me when I tell yeh, I have no problem with you, but take her out of here. I can't have her shaking her ass in me face and rubbin' her ghee all over yeh, now, can I? Can't have her cursin' out me bouncers. It's all very uncool."

"Look, I just met her . . ."

"I don't need details," he said. "I have enough problems. The only thing worse than having her be here dry humpin' another geezer is for me to fight over her. Makes me look desperate for her. If yer not here with her, I don't give a shite and I don't look like a clown in front of me mates, understand?"

"Absolutely," Colin said, trying but failing to find the eyes behind the sunglasses.

"She's a great chick for the lookin'," Mickey said in a reasonable tone. "But she's bad for business and totally feckin' *mad*. I even hear she's actually a feckin' *traveler* herself. That might explain it. Missin' one of the twenty-three chromosomes, because of inbreedin'.' "

"Traveler?"

"Yeah, tha's what I hear. Please, take her out of here."

"Right," Colin said.

The big guy appeared with their coats, and shoved them at Colin.

By the time Colin got to the door, three bouncers had herded the four cursing women up the stairs onto the sidewalk. Colin immediately recognized Gina's companions as the women from the dole office.

"I apologize for these two callin' you knackers," said one diplomatic bouncer, trying to make peace.

"That big lump a shite has a mouth as durty as his arse," Gina said, pointing to the one who'd called them knackers.

A police car turned the corner and slowed to a slither.

"Here's the cowboys now," said the reasonable bouncer.

"C'mon Grace," said Bridie. "We never win where the shades is concerned."

"To hell with the shades," Gina said.

"I gotta get back home to me babby, anyway," said Bridie.

Colin draped Gina's coat over her shoulders.

"You all right?" he asked. "Anything I can do?"

"I told you I don't need anybody, ever, righ'?" Gina said.

Is she really that hard? Colin wondered. *Or is that part of her act?*

The women drifted away from the club as the Garda car inched behind them in the gutter. The bouncers retreated back down the steps to the vestibule of the club.

"Who's yer mon, Grace?" asked the youngest one. "Looks like a buffer."

So her name is Grace, Colin thought, as he walked beside Gina. *But what the hell is a buffer? This is where Kieran's curiosity about the Gina character should deepen. And what the hell is a traveler?*

"And sounds like a Yank," said Bridie, rubbing her thumb and fingers together to indicate money.

"A bit of Christmas lolly," said the voluptuous one.

"At least one of us is in for a bit a crack, wha'?" said Bridie. "Well fer yeh, *laicin.*"

"Go way outta tha'," Gina said with a laugh. "He's gonna take us all back to the hotel for a nightcap, aren't yeh, gra?"

"Sure," Colin said, stifling a jet-lagged yawn.

"Another time for me," Bridie said. "I was only gowna have the one wine. There'll be killin's if I don't get home. Him-feckin-self is fresh outta nick and sniffin' around for lolly and ghee, neither of feckin' which he's gettin' from feckin' me."

"Aye," said the voluptuous one. "Mine's excuse for a father is up from the country and on the loose as well. I'd better go afore he breaks into me kip and empties me few sticks into his jam jar."

"I have a fiver toward a taxi," said the youngest one.

The women began pooling their money, pulling out their pockets and scouring the bottoms of their handbags, combining large coins with rumpled pound notes. Gina reached in her pocket, pulled out a wad of cash, and handed them a crisp twenty-pound note.

"The ride home's on me," she said, and the others kissed her on the cheek.

"Aren't yeh gowna introduce us to yer Yank?" asked the oldest.

Gina nodded, took a deep breath.

"Yer after making me go scarlet," Gina said, and then turned to Colin. "For the life of me, luv, I can't remember yer name, tha's why I didn't introduce yeh."

"Colin. Colin Coyne."

"'Course it is," Gina said with a snap of her fingers. "Sorry, Colin. These'ns is me cousins."

She introduced each one. The oldest one's name was Bridie; Philomena was the attractive voluptuous one; and the youngest, pretty, fashionable cousin was Susan.

They didn't shake his hand, just nodded and eyed him.

"Howayeh" was how each one formally introduced herself.

Gina asked Colin to hail a taxi and one sped from the rank. The three cousins piled into the back seat in an eruption of laughter, leaving Colin and Gina alone.

"Bally-feckin-tara, my Jaysus Christ," Colin heard the cabby exclaim before roaring off. "The gates is as far as I go."

The police car cruised past them again.

A soft black drizzle began to fall on the city and the streets were ghostly and empty. Colin and Gina walked along the wet cobblestones, echoes resounding off the stone buildings. *Joseph Cotten searching nighttime Vienna for Orson Welles in* The Third Man, he thought, cocking his head at an angle, taking his camera from his pocket, and fixing it to his eye, tilting it. *My movie is about a crooked girl. Maybe I'll shoot it at crooked angles the way Carol Reed shot that film. Everything and everyone could be off-kilter. Like Kieran's life. Shadows. Echoes. Night. Rain. Christmas.*

"You a snapper as well?" she asked, pointing to the camera.

"No, this is for scouting movie locations," he said.

"What's yer movie about?"

"A Yank looking for love," he said.

"The only thing they're ever looking for is ghee," she snapped.

"Sometimes that leads to love," Colin said.

"Most times not."

A burst of laughter carried from blocks away, and the thump of a bass line escaped from another nightclub they passed on Leeson Street. As they approached the taxi rank, Gina abruptly stopped him, got on her tiptoes, took his face in her small hands, and softly kissed him on the lips.

"Kiss me, yeh big bollocks," she said. Colin was startled and disarmed. He kissed her back. Her lips were soft, like little pillows, and warm and wet.

This would hook Kieran, he thought. *Here's the romance; the women in the audience will love it. Kieran is kissed by the pick-pocket while walking with her in the drizzly rain of Dublin during Christmas week.*

"Yer the first Yank I ever kissed," she said. "Had to give it an oul try, wha', or me cousins would be givin' me stick for days on end."

"Gina . . ."

"Yer a bit of all right. Now I could use that nightcap."

They had a quiet drink in the hotel lounge. "I'm banjaxed and in no humor for jettin' all the way home," she said. "Show me yer room and I'll show yeh me snorin', gra."

"What's that mean?" he asked. *"Gra?"*

"Gra, it means love," she said. "But only as a figure of speech, like. Don't get the wrong idea."

Colin was apprehensive. Gina Furey was a dangerous mix: a woman capable of simple kindness, gross larceny, embarrassing outbursts, fierce temper, sexy seduction. She had tried to rob him, aroused him on a dance floor in front of a room filled with gangsters, and then kissed him as gently as a fairy-tale princess. She was as fearless and crazy as anyone he'd ever met, yet it never occurred to him to say no, when she asked to be taken to his room.

While they sat on the bed drinking from a John Jameson bottle, Colin leaned over and kissed Gina. *This is what Kieran would do,* he thought. She responded and they rolled on the bed, kissing passionately, as Colin explored her tight body with his large hands. Fully clothed, Gina straddled him, grinding her pelvis into his, kissing his neck, then his chest and torso, leaving lipstick imprints on his beige turtleneck. Colin quickly pulled off his shirt, and she kissed his nipples, sucked them, nibbled them. He became very hard and excited. Then she quickly pushed herself off him.

"Stop and water the horses," she said, sitting on the edge of the bed, straightening her blouse and skirt.

"You're the one who wanted to come up here," he said.

"Aye, to sleep," she said, fanning herself. "By meself, not with you. Jaysus, you're a lovely fella, fit as a lifer-lag, but yous Yanks think yeh can just do the gonkey on the first bleedin' night. I see it all the time in them Hollywood pictures, but I didn't believe it was true. But then, yer a fil-um producer . . ."

"Director," Colin said, sighing in frustration, lying flat on his back, panting, trying to catch his breath. For the second time in three hours, his hard-on vanished.

"Kieran gets blue balls," he muttered.

"Who's Kieran?"

"Nobody you know," he said.

"Yer a right quare one," she said. "And I guess yeh thought I was gowna be a first-night ride for yeh. Well, I have front-page news for yeh, boyo. If yeh want to get in me knickers, the best way is not to try. G'night."

She kicked off her boots and climbed under the covers of the bed closest to the door and pulled the sheet tightly over her lips, as if afraid someone would put something in her mouth while she was sleeping. Colin sat up, taking big gulps from the bottle of Irish whiskey and looking over at Gina Furey, who was deep into worry-free sleep in less than two minutes.

God, she's beautiful, he thought. *Of course Kieran would fall for her.*

She's a dangerous woman, he decided in his half-drunkenness. *But that's exactly what attracts Kieran to her. It's the same magnetic pull that attracts some people to mountain climbing, skydiving, bungee jumping, and roller coasters. Gina has a perverse, nonsensical, ambivalent, challenging, death-defying allure. She brings Kieran to the edge.*

I have to find a way to show that Gina lives in that suspended nanosecond between inhale and exhale, that ephemeral pause between tick and tock that the Asian mystics call life.

If I succeed at that, then Kieran can think of Gina as more than a piece of ass. She's his dream come true, the elusive crock of gold, a reason to let go and fall in love. That, Colin decided, *will make the audience believe Kieran's character feels more than just immature infatuation. The actress I cast to play Gina needs to possess a mystical, hypnotic, inexplicable, almost otherworldly quality.*

Before it gets to the screen, he thought, *I have to get it on the page. Whether she knows it or not, the real Gina Furey is gonna help me write this script.*

Colin took a last gulp of the Irish whiskey and passed out with the open bottle in his hand.

December 22

Colin awakened with a woolly, dry mouth and a dull ache in his head. He was still wearing his black jeans but was barechested and barefoot. He didn't remember taking off his socks. With the heavy drapes pulled over the windows, the room was coal black. He looked around for the illuminated digital clock on the writing table, but he couldn't see it in the gloom. He sat up, groped for the lamp, and switched it on.

Through his parted fingers, he could see that the other bed was empty and stripped of all its bed-clothes. *She strips the bed after sleeping in it.*

"Gina," he called softly, but there was no reply.

His eyes slowly adjusted to the light and he stumbled, hungover, toward the bathroom, and looked inside. Gina was gone. Quickly he patted his front pants pocket where he kept his cash. It was still there. Relieved, Colin looked around the room, doing an inventory. The booze was also still there. Suddenly, he remembered hanging his jacket on the back of a chair, but it wasn't there. Panic shot through him. *My wallet!* he thought. *Passport! Plane ticket! Notebook! They're all in that jacket.* He searched the room, but couldn't find the jacket.

Bitch!

He yanked open the closet doors and found his jacket hanging neatly on a wooden hanger, the bottom button fastened to preserve its shape. Everything was still in the pockets. Gina's dole book was still in the inside pocket.

He felt terrible that he'd suspected her of robbing him.

Next to the jacket was his turtleneck shirt, looking as though it had just returned from the cleaners. He checked the front, where her lipstick stains had been—gone. The shirt smelled like his herbal shampoo.

He looked around the room, realizing Gina had also tidied up— all the newspapers were neatly folded and stacked in a pile, the glasses had been washed and placed upside down on a round serving tray, his dirty clothes had been washed and were hanging up in the closet.

He unbuckled and removed his jeans, pulled off his Jockey shorts, and went into the bathroom. Three pairs of socks and three pair of Jockeys were drying on a retractable line that she'd strung across the length of the tub. He felt the socks and shorts; they were dry. He shook his head and smiled as he pulled them down, placing them in a pile. Then he climbed into the shower.

The shower ran hot and cold and so he washed and shampooed quickly. *Who is this wacky broad?* he wondered. *Who and what the fuck is she?* He shivered under a cool rinse and stepped out and reached for a towel. There wasn't one. He glanced at the rack, where he'd seen a half dozen of them the day before. They were all gone.

"What the fuck?" he said aloud, as he stood dripping onto the tile floor. Now he noticed that the bath mat was also missing. He hurried into the bedroom, searched around for towels. There were none.

He looked at the bed in which Gina had slept and saw that it had been stripped of everything—pillowcases, sheets, bedspread.

He pulled the pillowcases from the pillows on his own bed and found a Temple Bar Hotel envelope with his first name written on it in a curiously spidery, childish scrawl. Colin quickly blotted himself dry with the linen pillowcases and tore open the sealed envelope. The note inside read: "Dear Yank Thanks for the nise time. Yore a fine fella. Don't look for me because I wont be there. Hapy Christmas. Grace. (The one and only, ha ha.) PS I borried a few ods end ands for silverneers too remember you bye."

He laughed and shook his head.

He did an inventory: She'd stolen the towels and bedclothes and the clock radio. He walked into the bathroom and reached for the hotel's wall-mounted hair dryer. Gone.

I should be pissed off, he thought. *But I'm not. I'm not because it suggests a new scene I wouldn't have thought of. Gina is unpredictable—a woman who turns dinner into a confrontation, almost gets you killed by gangsters, kisses you in the falling rain, comes to your hotel room, gives you a case of blue balls, washes and irons your clothes, and then robs your sheets and the hotel appliances before leaving a Christmas note good-bye.*

I simply have to see her again, he thought. *Kieran would certainly go find her. I need to find out more about her for the movie. Gina Furey's dole book is still in my jacket. With her Ballytara address.*

six

A half hour later, the taxi driver wished Colin a "Happy Christmas" as soon as he climbed into the backseat.

"Where to, youngfulluh?" the driver said.

Colin leaned across the front seat and showed the driver the dole book bearing Gina Furey's name and address.

"My Jaysus," the driver said. "I'll take yeh to the crossroads near the barracks but I'm not drivin' in."

"What's the problem?" Colin asked as the cabby pushed the computerized meter and headed out. "Too far?"

"Och, tha's no problem," said the driver, a man in his fifties who was wearing a flattened Irish cap and shifted gears with big thick hands. "But Ballytara is Apache territory. If we drive in there, 'specially three days before Christmas, the car would be surrounded by a war party, stripped, and sold for parts quicker than yeh could say yer last Hail feckin' Mary. What in the name of God possesses yeh to go to the like of Ballytara of a Christmas week?"

"There's a girl . . ."

"'Course there is," the cabby said, shifting gears and passing a rumbling lorry laden with coal. "That explains it. Isn't there always a bird behind every act of madness? Christ, I hope yer feckin' armed."

"Why's that?" Colin asked, amused, watching the cabby adjust the statues of Saint Christopher and Saint Jude on his dashboard.

"Ballytara is nicknamed Knackeragua, that's the feckin' why, son, righ'?" said the driver, who then fell into a long silence as he drove.

Colin also remained wordless for a brief spell, as he framed his fingers around his eye, imagining a traveling shot as they jolted along Templeogue Road through Rathmines, Rathgar, and Terenure, passing rows of grim and gray corporation flats as well as more appealing private homes, slowing through congested commercial strips. He took out his small camera, focusing on billboards: Guinness, Jameson whiskey, milk, Players and Silk Cut cigarettes. They cruised through upper-middle-class neighborhoods of stately dark-brick homes with neat lawns and private driveways.

The Dublin morning air was thick with the sulphurous odor of burning coal, and through the window Colin watched the way the older Irish women hurried along the narrow sidewalks, bent into the cold, carrying packages, heads bowed from years of common struggle. Many of the gray-haired ladies reminded him of his mother, inherently industrious and moving in a double-time step as if they were perpetually late for life itself.

Colin missed his mother, especially at this time of year, and in this place, where he could see her in almost every older Irish woman's face. *Maybe Kieran comes to Ireland to bury his mother,* he thought. *Maybe in his grief, he falls for Gina because of her Irishness, her accent.*

It was Colin's mother who left him the $10,000 it cost to start his short movie *First Love, Last Love. I wish I'd visited Ireland with Mom at least once before she died,* he thought.

"Knackeragua, meaning what?" Colin asked the driver, coming out of his reverie.

"Meaning it's overrun with knackers," the driver said. "So many knackers, living like Third World bushmen, like they do in South America, that Dubs call it Knackeragua, like Nicaragua."

There's that word "knacker" again, he thought, taking his tape recorder from his jacket pocket. "What's a knacker?"

"Tell me, son, is this girl yer lookin' for a re-lay-tive?" the driver asked cautiously, peeking at Colin in the rearview mirror. "Or your girlfriend, like?"

"I just met her," Colin said, pushing the record button.

"Fair play to yeh, all the same," the driver said as he sped along Templeogue Road. "Yous Yanks are a fair-minded lot, all right. No harm intended, but Dublin is filled with birds, son. With much better feckin' addresses than this one yer chasin', I can tell yeh that. But anyway, a knacker is a gypo, son, a tinker. The politicians and the newspapers call them itinerants. Travelin' people is what they like to call themselves, as if they were these romantic feckin' nomads, noble and all that shite. But the only place I fancy seein' them travel to is Mountjoy Prison. Durty robbers, every filthy one of them. They'd steal the milk out of yer feckin' tea if yeh blinked yer eyes to fart."

"They're not too well liked, huh?" Colin asked, smiling because the cabby reminded him of an Irish version of Archie Bunker.

"The knackers was fine when they stuck to the road, righ'?" the driver said. "When they kept to themselves. But now they're in the cities, big time. Moving into communities where normal workin' people are tryin' to raise families. Rubbishin' up clean respectable communities. The knacker kids give other children crash courses in robbin', pickpocketin', car strippin', scrap stealin', check forgin'. While men like me are out scrabblin' for a few Christmas bob, the knackers are all out stealin' and on the dole at the same time. And they teach their kids the thievin' and beggin' life from early age, like a knacker feckin' trade school. That's where your word 'gypped' comes from, the feckin' gypos robbin' ya. And every Jaysus one of the women is on the dole and up the pole. They might as well give 'em dole bewks with their birth certs, so they should."

"Most of them are on welfare?"

"Oh, Christ, aye," said the cabby. "Plus the stamp in your bewk says this young wan here yer goin' to visit is collectin' the children's allowance as well. Knackers multiply like Russian minks, tellin' you, son. Then they send the kids, as young as six and seven, out beggin' for money so the oulfulluh can spend it all on gargle. These kids are expected to bring home up to a hundred and fifty pound a week to the bastardin' parents. Or else they get clobbered somethin' terrible. The guards have picked these kids up beggin' in front of the feckin' Dail, the Euro Commission, even on the steps of the Irish Society for the Prevention of Cruelty to Children!"

"Does that mean this girl's married?"

"Och, that would be a right stretch these days, son," the cabby said, shifting gears and driving deeper into western Dublin. "Although with the knackers, they marry off their young wans as early as thirteen year of age, arranged marriages, mostly. But always amongst themselves. First cousins sometimes, mind yeh. You would have to feel pity for a young girl bein' forced to marry and lie with a big oul smelly drunken tinker cousin, poppin' out babbies when they're still babbies themselves. And then they send them out to Dublin with a blanket and the babby to beg for coins on O'Connell Street and Ha'penny Bridge while the so-called feckin' husband is off robbin' a farmer's furniture."

"Some marry first cousins at age thirteen?" Colin asked skeptically.

"Aye," said the cabby, nodding to Colin in the rearview mirror. "There's lots of crossbreedin', inbreedin' and sideways-breedin' amongst themselves, 'til they get the look off them like that wee fella in the *ET* fil-im. A special always-Jaysus-hungry look, yeh know? Rawboned, hollow-cheeked, teeth like a donkey, and deep-set in the eyes, a Romany schemer's grin on the face. Some of the blood is so closely mixed they get two different color eyes. A look so unique yeh could dress a feckin' knacker in a dickie bow and tuxedo and a feckin' penguin in the zoological gardens could pick him out of a lineup as a feckin' knacker. Most decent pubs won't serve the likes a them. Their reputation is so bad that even when one of them makes an honest success of himself no one will serve him. Like that Olympic boxer Francie Barrett, he was ejected from a Galway nightclub just for being a traveler. No restaurant in Dublin would bewk his family for a victory celebration. That's wrong, mind yeh. But Jaysus, son, the publicans and store dicks know most of 'em by sight. The guards have a file on every feckin' knacker family. They're feckin brutal, desperate they are. Drivin' all around the blessed country in their High Ace Toyotas, strippin' cars, collectin' scrap, robbin' farmers bleedin' blind, sellin' their antique furniture to the best shops in Dublin. And some knackers, the so-called kings, are dead rich, mind yeh, but not the ones out here in Bally-feckin'-tara. Even the knackers call the knackers who live here knackers."

"That bad, huh?" Colin said, listening closely and letting the recorder preserve it all.

"There was talk once of a pair of Bengal tigers escapin' from the Dublin Zoo and prancin' into Ballytara and never bein' seen or heard from again," joked the cabby. "Rumor has it the knackers 'et them in a feckin' stew and sold the hides to a rich Yank as rugs."

"I thought tinkers were these quaint gypsies who traveled around the Irish countryside in covered wagons repairing pots and pans," Colin said. "Tinsmiths and musicians, Irish bedouins."

"Yous Yanks is filled with fairy tales," the cabby said with a chuckle. "I hear them all, clay pipes and thatched roofs, banshees and dancin' leprechauns. This is a new century, son, all the Irish fairy tales have been bought up and sold abroad. Except for the knackers. They say there's twenty-five thousand of them still here and when they move into your street, by Jaysus, nobody lives happily ever after."

Not in my backyard, Colin thought. *It was* racism. *Xenophobia. Here in Ireland it seemed to be about class. Could be interesting if Kieran falls for a social outcast.*

Colin didn't argue with the driver over his views on tinkers or travelers. He wanted to hear the driver's views, and to know how people thought. Besides, he wasn't schooled enough on the topic to debate him.

The cabby pulled to a traffic circle near the Garda barracks. Across the road, a sign on a cement pillar read: THE BALLYTARA ESTATES. Everything was gray. From the taxi, Colin could see the massive, sprawling industrial housing tract of gray single-family homes spread out for as far as the naked eye could see. He lifted the camera and peered into a gray haze of belching chimney smoke and auto exhaust. Panning to the west, he saw a bleak cemetery with rows of simple crosses and plain gray headstones jammed into the muddied earth under an ashen sky. *It's like they live in a world before Technicolor,* he thought.

"You can pay me what's on the clock now," the cabbie said. "And if you want, I'll wait exactly fifteen minutes, to see if you come out alive. You won't find any taxis cruising out here. That address, according to my map, is three blocks straight ahead and one block to your left, son. Happy huntin' and God feckin' bless."

Colin paid the driver, asked him to wait, shut off his tape recorder, and put away his camera. He entered the first main street of the Ballytara Estates, where four young kids stood outside a grocery shop in tattered hand-me-down wool coats draped over gray undershirts. They were passing a cigarette around and gaped at Colin, who was wearing jeans and cowboy boots.

"Lookit yer mon in the bewts," said the oldest of the kids, about twelve, his red hair like a smashed pile of copper cable, badly bucked teeth jutting from his heavily freckled face.

"Clint Eastwood, wha'," said a short dark-haired kid who tried unsuccessfully to blow a smoke ring into the damp wind.

Colin walked deeper into the estates, past a traffic island, where head-scarved women stood chain-smoking, watching their wash flap from crude wire clotheslines. More badly dressed children, many with mismatched socks, stomped through black puddles, wearing shoes a few sizes too big for their feet. A young girl sat on a car battery, talking to a plastic milk bottle dressed to look like a doll. Unleashed dogs, most with rib bones protruding through mangy coats, stared up at Colin, their unblinking eyes pulsating with hunger.

Like fucking Bushwick, Colin thought. *Or Brownsville. Kieran comes looking for the girl from the Irish Spring commercial or* Riverdance *and falls in love with a knacker from the slums. When he brings her back to New York, Kieran's father is appalled.*

Some of the front gardens of the single, soot-covered houses boasted small flowerbeds and statues of the Blessed Mother. Other lawns were desecrated with the carcasses of stripped cars—old tires and abandoned car batteries piled together, bumpers bound in bundles by rough rope, different-colored automobile fenders, car doors, hubcaps, all separated into piles, ready for carting. Snarling pitbulls and German shepherds on long ropes stood guard, ready to attack anyone who dared come near.

Fucking place is like the documentaries of the Deep South in the early sixties, he thought. *A modern-day Tobacco Road.*

All the gray stucco-faced houses were identical in structure and many had their addresses removed from the front doors. Colin reached a corner where one house was missing the retaining fence and where an old-fashioned tinker's covered wagon—like the ones he'd seen on tea towels and old Guinness posters—was parked on the front lawn. A piebald pony cropped at a pile of hay, occasionally losing its nose into a pail of oats.

Two young boys, obviously brothers, raced out of the house, each grabbing large stones from the gravel bed of the flowerless garden and flinging the stones at the other's back and legs.

"Next time yeh 'et me feckin' ba-na-na I'll bleedin' kill yeh, yeh bastard, yeh," screamed the older boy, hitting his kid brother in the lower spine with a rock the size of a lemon.

The younger one stumbled, arched his back, but didn't go down, refused to cry. Instead, he turned and flung a rock back, hitting the older one in the chest. "I 'et it and I'd 'et it again, yeh bollocks, yeh."

Now the older one started chasing after the younger one and they raced up a side street and into a back alley behind the houses, out toward the cemetery.

Colin watched an elderly woman, bent in half, clearly suffering from osteoporosis, carrying a pail of coal. She passed Colin, paused when she saw his boots in her path, looked up, and said, "Feck off, yeh bollocks."

Colin stepped off the sidewalk into the gutter as the woman waddled past. He turned left at the corner, assaulted by rap music blaring from a boom box. Four teenagers hunched over a crackling oil-drum fire, dressed in frayed leather bomber jackets, hooded sweatshirts, and unpolished thick-soled shoes. They fed broken sticks and bags of garbage into the flames, and passed around a smoldering hashish pipe. *No different from the assholes who hang outside the high schools back home,* Colin thought.

"Yeah?" croaked the one, maybe seventeen, who wore his red hair and sideburns like Elvis, staring at Colin. He exhaled after gagging on his trapped cannabis smoke and hawked a phlegmy wad into the flames, watching it sizzle.

"Hi," Colin said.

"That we are," said a second one, who was short and muscular and had teeth dotted with little black holes of decay. He burst into laughter, the other three joining his infectious hashish giggles. "Higher than the price of drink, wha'. . ."

"A feckin' psychic," said the third, shaking dirty blond hair.

"Real swami, yer mon," said the fat one.

"I'm looking for Gina . . . um, Grace Furey's house," Colin said, reading from the dole book. "Whiterock Road . . ." The four men stopped laughing as Elvis toked the last of the hash.

"Give us a fag," said Elvis.

Colin pulled out a pack of the duty-free Marlboros and handed them to Elvis, who offered them around. He hadn't met anyone in Ireland older than twelve who didn't smoke.

"A Yank," said Elvis, with keen interest.

"With feckin' smashin' cowboy bewts as well, mind yeh," said the one with the bad teeth, unwrapping a Cadbury fruit-and-nut bar. He took a bite and passed the candy bar to the others.

"Howdy, Clint," said the fat guy, with an exaggerated John Wayne drawl. They dissolved in laughter again as Elvis lit his Marlboro with a stick from the fire and then passed the flaming stick to his buddies. Elvis tried to return the pack of Marlboros to Colin.

"Keep 'em," Colin said.

"Thanks, Yank," he said.

"Good title for a song, wha'," said the dirty blond, and they laughed in unison again, their mouths pasty with chocolate.

"Yeh ever see a red house in America?" asked bad teeth.

Colin looked baffled.

"Well, if yeh do, that's me Auntie Louie's house," he said.

"I'll look for it," Colin said.

"Show us the address you got?" said Elvis.

"You FBI?" asked the fat guy, and they started laughing again. "American Special Branch."

"CIA?" asked bad teeth.

"NYPD Blue?" asked dirty blond.

They kept laughing, but Colin's cigarettes lifted any menace from the exchange. One of the mangy dogs, its coat a checkerboard of bald patches and hairy clumps, came sniffing at Colin's feet, growling. Elvis took one step in its direction, stamping a foot, and the dog yelped and scampered in retreat.

"Go way outta dat, yeh mangy bitch, yeh," he shouted at the dog, and then handed the dole book back to Colin. "That's Cat, feckin' Patsy Donohoe's dog. What do yeh say about a cunt who names his feckin' dog Cat? There's even bad blood between the Furey and the Donohoe dogs. But never you mind that, righ'? The house you want is down the road there." He pointed to another corner house, where a different covered caravan, painted bright red and yellow, was parked. A piebald pony was tied to a leafless hedge in the same yard and scrap from several dismembered automobiles lay on the lawn, like the bones of jackal-ravaged animals.

"Thanks," said Colin.

"It's me cousin's kip," Elvis said. "She lives with me granda, who is a Furey, righ', and Granny, who's a bleedin' Lynch, righ'? But yeh can tell them for me that Luke—that's me, righ'—that Luke Furey, son of Rory Furey, toughest man in Ballytara, says all the Lynches is a bunch o' cunts and whores and ponces. And that Luke feckin' Furey—that's me, righ'—that Luke says to the Lynches that the Fureys rule the Ballytara Estates, cousins or no feckin' cousins, righ'? I got no problem with yeh, Yank, it's them'ns that I'm talkin' about, righ'? Are yeh righ', then?"

Colin nodded and said, "Right, thanks."

"Then tell them for me that I'm only jokin', righ'," he said, cracking up laughing. "Otherwise Granny'll 'et me for feckin' tea, wha'? We mightn't like each other, but we're family all the same."

"Right," Colin said. *Kid needs a fucking straitjacket,* he thought.

Colin walked down Whiterock Road, kicking aside milk cartons and empty cigarette packages. Orange and banana rinds, empty Tayto potato chips bags, and Cadbury candy wrappers clogged the small sewer grates. He put his camera to his eye and did a 360-degree pan of the scene, snapping several shots for details. *Gina's beauty against this blight will look great on film.*

He heard a mournfully sad reel being played on a tin whistle and realized it was coming from inside the covered wagon parked on the front lawn of the house Luke Furey had pointed out.

Colin paused in front of the house. The tin whistle stopped and an even sadder lament moaned from a set of bagpipes—the Irish kind, which are pumped with hand bellows rather than blown with the lips, as Scottish pipes are played. A musician in O'Donoghue's pub had told Colin they were called uilleann pipes. *Pretty damned good,* he thought. When he closed his eyes, he could be off in the glens of the Irish countryside instead of here in the midst of an urban slum. The music stopped abruptly.

Colin opened his eyes and walked through the gate. One of the numbers was missing from the address on the front door of the house, and the red paint on the lower-right panel of the wooden door had been scraped clean by the nails of some tenacious dog. The flap on the letter slot was gone, the gap stuffed with a rag. The canopy of the covered caravan on the front lawn was yellow and red and the spokes of the wagon wheels were painted the same bright colors. Outside the back door of the wagon, on the lawn, three automobile bucket seats were arranged around the large circular stones of an old-fashioned campfire, with an elevated metal grill positioned over the stones. There were double cinderblocks in front of each bucket seat, serving as crude tabletops.

A piebald pony with black-and-white patches, like a four-legged hobo, was tethered to the leafless bush, snorting around on the dead lawn, scrounging for something, anything, organic to eat. A gaunt nanny goat on a long rusty chain munched at a pile of composting garbage—fruit rinds, potato skins, vegetable leaves, fish skeletons, meat bones. The udders of the goat were swollen with milk. A dirty white infant's shoe with a small round bell attached was fastened about the goat's neck, dinging softly. The music again wafted from inside the covered wagon. *All the world's recycling ends up in this shit heap of a yard,* Colin thought. *Like a private Staten Island.*

The rest of the lawn was piled high with old drainage pipes, pieces of wrought-iron fencing, tires, car batteries, steering wheels, headlights, and dozens of other automobiles parts, along with motorcycles, bicycles, baby carriages, and lawn mowers.

The same mangy dog that had growled at Colin earlier tried his best to intimidate him again. Colin stamped his foot the same way Luke Furey had and the dog barked once, turned, tail between its cane-thin legs, and trotted off in an aimless sideways gait. The dog looked back once more and barked in a final attempt at bravery before continuing on its defeated way.

The knocker on the front door of the house was also missing, so

Colin rapped his knuckles on a small bubble-glass panel. There was no reply, but he could hear the voice of an older woman from within, singing in the babyish tones of a lullaby:

> *There was a little nigger*
> *He wouldn't grow any bigger*
> *So we put him in the windee for a show*
> *But he fell down in the windee*
> *And he broke his little fingee*
> *And he couldn't play his oul banjo . . .*

Jesus Christ, Colin thought. *We're starting a brand-new century and the last one hasn't even arrived here yet.*

He took an octagonal fifty-pence coin from his pants pocket and tapped it loudly on the glass panel of the door. Colin could hear the crying of the child grow louder and the footfalls of many young children slapping toward the door. An old woman shouted, "G'wan inside, the lot a yiz, or my Jaysus above there'll be the sally rod for one and all around here!"

Finally, the door opened, revealing an obese woman, maybe three hundred pounds, in her late sixties but with bright Kool-Aid orange hair spilling out from under a floral head scarf. *Bozo the clown's mother,* Colin thought. *Maybe Kieran's mother-in-law?*

She stood in the doorway, unfiltered cigarette dangling from her cracked, brownish lips, and holding a crying child in her arms. *This must be Granny Furey, maiden name Lynch,* Colin thought. He was trying to keep all of Luke Furey's data straight.

The baby in Granny's arms was definitely the same red-haired girl that Gina Furey pushed in the pram. *Right house,* he thought. "What about yeh?" Granny asked.

"I'm looking for Gina Furey," Colin said.

"Wrong house," Granny said. "Don't know anyone by that name. And I don't know my neighbors, whether they're my sons, daughters, brothers, and sisters or not, nieces and nephews or no, cousins or no cousins, or any of their kin, nor do I care to, thank you very much. If yer lookin' for somethin', pray to Saint Anthony." Granny wore a huge white cardigan, sooty with coal dust, the same soot forming black crescents under each of her fingernails. Her swollen feet were jammed into yellow plastic shoes, split at the sides, where sore-looking purple bunions protruded like grape-flavored sour balls. Her black-and-white polka-dot dress was the size of a small parachute, stenciled with dried white map lines of perspiration.

"Grace," Colin asked. "Is there a Grace Furey? Or Grainya?"

The other kids, whom Colin recognized as the ones Bridie, Susan, and Philomena had pushed in their prams, gathered around Granny's legs. An infant, whom Colin thought for sure was the same one the beggar girl had held in her arms the day before on O'Connell Bridge, crawled under the fat woman's legs. Its nose was blocked with green snot, a dirty pacifier plugging its chapped lips. The infant looked up at Colin with the saddest red-rimmed eyes he'd ever seen on a child, and he noticed the kid was hugging a Temple Bar Hotel towel as though it were a security blanket.

The old lady who lived in a fucking shoe, he thought.

"Grace . . . that sounds like a name on a bank bewk, wha'?" said the fat woman. "Or on a letter from Australia, wha'? No one here uses a bank. I don't know anyone from Australia. May the wind be at yer back with a knife in your bewt."

She attempted to close the door, but Colin took a step closer, put his shoulder against the door, and looked past her into the house, searching for Gina or anyone else. In contrast to the landfill that was her front garden, the inside of the fat woman's house was spotless and cozy. The living room boasted a glowing coal fire topped with a block of beautifully aromatic peat and was furnished with simple couches piled with brightly colored throw pillows and quilts. Clean, if worn, rugs covered the floors. A gleaming round oak dining table squatted on lion's-paw feet, surrounded by matching high-backed, ornately carved chairs. A matching oak hutch displayed a sparkling set of blue delft, polished silver bowls, and candlesticks. A collection of old briar pipes lined the fireplace mantel next to a display of old, cracked family photos in hand-carved wooden frames, many depicting gatherings of a tinker clan around country campsites.

A digital clock radio on the mantel—one that looked a lot like the one from his hotel room—told Colin he had six minutes before the cab driver took off, leaving him marooned out here in Knackaragua.

"You can break your skinny neck lookin' but you won't get past me," said the fat woman. "No Yank will ever darken my feckin' door."

"I have something of Gina's or Grace's I'd like to return."

"A Yank already brought rack and ruin to this family the one'st," she said, anger rising in her strong voice. "I'll not sit by and watch it happen the twice't. I heard of another Yank once. Jesse James, that's him. The cowboy. Shot in the bleedin' back, he was, wha'? Prolly a re-lay-tive of me useless husband's. Ask him."

She pointed at the covered caravan parked on the lawn. Colin turned and saw a gray-haired man with his head bowed out the small back door of the wagon. His jaw was moving up and down— the lips pursed out, cheeks hollow, as though he had no teeth in his mouth. *Must be Granda Furey,* he thought. *Gabby fucking Hays with a flute.* Granda was working with trained skill and a special kind of whittling knife on the odd-looking uilleann pipes.

"No Yank'll darken my door again, hear?" the fat woman shouted and slammed the front door. Colin heard the baby continue to cry from within and the old woman once again began to sing the racist minstrel song to the crying child.

There was a little nigger
He wouldn't grow any bigger . . .

Colin walked to the gray-haired man.

"I'm looking for Gina or Grace," Colin said.

Granda Furey looked up sideways at a loud, shiny black crow on an overhead wire, narrowed his eyes, and slowly blew out an ominous stream of breath. Gray stubble matted Granda's old, weathered face.

"A crow over yer home means someone's gonna die," Granda said.

"Look," Colin said, getting annoyed. "If you see her, tell Gina that Colin was here to return something to her."

Now Colin saw a red and muddied High Ace Toyota van pull to

a brusque halt on Whiterock Road, just outside the gate. The back of the van was piled high with old furniture and pieces of scrap metal. Two men got out, slamming the doors. They wore scuffed bomber jackets, muddy motorcycle boots, and flat caps and they approached with alacrity, their eyes fixed on Colin, arms swinging menacingly, faces hardened from years of weather, booze, poverty, and rage. One carried a hurling stick. Then Colin heard footsteps from behind him, from the direction of the cemetery. He turned and saw another man leaving the house to the right of the fat woman's.

Colin recognized him by his brand-new tweed sport jacket—the one Gina gave him in the McDonald's on Grafton Street.

Oh, Jesus, Colin thought. *Gina's husband, the father of her kid.*

Adrenaline pumped in him like heavy-metal music—frantic, undisciplined, desperate. *Nowhere to run,* he thought. *No wonder they built this slum next to a fucking cemetery.* He thought of himself as a cheap headline in the morning's *Irish Independent,* YANK MURDERED IN BALLYTARA! He would be the subject of a protracted exchange of readers' letters in *The Irish Times.*

"I must have the wrong house," Colin said to the old man, barely able to get the words out of his dry mouth. "Sorry."

Colin turned again, began walking toward the gate when Granda said, "Are you a re-lay-tive of hers from the States? A brother, maybe?"

Colin looked at him and shook his head.

"No," he said, curious, licking his dry lips. "I just met her."

"Oh, my Jaysus," Granda said. "Just like her mother. I warned her. If she kept lookin', she'd be put aside by her own kind. Bad enough she's mixed herself."

"Excuse me?"

"Should've known there was killins coming with a crow over me feckin' wagon."

Shooting Colin an anguished look, he disappeared into the caravan. Colin turned toward the gate and then suddenly felt something touch his leg. He jumped in horror, his fist balled, ready for action. The nanny goat bayed and moved closer to him, licking his jeans. The man with the hurling stick laughed uproariously.

"Nanny got yer feckin' goat, Yank?" he said, his voice a low menacing whisper. "The oul goat knows yer scared, see. He smells the fear by the sweat off yeh, see. He's looking to lick the Yank salt from yer sweaty Yank fear off yer Yank trousers."

The one in the tweed jacket remained silent, but indicated with his shifting eyes that Colin should leave.

Colin checked his watch; three minutes before the cabby would leave.

"Where in them States is yeh from, cowboy?" asked one of the men, removing his cap and shoving it into his jacket pocket, revealing dark unwashed hair. He slowly unzipped the jacket, hung it on the gatepost, and pushed his sweater sleeves up over thick, veiny forearms. His bulging muscles under the tight green sweater looked like they had been spot-welded together from iron scrap from the lawn. *Jesus Christ, this is outta* Deliverance, Colin thought.

"Said where yeh from?"

"New York City," said Colin.

"That a fact?" said muscles. "What might yer name be, then?"

Colin told him.

"Yeh look like yeh could be Eyetalian," muscles said, and then looked to the others. "Doesn't he look like he could be a smelly Eye Tai from New York instead of a Coyne, lads?"

"Aye, Rory, he does at that," said the shorter man standing with muscle-bound Rory. "Maybe he needs the oul garlic test."

"Leave it out, Derek," said the man in the tweed jacket.

"Shut yeh up, Paul Lynch, this is Furey family business, so it is," said Derek, twirling the hurling stick. "I says maybe we takes the Yank up to Garlic Hill. Show him how many unmarked Eyetalian graves there are."

Paul Lynch took his hands out of his tweed jacket pockets, quickly stepped toward Colin, and said, "Listen, fella, what are yeh doin' asking about Gina Furey? For what, like?"

"I found something of hers," Colin said.

"Show us," said Rory Furey, holding out his callused hand.

"It's in the hotel safe. A document, written in Gaelic."

"Yer here on yer holliers, just?" asked Paul Lynch.

"Right, holiday vacation," Colin said, recognizing the slang.

His watch told him the cabby was leaving in a minute.

"Nice watch," said Derek, lifting and batting a pebble with the hurling stick. "Whadda yeh think of his timepiece Rory?"

"Now all yeh need is learn to tell time," said Paul Lynch.

The other two laughed. Derek brandished the hurling stick in a mock threat and said, "I'll put me big hand in yer gob and me little one in yer bollocks, Paul, so I will."

"Yeh waiting for someone, Yank?" asked Paul.

"Taxi waiting by the barracks," Colin said.

"Yeh didn't come from America looking for Gina?" asked Rory, his flexed muscles starting to relax under the sweater.

"No," Colin said. "Never even heard of her before."

Now Luke Furey, the Elvis wannabe, approached Rory, shaking the Marlboro box. "Daddy-o, the Yank gimme these, so he did."

The men each took a cigarette from the pack and Paul Lynch lit all of them with an ornate lighter boasting a huge flame.

"Gina's no kin to yeh, then?" asked Paul Lynch.

"My parents are from Tipperary and Derry," said Colin. "No relatives in Dublin."

"Fine halting sites once upon a time, Derry and Tip," said Rory. "But now they put up all the feckin' boulders and dug trenches on the sides of the road like the rest of the country. Nowhere wants us. That's where they want us travelers to live, County Nowhere. That's why we're here, but come spring we'll be back on the road, sure."

"You guys related to Gina?" Colin asked, checking his watch, hurrying to the gate.

All four men looked at each other, considering the question.

"Aye," Paul said. "What time is your taxi leaving?"

Colin checked his watch. "Less than a minute."

"I'd get marchin' if I was you," said Paul Lynch. "This isn't the safest place for a geezer from America who looks like an Eyetalian to be asking about Gina Furey. If yeh folly me drift."

Colin didn't understand all of it but he'd heard enough to know that this was all about the blood secrets of a tinker clan and that it was time for him to go. He nodded and backed away from the four men, turned, saw Granda peering from inside the covered wagon, saw Granny spying through the window of the house, saw the loud black crow take flight from the overhead wire, heard the goat bah, the pony whinny, and then Colin started to run, past the barrel fires, the dirty children, and the barking dog named Cat, out of Ballytara Estates, which they also called Knackeragua.

seven

After changing into his bomber jacket at the hotel, Colin spent the better part of the day Christmas shopping for his brothers and picking up Irish gifts. His father would love the tweed jacket and matching Irish walking hat. And his two brothers—Jack, four years older and a fledgling architect, and Eddie, three years younger and working for the telephone company while waiting to get on the police force—were getting white Irish wool Aran sweaters.

As he drifted up and down Grafton Street, window shopping and girl-watching, Colin also searched in the thick crowd for a blond girl in a floppy hat. He passed the busking musicians and several dirty traveler women begging, with young kids and infants at their sides, like something out of an old movie. *They do exploit their kids,* Colin thought. He paused to watch the women begging for a few minutes, the pickings slim from natives, generous from tourists.

But he couldn't see Gina anywhere.

He was scheduled to go back to New York in three days, and wasn't sure he'd ever see her again.

He popped into Bewley's on the odd chance that she'd be in there, having a cup of tea. The place was mobbed with shoppers and their children, loud with the clatter of cups and saucers and silverware. *Like a Foley sound effects room,* he thought. He found a seat at a table with three elderly strangers, where he sipped an excellent cup of coffee, ate a scone, and read the *Irish Independent*. There was a page five story about Christmas begging in Dublin, with excellent photographs of traveler women beggars using their infants as props. There were also photographs of traveler children on their own or in pairs, begging in front of the swankiest clothes stores and restaurants in town. *That cabbie wasn't exaggerating this part of his rant,* Colin thought.

The *Independent* story said that there is an urgent need for a clampdown on so-called Fagin-families, who force their children to beg to support their parents' drink and drug habits. The chairman of something called the Eastern Health Board's Community Care Program said that "these children are being systematically abused in what is part of a very serious racket in Dublin city."

The Health Board chairman also claimed that nothing was being done about the problem because of "the new political correctness that shields these so-called travelers, many of whom are nothing more than Dickensian child abusers of the worst sort."

Colin was reminded of the young beggar woman, still a teenager, who the day before had been begging with her cold and hungry infant on O'Connell Bridge before Gina came along and angrily shoved her and the baby onto a bus. He'd seen that same baby with Gina's red-haired child at the house of the fat granny with the orange Kool-Aid hair in Ballytara.

With the fat lady's husband living in a caravan on the front garden with a piebald pony, there was no doubt that Gina was somehow connected to a tinker family.

Even Mickey, the gangster in the Leeson Street nightclub, said Gina might be a traveler. The bouncers barred her three cousins because they were "knackers," the derogatory term for traveler.

Colin realized that Gina Furey was more than just some girl from the Dublin slums. She came out of an Irish subculture he knew very little about. Had the cabbie been telling the truth when he said traveler women were forced into arranged marriages as young as thirteen? To first cousins? Like the mutant banjo players in *Deliverance? Does Kieran come all the way to Ireland to become smitten by a thief, a liar, and a genetically inbred, backwoods Irish hillbilly?*

This scenario intrigued Colin all the more. *It's fresh,* he thought. *It hasn't been done before. I need to find out more. The truth is always stranger than fiction. Gina Furey is beyond different; she's even different to the Irish, who were already different from everyone else. That's living way out on the edge, and Gina Furey has more edge than a straight razor because she lives on the edge of the world.*

I have to know more about Gina, about what her life on the road has been like, where she comes from, how she was raised. I want to know everything there is to know about Gina Furey. For Kieran, for the movie. But how can I find out more? I'm not going back out there to Ballytara. And chances are slim that Gina will be coming around to see me after looting my hotel room.

He left Bewley's and walked back to the Temple Bar Hotel.

A knock on his door came a little past 7:00 P.M. He opened the door, expecting a maid to turn down the bed.

Gina Furey was encased in a chocolate-brown, beautifully tailored, crushed-velvet pantsuit and high-heeled ankle boots. Her freshly blown-out hair spilled over her padded shoulders. Her jacket, scoop-necked at the top, was fastened tightly around her wasp-thin waist, accentuating her shapely figure. Leaning against the door frame, winter coat draped over her arm, with a familiar-looking black canvas bag slung over her shoulder, she looked even more beautiful than he remembered.

"Alone?" she whispered.

"Not anymore," he said.

"Busy?"

"Wanna get?"

She smiled and he opened the door wider, stepping aside as she humbly walked into the room.

Gina dropped her canvas bag on the bed and pulled open the zipper. "Yer not yer typical gobshite Yank so I felt a wee bit guilty about leaving yeh to explain all this to the manager," she said as she dumped the sheets, pillowcases, and bedspread onto the bed.

"Jesus," Colin said. "I'm flattered."

She removed the clock radio and placed it where it belonged on the bureau top and bent to plug it in. As she leaned forward to reach the outlet, Colin could see down her loose silk blouse. She wasn't wearing a bra and her small firm breasts were visible, the nipples as dark as her eyes.

The radio came to life, Madonna singing "The Power of Goodbye." Gina looked up, catching Colin staring down her blouse.

"I used to know a girl who charged her parish priest five quid for a cheap look like tha'," she said, standing up, lightly cupping her breasts. "A tenner for an oul feel."

"She let a priest feel her up?"

"Better'n beggin'," she said. "And it bought her coal."

He wanted to tell her about watching her put the beggar woman on the bus, but he didn't dare tell her he'd spied on her.

"Hungry?"

"Wallfallen," she said. "But no French feckin' snails, thank yeh very much. Tell yeh what I never 'et in me life, though."

"What's that?"

"Room service," she said. "I've heard of it in the pictures. What is it?"

Colin rummaged in the top drawer of the bureau and took out a room-service menu and handed it to her.

"Read it to me," she said. "I like your American accent. It reminds me of that Robert De Niro fella. I always imagined having an Eyetalian father like him . . ."

Colin squinted at her. "Most women dream about having a lover like him," he said.

"Och, no, he's the perfect age for me father," she said.

Different, he thought. *She's not just contrary. She's different. An Irish tinker who wishes she had an Italian-American father like Robert De Niro. Wait, the mutant cousins out in Ballytara grilled him over whether he was Italian. And Gina says she only picks the pockets of Italian Yanks. Why? What's with this Italian shit?*

He began to read aloud. When he came to salmon steak, she stopped him.

"That'll do me like a dog on a rat," she said. "A bit of lovely salmon, some carrots and a few oul chips . . . I remember a time we caught some salmon straight out of the River Suir and cooked them on the riverbank in Carrick with a bit a buh'er and salt and they were only gorgeous, so they were."

"Who were you with?"

"None of yer business, nosy hole," she said.

"Should I order wine?" he asked.

"Oh, aye," she said. "And a pot a tay, and Irish brown bread and buh'er, and a sweet for after."

"Chocolate mousse?" he asked.

"Jayz, wha's dat?"

"You'll like it," he said.

"Grand," she said, rubbing her hands together like a kid.

Colin phoned room service and placed the order. Then, for the next fifteen minutes, he watched her busy herself in the hotel room. *She looks like a woman preparing a nest,* he thought. She hung up her winter coat, removed her velvet jacket, and put that on a hanger. She then hung Colin's jacket next to hers and carried the returned hair dryer into the bathroom. She folded the rumpled towels, neatly arranged Colin's various newspapers, took used glasses into the bathroom and rinsed them out, and arranged all his toiletries in a neat corner of the bathroom vanity. She walked back into the bedroom area, removed her boots, and as Celine Dion sang "Because You Loved Me" on the radio, Gina finally sat next to Colin on the bed closest to the window.

"Yeh were out in Ballytara looking for me," she said.

"Yeah."

"Why? I don't live there. Me cousins do. The ones you met last night. Third cousins, mind yeh. From the poor side of the family. Their mother married bad. How'd you know to go way out there?"

He was at a loss for words and then said, "I heard one of your cousins say they were taking the taxi to Ballytara."

"Load of shite," she said. "Yeh were lookin' for the stuff I nicked, weren't yeh? A few measly bits and pieces."

"I was not," he said. "I was looking for you."

"Told me distant auntie you'd something to return of mine."
Distant aunt, my ass, he thought. *That was her grandmother. More
bullshit . . .*

"Just said that because I wanted to see you again," he said.

Flatter her, Colin thought. *The way Kieran would.*

"Why'd you want to see me?"

"I don't know . . . because you're you, because I like you."

"Or because you were after a cheap ride?"

"You're a beautiful woman," he said. "I'd be lying if I said I
didn't want to sleep with you. Plus, I like you, you're different."

He shrugged. *Half of it's true,* he thought.

Gina stared at him in silence. "Yer different yerself," she said.
"No Irish fella would ever let all them words come out of his mouth
about what he was feelin'. Irish men are incapable of tellin' yeh how
they feel until they've had one too many gargles. And even then, the
only t'ing they ever feel is your ditties."

"Well, that's the reason I went out there," he said.

"The reason I took yer t'ings was to have a reason to come back
and see yeh, meself," she said. "Without lookin' like the righ' eejit.
Which I feel now anyway for admittin' it."

*It seems like a giant step for Gina Furey to display this kind of
emotion,* Colin thought. *Maybe she's horseshitting me, like I'm shitting her. The old scammer's routine, make good on a few small
loans to gain trust for the big one you never pay back.*

He didn't say any more about what he'd seen and heard in
Ballytara. Gina was obviously embarrassed. Or she wouldn't have
kept up the charade of a fake name and the pipe dream of the cottage on the sea, ignoring talk of her child, claiming her space-case
grandmother was some distant aunt.

Gina sat up and said, "Well, aren't yeh goin' to at least Jaysus
kiss me hello? I'm only after gettin' a new outfit just for you and
havin' me hair and nails done up professional. Good job yeh weren't
here with a durty oul ride or I . . . ."

She didn't get to finish the sentence, as Colin smothered her
mouth with his, kissing her deeply, clutching her small face in his
right hand, feeling her go limp as he put his left arm around her.

Her loose breasts pressed against his chest as she ran her long nails through his hair. She draped a leg over his, pushing him onto his back, her right thigh rising between his legs, rubbing him up and down, making him writhe. He cupped her behind, pulling her closer. He slid a hand down the back of her tight pants.

And the knock came on the door, accompanied by a pleasant, singsongy voice. "Room service!"

"Fuck," Colin said, freeing his hand from her pants.

"Almost," she said, laughing and straightening herself as Colin hurried to the door, adjusting his pants.

Gina devoured her salmon steak and fresh chips with peas, carrots, and brussels sprouts and several slices of brown bread and butter. *She eats like a fucking racehorse,* Colin thought.

Halfway through the second bottle of chardonnay, she said, "Tell me about New York."

"Huge," he said. "Eight million people. Greatest night-life in the world. Best food anywhere . . ."

"How many Eyetalians live there?"

Colin looked at her in surprise. *Again with the Italians,* he thought. *Italian-obsessed. Why?*

"Lots of Italians," Colin said. "Some of our most famous mayors were Italian. There's also lots of Irish, Poles, Russians, Jews, Asians, blacks, Latins. Lots of everything. New York is the world."

"How many Eyetalian gangsters?" she asked.

"Enough," Colin said.

"Are the Eyetalians hard to find in New York?"

"No," Colin said. "All you have to do is cast a mob movie. Thousands show up."

She looked at him blankly, not understanding.

"Seriously, there're loads of Italian neighborhoods," he said. "In Brooklyn, there's Bensonhurst, Dyker Heights, and Carroll Gardens. Staten Island has tens of thousands of Italians. In Manhattan, there's a place called Little Italy. In the Bronx, there's Arthur Avenue. In Queens, there's Ozone Park, Middle Village, and Howard Beach, where John Gotti came from . . ."

"I know who he is from the telly," she said. "He's lov-e-ly."

"Where he's spending the rest of his life isn't."

"Pity," she said. "Smashin' dresser. Killer smile."

"Can say that again," Colin said. "You have a thing for Italian gangsters?"

Is there a touch of jealousy in my voice? he wondered. *Kieran would be jealous.*

"I thought yeh were an Eyetalian," she said. "That's why I went after yer wallet."

"The fat guy you dipped downstairs also looked Italian."

"Aye," she said. "I looks for the Eyetalian Yanks. Not the chip-shop and ice cream Eyetalians we have here, mind yeh."

Colin knew from the travel books that most of the fish-and-chip shops in Dublin were once run by Italians, but their stranglehold on the fast-food trade was quickly being replaced by Vietnamese, Indian, and American fast-food emporiums.

Gina took a final bite of chocolate mousse and a sip of tea, followed by a gulp of wine. He poured two more glasses of wine and the second bottle was now gone.

"Jaysus, I'm as stuffed as a fat bishop's mistress," she said.

"So what's with the Italian fascination?" Colin asked.

"None of yer business is what it's with," she said.

Feeling the wine, he pushed the room-service tray into the hall. He closed the door and walked to her, kissed her. But this time she didn't open her lips.

"I couldn't put another blessed thing in me mouth," she said with a laugh, using a remote-control switch to turn on the TV.

Frustrated, Colin rolled away from her, got up, and made himself a cup of instant coffee at the small self-service machine on top of the refrigerator. *Fucking broad plays games,* he thought. He half filled the cup with coffee and topped it with Irish whiskey. Gina sensed that he was slightly annoyed.

"I told yeh, the best way to get in me knickers is not to try. Besides, not even a durty whore in a harem could do the gonkey after a huge feed like tha'."

"It's okay," he said, sitting on the bed.

"Have a wee nap," she said, kissing him on the lips.

He drank the whiskey, took off his pants, and got under the sheets. She turned off the TV, wiggled under the covers with him, and they kissed again. Then she retracted into a fetal ball, pulled the sheet tight over her mouth, hit an off switch in her head, and was quickly lost in slumber.

Fucking tinkers can probably sleep on broken bottles, he thought. *They live most of their lives under the stars on the rocky ground. Give them a hotel bed and they'll sleep like cadavers.* Colin watched Gina sleep and wondered what really went on behind those eyes. *What does she dream about?*

He had one more whiskey and then in frustration he turned his back on her and fell asleep.

December 23

In the morning, Colin reached across the bed for Gina. She wasn't there. He looked at the clock: 6:13 A.M.

"Gina," he called in the dark, but there was no reply. He switched on a lamp and saw that this time all the bedding was intact; the hair dryer and the towels were still there.

Every time I close my eyes she splits, he thought.

He showered, dried his hair, and put on a starched denim shirt and clean blue jeans. He took the black jeans from the hanger, removed the belt, and grabbed the cash from the right-hand pocket. His 1,500-pound cash wad was diminished by at least half. The wallet was also missing, along with his credit cards. "Fuck," he shouted.

In a panic, Colin checked his bomber jacket pocket and found that his passport was also missing. He searched the sport jacket he had worn the previous morning and, sure enough, Gina Furey's dole book was still there.

Ingrate bitch eats my meal, drinks my booze, teases my prick, and then robs me blind two days before Christmas, he thought. *What an asshole I am.*

Then on the top of the TV he spotted the hotel envelope with his name on it, in Gina's printed spidery handwriting. *Another one of her illiterate fucking letters,* he thought. *Telling me what a nice fella*

I am and thanks for everything she robbed and good-bye, chump.

He tore open the envelope. The letter inside read: "Colin Luv, I'm at the Wavefront Hotel in Howth. Under yore name. Ha ha. Hury, Grace. PS. Bring Willie."

eight

Colin called the Wavefront Hotel and, sure enough, there was a Colin Coyne booked there, with his *wife*. "Sorry," said the receptionist. "The private seaside cottage Mr. and Mrs. Coyne are sharing has a Do Not Disturb on the phone."

The skinny, thirty something taxi driver knew the Wavefront Hotel. "Yeh must be paying a pretty penny there," the driver said.

"I guess I am," Colin said.

"I betcha the missus picked it, wha'?"

"You could say that," Colin said.

"Well, she better make it worth every penny, boyo," the driver said with a dirty laugh, as he maneuvered through the empty early-morning streets of Dublin. "I know I feckin' would, wha'? If mine ever dared make me fork up for a place like the feckin' Wavefront, by Jaysus she'd go home bowlegged as a jockey."

"Good advice," Colin said.

Colin lifted his camera, looked through the viewfinder, and panned the rocky winter seaside as the driver sped up the empty coast road to Howth. The morning looked like early evening as rain clouds swelled in a heavy gray sky and whitecaps rippled the sea. An oil tanker sat on the horizon like a dirty child's toy.

"Looks like rain," Colin said.

"All the better for what yer after," the driver said.

The taxi mounted the road to the Gothic estate atop a sea cliff.

The main house was a century old, surrounded by a half dozen private cottages discreetly spaced along the bluff overlooking the edge of the Irish Sea. Colin overtipped the driver—giving him ten pounds for Christmas.

"Happy Christmas, and don't do anything I wouldn't do . . . unless you do it twice," the driver said with a laugh before speeding off.

Colin carried his bag into the main house as the first drops of morning rain began to fall. He stopped at the front desk, where the receptionist asked him to sign the American Express imprint Gina had presented earlier. He did and she handed Colin a room key.

"Now, first cottage up the path to your right," the woman said, in a rushed breathless whisper, blushing. "There'll be music in the Robert Emmet lounge this evening. Room service is available twenty-four hours. Enjoy your honeymoon, Mr. Coyne."

Colin nodded and took the key and said, "Thanks."

He walked out of the main hotel building into the mounting rain and followed an old stone path toward a bluff overlooking the sea, where waves were crashing on the ancient breakers in a stormy fit. The smell of the sea and the roar of the wet wind were exhilarating as Colin approached the rugged squat cottage that sat on the very edge of Ireland. Wood smoke billowed out of the red brick chimney and scattered in the gale. Colin grew excited as he approached the front door and put the key into the lock.

He opened the door and stepped inside, closing it behind him. Gina Furey lay under the sheets of the king-size four-poster bed, a bottle of champagne chilling in a silver ice bucket beside her. A roaring wood fire crackled from a deep-set fireplace, casting an undulating orange hue over the large room. The curtains on the big bay window were open wide but no one could look in from the sea. The cottage was as private and romantic as the one Gina Furey had described in her fantasy that night in the French restaurant.

Gina poured a second glass of champagne for Colin. He slipped off his jacket, dropped it onto an overstuffed chair, and walked to her. He took the glass and she pulled back the top sheet. Gina wore the fishnet teddy she'd shoplifted from Green and Timothy's department store. A pelt of bright copper-colored pubic hair peeked through the black teddy. *A natural redhead,* he thought.

"I was afraid you'd never come . . ."

"Pun intended?"

She narrowed her eyes. "What is it?"

"Never mind," he said. "What about protection?"

"Not to worry," she said.

They made love for more than an hour. He imagined it on film. Boiled down to two horny minutes: *A lot of cutting. Crooked angles. She's trying to steal Kieran's heart. Firelight. Rain on the windows. The sound of the sea. Needs to start romantically, with awkward foreplay, and build to an animal lust. Sweaty. Groaning. Contorted. Front, back, sideways. Think William Hurt and Kathleen Turner in* Body Heat.

Gina led him to a full-length mirror, making him stand as she knelt and filled her mouth with him. He watched her in the mirror in a mounting frenzy. When she sensed he was ready, she spindled herself on him and he danced in a crazy circle, with her arms around his neck, looking him square in the eyes, ferociously, while he emptied himself inside her.

If I can get this on film, the audience has to believe Kieran's obsession with her, he thought. *It's sexual skydiving, bungee jumping, a launch into deepest, darkest space with a woman as unpredictable and scary as any he's ever met.*

When they were finished, Colin was weak in the legs. Gina smiled and dismounted him. She walked confidently to the fire, which she fed with bundles of driftwood. Colin plopped in an armchair and poured the last of the champagne, his eyes feasting on her nakedness. *Kieran feels victorious,* he thought. *He's triumphant, in charge, and ready to be fleeced.*

They sat on facing chairs, sipping champagne. Gina draped a leg over the arm of her chair, the fire reflecting in her big dark eyes. She stared at him in eerie silence. He leaned toward her, drizzling champagne between her legs. He knelt and gently munched it off.

"Did you grow up in Dublin?" he asked, looking up at her.

"The less yeh know about me the more you'll like me," she said, grasping a handful of his hair, pulling his face into her.

Gina lifted the phone and ordered more champagne and a huge Irish breakfast of rashers and eggs and porridge and toast and scones and raspberry jam and orange marmalade and Irish tea. She hung up. She screamed. She grabbed his ears. Clamped her thighs. Went limp.

Later, as Gina staggered dreamily to the bathroom, Colin pulled on a hotel robe and answered the knock on the front door. The room smelled heavily of sex. He tipped the blushing room-service girl. They ate, naked and silent. He stared at the red V between her legs and then at the blond curls on her head. She noticed, said nothing. He didn't mention it. They fed each other, playfully finger-painting one another with jam and marmalade and soon began licking one another clean. She lifted a butter patty, very slowly, very delicately, unwrapped it, and then buttered herself thoroughly. *Last Tango in Paris,* Colin thought. *No dialogue. Action. Music. All pictures.*

Gina lay on the carpet in front of the fire. "Manlier this time," she said, lifting herself to him. "Yeh don't have to be nice."

Gina's was so loud it scared Colin. *Fucking banshee,* he thought. *She makes Kieran feel like royalty. Brian Boru, king of all Ireland, fucking some gypsy queen.*

Finished. Heart pounding. Limp. *Friction sores on my prick,* he thought. Her giggles turned to uncontrollable laughter.

"What's so fucking funny?" he asked.

"This all cost yeh a lot more than was in yer wallet that first day."

"Worth it."

Gina turned on the radio, Sinead O'Connor singing "The Foggy Dew" from the Chieftains album.

"She never recovered from tearing up the picture of the pope on American TV," Colin said.

"Aye, she sings like an angel, but," Gina said. "She's just a bit touched, like three-quarters of Dublin, wha'?"

"You're fond of music, aren't you?"

"I am and I am'nt," she said. "Some of it brings back memories that are terrible sad."

"Like what?"

"Like memories that belong to *me,* righ'?"

He nodded. "Sorry," he said.

They kissed and touched and drank more champagne. After long minutes of silence, Gina wordlessly walked to the bathroom and took a shower. Colin dozed. A zombie nod, half awake, half asleep, sexually satiated. He awoke and showered.

By the time he had finished, Gina had ordered a lunch of three dozen oysters and bowls of steaming oxtail soup, plus assorted bread and rolls.

"Feed that willie," she said, holding it softly in her hand.

He devoured the soup and bread. She fed Colin the oysters from the half shell, whooping with laughter at the way he scooped the raw shellfish through his curled tongue.

"I fancy the way yeh do dat."

"Then gimme that bearded oyster, sweetheart," he said.

"The wha'?"

And he buried his face in her. She laughed in a roaring fit as rain streaked down the windows and the waves smashed into the breakers. He thought, *Cutaways. Do some coverage to keep this from becoming NC-17, no* Nine ½ Weeks *on my first film.* The laughter soon stopped, replaced by Gina's soft sighs, and then her mounting moans, her urgent cries, and finally the steamy steady climb to the banshee wail.

She is easily the best piece of ass Kieran has ever, ever had, Colin thought. *Savage.*

In late afternoon, they napped, her head on his shoulder, the golden locks spilling down his bare chest and abdomen.

That night, they sat at a table in the Robert Emmet lounge overlooking the roiled and rugged coast of the Irish Sea. The crowd was mostly middle-aged and affluent, a few European tourists. Colin could hear French and German being spoken. The band was playing James Taylor's "Carolina in My Mind," with the lead singer strumming a Martin acoustic guitar and singing in a pleasant voice, backed by a drummer, a bass player, and a keyboard player.

Colin and Gina were reading the menus when the manager, a gracious white-haired man in an open-necked shirt and blue blazer, came to the table and introduced himself as Vinny Ford. "We'd like to honor your honeymoon with a complimentary bottle of champagne."

"Och, you're too kind," Gina said, beaming, as she reached across the table and took Colin's hand in hers.

A waiter appeared and popped the Moet champagne, while the manager signaled the band leader.

"A nice hand and for the newlyweds," the Dublin bandleader said. "Mr. and Mrs. Colin Coyne."

The other diners clapped politely.

"What did you tell these poor assholes?" Colin whispered.

"Och, it's only a bit a feckin' crack," Gina said.

"Now will the happy couple come up and have the first dance?" the bandleader said, and the crowd applauded again.

Colin downed a glass of champagne as the bandleader said, "The bride has requested we play a Strauss waltz. Tall order, but we'll give it our best go anyway. G'luck a hundred babbies for yous."

"I don't know how to fucking waltz," Colin whispered as Gina pulled him up.

"It's the gonkey standing up," she said. "Folly me, yeh big bollocks."

She took Colin by the hand and led him onto the dance floor. She grasped both his hands, put one around her waist, one held high, and began to waltz him with perfect grace, in her high heels and black minidress, sweeping Colin around the polished floor with a skillful, swirling majesty.

"Where did you learn to waltz?" he asked as they glided.

"From the fat man's arse on Moore Street, righ'?" she said.

He leaned back in confusion as she dipped him to the right and then to the left, and then spun him in a dizzying circle.

"What fat man?" Colin asked as the ceiling whipped past him.

"It's an expression meanin' none of yer flippin' business."

"Whatever," he said, and followed her moves.

Colin imagined it all as a movie: *the band playing. Gina waltzing him all over the dance floor in a circular frenzy. Faces. Envious women. Horny men. All gaping at Gina. Jealous wives elbowing their ogling husbands. Drunks clapping out of time. Gina's skin-tight dress. The choker of white pearls. Her high heels. Waltzing magnificently.*

Then the band abruptly finished and Gina did a small mock curtsy. The diners clapped while Gina and Colin sat down. They ate poached cod, potatoes, and assorted green vegetables. A couple sent over a second bottle of champagne. Colin felt tired from all the fucking and dancing and drinking and the food. A second couple bought them a round of thirty-year-old Napoleon cognacs. Requests started coming in for dances with the bride. And Gina accepted every one of them. Colin watched Gina dance animatedly to songs like Cher's "Believe," and lyrically to slow ones like Eric Clapton's "Wonderful Tonight."

Some of the women in their forties and fifties wanted to dance with the handsome young groom and Colin obliged as many of them as he could. As he danced, they whispered good luck and first-night advice. One warned him that the drink could spoil his erection and offered him some of her husband's Viagra, which *she* happened to carry with her. Colin declined. "Be gentle with her on the first night," said another, who rubbed herself against him. *Christ, if she only knew about the friction sores on my dick,* he thought. The band finally took a break. When Colin lurched back to the table, Gina had another couple spellbound and leaning in close to her like a pair of kids listening to a ghost story around a campfire.

"Hi," Colin said, sitting down.

"Hi. I was just telling Janice and William here, from Kent they are, how we met," Gina said.

"Oh," Colin said, thinking, *This oughta be a fucking corker.*

"You're a very brave young fella," said Janice, the middle-aged woman with a sophisticated but not pompous British accent.

"I am?" Colin said.

"You could have gotten killed," said William, the pink-faced, graying husband. "If I saw a drug-crazed skinhead with a gun in New York, stealing a young woman's handbag, I'd call a copper. But I don't think I'd confront him, the way you did."

"Well . . ." Colin said, looking at Gina, who took a sip of cognac. He was hoping she'd pick up the ball.

"Daring him to shoot you," the woman said. "What if he would have?"

"Then I guess . . ."

"Och, but my Colin has a way of lookin' yeh in the eye and lettin' yeh know when he's in charge," Gina said, turning to him in admiration. "Don't yeh, darlin'? The durty skinhead handed him me bag, said he was sorry, and raced off like a puppy with his tail between his legs. I bet he ran all the way to Queens. Naturally, it was love at first sight."

She took Colin's hand and guided it under the table and up between her legs. She pushed his thumb inside her and tightened her muscles. He began to harden again.

"Was it love at first sight for you, Colin?" asked Janice.

"'Course it was," said William. "Just take one look at that face of hers."

The woman looked at her husband, slightly offended, and dug an elbow into his soft belly.

Gina pressed her hot, sweaty thighs around Colin's hand.

"She was like no one I'd ever met before," Colin said. "That's for sure. So open. So warm."

Now Gina reached over and squeezed the bulge in Colin's pants.

"And I knew he was strong," she said. "A real man's man."

"He didn't know you were a singer on tour?" Janice asked.

"No," she said. "Did yeh, darlin'?"

"No," he said, looking at her in surprise. "No, I didn't know she was a singer."

"But he came to the club where I was singin' and I sang a song just for him, didn't I, darlin'?" Gina said, kneading him.

"She sure did," Colin said, playing right along. Thinking: *What if she does a fucking* When Harry Met Sally *right here?*

"Why don't you sing us a song, Gina?" said William.

"The one you sang to Colin that first night," said Janice.

Gina turned to Colin, her eyes gleaming with devilish mischief, as he plunged his thumb in and out of her. She closed her eyes dreamily, then used her pelvic muscles to urge him out of her.

"Ahhhh . . . should I, gra?" she asked, giving Colin's cock one final hard squeeze, his friction sores anesthetized by arousal.

"Oh, sure," he said. "I'd love to hear you sing it . . . again."

Gina walked to the stage and chatted a moment with the band-leader, who was sipping a pint of Guinness. He nodded and eagerly handed her his Martin guitar, which she strapped across her narrow shoulders.

"I don't need the mike," Gina said. "This is grand."

Colin sat in awe of Gina's confidence as she climbed up on the stool, did a slow, deliberate Sharon Stone leg cross, tuned the guitar to her liking and then began to play a slow, catchy ballad called "Baby, You Keep Stealing Up on Me." She sang every single word of it while staring directly at Colin.

> *Baby, you keep stealing up on me*
> *In the moments I am certain I am free*
> *In between my waking hours and memories*
> *Baby, you keep stealing up on me.*

Everyone in the restaurant suddenly went still, knives and forks sus-pended or laid beside plates, the manager bringing waiters and bus-boys to a halt in their rounds, as Gina Furey sang the ballad with a pure and powerful voice.

> *And baby, I can't shake you from my mind*
> *When the snow is on my shoulders or it's fine.*
> *When I'm lost within my head*
> *Or just confused by time*
> *Baby, I can't shake you from my mind.*

Gina Furey kept looking directly at Colin as she sang:

> *Because baby, you have taken part of me*
> *You took it and I didn't even see*
> *Like the autumn steals the summer off of every tree*
> *Baby, you have stolen part of me.*

When she finished, the whole restaurant rose to a standing ovation. Gina was still looking directly at Colin, who was thinking: *Kieran would be eating out of her thieving hand right now.* Gina winked at

Colin and blew him a soft kiss. *Christ almighty,* he thought. *Who wouldn't be in love with Gina Furey?*

Gina spoke to a waiter before returning to the table, giving him an order. When she finally reached the table, Colin stood, smiled, and kissed her, wrapping his arms around her. The older couple beamed.

"Where do we buy an LP of your songs?" asked William.

"I haven't recorded one yet," Gina said.

"C'mon, you, leave the lovebirds alone," said Janice.

Two more people approached to ask Gina if they could buy her recordings. She told them that Colin was working with a record company on a contract. Colin nodded, knowingly. "That's right, next week, in New York. We're meeting with Tommy Mottola, making a video for Clear Conscience Videos, SoHo."

Finally, they were alone at the table again while the dance floor filled with couples.

"You've done this before," he said.

"In me dreams," she said, as the waiter brought a small pot of coffee and a half-dozen oysters on the half shell and placed them in front of Colin.

"Did you write that song?"

"I wish," she said, pouring him a cup of coffee and lifting an oyster. "Actually, a barrister named Adrian Mannering, from Kimmage, he wrote it. Good song. Good singer. Good lawyer."

"How'd you pick this place?"

"Seen it in a magazine and thought it looked lovely," she said, placing the oysters in front of Colin's mouth. Colin sucked one through his curled tongue.

"It is lovely."

"Aye," she said. "And so are you. Big strong fella, good in the heart, as well."

You will never know the horseshit from the sincerity with Gina, he thought. *That will be what brings down Kieran in the second act. I still need to work on the third act. Don't push it, don't contrive it, it'll come. From Gina.*

"You dance like Ginger Rogers, you sing like Shania Twain," he said. "So why don't you . . . ?"

"Why, me arse," she said. "Questions, questions, questions. I likes to dance for the hooley. I sings for the crack. I drinks for the madness. Look, I knows good dancin' when I sees it. And I knows good music and singin' when I hears it. I'm not good enough to do it for a feckin' job, like. I'm just a simple Irish girl. I don't have big silly American dreams. I have just one thing I'm looking for and I'll find it eventually. Udder den dat I'm me and I'm grand. Get it straight, I'm like Popeye the sailor man, righ'? I yam what I yam. And I yam'nt what I yam'nt. Toot toot."

"Tell me more about who you yam," he said.

"No," she said quietly, and handed him the coffee and lifted another oyster to his mouth. "Dere, now, get that inta yeh. You'll need yer manly strength cause I'm not even half done with yeh yet, boyo."

As they rushed through the rain, they heard the band play in the distance. As soon as they entered the room, she began to undress. Colin watched her, framing her with his bracketed fingers against the fire embers. *As Gina wiggles out of the wet dress, Kieran sees what other men will masturbate to tonight,* Colin thought. *Or think about as they bang their faithful wives.* She hung the wet dress from the bedpost. He removed his pants, draped them on the back of an arm-chair, and plopped naked into the big overstuffed chair in front of the bare bay window sipping a big snifter of brandy and port that he'd carried through the rain from the lounge. He watched Gina as she revived the guttering fire, adding more wood. Brushing her long hair in a hypnotic feminine ritual. Applying fresh lipstick and perfume. Hooking a thin gold chain around her waist, more golden chains around her neck, and holstering her feet into red stiletto heels.

For Kieran, he thought, *this is like a live show, with the woman of his dreams on stage for an audience of one—him.*

When she saw that her performance had fully excited Colin again, she walked slowly to him, straddling him in the big armchair in front of the bay window as lightning scribbled in the sky above the Irish Sea. She mounted him, all 110 perfect pounds of her, and rode him front and back, bringing herself to climax twice, sounding like part of the crazy storm. "I feel like a milked cow," she said. She poured more champagne, brushed out her pubic hair in front of the fire. *She yam what she yam,* he thought.

He fell asleep in the big armchair to the sound of the drumming of the rain.

nine

December 24

He awakened as dawn cracked on the horizon, feeling hot and wet and hard between his legs. Gina was kneeling in front of him in the muted first light of morning, looking up at him with her big dark eyes. She smiled with swollen lips, brushed her wild hair from her face.

"Mornin'," she said, her voice a soft purr. "Happy Christmas." And then she selflessly finished.

As seabirds circled in a baby-blue sky and sun burned through the morning mist, he lay motionless in the big chair.

"Was I all right?" she asked, more vulnerable than he'd yet seen her, naked and flawless.

"No," Colin said, intentionally pausing for a movie beat.

"Feck off, then."

"You were magnificent."

"Go way outta dat," she said, blushing, tearing a filter off a Dunhill cigarette and lighting it, pulling her knees up under her chin. "I bet I'm no match for them fil-um stars."

"You're right," Colin said, thinking of many struggling actresses he'd slept with, some as pretty, in a false, desperate way, as any of the famous stars. "No match at all. You leave them all in the star dust."

"I'm tellin yeh, boyo, we did things last night I never knew were possible in a Catholic country without gettin' struck with lightning," she said. "Does everybody in America do all them things?"

"No," he said. "I guess it's what's called the right chemistry."

"Planets lined up, like?" she asked, cocking her head.

"Maybe," he said.

"Load of shite," she said, that familiar chilly look returning to her eyes. "Sounds nice but, ah, well, it was just a bit a fun. The oul crack. A good night, as they say. Don't let's make it more than it was. We live worlds apart. You'll be goin' home to New York in a few days and I'll be back to me own little life. Still, the crack last night was ninety, wha'?"

She smacked his ass and exhaled smoke.

"The crack was a hundred and ninety," Colin said.

"When do you have to leave, then?"

She took a deep drag of the cigarette, suddenly unable to look him in the eyes the way she had when she sang to him. All at once, as the sun backlit her hair like a spool of Coney Island cotton candy, she looked much younger, vulnerable, sadly alone.

"On the twenty-sixth," he said.

"Saint Stephens's day," she said. "And I have to be with my re-lay-tives on Christmas Day." He knew she meant at least her daughter, and probably her cousins, the Lynches, and fat Granny, and Granda, the old loon in the covered wagon who could play beautiful music but who foresaw death in the cold eye of a crow. Maybe it included the four screwballs who confronted him in front of the house in Ballytara. *What a fuckin' crew,* he thought. *How does she fit in with them?*

"Can you stay another night with me?" he asked, eager to pick her brains for his script before he left Ireland.

"Och, I'd need to go into town to make arrangements," she said. "There's a bit of business I have to see to. I'd like to, mind yeh, it's been a long oul while since I been with a fella . . ."

"What about your friend Mickey, the gangster?" he asked.

"Don't be feckin' annoyin' me with that right eejit," she said. "I don't sleep with married men. I don't sleep with many fellas, period. It's been almost a year. It's usually too sloppy afterward, them always wantin' to marryin' me, or ownin' me. That, or a bunch of wankers lookin' for a new mammy. I won't play mammy to some big hairy Nancy, and no one will ever own me, righ'?"

"You've already made that perfectly clear."

She leaned back on the floor, letting the sunlight shine on her face and her body. In the sunshine, Colin could see filaments of red hair on her arms and red downy swirls on the nape of her neck. For the first time, he could also see red roots at the very base of the hair on her head.

"Can I ask you a question?"

"Maybe," she said.

"Why dye such beautiful red hair blond?"

"You mean why don't me drapes match me rug?"

"Yeah," he said, laughing.

"Red's too Irish," she said, blowing out the smoke. "Besides, me ma had red hair. It always made me sad to see it in the mirror because it made me think of her."

"Sorry."

"Yeah," she said, flicking her cigarette with perfect aim across the room and into the fire. "Me as well. I was very young but I can remember her. I remember when it happened, sure."

"Jesus, I didn't mean to pry that far," he said. But he didn't really know if this was just another of the many fictions Gina had created for herself.

"It's okay," she said with a dry sad laugh, blowing out her last stream of smoke. "Actually, I was thinking of dyin' me hair dark brown, like an Eyetalian. But then I saw in all them movies— *Goodfellas, Casino, Donnie Brasco*—that the Mafia wives always dye their hair blondie. That must be how the Eyetalians like their women, dyed blondie, so I did it this color. Doesn't it suit me, Colin?"

"You couldn't be any more beautiful. But what's your obsession with Italians? You think they're hot?"

"Nothin' like that, atall," she said. "Although some of them are. Never yeh mind, it's personal, like. Leave it out, righ'?"

"Sure."

"Now, I better go take care of a bit a business," she said.

"Should I hold on to this room?"

"Too dear. I thought it would be grand for one special night."

"That it was."

"Yeh t'ink so?" She looked him in the eye as if she wanted to say something more. She didn't.

Gina took a pair of blue jeans from her black canvas bag and snapped the wrinkles from them. Colin was entranced as he watched her wiggle into them, a pure male fantasy. It made him half erect again.

"Jaysus, there's no stoppin' you, boyo," she said. "When you go back home you can leave that on loan with me if you like."

She laughed as she reached in her handbag and took out his wad of cash, his passport, and his wallet and handed them to him.

"Why don't we share a taxi into town?" he asked.

"It takes two to tango," she said, "but one to live yer life. And I have to get back to mine."

He tried to hand her some bills for a taxi. "No," she said as she pulled on a sweater over her small breasts. "You've spent enough. I have me own money for a taxi, sure."

"I'll be at the Temple Bar Hotel, then," he said.

She walked to him and kissed him on the lips and grabbed a handful of the back of his hair and yanked it with a soft growl.

"Grand fella," she said through clenched teeth. "For a Yank."

And then she was gone, out the door into the sunny morning, her black canvas bag slung over her shoulder.

ten

After showering and eating breakfast, Colin checked out of the Wavefront and took a taxi back to the Temple Bar Hotel. He realized he'd left his Temple Bar Hotel key back at the Wavefront, and asked for another at the front desk.

He spent another two hours in the gym, most of it on the stationary bike, trying the morning tabloids, both British and Irish. He couldn't focus on anything. Colin's mind was filled with movie ideas and images. *Kieran waltzing with Gina Furey. Her singing to Kieran. Food. Drink. The fireplace. The storm. The sea. The sex. Butter. Laughter. As the song says, Gina keeps stealing up on Kieran,* he thought. *All too good. Too positive. Kieran has to be getting set up for a major fall.*

After shaving, Colin donned clean black jeans, an Aran sweater, and his polished cowboy boots and went out into the day. The streets were crowded with last-minute holiday shoppers. He strolled Grafton Street in the Christmas Eve madness, drifting into a few stores, buying some presents for his brother Eddie's kids. He saw something Gina might like. *Fuck it, I'll buy it,* he thought. *Just to register her reaction. It's R and D. I need to be nice to her, to mine her for character, dialogue, and story. To get a script done, to make some dough. After the three-hundred-pound Wavefront bill, smoke should start curling from the edges of my American Express card.*

Hungry after his workout, he walked ten minutes across town to the Christ Church area and stood on line at Burdock's famous fish-and-chips shop. He ate sitting alone in a small park around the corner, washing the fish and chips down with a cold Coke. The greasy chips tasted strongly of the rich Irish earth. The fish inside the thick crispy batter was fresh and moist and worth every indulgent bite.

Walking alone through the Dublin streets, he took out his tape recorder, speaking notes into it, hitting the pause button, and then the record button when another idea struck, trying to make sense of Kieran's feelings for Gina.

"If Kieran knows Gina has a kid he's gotta know that it's madness to get involved with this crazy dame," he said into the microphone. "The kid part is a lifer. You take a kid into your life, present yourself as a father figure, you've taken on a moral, emotional, and financial responsibility for life. Like the promise I made to Mom about never walking away from a child. So when Kieran steps into that role, remember what that role is: It's shit on the rug, crying in the night, tuition, homework, bedtime stories, Girl Scouts, doctors, boys looking up her dress, puberty, falsies, dating, marriage, grandkids, and probably divorce. And, remember, the kid's mother is Gina. And she's a thieving, conniving, scamming, lying, hard-drinking, cursing knacker. She's also good-hearted, generous to strangers, loyal to friends and family, God-fearing, self-reliant, resourceful, resilient, contrary, sweet, funny, unpredictable, beautiful, and the best piece of ass he's ever had."

He hit pause as he looked the wrong way for traffic while crossing Lord Edward Street. A Cara Irish Butter truck skid to a stop inches from Colin whose instinct was to race ahead, where he almost got hit by a sixtyish man on a bicycle.

"Christmas in the graveyard, yer after," shouted the truck driver. The man on the bike just blew out a long stream of breath, his ruddy cheeks deflating like a bellows.

"Sorry," Colin said to the bicyclist, and headed toward Dawson Street. He lifted the tape recorder back to his mouth.

"How does Kieran deal with the public outbursts? The defiant attitude? The portable grievances? All that crazy shit is scary, dangerous, and destructive. Does she start making Kieran just as antisocial? Instead of taming and changing her, does she change him? Or is their relationship a drag out brawl?"

He hit the pause button, knowing that was the rational, sensible Colin thinking. He pushed record again as he approached Saint Stephen's Green, people gawking oddly at him as he walked and talked into his tape recorder.

"Kieran thinks of ways he might explain his feelings for her to his brothers. I want her because she doesn't want or need anyone, never mind me, he'd say. I've never met anyone so free, so independent. I want her because I can't have her."

He hit the pause button because Colin knew none of those explanations would make any sense to his own two brothers if he ever brought home the likes of Gina Furey. *Jack had turned down a job with the telephone company to become an architect,* Colin thought. *He understands passion and risk, but Jack would never gamble with his emotions or his life. Eddie wants to be a cop because he likes the job security, the health plan, and retirement after twenty years. His life will be orderly and normal and law-abiding. He's already living out on Long Island in a four-bedroom house, with a mortgage, a couple of cars, a bunch of kids, and a dog.*

Eddie thought Colin was nuts when he told him he was going to major in filmmaking in college. "Why waste a fortune in prestigious New York University to make little movies?" he'd asked. "Where's the security?" But Jack supported the idea. "Be a fucking Irish Spike Lee, Col," he'd said. "Money, broads, and courtside Knicks tickets."

But if Colin ever told either of his brothers that he wanted to shack up with an Irish tinker who already had a kid, a woman he'd met while she was picking his pocket, they'd probably try to put him into a conservatorship, declare him incompetent, and book him a charter flight of shrinks.

Colin agreed with them. He was from the real world.

But the romantic and naive Kieran doesn't agree, he thought.

As he entered the great emerald park, Colin pressed record and took a seat on a bench facing a statue of James Joyce.

"Kieran would have to explain to his fictitious brothers how he met her," Colin said into the tape recorder. "How he followed her, stalked her, and finally banged her. That it was the best sex of his life, a blow job whipped up on Mount Olympus. He'll try to make them understand. But they won't. And it's probably better drama if they don't understand. If they think Kieran's nuts, it'll cause conflict, which is something Gina Furey lives for and excels at. Maybe in battle with her they'll come to respect and understand her as a worthy opponent. Ultimately, Kieran says, 'Fuck the family.' And chooses Gina Furey—his tinker gypsy queen. And in doing so accepts the inevitable consequences. Breaking from the family, friends, the neighborhood, into the unknown."

Colin pushed the off button and put the tape recorder away for later transcription.

The real-life Gina Furey is too free an Irish spirit to ever go back to New York with the likes of him, Colin thought. *And thank God for that. She's the crazy one but she would be the one who would ultimately make the sanest decision and accept their brief holiday encounter as just that. A bit of crack.*

Once he got to know her a little better, he'd have to imagine Gina in New York. That part would be pure fiction, total imagination, but at least he'd be on his home turf. He'd get to see New York through the fresh eyes of a stranger. *I'll have to try to see the New York part of the film through Gina's eyes,* Colin thought. *From her point of view. When I get home, I'll have to walk through New York imagining I'm Gina seeing it for the first time.*

When Colin got back to the hotel, a skeleton crew of Indian and Arab workers, all non-Christians, were working the Christmas Eve shift. The Irish were out shopping, crowding into pubs, playing Christmas music, wrapping presents, and preparing for the big holiday meal. Colin checked at the front desk for messages. There were none. *Gina is probably out last-minute shopping,* he thought. *For her baby and the rest of her wacky family. Probably be busy all day and all night. If she doesn't call, I'll understand.*

As carols played on a hidden PA system, he walked across the lobby, which twinkled with Christmas lights, and into the holly-draped elevator. Suddenly, for the first time, he felt alone. He thought of his mother, of all the Christmases with her. *Holiday horseshit,* he thought. *Cheap sentimentality, there'll be other Christmases. Forget Gina Furey, you're here to work. Get the fucking notes on paper, sketch out scenes, and transcribe the tapes. There's no such thing as loneliness when you're working.*

At the door of room 221, he fumbled for his key. He found it, opened the door, and went in.

Gina was in his bed, under the sheets, her shoulders bare.

"The shops were black with people but I got all me messages in as fast as I could and so here I am and what about yeh?" she said.

"How . . ."

She dangled the key he thought he left behind in the Wavefront.

"You're gonna make my dick fall off," he said.

"Yeh can leave it with me for safekeepin'."

After sex and a shower together, Gina dressed in an elegant black pantsuit, ankle boots, a forest-green turtleneck, and a waist-length black leather jacket crisscrossed with silver zippers. She placed a green floppy hat on her head.

"I want to show yeh around," she said, "to a few rare oul Dublin pubs yeh should put in yer movie."

Colin couldn't keep track of all the pubs they visited, but she limited them to one drink in each place. Most of them had music, all of them were packed, and most of the joyously drunken men who saw Gina on his arm gave Colin a certain slow half-nod of the head that was indigenous to Dublin, a silent signal of approval that said, "All right, mate." *Kieran would swell with pride,* he thought, *with the euphoria of conquest. Kieran has come to their country, their city, and he has one of their most desirable women on his arm.*

That's what Kieran will feel, Colin thought. *For all I know, that nod they're all giving me might be one of pity for being with a psycho who once robbed them blind.*

They bounced from The Stag's Head to Slattery's, the Brazen Head to McDaid's, The Long Hall to Doheny & Nesbitt, the Palace to the Baggot Inn. The pub crawl was more like an out-of-body experience, floating, pints and cognacs, faces popping out of crowds—bearded men, white-skinned women, mouths moving, eyes staring, loud disconnected words bouncing off tin ceilings, frazzled barmen, clouds of smoke, Colin's head getting lighter, his motor skills slower, the smell of body odor and farts and perfume and whiskey and beer. Dirty, piss-puddled mens' rooms. He heard folk songs and pieces of rock and roll, Christmas carols and pop tunes, a cappella and full show bands. *It's like a disjointed montage from a 1960s acid flick,* he thought. The Trip, *or* Easy Rider.

When they got back to the Temple Bar pub, near his hotel, Colin was shitfaced. He listened to several singers belt out songs like "Rare Old Times," "Raglan Road," "Clare to Here."

Then, sitting in a tight collection of tiny tables, jammed with late-night drinkers, cigarettes smoldering in small glass ashtrays, bottles and glasses bunched together like bowling pins on the table-tops, coats piled in a heap on a widowsill, surrounded by a group of traditional Dublin musicians, Colin asked Gina to sing "Baby, You Keep Stealing Up on Me." The way she had sung it to him the night before. She turned to him, anger glittering in her dark eyes, and softly said, "Yeh know I can't sing."

And she stormed out of the pub in front of the crowd. Colin looked at some of the men who had earlier given him the "All right, mate," nod, and now they were giving him nods of sympathy. A few laughed.

Colin chased Gina into the street, looking both ways. He saw a street sign that said he was in the middle of something called Meetinghouse Square. Then he saw her—the blond hair under the felt hat, skin-tight pants, walking in a slight stagger on the cobbled street. *Bitch never looks back,* he thought.

Colin began to run, his feet twisting into the crevices between the cobblestones. He lost his balance, careened against a parked Volkswagen. Grabbed onto a light pole. Passed a Garda on the beat. "Easy does it, lad," the guard said. *One of my old man's AA mantras,* he thought.

"*Slainte,*" Colin said, saluting the guard.

"G'wan outta it," the cop said.

Colin finally caught up to Gina.

Gina was waving for a taxi.

"Gina . . ."

"Feck off, yeh," she said, the booze fueling her anger. "Made a holy show of me in front of all them fellas. Fellas I'll still see long after yer gone."

"For chrissakes," he said. "All I did was ask you to sing . . ."

"I never sing where I'm known," she said. "Singin' is dead serious business in this country. Not for posers. Or Yanks . . ."

"You sing beautifully," he said.

"As if yer opinion is worth two buttons and a donkey's fart," she says. "Yeh heard me sing for a roomful of tourists and suburban wankers. What would they know? You made a holy show of me."

"The nicer someone is to you, the more you treat him like shit. Fuck you, Gina."

She raised a hand, her eyes glowering.

"Hit me and you'll fucking regret it," he said.

"Yeh gonna hit me, yeh big Nancy, yeh?"

"I don't punch girls, but I'll kick you so fuckin' hard in your cute little ass you'll be pissing standing up for a week."

She took a step closer to him, staring him in the eye. He stood his ground, face jutted forward, wobbling.

"Go back to New York and your fancy women."

He pulled three small wrapped gifts from his jacket pocket and handed her the largest one.

"Here, hard ass," he said. "Merry, um, Happy Christmas."

She gazed down at the brightly wrapped package, topped with a red bow. For the first time, her eyes were unable to hold his stare.

"Yeh bought me a Christmas present?" she whispered.

He nodded, thinking, *Kieran did, to see your horseshit reaction.*

"Och, Jaysus, yeh don't make sayin' good-bye easy, do yeh?"

She took the present from him and they stepped closer to a wall, while the music of three bands merged incoherently from the packed pubs. Tenderly, she untied the bow and peeled away the cellophane tape.

"I hope it fits," he said.

Gina opened the jewelry box and took out the gleaming gold Claddagh ring encrusted with emeralds.

"Oh . . . my . . . God," she said, drawing in a shock of breath.

She slipped several silver rings off her left ring finger and placed the golden Claddagh on it. She stepped from the wall to see it shine in the light of the streetlamp. "Yeh sure this is for me?"

The things men do in the pursuit of art, he thought. *And women.*

He handed her a second gift, which she tore open like a child with a box of candy. She removed a gold bracelet with emerald studs and matching Claddagh earrings.

"Och, it's too much," she said. "Yer too kind, altogether. Now I feel the right gobshite for rearin' on yeh."

It was close as she could bring herself to apologizing. Gina clipped on the bracelet and the earrings, yanked the side mirror of a parked car her way, crouched, and looked at herself.

"Jaysus, they're only gorgeous," she said and turned to him and threw her arms around his neck and kissed him. Then followed a series of small kisses as he handed her a final box.

"*Hear,* now," she said.

She opened this box with her eyes wide, her smile dazzling. Then her expression grew suddenly grave as she looked at the gold nameplate with emerald chips spelling the name *Brianna.*

"What exactly is your fuckin game?" she said, holding the nameplate as if it were incriminating evidence.

"It's not a fucking game," Colin said. "I thought it would look adorable on your daughter."

Gina moved toward him.

"How do yeh know about my child? What else yeh know about me?"

Colin reached in his inside jacket pocket, took out the dole book, and handed it to her.

"You dropped this in the Shelbourne the day you tried to rob me," he said. "Little Miss Don't Call Me Gina Furey."

She snatched the dole book out of his hand.

"The feckin' cheek of yeh," she said. "What am I to yeh? A laboratory rat? Something you study? An experiment? I had to apply for emergency funds to feed my child because I lost my bewk. Alls the while yeh have it. And where did yeh see me with me child?"

He told her about following her from the dole office, about the beggar woman, the scene in the department store. He told her everything he'd seen her do.

She began taking off his earrings, bracelet, ring.

"Yeah, I checked you out," he said, defiantly, his steel beer balls clanging. "That's right. I wanted to know who this little bitch was who tried to rob me."

Gina took his right hand and placed all the jewelry into his palm and closed it. "I don't need yer charity and I don't want yer company. Happy Christmas and bon voyage, Yank."

Gina walked proudly down Dame Street and finally hailed a taxi. She never looked back.

eleven

December 25

On Christmas morning, Colin ate breakfast alone in his room. The old man with the turban who brought him his room-service tray told him that only a skeleton staff was working. There were no newspapers to read. A gray drizzle fell on Dublin.

Colin poked at his eggs, ate one slice of toast with jam, and sipped the hot, sweet tea. He felt lousy. Hungover. Worse, dirty. Gina was partly right; he'd followed her and observed her and made notations in his notebook as if she were some object. He'd treated her as a character instead of a person. He'd spied on her, like a voyeur, a Peeping Tom, peeking behind the curtain of her life.

He couldn't breathe properly. He needed air. Space. He wanted to run. From Gina. From himself.

He pulled on his sweatshirt and sneakers and hurried down the stairs and out of the hotel into the early morning rain. He started to run—down to the banks of the Liffey, along the quays, and over the Ha'penny Bridge. He stopped for a brief moment to watch the river flowing in a westerly direction, as Gina had told him it always did. It was a factlet he'd remember for the rest of his life.

Church bells pealed for eight o'clock Christmas masses. Even the bells sounded empty and hollow and wet.

He started running again and passed an old man in a frayed tweed cap walking an ancient, arthritic dog on the other side of the bridge. "Howayeh," the old man said with that odd Dublin nod. "Happy Christmas."

"Merry Christmas," Colin said and kept running.

Gina had wished him a happy Christmas before walking out of his life the night before. All logic told him she'd done him a favor. He could give the jewelry to some new chick back in New York. He'd seen enough of Gina's life to build a character. *Even Kieran,* he thought, *after a given amount of time with Gina, would want to get involved with a normal woman who works for a living and aspires to a civilized life instead of a gypsy thief who collects the dole and sees the world as a game of Supermarket Sweep, calculating the amount of free lunch she can load into her basket before someone finally stops her.*

He ran along the quays on the northern side of the Liffey and passed Monet's Garden, the French restaurant where he'd dined with Gina. He couldn't help smiling, thinking of the waiter's face when she asked for eggs and chips.

He splashed up O'Connell Street, the shops all shuttered, mournfully empty and still, his wet footfalls squishing in the hallowed ground of Irish history and martyrdom. He glanced again at the bullet holes in the stone walls of the General Post Office and realized he didn't know how many had died there in 1916. At Parnell Square, he passed the gated cafe from which he'd watched Gina meet her cousins outside the dole office. He jogged by the bank where Gina had cashed her check. And then he ran down empty Moore Street, where a mindless dipso stood talking to his wet cigarette. The street smelled of old fish and rotting produce and Colin grimaced as he looked at the padlocked luggage store where Gina had robbed the canvas bags from the Pakistani. *Even Kieran must think there's nothing romantic about stealing from an immigrant trying to make an honest living,* he thought.

A gypsy thief calling the working man a dirty Arab, Colin thought. Her racist, xenophobic remark even got his race and ethnicity twisted. She only knew that he was *different* and mocked him for it. A woman whom others called a knacker needed someone to denigrate in the mean human pecking order. Someone to feel superior to. The way the fat woman in Ballytara sang a nursery rhyme about a "little nigger" whom they put in a window for "a show." *Thank God I'm rid of that whole family,* he thought as he picked up the pace, feeling his body returning to life, as he breathed in through his nose, out through his mouth, arms pumping, fists balled, rain in his face. *But what a great character Gina Furey is, and what a great piece of ass.*

He crossed back over on O'Connell Bridge, remembering the beggar woman, who was probably another of Gina's cousins. *Kieran must be tormented,* Colin thought. *He must ask himself why the hell he would want to get involved with a clan that sends teenage mothers out begging with pathetic, hungry, cold, and dirty children.*

Colin had gone as far as he could with Gina. And the moment he'd confronted her with the truth in the middle of her fictional performance, she had short-circuited and stormed off. Colin had decided that it was her own life that Gina was furious about. When she learned that he knew who she really was, she had blamed him for her fucked-up life. She shot the messenger who reminded her of her own reality. *Let her go,* he thought. *Let Kieran chase her—in fiction.*

He felt a sudden wave of relief that Gina Furey had returned to her life and that the next day he'd be returning to his. Normal, free, and in one piece. *Christ, I almost got sucked in,* he thought.

He ran through Temple Bar, remembering almost every pint and every song in every pub he'd shared with Gina. Then he ran up Grafton Street, which was eerily empty. All of yesterday's frantic shoppers were home with their families, the money of another Christmas spent. The children were waking up now all over the city, tearing boxes open as women prepared roasts for big family dinners. He passed Green and Timothy's, where he'd watched Gina steal the teddy that she'd worn the night they made love. He passed the jewelry store where he'd bought Gina the Christmas presents that had sealed the end of their brief relationship. *I spent three hundred pounds for her to tell me to fuck off,* he thought. *She's a total wack job. Good riddance; I'll find a chick who'll appreciate the jewelry.*

Colin ran up to St. Stephen's Green, trying to outrun the specter of Gina Furey, hoping to jog in the company of the ducks and swans, who lived stable, ordinary, respectable lives. But the green was locked. He circled the park, trying to launder Gina from his brain, and then he ran past the Shelbourne hotel, where he'd met Gina, and the bus stop where he'd chased after her with the dole book. If he'd caught her then, it would all have been different.

Bitch tried to rob me, he thought.

He jogged back through the streets, passing more pubs, and finally back through desolate Temple Bar. And then there was no running left in him. He walked slowly through the stretch of glistening cobblestone where she had sarcastically wished him a happy Christmas and a bon voyage.

Back in his hotel room, he peeled off his wet clothes, showered and dressed in black jeans, boots, and a dark blue sweater.

After two whiskeys, Colin went down to the restaurant. He ordered soup and sandwiches and saw Deke walk in wearing a tight green corduroy pantsuit. She was holding the arm of a handsome man in his mid-thirties, wearing a tapered, expensive blazer, open-necked white silk shirt, pleated gray wool slacks, and polished black leather loafers. Both of them had that fresh, sparkling look that made Colin suspect they'd just gotten out of the same bubble bath. He remembered what Deke looked like naked—tall, eggshell-white, long-legged, firm-assed, and small-breasted. He imagined the man soaping her and her soaping him in the bath.

I'm fucking nuts, he thought. *I could have spent Christmas week with this knockout, had Christmas dinner with her, partied with her, and said a pleasant good-bye. We could have kept in touch by phone until she came to New York on a shoot, where I could have showed her off to all the horn-dog neighborhood guys. She would have driven my brothers nuts with her sexy Dutch accent.*

Instead, I'm eating alone on Christmas Day, making notes about a wacky welfare artist pickpocket with a kid.

He heard the man with Deke order for her in a deep French accent. *He's as handsome, smooth, and urbane as Alain Delon,* Colin thought. Colin's soup and sandwiches arrived and he asked the sixtyish waitress for a pint of Harp. He watched Deke's hand move across the table and take the Frenchman's hand. Colin noticed her intentionally glare at him, a very large "fuck you" dripping from her dreamy eyes. *Fuck you, asshole, I'm fucking him instead of you,* she seemed to be saying with that one fleeting look. Colin even thought the middle finger she was using to scratch her nose was intended for him, before the Frenchman gripped the finger and kissed her hand.

Colin ate in silence, sipping the soup, devouring the sandwiches, and gulping the Harp. He watched the waitress bring Louis Roederer Cristal champagne and smoked Irish salmon dotted with caviar to Deke's table. He saw the Frenchman and Deke clink bubbling glasses and each lean over the table for a joyous Christmas kiss.

Colin got up and left his table. He walked past Deke's table but she didn't so much as look up at him, just scratched her nose with her middle finger as she and the Frenchman laughed and fed each other wedges of salmon on Irish brown bread followed by champagne.

Fuck you, Gina Furey, Colin thought.

twelve

December 26

The next morning, after checking his luggage and getting his Aer Lingus boarding pass, Colin stood at the bar in Dublin Airport sipping an Irish coffee, reading *The Irish Times,* when he felt a hand on his ass. Near his wallet.

He quickly grabbed the hand, turned, and Gina said, "I've thought it over and I'm goin' to New York with yeh."

Brianna, her red-haired daughter, maybe eighteen months old, sat in her pram, sucking on a pacifier. Slung over Gina's shoulder was her black canvas bag, bulging at the zippers. She held a large overcoat over her left arm, satin lining facing out. Gina's hair was piled under the green floppy hat and her eyes were sparkling almost as bright as her teeth.

"I'm away wit' yeh, so I am," she said.

Kieran would love this fucking act, Colin thought. *The gypsy arrives at the airport, ready to hit the road with him.*

"Jesus Christ, Grace . . ."

"Gina," she said with finality. "Gina Furey, the one and only. That's the one me mammy gave me. So, dere now."

"Do you have a passport?"

"No, but, I borried one from me cousin Bridie and I've got me child and I've got a few oul bits and pieces in me kit bag," she said. "That's me packed for America."

"You also need to have a visa," Colin said.

"Och, no problem, I've nicked loads of them," she said. "Master-Cards as well." She looked around the airport at the passengers awaiting departures. "Give us a few wee minutes and I'll get a new one."

"No, Gina," he said. "A visa is a stamp from the American embassy. In your own passport, because you don't look anything like Bridie."

"You're a big-time fil-um fella," she said. "Tell them yeh wants to takes me to New York to star in yer movie."

He ordered Gina an Irish coffee, and over the next twenty minutes, before boarding, he explained how she would have to get Irish passports for herself and Brianna, and then apply for American visas.

"After you do all that, give me a call," he said, knowing he'd have some time convincing his brother Jack to let an Irish tinker and her brat stay in his pad for a couple of weeks as part of his research. But Colin also knew that just watching Gina in New York would almost write the middle act of the script for him.

"Feck all that malarkey," she said.

"Going to America is not like hailing a taxi, Gina."

"Why not?" she asked. "It's just across the pond, as they say."

Brianna dropped her pacifier and Gina bent, picked it off the airport floor, dipped it into her Irish coffee, and plugged it back into the baby's mouth.

"Gina, I need to ask you a few questions before I leave," he said. "Just so I have some things straight in my head."

There was a long silence as she looked directly into his eyes, again with that unblinking, confident stare. *Like a very good poker player,* Colin thought. *Or a fucking alien.*

"G'wan, then."

"What about Brianna's father?" he whispered.

"Kilt in a bank robbery in England before Brianna was hatched," Gina said quickly, without emotion, like a rehearsed alibi.

"Those people out in Ballytara . . ."

"Me granny and me grandfather," she said.

"What about your own parents?"

"Me da kilt me ma when I was three," she said. "Then he was kilt by me ma's brudda and he's doin' life for tha'."

"What the hell was all the killing over?"

"Me," she said. "That's all I'm sayin' for nothin'."

Holy shit, Colin thought. *If this is true, this poor girl carries an awful heavy load of bricks on her back.*

"Does the family hold you responsible or something?"

"Just the men," she said. "Anyway, I can't go back out there. I told the lot of them to feck off last night, that I was away to America. They had a good oul laugh on me. Now they'll have an even bigger one that yer leavin' without me, wha'?"

A voice announced last call for boarding for Colin's flight to New York. He took out the last of his Irish cash from his pocket, totaling about one hundred and fifty pounds. He still had about two hundred bucks in American dollars in his wallet. He tried to give her the Irish money. She waved him off.

"It's not money I'm after," she said.

He shoved the cash in her canvas bag. "You'll need money for visas and passports," he said.

Colin took the jewelry he'd bought her for Christmas from his own carry-on bag. "I bought it for you," he said.

She glided the gold Claddagh ring onto her finger. "The crown's facing me heart," she said. "Meaning me ghee's spoken for."

Kieran would die to hear her say this, Colin thought.

"Jesus Christ, Gina, I don't expect that."

"Yeh don't buy a gold Claddagh for any oul whore, yeh know."

Now she draped the nameplate necklace around Brianna's neck.

"There, now," she said. "That makes two Irish girls yer after claimin' and leavin' behind."

She stood and unfolded the large overcoat she had placed on the chair next to her. She snapped out the wrinkles and held it up for Colin to put on. He shook his head as she helped him on with the expensive navy blue wool coat.

"Hear it's as cold as a Brit judge's heart in New York," she said. "Did you . . ."

"I bought this one," she said.

"Love it," he said, buttoning the knee-length coat.

The PA crackled, this time paging him by name.

"How do I get in touch with you?"

"You can't," she said.

He quickly wrote down his phone number and gave it to her.

"Call me," he said. "Go to the American embassy. For God's sake, tell them the truth."

He walked toward the metal detectors and she pushed the pram alongside him, shouldering her own bag.

"Good-bye, Gina," he said, kissing her, imagining the scene on film, in a wide shot. *Like* Casablanca, he thought. *Two lovers separated at an airport. Except Ingrid Bergman didn't have a kid, and three homicides in her family, and she got on the plane. And instead of the beginning of a beautiful friendship, this was probably the beginning of one huge fucking phone bill.*

She put her bag down and held his face in her ringed fingers, the emeralds of the Claddagh sparkling, and kissed him. "May the tobar rise to meet yeh," she said.

"What the hell's a tobar?" he said.

"It's gammon for road," she said. "Traveler language. Gammon or shelta or cant. Road rap."

"Gina . . ."

"Say no more."

He wanted to tell her not to put too much hope in getting a visa. Because she was a traveler, because she probably had a police record, because she had no Irish real estate or business, she'd probably get denied. He also wanted her to know that although their time together was fun, that the sex was great, that the crack was ninety, he only wanted her to come for a *visit*. He wanted to tell her that because he was an artist, a filmmaker, there was no way he was getting seriously involved with any woman—especially a thief, a tinker, with a kid.

"I have some things I really should say."

"Yer plane'll go without cha," she said, shooing him away. "Crush on, boyo, time to misli."

"What's that mean?"

"Time to go on, now," she said.

"Call me," he said. Thinking: *Kieran would tell her that he loves her.*

"G'wan, yeh big eejit," she said. "Shift. Crush on, sham."

After he hurried through security, he turned to wave but all he could see was Gina's floppy hat bobbing toward the exit. She didn't look back.

Part II

New York

thirteen

January 21

Colin walked from his bedroom across the second-story landing and leaned against the door frame of his brother Jack's spacious bedroom, holding a steaming mug of tea with milk and sugar, scratching a three-week shag of hair on his face. Jack was huddled over a drafting table, a gooseneck lamp yanked tight above his drawing of a new branch of a restaurant chain he was designing. The wall in front of Jack was completely covered in cork, clear pushpins pierced through three earlier drafts of the same restaurant project, all straight-ruled white lines on denim-blue backgrounds. "You look like Robert Redford planning the museum heist in *The Hot Rock,*" Colin said.

"Only this ain't make-believe," Jack said. "This is called making a living. If I looked like Robert Redford, I'd be getting laid right now instead of busting my hump designing yet another Brew and Moo Saloon."

The other walls of the bedroom bore the weight of custom-built floor-to-ceiling bookcases fastidiously lined with Jack's old textbooks—fat books on municipal building codes from a dozen major American cities, filled with rules and regulations on fire, flood, and hurricane standards, books on zoning, water, steel, lumber, cement, sewage, electricity, plumbing, tools, engineering. Big expensive oversized hardcovers with color photographs, and coffee-table volumes on Frank Lloyd Wright, Frederick Law Olmsted, I. M Pei, J. A. Roebling, William Van Alen, and the Rouse Company that Colin had given Jack on Christmases and birthdays past.

A single window of the corner bedroom in the two-bedroom Tudor-style duplex apartment looked out onto slushy Thirty-fifth Avenue. Outside, the Queens curbsides were piled high with drifts of grimy snow, glinting in the high mid-January sun. Jack's bedroom was as neat as his short, parted hair. The full-size bed was made with hospital corners as tight as the folds on a cigarette pack. The parquet floors gleamed. The small Persian rug was spotless, its nap running in one uniform direction, undisturbed by shoeprints.

"Don't you dare leave one of those silent Guinness farts in my fuckin' room again, pal," Jack said, without looking up.

"It's tea."

"Since you came home from Ireland, all you drink is stout and tea, tea and stout," Jack said, using a T square on the drafting table, and then tapping some keyboard commands and making mouse clicks to duplicate on the color computer screen what's he'd done on paper. "Have a goddamned coffee or a Bud, for chrissakes, Col. This is America. Welcome home. The plane has landed, the vacation's over, and there's a new year. It took three mailmen to carry your latest Amex bill and the February rent is due next week. But I haven't seen a check with your name on it since October."

"I still have a few grand from the option money," Colin said, suddenly wondering if Gina had sold the jewelry he'd bought her.

"Won't last long not working," Jack said. "Go back to your own cave. Do whatever the fuck it is you do in there, all day and night."

"Research and writing," Colin said, taking a gulp of tea, remembering Gina drinking her tea with champagne and egg and chips. He hadn't heard a word from her since he left her at Dublin Airport. He wondered if he ever would. "But now I need to bounce it off someone, before I do more research."

"More research?" Jack said, looking at Colin. "You spent ten days in Ireland doing so-called research, which is a great excuse for pub crawling and chasing broads. You've been holed up in your room for three weeks like a con planning a break, and now you're talking more research? What the hell are you writing? A six-part miniseries? I thought this was a two-hour movie."

"It is," Colin said. Trying to fit Gina into two hours was like trying to fit the Liffey into a baggie.

"What's it about?"

"A guy and a chick," Colin said. "Sort of a love story."

"So where the hell's the research? *The Oxford History of the Knobjob?* What?"

"The high concept is that a naive Irish-American guy goes to Ireland to find a wife," Colin said. "An old-fashioned Colleen, and winds up tangled up with a tinker girl."

"A tinker?" Jack said, laying down his T square. "You mean an Irish gypsy?"

"Yeah. Problem is there isn't much shit written about them. They're like a subculture. They have their own secret language called gammon, or shelta, or cant, a sort of Irish pig Latin. They've lived on the road for centuries. They don't mix well with what they call 'settled people.'"

"Sounds like a tribe of nasty asses to me," Jack said. "No running water? They must shit on the side of the road and wipe their ass with leaves. If I met a broad like that, the first thing I'd do is boil her in the shower and douche her with a bottle of A-2000 for cooties and crabs."

"They're not all dirty," Colin said.

"What the fuck they do for money? Pick garbage? Collect bottles? Panhandle? What?"

"Odd jobs," Colin said.

"Oh, okay, *thieves*," Jack said, getting up from his workstation and walking toward Colin. "A guy tells me he does odd jobs I make him right away for a second-story artist."

"Some are," Colin said.

Jack's always fucking right, Colin thought.

"And some usually means most," Jack said, faking a right hand to Colin's gut, steering him by the shoulders across the landing, past photographs of their mother and father at Eddie's wedding six years ago. "This 'naive Irish-American guy' falls in love with a thief or something? Come on, show me some of this shit you've been so busy working on that you only seen the old man once since you came home. That you don't return calls from hot babes. Show me what has you sitting by the phone, screening calls, checking the mail, running to libraries, bookstores, Irish archivists. Who is this broad you met, anyway?"

"She's just a chick I'm using as a sort of prototype," Colin said as his big brother backed him into his smaller bedroom. "The rest will be fictitious. But I need to get her background and the cultural trappings down right."

Colin's room was more crowded than Jack's, neat but not to the point of compulsion. A plain black comforter covered his queen-size bed. A couple of books—*Nan* by Sharon Gmelch and another book of essays called *Irish Travellers*—sat on his night table under a green-shaded desk lamp. Bookcases covered two walls. They were overflowing with old, dog-eared scripts, NYU textbooks, film magazines, biographies of Truffaut, Hitchcock, Welles, Spielberg, Lucas, Kubrick, Kurosawa. There were more books on film editing, cinematography, lighting, and sound.

A single poster from *Close Encounters of the Third Kind* showing a wide-eyed boy opening a door to a blinding glow of light, adorned the space between the two windows. A Compaq laptop sat open on the wooden desk, with the screen displaying a page of his screenplay-in-progress. The page number was thirty-two. Three separate bulletin boards hung on the big wall in front of his desk. The first board was covered with sixteen white index cards with hand-scribbled notes. They all had X marks slashed through them. A few baby-blue index cards were pinned to the middle board. The last board was empty. Color photos were jammed into the frame of his bureau-top mirror, three by five inch prints of Gina on Moore Street, Grafton Street, in front of the dole office, in Temple Bar, and various other locations in Dublin, and a series of shots of the squalor of Ballytara.

"This is it?" Jack said.

"Each bulletin board represents an act in the screenplay," Colin said. "I have my whole first act."

Jack walked closer to the first board and looked closely at the first index card and read the scribbling aloud. "Pre-credits. Shelbourne bar. Kieran having pint. Feels someone touch ass. Grabs hand. Turns. Pickpocket a beautiful woman."

Jack turned instantly to Colin. "I nailed it, asshole," Jack said. "Tinker broad is pretty. But she's a thief. And she's pushing a kid in a stroller. Please, tell me this shit ain't for real."

"'Course not," Colin said, shrugging. "But it's a good way to introduce the two of them. Before she steals his heart."

"And all his common sense," Jack said.

"I'm stealing that," Colin said, picking up a felt-tip pen and scribbling *steals common sense* on the index card.

Jack moved from card to card, mumbling to himself: "She drops something. K chases chick. Street. She gets on double-decker. K tracks her down. Dole office. A *kid.* K goes to address in *slums.* Ballytara, the house, covered wagon."

Jack turned to Colin, his finger on the index card containing the words "covered wagon," and shook his head. "Lemme get this straight, case I'm not following. A Queens mick goes to Dublin and chases after an Irish trailer-trash thief with a brat? This is a fucking love story?"

"Sorta."

"What do I know?" Jack said, shrugging. "I'm no film critic. In *Titanic* I rooted for the iceberg."

He walked to the night table and picked up *Nan* and leafed through it, looking at the photographs of dirty-faced traveler kids living in total squalor. Then he looked at the shots of Ballytara on the mirror.

"It ain't Disney," Jack said. "Look at these poor tinker bastards. Look like Kosovar refugees."

"They don't like being called tinkers," Colin said. "Or knackers, pavies, or gypos. They prefer travelers."

"Excuse fuckin' me," Jack said. "But I'm only politically correct to people who are hygienically correct. Call me an old fogey, but, you don't wash, I call you a dirty fuck. Period. Not *Mr.* Dirty Fuck or *Ms.* Dirty Fuck. Just a dirty fuck. When these skanks give their kids a bath, I'll wash out my politically incorrect mouth."

"You have to try to understand them on their own terms, Jack," Colin said. "You don't know the first thing about them. These people are *us,* our *tribe,* they're *Irish.*"

Jack looked at him, and then at the photographs, held the book by a corner as if it were a shitty diaper, and dropped it back on the night table.

"Okay, so tell me, what's the deal with these people? And why should I give a rat's ass about them? Or pay to see a movie about them?"

Colin told Jack most of what he gleaned from the Internet, the library, and the Irish bookstores about Irish travelers.

He explained that most travelers used to live in covered wagons on the back roads of Ireland. Today, most have been forced off the road and into public housing in the slums of the big cities of Ireland. They are still a subculture, mostly demonized by modern Irish society.

"We got the same shit here," Jack said. "Young bums, Rikers grads, who won't work and think you should give them your money. Lazy, dirty fucks."

"You want to hear about this or not?" Colin asked. Jack waved for him to continue.

Colin explained that, after the famine of the late 1840s, most male travelers made their living as tinsmiths, traveling the countryside repairing pots and pans and other metal possessions. Thus the name "*tin*kers." They also dealt in horses, the distilling of Irish moonshine called poitin, repairing china, chimney sweeping, and the crafting and repair of musical instruments, such as fiddles, tin whistles, and uilleann pipes.

"Hillbillies," Jack said. "Moonshine, poontang, and banjos. Jed Clampett, Jethro, and Elly May come to mind."

"Not exactly."

Colin told Jack that some Irish travelers forced pubescent teenage daughters into arranged marriages, often with kin, to keep their traveler bloodlines pure.

"Some of these girls are as young as thirteen," Colin said. "The men claim they want the females to have as many children as possible so the clan can survive."

Colin wondered if Gina's had been an arranged marriage. If she'd been forced to have a child with a member of her own clan. He wondered how much time she had spent on the road as a child, getting porked by dirty, drunken men in the name of perpetuating the clan.

"Barbaric," Jack said. "Not your average Irish Catholic behavior. Confess that shit to a priest up at Sacred Heart and he'd stage a new crucifixion in the schoolyard on Good Friday."

"Anti-traveler critics say the men do it to collect more money for each child from the state," Colin said. "The young mothers are forced to go out and beg in the streets of the large cities, with the infants as props."

Colin wondered if Gina had ever been exploited into begging or reading palms as a child or a young mother. Begging was clearly not something Gina approved of because he remembered how upset she was with the young beggar woman on O'Connell Bridge.

"Okay, I get it," Jack said. "You're making a nice little Christmas movie?"

"I'm being serious here," Colin said. "This is rich background for a film."

"Sorry."

Colin explained that some traveler men forced their young women to carry their infants in their arms as they begged or sold novelties they called swag—shoelaces, pocket combs, needles, and thread—from door to door. The women were also trained in the rituals of "gypsying"—reading palms, tea leaves, and tarot cards.

"Like Coney Island carnies," Jack said.

Colin said that in the 1960s, with the introduction of plastics and aluminum, tinsmithing became an obsolete profession. Tinkers adapted to a changing society by collecting and selling scrap metal, earning them the nickname knacker, a term traditionally used for scrap dealers. Others quickly became skilled in the crafts of laying carpet and linoleum and the restoration of antique furniture. Travelers also roamed middle-class neighborhoods, putting tarmac on driveways and paving dirt roads, which earned them the nick-name pavy.

"Enough, I don't need any more anthropology to get the picture," Jack said. "You might call them travelers. To me they sound like skells on the lam. They live on the road because the cops are always two steps behind them, as they should be. With nets."

"Some of the women are pickpockets and shoplifters. The men do burglaries and con games, that's true. But people are always blaming everything on the knackers, the way people here stereotype blacks."

"And you want to make a broad like this your leading lady?"

"Yeah," Colin said. "Like a modern-day *Moll Flanders.*"

"How many of these people are there?"

"No one knows for sure," Colin said. "Some people estimate about twenty-five thousand."

"You sure they're really Irish?"

"Some theories say they're descended from the Celts," Colin said. "Others claim they were settled people uprooted by the famine of the late 1840s. Still others claim they have Romany blood and were a branch of the European gypsies, who lived the nomadic life all over the European continent."

"That might explain it," Jack said. "Even the shantiest mick I've ever known was never as dirty as the slobbos in that book."

Colin shook his head.

"You sound like cabbie I had in Dublin," Colin said. "The truth is that the travelers have a peculiar fixation with cleanliness."

"Yeah," Jack said. "Dry cleaning—no soap and water."

"You're an ignorant fuck sometimes, know that?" Colin said. "Travelers use separate basins to wash dishes, clothes, sheets, themselves. If anything is cross-contaminated, like if a cup is accidentally washed in a linens basin, they throw it away. Any food even remotely thought to be 'polluted' or spoiled is shitcanned. Travelers believe that this code of cleanliness keeps them from getting sick, so they don't have to rely on doctors."

"You can blab your research all day long," Jack said. "But answer me one question."

"What?"

"Would you let one of these mud balls wait on you in a restaurant?"

"Most of the ones I met were clean," Colin said.

"Colin, for chrissakes, look at the way these people live," Jack said, picking up the book, pointing to photographs of people sitting outside their trailers amid strewn rubble and trash.

"I know, but it's weird," Colin said. "Travelers throw garbage just outside their door because they think of that as property that doesn't belong to them, as someone else's problem or obligation. Responsibility stops at the threshold."

"Great fucking neighbors, huh?"

"But the inside of a traveler's home, whether it's a covered wagon, a trailer, or a regular house, is usually immaculate."

"You must have a thing for this broad, Col," Jack said.

"No fucking way."

"Oh, yeah."

"Why do you say that?"

"You keep sticking up for these mutts," Jack said. "They look like mutts. The live like mutts. They treat their women and their kids like mutts. But to you they can do no wrong. You must dig her."

Jack walked to the middle board and pointed to a blue index card. "What's this card in the second act all about?"

Colin looked at the card. G'S FLASHBACK MURDERS was scribbled across the top. Underneath it was an alphabetized list:

a) G. Mother killed by father
b) G. Father killed in retaliation by G. mother's brother
c) G. Uncle doing life
d) G. Other uncles hate her because their brother doing time
e) G. Husband killed in bank robbery

"Any of this crazy shit the real deal?" Jack said.

"Nah," said Colin, remembering how nonchalantly Gina had told him about all of this as they sat together in the airport. *She'd said it all without emotion,* Colin thought. *Which made it all the more believable.*

"What happens in real life when a tinker broad gets involved with a normal non-tinker guy?" Jack asked.

"That's part of the main conflict," Colin said. "If a traveler woman mates with a non-traveler man, she's usually ostracized by her clan. Even if they forgive her, the non-traveler man is never accepted as a traveler."

"What if they have a kid, God fuckin' forbid?"

"The kid is considered a traveler. Just as any child of a mixed marriage between a Jewish woman and non-Jewish man would be considered a Jew."

Jack looked at him and shook his head. "I'll give you this much," Jack said. "It's *different*. It ain't another Brew and Moo."

"I need my middle act," Colin said.

"Where's that take place?"

"New York."

"Oh, Jesus," Jack said. "You want to fly her over?"

"Maybe for a visit," Colin said.

Jack looked at him, at the bulletin boards, at the index card marked G'S FLASHBACK MURDERS. He widened his eyes and walked back toward his own room.

"I'm going down Grogan's to meet Eddie for a beer," Jack said. "Wanna come? Never know, you might get laid and get this tinker chick out of your system."

"I'm gonna shave and shower first," Colin said.

An hour later, when he entered Grogan's Tavern, Colin saw Linda Parks, an old college girlfriend, sitting on the first stool near the window of the L-shaped bar.

Little daggers of dirty-blond hair jabbed from under a red beret and a gold stud pierced her tiny nose. The stud was new. The half-dozen gold hoops piercing her left ear from lobe to top were not new. Her scuffed combat boots and camouflage pants looked like the same ones she wore when they were film students together at NYU. A simple gold chain dangled around her long neck and she smiled with a set of brilliant white teeth when she saw Colin step in from the cold.

For all her dressing down and lack of makeup, Linda Parks couldn't hide her natural beauty—her big, startled-kitten eyes, real long lashes, small jump nose, and full, moist lips.

She raised a mug of beer, and took a soft sip through the foam.

"You don't answer my calls," she said, slowly licking her upper lip. *She used to lick my lips the same way,* he thought. "But I knew I'd find you here for Sunday afternoon football. You never missed a Sunday afternoon in Grogan's during football season . . ."

"How are you, Linda?"

"I'm here to congratulate you," she said. "On all your awards, for selling the option on your script."

"I heard your messages," he said. "Thanks."

Without being asked, the bar owner, Davey Grogan, brought a frosted mug of beer and placed it in front of Colin. He lifted it, shivered involuntarily at the cold prospect, and took a deep drink.

"On your brother Jack, Col," Davey Grogan said, knocking the wooden bar and nodding toward Jack and his kid brother, Eddie, who were standing in the middle of the crowded smoky bar. Colin raised his glass at them and they did the same. Colin saw a young, dark-haired woman named Peggy Johnson standing near the phone booth, sipping a screwdriver. She gave him a long, injured look and turned away. Linda Parks noticed.

"How come you didn't answer any of my calls?" Linda asked. "You a fucking star now, or something?"

"You never answered any of mine before I won a few awards."

"Touché," she said. "But the truth is . . . how can I say this without making myself sound like an asshole . . . I was trying to get *over* you."

"You're the one who ended whatever the hell it was we had," Colin said. "Fine by me. 'A good college romp.' Remember? You said that when we graduated from school . . ."

"I know. Those were my words. They haunted me. But it's been a few years. I'm over you now, but not over your talent. I've started a music video production company and I'd love you to direct some videos for me."

"Sorry, Linda," Colin said, stealing another glance at the sad-looking Peggy Johnson, who sat on the jukebox. "But I'm trying to get a feature on the boards."

Linda took a slow drink of her beer and Colin watched her swallow, studied the contours of her elegant, Audrey Hepburn neck. *I'd love to shoot her drinking like that in slow motion,* he thought. Linda was a downtown girl, pure Manhattan, sporting willfully ugly rock-climbing clothes and probably a pierced belly button. Unless she'd had it lasered off, he knew she had a tattoo of a rosebud (in honor of Orson Welles's *Citizen Kane)* on the left cheek of her ass. On the right cheek, there were the initials CC—for Colin Coyne— which she'd gotten when they were at a student film festival together in New Orleans. He'd tried to talk her out of it, but she was drunk.

In the morning, Colin told her that as far as he was concerned the initials would always stand for Clear Conscience.

She was a great lover who tried to live as a free-love hippie chick in the late 1990s but wound up falling in love with Colin and then hating herself for it. So she deep-sixed the relationship to prove she was tough and liberated. She was both. She was also a very talented filmmaker.

Now, in this bar in Bayside, Queens, far from her chic downtown turf, she held out her hand to shake his. He took it and she drew him close and kissed him on the cheek and whispered in his right ear. She pushed the fingers of her other hand into the back pocket of his jeans, the goose thrilling him, and he thought of Gina picking his pocket.

"I better scram," Linda said. "I think there's a chick by the pay phone waiting to get you naked, and your brothers are waiting to get you stewed. But if you ever wanna get rich making videos, gimme a call. My card's in your back pocket. I'm on Mercer Street in SoHo; the name of my production company is Clear Conscience. I had to justify the fucking tattoo to new boyfriends somehow. Be good to yourself, Colin, you deserve it."

"Good luck," Colin said, and she was gone.

A few minutes later, Jack stood at the crowded bar on Colin's left, Eddie on his right. All three of them were wearing white Irish wool sweaters and a lot of the guys in Grogan's Tavern were goofing on them, calling them the Clancy Brothers.

"Come on, lads," yelled Davey Grogan, in a mock Irish accent. "Give us 'It's a Long Way to Tipperary.' Give us a wee song."

"You got broads calling you every day," Jack said to Colin above the boozy din of the football fans. "Including that Pam Larsen, the law student, whose father is richer than God's boss."

"Yeah, and all she talks about is her father's money," Colin said, "and how much of it she's gonna get when she gets married. Like it was a sales pitch."

"Have her pitch it my way," Jack said. "Then you have that Linda Parks calling, Miss SoHo, coming around here to see you in person in deepest darkest fucking Queens."

"She's just an old friend now," Colin said.

"But she's still hot to trot," Jack said. "Meanwhile, while all these broads are calling and tracking you down, you're waiting for a call so you can fly over some Irish tinker broad with a kid."

Colin drained his beer mug, placed it on the bar, shrugged.

"It's work," he said with a shrug. "If I was doing a picture about a whore, I'd hang with whores. If I was doing one about a waitress, I'd talk to waitresses until I shit apple pie. Gina is a traveler, a unique woman."

"*Woman,*" Eddie said, turning to Jack, looking past Colin and taking a slug of his own beer. "Jack, he called her a *woman.* Not chick, dame, bitch, bim, or broad. He said *woman.* Which means only one thing . . ."

"He's in fuckin' love," said Jack, shaking his head.

"Who's the father of her screamer?" Eddie asked.

"He's dead," Colin said, imagining some stringy-haired asshole getting blown away in some little two-teller London bank.

"A widda," chimed in Davey Grogan, who was listening as he refilled their three beer mugs from the Budweiser tap and then turned to the rest of the Sunday afternoon football crowd watching the Giants game on the big screen TV. "Colin Spielberg here is courtin' an Irish widda with a brat, no less. Some guys go Hollywood and wind up with Julia Roberts or Sharon Stone. Genius here wins an award and falls for a Irish widda with a kid."

Everyone at the bar started laughing at Colin. Everyone but Peggy Johnson. She was standing by the telephone, sipping her screwdriver, wearing tight jeans and boots, a loose red sweater. Peggy was twenty-two and a nurse at Flushing Hospital. *Guys all over Bayside would get in line to bang her,* Colin thought. She'd been nuts about Colin Coyne since she was a freshman and he was a senior at Bayside High.

Colin, reddening, picked up his beer mug, looked at Davey Grogan, and said, "Fuck you, Davey. You couldn't get laid in a female prison with a fistful of pardons."

Colin took a sip of his beer as Davey carried a handful of beers down the bar to a group of guys wearing green Grogan's jackets. In the reflection of the bar mirror Colin saw Peggy Johnson staring at him, her face a jumble of anger and hurt.

Colin watched a big, young, good-looking jock walk over and offer to buy Peggy a drink. She looked past the jock at Colin in the mirror, drained her glass, and handed it to the jock, who moved to the bar. Her eyes held Colin's in the mirror, and Colin felt a pang of guilt rise in him. He also felt his dick twinge. He was twenty-five and it had been three weeks since his last sex. Peggy broke the stare, and looked up at the TV.

"And I don't know what the fuck you're laughing about, Jack," said Davey Grogan. "I bet damp dollars to Dunkin' Donuts that the widda and her little shit factory move into your apartment."

"Holy shit!" said Eddie. "Jack's Irish B&B—Bim and Brat!"

Jack stood up from his leaning position against the bar and looked directly at Colin, his eyes asking for an answer.

"A visitor's visa is only good for three weeks," Colin said humbly. "If she even gets one, and if she ever calls. It's been almost a month and I haven't heard a peep from her yet."

"Why don't you call her?" Eddie asked.

"She's gonna stay *three weeks?*" Jack said. "As in twenty-one fuckin' days? Colin, bro, I love ya, but I can't let our pad become Sesame Street for twenty-one days. I work home, you know that. Kid'll be finger painting with Bosco on my blueprints."

"Big Bird'll say they're gonna learn the letter *S,*" Davey Grogan said, "and the brat'll start finger paintin' with S-H-I-T!"

"Why don't you call the broad?" Eddie asked again.

"Can't," Colin said, taking a gulp of his beer, catching Peggy Johnson in the mirror. She was still staring at him with those angry, injured eyes, as the jock brought her a fresh screwdriver.

"Why can't you call her?" Jack asked.

"She only speaks Gaelic," Davey Grogan said. "Or quaaludian."

"Well . . ." Colin was trying to think of a good answer.

"She's deaf and dumb," Davey Grogan suggested, distorting his face and miming sign language. "She only knows Gaelic sign lingo, but what a fuckin' great personality."

"She got no phone, does she?" Eddie said.

"Well . . . no," said Colin, followed by a gulp of beer.

"Dial 1-800-S-H-A-N-T-Y," said Davey Grogan. "Another *S* word. Shit and shanty go together like bank and ruptcy."

"Knock it off, Davey," Colin said, a bit miffed.

"Ooooo," said Eddie. "A sore spot. Which means . . ."

"True love," said Jack.

Davey Grogan held the neck of a booze bottle as a mock microphone, pretending to be an interviewer, and asked, "So, Mr. Coyne, how does it feel to be the pot of American gold at the end of a shanty leprechaun's rainbow?"

"Up yours, Davey," Colin said as the bar rocked with laughter. Colin turned to Peggy Johnson, who looked like a woman learning she'd just become a widow. The jock tried to plant a kiss on her lips, but she gently pushed him away. All the jock could do was blink. Peggy turned away from him and staggered into the smoky back room of the bar.

What a fuckin' body, Colin thought, watching her move through the crowd of admiring men, remembering how tight and perfect it looked naked. She looked back at Colin before making a turn down a corridor marked REST ROOMS.

"Sorry, Col," said Davey Grogan. "Didn't know this Irish broad was special."

"She sort of is," Colin said. "In a purely professional way."

Grogan rolled his eyes and moved down the bar to wait on other customers, leaving the brothers in a private knot at the loud bar.

"Did you tell the old man about her yet?" Eddie asked.

Colin shook his head.

"You should," said Jack. "But lie. He'll never understand the concept of flying in a mother and child for *research*."

"Oh, he'll be thrilled," said Eddie in a low grumble. "Thank God Mom ain't around for this."

"That's unfuckin' called for, Eddie," Colin said.

"Hey . . . sorry." Eddie held his hands up, palms out.

"Calm down," Jack said, looking around to make sure no one else was listening. "Anyone should have an attitude here, it's me, Col. You invite a chick and her kid to come stay in my pad without asking me. I could say that's uncalled for, too. Eddie has a point. When the old man hears this, he's gonna go into one of his Trappist monk silences. If Mom was around, she'd be doing novenas every night."

"You guys are too fuckin' much," Colin said. "I just invited a chick I'm mining for a movie for a visit. If you don't want her in your pad, Jack, fuck it, I'll move out. It's your pad, but I do pay you half the rent. Say the word, and I'll rent my own place. I don't need anyone's bullshit. I'm twenty-five years old. I don't need Dad's permission or either of your snide remarks. This is fucking *work*, not romance. It's okay that you got an annulment from Barbara, Jack. Or that you dropped out of college to work at twenty, Eddie, because you knocked up Helen."

"Now you're insulting me," said Eddie, under the roar of the bar crowd as the Giants scored a touchdown. "I took the ball-busting for my mistake from both of you guys, from Mom and Dad and all the guys in the neighborhood. But I was thick-skinned about it. I acted like a man. I went to the altar with her. Took the responsibility by the balls. Today I'm happily married. I got my own house on the Island, I'm on the cops' list, and I don't ask anyone for shit. And I don't like anyone referring to my oldest kid's conception as 'knocked up' no more."

Colin was about to answer but stifled himself when he saw Davey Grogan returning their way. "Excuse me," said Davey Grogan, leaning into the trio of Coyne brothers. "Any truth to the rumor that you Clancy Brothers are disbanding?"

Colin couldn't hold back his laughter. Eddie immediately joined him. Jack just shook his head and said, "Give us another round, ya fuckin' outside agitator."

"You drink the shit," Davey Grogan said. "I just stir."

"Look," said Eddie. "If your 'woman' has no phone, send her a telegram. They have Western Union over there, don't they?"

"That's just for Western civilization," said Davey Grogan. "They use Donkey Express, guaranteed next-century delivery."

"Dublin is almost as cosmopolitan as New York these days," Colin said.

But Colin realized he didn't have an address. Even if he could remember the Ballytara address, he wouldn't send anything there. It would be used to light a campfire or to feed the goat.

"She'll call," Colin said. He placed his beer mug on the bar and walked toward the men's room.

He stepped into the men's room and there was Peggy Johnson sitting on the edge of the sink. She slid the lock closed on the inside of the door when Colin entered.

"Hey, Peggy."

She grabbed his belt buckle and started unfastening it, began to kneel. He hoisted her upright.

"Hey, christsakes, Peggy."

"That's how you did it to me," she said, her voice a fractured whine. "Friday night, September twelfth, you followed me into the ladies', locked the door, kissed me, I unbuckled your pants. I waited since I was fourteen and you waited until you were drunk, a big shot, with the film awards, to let me suck your precious dick in the ladies' room of Grogan's Tavern. Come on, let me do it again now, big shot. Come on, you fucking big-shot Hollywood bastard!"

She opened his belt.

"Knock it off," he said.

"Like you knocked off a piece of me? Treated me like one of your long line of actress bimbos? Or that hippie punk slut that you were talking to at the bar before? Now you have some Irish whore coming over here. You fucking bastard!"

"Get it straight. You took me by the hand that night, led me into the ladies' room. You said you had a joint you wanted to share. You did *me,* Peggy. Not the other way around."

"You didn't stop me!"

"Why would I?" he said. "I'm a twenty-five-year-old practicing heterosexual. You were pretty, legal, horny, and eager."

"Good ole Peggy Blow Job," she said.

"Hey," he said. "I never said it was serious. We always liked each other. You went out with Johnny Kirk for the last three, four years, I thought you were just looking for some strange."

"You act like it was just one night," Peggy said. "You fucked me whenever you wanted for three months after that. In the same bed you're bringing this Irish bitch to . . ."

"Hey, Peggy, you fucked me, too. It was mutual, adult, consensual. But no commitment, remember? I don't 'go steady.'"

"Why, too good for anybody else?"

"No, because the first time I gave a chick my heart she stepped on it with high heels. So, yeah, I'm into recreational sex. And the only thing I go steady with is my career."

His bladder was swelling now but he didn't want her watching him piss. He stepped into a toilet stall, locked it, relieved himself. Beer drinkers started banging on the mens' room door.

"Yo, Colin, call from Dublin on the phone," yelled one guy and a bunch of others started laughing. Now all of them started thumping on the door.

"It's fucking halftime," yelled one guy. "Miller Piss Time, Coyne. C'mon, open the fuckin' door, we'll cross swords."

Colin zipped up, flushed, and stepped out of the stall. Peggy sat on the sink edge, her sweater pulled up over her bare breasts.

"Take me home and fuck me," she said. "Recreationally. No strings attached."

"Peggy, christsakes, guys are banging on the door."

"If I asked any one of them they'd *bang me* on the kitchen table in front of their wives," she said. "I have doctors making millions at the hospital chasing me all over the wards for an ass grab. Guys stop me on the street asking me for my phone number, asking me to fucking *marry* them. Why don't *you* want me, Colin?"

"Peggy, you're half in the bag," he said.

"I'm a good nurse, and a good person," she said. "Clean. Besides you, I've only been with three guys. I'm no whore. Don't tell me you're in love with some Irish shanty slut."

The commotion at the door was getting louder and more agitated now. Colin walked to Peggy, kissed each hardened nipple, pulled her sweater down over her breasts, ripped a paper towel out of the rack, and dabbed a muddy tear from the corner of her left eye.

"You know I'll do anything you want," she said.

"Let me take you out of here. You're better than this."

Colin unlocked the door and led Peggy out of the men's room. She carried her screwdriver with her.

The crowded corridor exploded into applause as Colin and Peggy walked through it as though it were a gauntlet. The jock who had bought Peggy the screwdriver glared at Colin as he passed. Colin looked him in the eyes and nodded.

"Gotta be a boy if it was conceived in the men's room," shouted one guy.

"Either that or a camphor ball with a dick," said another.

"Talk about going to the head," shouted another.

"Hey, nurse," shouted another, "can we play doctor, too?"

Peggy Johnson seemed unfazed as Colin led her toward the back door of the bar. Colin left her by the door a moment as he went to the coatrack by the front door and retrieved the overcoat Gina had given him. He shrugged it on and passed Jack and Eddie at the bar.

"Peggy is sure looking good to me," Eddie said.

"I gotta get her out of here," Colin said.

"I'll see you back home," Jack said. "Unless I can convince one of those rich broads calling for you to go out with me."

Colin pulled the collar of Gina's coat up around his neck as he helped Peggy into his old white Ford Explorer.

"Where we going?" she asked.

"I'm taking you home."

"To fuck me?"

"Yeah."

Why not, he thought, as he drove down crowded Bell Boulevard. *It's what she wants. Everybody needs to get laid. Gina's probably getting laid back in Dublin somewhere. I am Peggy's first true love, but I won't be her last love. She'll learn that a broken heart is part of falling in love. The way Gwen Liori broke mine when she dumped me. Little did Gwen know that she gave me the material for my first successful movie.*

He realized, as he waited for a red light, that it had taken him from age seventeen to twenty to get over Gwen. When Colin was finally over her, he'd promised himself that he would never be that vulnerable again. They broke up when Colin found out Gwen was cheating on him, and had been for a long time. She'd even slept with some of the guys he hung around with. He felt like the biggest asshole in the neighborhood—which for a kid from Bayside, Queens, is the whole world.

He'd unloaded most of that pain with his short film, *First Love, Last Love.* The movie was shot in the streets of Bayside in seven days and nights. Colin used old NYU buddies as his crew and neighborhood people as actors. He plugged his lights into the local lampposts, worked without permits, raised the ire of neighbors, and haggled with local cops. He'd rented all the camera and sound equipment with one credit card, bought all the film stock on another credit card, and used the ten thousand dollars his mother had given him to do the postproduction work.

After he won the awards, the movie was broadcast on Bravo and the Independent Film Channel, which brought it to the attention of Bonnie Corbet, his agent. She encouraged him to write a feature-length screenplay. He wrote *Death Dunes* but wasn't allowed to be the director. Bonnie suggested that now that he had a toehold in feature films as a writer, he should write a low-budget feature that one of the smaller studios might let him direct. She pointed out that if he got nominated for an Oscar for best short film, he had an even better chance of making this happen.

Colin was aching for a nomination, which would be announced in a few weeks.

But he didn't want to do a sequel to *First Love, Last Love.*

He never wanted to relive the pain that had inspired it. Besides, time and fate had not been kind to Gwen Liori, who had once been so hot and beautiful. She was now twenty-four, with three kids from three different fathers—one dead from an OD, one doing seven to fifteen in Attica for armed robbery, one on the lam. The once-svelte Gwen was now fat and living with her mother in the same roachy rental house in Flushing, south of Northern Boulevard, where she'd grown up. *The only one she ever really fucked was herself,* he thought. *She cheated herself out of a life.*

"What's she like?" Peggy asked, his reverie abruptly interrupted like film jamming in a projector.

"Who?"

"Your Irish girlfriend," she said.

"She's different," he said. "And she's not my girlfriend."

"I'm sorry I called her names. It's unfair."

"It was the booze talking," he said.

"Nah," she said. "It was jealousy. You know how I feel about you. I lost my virginity to Johnny Kirk just to get experience for you because I heard you didn't like doing it with virgins. But when I slept with Johnny, I always pretended he was you. Every other guy I've been with, same thing. Well, maybe I fantasized on Johnny Depp once or twice."

Being a beautiful woman's masturbatory fantasy was Miracle-Gro for the dick, Colin thought as he felt his rise. He said nothing, knowing he would never feel the same way about Peggy as she felt about him. She loved Colin the way he had once loved Gwen Liori. So he empathized with Peggy as she learned her wicked little life lesson. He knew someday Peggy might despise him for rejecting her love, but right now she wanted him to fuck her, and he wasn't going to reject that. *I know I'm going to hell anyway,* he thought.

Peggy fell silent as Colin drove past nail parlors, saloons with green neon shamrocks glowing in the frosted windows, and the Bayside UA Cinema movie house, where he'd worked through high school and where he'd seen all the movies for free. He'd watched the movies over and over until he broke them down into cuts and camera angles. He studied them for technique, lighting, framing, master shots, close-ups, and dolly shots. Then he'd graduated to assistant projectionist and started buying books on filmmaking.

His brothers had bought him a ticket to the two-day seminar on screenwriting by Robert McKee, which he thought was a little like sitting through a cult-a-thon but was extremely helpful in understanding the structure of screenwriting.

By the time Colin finished high school, intoxicated by the smell of popcorn and hypnotized by the sound of celluloid slithering through the projector, he knew what he wanted to be when he grew up. He chose NYU because of their film school, which had produced Martin Scorsese, Spike Lee, the Coen brothers. Colin had won a partial scholarship there.

"How is the Irish girl different?"

"Why do you want to know?"

"Because I want to know what I'm not," Peggy said.

"Worry about what you are," he said. "Not what you're not."

He took her to her place, a basement apartment in an old Dutch colonial near the Clearview Expressway. She led him through the living room, which was carefully furnished with antiques, a small Iranian rug, Tiffany lamps, a mahogany coffee table and matching end tables, an old overstuffed sofa piled with satin throw pillows, and heavy velour drapes. When she reached the pink-and-white bedroom, she immediately undressed. Then he fucked her in the spirit of Christian mercy. He used a condom. *Peggy is a truly great fuck,* he thought, but before he came his mind flooded with images of Gina Furey in the Wavefront.

As he dressed to leave, Peggy said, "I know what you did."

"What?"

"You made believe I was her, didn't you?" she said, pulling her legs up to her chest. "The way I always think of you when I'm with someone else."

"No."

"Thanks for lying," she said. "But you're in love with this Irish girl."

"Nah."

He kissed her and left, feeling like a real prick.

February 3

Over the previous ten days, using the notes he'd made in Dublin, Colin had worked very hard tightening the first act of his script. He had written a loose outline of the rest of the Irish love story, sent it to his agent, then met her for lunch.

Bonnie Corbet was a sassy thirtysomething woman who'd signed Colin at the Seattle festival. She and Colin met for lunch after she'd read his outline. "Great first act, I love the woman character, but the outline needs work," she said over a Caesar salad in the Trattoria Dell' Arte on Seventh Avenue near Fifty-seventh Street. "The middle act needs to be funnier, crazier, wackier. You need to take some chances, like this Gina character. Make the script less conventional, go out on the edge. Also, the end is way too fucking soapy. There's no way these two people can ever have a happily ever after. The script has real promise, though."

"Think so?" he asked, panning the other tables, where Sydney Pollack was having lunch with Robert Redford and Susan Sarandon was eating with her agent.

"It's the kind of movie that could look expensive but could be made cheaply," Bonnie said. "If you get the American actors to work for SAG scale with deferred points, there's a good chance of getting it set up as a development deal at one of the independent studios. It's a love story with a turn-of-the-new-century edge. I can always sell a love story with an edge. Humor, sex, and a little violence don't hurt, either. You rework it and I'll talk it up, create a buzz. Before I send it out, let's see if you get nominated for an Oscar."

Every morning for the next few weeks, he dedicated four solid hours to work on the film treatment, shuffling his index cards, imagining Gina in New York settings, while listening for the phone to ring, hoping to hear Gina's voice. He let Jack's machine screen the calls. He received messages from several other girls, including Linda

Parks, Pam Larsen, and Peggy Johnson, none of which he returned. But nothing from Gina.

Having Gina and the kid here is gonna be a real ball-buster, he thought one afternoon as he watched Jack working in the downstairs dining room, his blueprints spread across the big tabletop. *Fuck it, it's only three weeks. If she comes at all.*

After an hour in the gym, he usually popped in to see his father for a cup of tea and to talk about the winter baseball trades, politics, the headlines in the *Daily News,* and always some story about his mother. Colin never mentioned Gina Furey, or the film script he was working on.

In the afternoon, he'd mark up the printout of the morning's pages, refining lines of dialogue, remembering details, honing his characters. A movie treatment was like a stick-up note you presented to the studio when you were looking for them to hand over millions of dollars. He knew it had to be right. "Executives rarely read anything once," Bonnie Corbet said, "never mind twice."

February 28

After another complete rewrite, he handed in his outline to Bonnie Corbet and waited for her response. He went to the local Citibank and checked his account balance. He had just shy of six thousand dollars left, after taxes and the Ireland trip.

When he gave Jack his five-hundred-dollar share of the March rent on the first of the month, Gina Furey had still not called.

fourteen

March 2

His mother's silver bells rang when Colin opened his father's door. Every time he heard the silver bells, he felt his dead mother saying hello. She had been a collector of bells, and these six silver bells on a green satin rope, her favorites, were strung over the door after her death to ring her to life whenever anyone entered or left the Coyne house.

On the small wall panel next to the bells was a holy-water font that his father kept replenished with bottles from Sacred Heart church. Colin didn't believe much of the mumbo jumbo of the church anymore, but he was still fascinated by the spell it cast on so many of his family and friends in Queens. The closest his filmmaker friends in SoHo came to a church was the Angelika movie theater on Houston Street. Colin was still superstitious enough to dip his fingers in the holy water and bless himself in deference to his mother, who had been a great believer. As he did, he thought of Gina Furey blessing herself with holy water in the church in Dublin, where she had prayed in front of Saint Brendan the Navigator.

He also did it for his father, who usually glanced up from his recliner in front of the TV to make sure that all who entered blessed themselves for their dead mother's soul.

"Hey, Dad."

Liam Coyne grunted as he watched the news on NY 1. *Uh-oh,* Colin thought, knowing from the response that his father was angry. As always, Colin walked into the kitchen and lifted the kettle. It was half full and the bottom still warm from recent use. He placed the kettle back on the burner and lit the gas. He took four Red Rose tea bags from a mason jar and plopped them into a flow- ered ceramic teapot, the one his mother had always used. Then he walked around the counter into the living room.

"So tell me about the Irish woman," his father said.

Colin looked surprised, wiped the holy water from his fingers onto his pants, and took a seat on the couch.

"Jack told you?"

"It wasn't your brothers who told me," he said, his accent still as thick as ever after thirty-seven years in New York. "But wait'll I catch hold of them blackguard brothers of yours for not telling me. On the other hand, I suppose I shouldn't blame them for not being quislings. The only thing worse than a conspirator is an informer. I'll tell ya, I'm raging at you for not telling me about this Gina Furey."

"You even know her name?"

"Aye, I know her name," he said. "The operator is after telling me her name loud and clear. 'I have an emergency collect call for Colin Coyne from Gina Furey in Dublin,' said she. 'Will you accept charges?' said she."

"Oh, Jesus . . ."

"And leave him out of it," he said. "If anyone ever paid his own way it was Jesus Christ."

Colin smiled, felt excited that Gina had reached out for him.

"What did she say, Dad?"

"She sounds very common, Colin," he said.

"What is that supposed to mean?" Colin said in an annoyed way. "What are we, uncommon? We Castle Irish all of a sudden?"

"She told me her *child* had lost your number." Liam said. "So she had the operator look up all the different Coynes in the borough of Queens. She finally got to me."

"Jack's number is unlisted," Colin said as he heard the kettle whistle. He got up, poured the boiling water over the tea bags, and put the potholder on top of the pot to keep it warm, the way his mother always had.

"I can never understand anyone paying to be unlisted," Liam said. "If he's always looking for this freelance work, how in God's name does Jack expect anyone to find him if he's unlisted?"

"His business number is listed," Colin said. "What did Gina say, Dad?"

"She said something about having a hard time getting a visa," Liam said. "Thank God for small favors. She had the child with her and she was calling from a pub. I always hated a child in a pub."

"What else did she say?"

"She asked for your number," he said. "I gave it to her. I don't know if that was wise."

"What's the matter, Dad?" Colin asked, as he stirred the tea bags in the pot and poured two cups, adding milk and sugar.

"Is she raising this child alone?"

"Yes," Colin said.

"What bloody age is this Gina Furey?"

"Twenty-one."

"Shit, damn, and corruption, man," Liam said as he reached for a pack of Vantages from an end table and lit one. Colin placed the cup of tea and saucer on the table next to the cigarettes.

"I guess you'd like to know what happened to the father," Colin said, perching on the edge of the couch, sipping the tea.

Liam Coyne took a deep drag of his cigarette and blew the smoke out in the general direction of the TV, on top of which were family photos. The smoky silence was full of questions.

"He was murdered," Colin lied. "Dublin is crime-ridden now."

Liam took another drag of the cigarette.

"She's on her own with the kid," Colin said. "She's sort of the model I'm using for the character in my script. I only offered her to come for a visit, Dad. So she could see what it was like. So I could see what she would be like here. Like that."

Still, Colin's father remained silent as the room continued to fill with smoke.

"I thought if anyone would understand what the dream of America means, it would be you, Dad," Colin said.

And at least she didn't give her kid up when the going got rough, like Mom did, he thought, wishing he had the balls to say it to his father.

"Bollocks," his father said.

"She's just an Irish girl like Mom was an Irish girl."

"Your mother never called anyone collect in her life," Liam Coyne said.

"Dad," Colin said. "This is a new millennium."

"Exactly," he said. "Even Dublin has direct-dial phones now."

"She doesn't have a phone," Colin said.

"That means she must have bad credit."

"Jesus Christ," Colin said. "How the hell can you judge somebody by whether or not they have a goddamned phone? I'll pay for the goddamned call, Dad."

"And her fare over, I suppose," he said. "You'll pay for her child's and for her American holiday, for the lot."

"It's my money," Colin said.

"And you're my son," he said. "So I can go on record that you're a fool and you'll live to regret it. Mark my words."

"Duly noted, Dad," Colin said, abruptly placing his cup back on the saucer and walking toward the door.

"She said she'd call before noon," the father said as Colin pulled open the door, hearing his mother's silver bells.

"Thanks," Colin said, and left.

fifteen

March 3

At 9:55 A. M., the phone rang, forever changing the life of Colin Coyne.

"I have a collect call from Gina Furey in Dublin, will you accept charges?" the operator said.

Colin accepted the call.

"Yer a hard man to track down, yeh are," said Gina after the operator connected the call.

"I've been waiting by the phone every day," he said.

"Sure yeh have," she said with a laugh. "With a beer in one hand and yer mot in the other."

"Why didn't you call sooner?"

"I threw yer number away," she said. And now Colin could hear Brianna in the background, asking for Tayto, the Irish potato chips. The background din of conversation and the rattling of glasses and bottles told Colin she was calling from a pub.

"Threw it away? Why?"

"I got browned-off at yeh, that's the why," she said. "I went down to that feckin' American Embassy like yeh says. But I had a bit of trouble doing all the writin' on them forms. You'd think I was asking to have a death sentence commuted. Then they started askin' for documents and asking all kinds of personal questions."

"What did they say?" Colin asked.

"Yeh told me to tell the truth, right?"

"I did," Colin said.

"So they asked how I supported meself," Gina said. "And I tells them I'm on the dole and the children's allowance, righ'? They looks at me like I have two heads and three arms. They asks me about me husband. 'Me husband is dead,' says I. 'How did he die?' says this oul wan, face on her long as a fiddle. I tells her he was shot dead in a bank. They asks if he was a teller and I tells them no, he was robbin' the teller. Now she calls over a geezer in a suit. He asks why I want to go to America. I tells him there's this fella I met who is a producer for the pictures."

"Director," Colin said with a heavy sigh, letting his head fall into his hand, smiling. "Gina, hold on, you didn't actually tell them your husband got killed doing a bank heist, did you?"

"Yeh told me to tell them the bleedin' truth, didn't yeh?"

"Yes," he said. "But tempered with a little common sense."

"Now yer sayin' that I should've lied about the truth?"

"So what happened next?"

"So then this fright-faced whore's daughter—God help us—asks me where I lives," Gina said. "So I tells her, here and there, like. She asks what I mean by that and I says I shift around a lot. She asks if I have a home of me own and I tells her that when I was growing up, in the spring and summer months, I spent most of me time in a caravan and winters in a settled house. Not many people use the old barrel-top caravans anymore, mostly they live in trailers, says I. But, says I, me granda still has a fine caravan. Then she asks if I'm a traveler, and I says, 'Yeah, course I'm a traveler, that's why I want a visa, so I can travel to New York to see me fella.' She asks where my permanent residence is and I say I'm kippin' with me granny out in Ballytara while I wait for the corporation to find me a settled place of me own next door a them. Right away she asks what incentive I have to return to Ireland. So I tells her it's a nice spot and I likes the people."

"Oh, God. . ."

"That's exactly what she said. Did I say something wrong?"

Colin felt his heart sink; his head began to pound. "Gina, they turned you down for the visitor's visa, didn't they?"

"Aye," Gina said, "they said since I had no spouse to return to, or child to come home to—because I wanted to bring Brianna with me, a course—and no permanent residence that I was not a candidate for a visitor's visa. Unless I had someone put up a bond, like I was a criminal or somethin'. So I walked outside and I tore your number up and that was that. Until . . ."

There was a long silence as Gina rattled cellophane and told Brianna to take a sip of a drink, talking to her as the phone obviously dangled and knocked against the wooden wall. After what seemed like a full minute, Gina came back on the phone.

"Sorry . . . I was just giving Brianna a bag of Tayto and asking the publican for another Club orange," she said. "You'd think I was asking for holy water in hell because I have a child in a pub. Barman has a face on him like a vampire's mirror. Big feckin' mammy's boy . . . that's right, yeh heard me, yeh bollocks yeh . . ."

She's fighting with a bartender three thousand miles away, he thought.

"Until what, Gina?"

"Until what, what?" she said.

"You said you tore my number up and that was that until . . ."

"Oh, right," she said, and paused to take a sip of a drink. "Until I didn't get a visit from Mary."

Colin was silent a moment as he heard the murmur of the pub, phlegmy Irish voices and beery laughter in the background, an ocean away. "Who the hell is Mary?"

"*My* Mary," she said. "The Mary what visits every month."

"Your period?" he asked, his heart pumping faster, his head doing an extra thump.

"Aye, but we were never allowed to call it that," she said. "You'd get clattered for using that word in my family."

"What made you change your mind about calling me?" Colin asked.

"How thick are yeh?"

"What do you mean? I'm confused."

"All right, then, I'm up the pole."

"What pole?" Remembering the cabbie on the way to Ballytara

saying most knacker women were "on the dole and up the pole."

"Your pole, yeh gobshite. I'm with child. *Your* child. And very good-lookin' it'll be, too. Mind yeh, it won't be lickin' its looks off the stones, either."

"Pregnant?"

"Oh, aye," she said, matter-of-factly, as if she were saying she was hungry. Or sleepy.

"Gina, I asked you about fucking protection!"

"I thought you meant was I infected," she said. "AIDS or a dose or somethin'."

"What about fucking birth control?"

Gina laughed. "I use Irish birth control," she said. "Five Our Fathers and five Hail Marys."

Colin fell very quiet, thinking of the gravity of this news. He considered the consequences. This was what Jack always called a lifer. Gina Furey, in one phone call, had just transformed an aspiring young bachelor filmmaker from Queens into a father of two with an Irish common-law wife. Who could not get an American visa. Suddenly, the six thousand he had in the bank seemed like petty cash instead of a small nest egg.

"What's wrong, luv," Gina said with a teasing laugh. "The boy all a sudden afraid of being a man?"

"You want me to arrange for the abortion?" Colin asked. "It's legal in Ireland now, right?"

Now it was Gina's turn at silence.

"Did yeh say *abortion?*" she said after a long pause. "If you said abortion, it's a good job yer not standing in front of me or I'd abort you. You'd be swallying this ring yeh gived me with me fist attached."

"You don't mean you actually want to *have* this baby?" Colin said, incredulous.

"A course I'm havin' me babby," she said. "Yeh think I'm gonna let someone else have it?"

Colin thought of his mother letting someone else have hers. Then he remembered the promise he'd made to her as she lay dying.

"Gina, you have to have a goddamned abortion," Colin said.

"It's not like there's a choice. Me and you, we can't have a kid. You fucking nuts?"

"Colin Coyne, yeh listen to me," Gina said, her voice as stern as a schoolmarm's. "I might be a lot of things, and most of them don't get yeh a visa to yer precious America, but one t'ing I'll never be is a babby killer. And one t'ing I'll always be is a Catholic and a devoted mother. I believe in the life of the child in me belly as if it were me own, because, well, because it feckin' is. Me an you, boyo, we both had our Christmas fun doing the seashore gonkey, and now the fun's become a son. I know it'll be a boy, that was in me tea leaves. If yeh want to walk away from that responsibility, you won't be the first coward with a willie but no balls to do it to his child. A man who knows he has a child somewhere and walks away from the responsibility isn't a man atall. But, not to worry, I won't lower meself by trying to track yeh down for money. I'll get along."

He thought again of his mother, alone, with a baby by a dead British soldier, her family ridiculing her until she gave it up. *I promised her I'd never do the same thing,* he thought. *Why the fuck did I ever make a promise like that?*

"How do I know it's even mine, for chrissakes?"

"Who else's could it be?" she snapped.

"Only you really know that."

"Yer the only man I've been with in a long, long time."

Colin could hear the barman in the background shouting for everyone to drink up before closing for the afternoon Holy Hour. Colin suddenly realized that a woman like Gina Furey, who lived on her wits, robbed and swindled and scammed, would still draw the line at something as precious as a baby. He remembered her lighting two candles and stealing one in the church in Dublin. She probably was a devout Catholic, did not believe in abortion, and Colin simply believed her when she said the child was his.

"Look," she said. "I have to go."

"Will you call me again tomorrow?" he asked.

"Does my unborn child's daddy want me to?"

"Yeah," he said.

"For a minute there, I thought yeh thought I was snookerin'

yeh," she said. "Let me tell yeh, the only thing worse that a man walkin' away from his child is a woman who deceives a man into believing one that isn't his is. I'm not that kind of laicin."

"Will you call?" Colin asked.

"Aye," she said. "Bye-bye, da-da."

Sweat broke out on his brow. *I'm gonna have a baby with an Irish tinker girl,* he thought. *In other words, I'm fucked.*

sixteen

"How the fuck do you know it's even yours?" his brother Jack said, pacing the living room as if he were trying to locate a solution. He fussed with the family photos on the mantel, straightened books in the bookcases, walked to the kitchen, opened the fridge, looked inside, closed it in disgust.

"I can't quite explain how I know," Colin said, plopping into an overstuffed armchair, draping his right leg over the arm. "Because if she was husband-hunting, she would have slept with me the first time I tried and she didn't. I had to chase her."

"I think you're in love with the idea of being in love with an Irish dame," Jack said.

"Nah," Colin said. "I was a character named Kieran, from my movie, chasing the Gina character. At the risk of sounding, well, pompous, it happened in the pursuit of art."

"Art?" Jack said. "Knocking up an Irish welfare artist is not *art!* Where we come from it's called fucking insanity!"

"Kieran was falling in love with her so he had to make love to her and, well, you know the rest."

"You, Colin," Jack said, "not this figment of your imagination, this alter ego called Kieran, you fell for this chick. You fell in love with the kiss-me-I'm-Irish, descendant-of-the-Celts, up-the-rebels, horseshit-romantic notion of it all. You don't know this broad long enough to be in love with her. But now you're the father of her kid—for-fuckin'-*ever*. Unless she goes to a clinic."

"Catholic," Colin said, suddenly thinking, *What about Kieran? How would he react to this news? Jesus Christ, Gina just gave me my middle act!*

"Eddie, please, talk to him," Jack said.

His brother Eddie sat on the couch to Colin's left, bending the can of a beer he'd just finished, looking from brother to brother. "I been there, done that," Eddie said, walking to the kitchen, tossing the empty can in the trash, and grabbing a fresh brew from the fridge. "Mine was a little less complicated. My wife lived two blocks away. But when you're faced with fatherhood, you do what you gotta do."

Colin stood silently, then hurried up the stairs.

"Where the hell ya going?" Jack said, following Colin upstairs, Eddie traipsing after them.

Colin entered his bedroom and took the cap off a felt-tip pen and began scribbling quickly on a blue index card. He pinned it to the middle bulletin board.

The card read: K. GETS CALL. G. SAYS SHE'S PREGNANT.

Jack read the index card and looked at Colin incredulously, then at Eddie, eyes wide. Colin scribbled another card.

K. HAS CONFRONTATION WITH FAMILY. MUST GET G. INTO USA.

"Are you losing all your marbles or what?" Jack said. "Your life is only about to change forever and you're still seeing it as a fucking movie! This is *real*, Colin!"

"I know," Colin said. And thought, *The middle act will write itself. Maybe the baby being born starts the third act, or it can be the mid-act plot point of the second act. This is the movie!*

"I'll keep an eye out for a house on my block in Babylon, Col," Eddie said. "Great town for raising kids."

The phone rang and the answering machine on Colin's desk clicked on. "Hi, I'm looking for Colin, this is Linda, *again*, Linda Parks. Hey, Col, call me, honey, will ya? I'll make it worth your while. I have a few hot jobs I wanna discuss with you. Bye, babe."

Colin affixed another index card to the board: G. MEETS K.'S OLD GIRLFRIENDS.

Jack read the card, pointed at the tape machine, and looked at Colin, who was busy writing more cards.

"I walk around with a boner all day just listening to your messages," Jack said. "Poor Peggy Johnson, who is a total ten, calls three times a day. Pam Larsen is ready to buy a house, move you in, and sign over the deed. Every week, that casting agent, Kim Baker, asks if you're available for a date to a client's premiere. You have starlets and ingenues up the kazoo calling day and night, but you're having a *kid* with this Gina Furey—and about to become a father of *two* and breadwinner of *four* with *one* Aer Lingus touchdown at JFK? We're talking a *lifer,* here little brother."

Colin pinned a new index card to the board: AER LINGUS JET TOUCHES DOWN. G. AND B. GET OFF.

I'll have to trim Jack's dialogue way down for the script, Colin thought.

"Colin, you can't let her have this kid," Jack said, sitting on the edge of Jack's bureau.

"Like I said, Gina's a devout Catholic," Colin said.

"So's the pope and even he wouldn't do this!" Jack said.

"Gina'll love the church out near us," said Eddie. "Cushions on the kneel-down things. Modern sound system."

"In fact, there was an Irish bishop, from Galway, I think, he knocked up an American dame," said Jack, cutting Eddie off. "And he didn't chuck the collar and say, 'I do.' He sought divine intervention and paid her off with parishioners money."

"Ultimately, it's her decision, Jack," Colin said. "If she wants to stay in Ireland, I'll send dough. If she wants to stay in America, I have to give the kid that shot."

"Buy in Babylon, we can carpool," Eddie said, wiping beer foam from his upper lip.

"I'll move to L.A. as soon as I sign a movie deal," Colin said.

"The old man is gonna have kittens over this," Jack said, waving his arms, pacing. "No, fuckin' mountain lions."

Colin pinned a card to the board that read: K. AND G. TO L.A.

"Don't worry, Col, Dad's a wonderful Gramps," Eddie said.

"You want me to tell him?" Jack asked, still pacing, looking out the bedroom window at the sun melting the snow. "I'll make sure he takes his nitro pills first."

"No," Colin said. "I will, when Gina gets here."

The next card read: G. MEETS K.'S FATHER.

"Christ," Jack said, and plopped on the bed. "Okay, so you're gonna fly her in. Then what is this . . . Gina Furey, the Irish tinker girl, gonna *do*, Col?"

"Do?" Colin asked.

"With her life? Put a card up on the board that explains what the fuck she does with her life here."

"If she stays, she'll raise her kids," Colin said.

"Colin, my brother, listen to me, carefully," Jack said, walking toward Colin, who stood in front of the board, rearranging the order of the cards, building his script. "You're a filmmaker. A creative person. An *artiste*. That's what got you in this jam. I understand what that means, because I'm an architect. In order for your creativity to flourish, you need solitude or a soul mate who is also creative. Someone who nourishes you. Someone who understands your search for the elusive muse. Knows when to leave you alone when you're fertile with ideas and busy working and when and how to inspire you when you're arid or blocked. You can't just bring a woman into your life who doesn't understand or respect your talent. It's not fair to you or *her,* because an artist is a fucking monster, Col, filled with mood swings, a life of deep depressions, and periods of giddy euphoria. You're young, Col, gifted, free, ready to explode onto the world. And you're about to chain three human beings, high-maintenance, needy dependents, onto your ankle while you try to push that boulder called your career up a mountain."

"That's pretty good shit, Jack," Eddie said. "Where'd you learn all that?"

I'll steal some of it, Colin thought. *Some as dialogue. The rest as thematic conflict.*

"I hear ya, Jack," Colin said, pinning a new card to the board. This one read: K. AND G. BATTLE OVER HIS CAREER. CONFLICT.

Jack read the card and threw his hands in the air.

"What happens after this movie?" Jack asked. "She inspires this picture, fine. How does she help the next one?"

"Right now, she's just a chick having my kid," Colin said. "I'm not married to her. Who knows? Maybe she'll help my career. She cuts through bullshit like an ax through chopped meat."

Colin was filled with excitement about the new possibilities of his movie, as well as with a surge of real-life dread.

"How the fuck are you going to go off shooting a picture on location?" Jack asked. "Say, in some jungle, desert, the Arctic, if the script calls for it, and expect some chick from Dublin, who doesn't know anyone here, with two kids, to get along without you?"

"Other directors do it," Colin said, although he couldn't think of one.

"And most of them wind up with five divorces," Jack said, "directing any hack shit that comes their way just to meet the five alimony payments. You want that? You want to have a kid, get married, and then get divorced, with your ex-wife going back to Dublin with your kid? Colin, you aren't thinking clearly. Relationships between the talented and the untalented almost never work, because one always winds up resenting the other. Unless, of course, the untalented one is ready to totally subjugate his or her life to the talented one."

"What's subjugate mean?" Eddie asked.

"Or unless the talented one is ready to compromise his or her talent," Jack said, ignoring Eddie. "Which is a crime against yourself and your talent. Just remember, anyone who lets the crop rot in the field dies with it."

"Are these, like, song lyrics?" Eddie asked, laughing. "Chill out, Jack. Relax. So Colin gets married, has a kid. If the film shit don't work out, the old man gets him in Ma Bell, he puts ten percent down on a house, thirty-year mortgage. With his college education, he becomes management in two, three years. The kids won't starve as long as he has two hands."

"I'm sorry if I'm big brothering you to death here," Jack said, looking at the index cards and shaking his head. "But I'd be a shitty brother if I didn't tell you how I feel. I think you're making a very big and very complicated mistake."

"I appreciate your concern, Jack," Colin said. "Really I do. But I've gotten this far in my life on my own instincts. I have no choice but to deal with it as it comes. I'm scared, yeah. But it's a fear I kinda like."

Jack plopped in Colin's desk chair, yanked the lever to recline it, put his feet up on the desk, and closed his eyes.

"Okay, I've had my say," Jack said. "Now I can wait for the I-told-you-so's to come home to roost. Meanwhile, just do me and Eddie and yourself a favor; be up-front with the old man."

Colin looked at Eddie, who nodded agreement.

"Okay," Colin said. "But first I gotta go see that lawyer, Brendan O'Dowd, about the immigration problem."

He put a new blue card on the board: K. HIRES IMMIG. LAWYER.

"Leave him a down payment on the divorce," Jack said.

"If I'm a father," Colin said, "I gotta do the right thing."

"You're doomed," Jack said.

"That's what's so exciting to me," said Colin.

Colin pulled on the coat Gina gave him and left.

March 4

Colin was alone in the apartment when Gina's next collect call came.

"The lawyer says that I'll have to fly to Dublin and have you apply for a spousal visa," Colin told her. "Then it could still take up to six months to get the visa if we get married."

"Married!" she said. "Who said anythin' about gettin' married? I did that once. I didn't like the way it turned out. This laicin is not gettin' married just to get through the door of America."

He felt a wave of relief. *A chick who doesn't want to get married,* he thought. *Makes her character even better. Maybe Kieran wants to get married and she doesn't.*

"What do you propose, then?"

"Anythin' but a marriage proposal," she said.

"I can't live in Dublin. My work, my career, is here."

"They make the pictures everywhere, don't they?"

"Yes," Colin said. "But this is where I make them."

"Well, then," she said. "If you ever do get over here, in, say, eight months, drop by and say hello to your son. Bye-bye and may the tobar rise . . ."

"Hold on!" he shouted because he knew once she clicked down that receiver there would be absolutely no way to reach her.

"What is it, gra?" she asked.

"Someone told me of another way to get you into the States."

Part III

Dublin, Ireland

seventeen

March 6

STRIKE! proclaimed the headline of the *Irish Independent.*

Colin stopped to buy the newspaper as he moved through the Dublin Airport. Dropping his single bag, he yawned and stretched and shook his head like a dog who had just climbed out of a pond. He'd been traveling for twenty-three hours, imagining himself as a jet-lagged spy who had just completed half of a covert mission. His eyes stung, his stomach was sour, his muscles ached, and he could smell himself ripening like an old banana.

His trip originated in New York's JFK airport, where Colin caught a seven-hour AeroMexico flight to Mexico City. In Mexico, he'd rented a car and made all the arrangements necessary to sneak Gina and Brianna into the United States. Then, because there were no direct flights from Mexico to Ireland, he caught a ten-hour flight to London, where he changed airports and planes for a flight to Dublin.

Colin had taken along his laptop computer and worked on the movie treatment, which he called *Across the Pond,* on the various plane rides. On the final flight, he had E-mailed his new treatment to his agent. If Bonnie Corbet liked it, she would try to get a bite on it.

Exhausted, Colin glanced at the newspaper headline story and learned that all the hotels, buses, milk, bread, and coal deliveries were affected by the strike. Banks and a half-dozen other services were ready to close. Even McDonald's was on strike.

Colin had a reservation at the Temple Bar Hotel, but after reading the newspaper story he drifted over to the mobbed traveler's information booth. Tourists from all over Europe and America had descended on the booth as they tried to sort out their travel and lodging arrangements.

"I'll give yeh all the traveler's information yeh want," said the familiar voice from behind him.

He spun around and embraced Gina. Standing off to the side was a young man—Paul Lynch, the one with the distinctive tweed jacket who had confronted him with the three other men in front of the fat granny's house in Ballytara.

"Gina, I told you I'd get a taxi to the hotel," Colin said.

"Taxis are on strike," Gina said. "Everything's on strike. You'd be kilt and served for dinner if you crossed the picket outside any hotel."

"Christ," Colin said. "What the hell am I gonna do?"

"You've met me cousin, Paul," Gina said.

"Yeah, we've met," Colin said, nodding to Paul.

"Howayeh," Paul said, and grabbed Colin's suitcase. "I have a wee jam jar parked outside. Hurry before someone notices it."

Colin looked at Gina, who took him by the arm and whisked him out of the airport. She pushed Colin into the front passenger seat of an Opel Kadet station wagon and climbed into the back. Paul slid behind the wheel and peeled away from the curb like a man who had just done a stickup.

"Where we goin'?" asked Colin.

"Now that I'm havin' yer babby," she said, "me family wants yeh over for tay."

"Great," Colin said. *Gotta get this on tape,* he thought.

They fell silent as Paul drove through police checkpoints.

"Nice car you have here, Paul," Colin said as they passed the final checkpoint and took the road toward the city.

"Yeh think so?" Paul said. "I'm thinkin' of tradin' it in."

"Really?" Colin said. "How long you have it?"

"Few hours," Paul said.

"Just bought it?"

Paul looked at Gina in the rearview mirror, smiling. "Nicked," Paul said.

Colin twisted in his seat, looked at Gina for a translation.

"It's kind of not his," Gina said. "It's on loan. Fella left it running and ran into the bank in a panic just before the banks went on strike this mornin.' At a bus stop, mind yeh, with the buses on strike. Cheek of 'im, he deserved it, so he did. Half the motors in Dublin will be nicked by the end of this oul strike."

"You picked me up in a fucking stolen car?"

"Aye," Gina said. "Least yeh can do is say t'anks to Paul. He could be out makin' a bomb pickin' up people at bus stops."

"Jesus, thanks, there, Paul," Colin said. "Thanks so much, pal, for picking me up in this lovely stolen car."

He turned to Gina in the back seat.

"What happens if we get stopped?" Colin asked.

"If yeh get nicked in a nicked car, yeh usually wind up in the nick," she said.

Colin stared ahead as Paul zoomed south on the main road into Dublin until he arrived at the outskirts of the city, where he passed a few Garda cars. Paul then slithered down back streets and narrow lanes. From his jacket, Colin took out his small camera and put it to his left eye. *I could track down these streets,* Colin thought, making mental notes of the bleak landscape. *Or I could use hand-held digital cameras and wild-track sound, cinema verité. I need to get the claustrophobia, the stagnant, airless, hopelessness of it.*

Colin clicked his pen and jotted down notes as Paul raced past closed factories, public utilities, and grim concrete blocks of corporation housing. They jolted through the abyss of the city, where news of the bank and hotel strike might never touch a single citizen—but where the coal and milk strike had an immediate impact.

As Paul drove, Colin asked Gina about the baby, and what the doctor had said. She said she hadn't been to a doctor, she didn't like doctors, and she didn't trust doctors.

"You have to have prenatal care," Colin told her.

"Nothing wrong with me sinuses," she replied.

Colin closed his eyes and changed the subject, for now.

"Did you get passports?"

"Aye," Gina said. "All ready and rearing to go."

"That's good," Colin said. "Tomorrow we have a 9:00 A.M. flight to London, where we catch our connecting flight to Mexico. The sooner we get out of here, the better."

"That's insultin'," Gina said.

"I was talking about the goddamned strike."

"A strike is always a bit of crack, but," Gina said.

"I wish we were staying in a hotel," Colin said.

"We'll have great gas with me family, sure," she said. "Won't we but, Paul?"

"Ninety," Paul said. "It'll be fuckin' ninety."

As they finally wound through the gates of Ballytara, Colin saw a collection of women and children running in circles around a milk lorry, which was pulling away from the lone shop on the corner. The young truck driver swerved to keep from hitting the group of people. The shopkeeper, wearing a dirty apron, was waving her fist at the delivery man.

"Thievin' bastards from the North chargin' three times the price of milk," she screamed at the women, her regular customers.

"What the hell are the women gonna to do?" Colin asked.

"Make the cow jump over the moon," said Gina, laughing.

"They hijacking the goddamned milk truck?" Colin asked, putting the camera to his eye, panning and clicking on the the faces of the angry women, who looped around the truck.

"Milk deliveries is on strike so they sussed out these'ns must be culchie scabs from across the border trying to cash in on desperate women with babbies," Gina said.

"Paul, stop a minute, will ya?" Colin asked.

Paul pulled the car to a sudden stop at the mouth of the quadrangle. Colin searched his carry-on bag for his compact Sony video camera, with zoom lens, which fit snugly into his right hand. As Paul lit a cigarette with the car lighter, Colin began videotaping the scene through the car window. He began to smell the acrid odor of burning plastic and turned to see Paul sizzling the bright hot coils of the car lighter into the Naugahyde dashboard.

"Why the hell are you doing that?" Colin asked.

"For the beautiful badness," Paul said, a glint in his eye like a jeweler's after finding a flawless stone. "Let the cunt who owns it know I owned it too, for a wee while, anyway. Him and his feckin' bank bewk and his Blackrock home, wha'."

Colin looked from the smoking gouge on the dashboard back out into the quadrangle of Ballytara, where the driver of the lorry was desperately trying to leave the compound. Colin lifted the video camera to his eye and with the zoom lens saw a terrified young helper sitting next to the driver. Colin slowly widened the angle to reveal the mothers—hard-faced, wearing head scarves, cigarettes dangling from unglossed lips, toting dirty-faced kids. They pushed old baby carriages, rolled bald tires, and threw bags of garbage in front of the milk truck, trying to make it stop. The driver saw an opening in the crowd and floored the accelerator.

One defiant woman stepped in front of its path and upraised the middle and index fingers of her right hand.

"Get yeh out of that feckin' truck, yeh big bollockses, yeh," shouted the woman. Colin zoomed in on her. She was in her sixties, with a nose that had been broken as many times as a prizefighter's, shaking a swollen-knuckled fist. "There's hungry childer here and that feckin' moo juice will never leave these feckin' flats. We can arrange the same for the both of yiz as well if yiz like, or yiz can feck off now."

"Great stuff," Gina said, leaning forward from the backseat. "Fair play to Auntie Tesey, even if she is a miserable oul whore . . ."

"She's your aunt?" Colin said, still taping.

"Aye, but on me granny's side," Gina said.

"A Lynch," said Paul. "Mad as a March hare, she is. She'd slit your throat to make a pie of yer Adam's apple."

The truck driver slammed on his brakes, stopping inches from the woman. The other women and their kids surrounded the truck, clutching stones and waving broom and mop handles at the driver's window, battering the cab. One woman smashed a rock against the driver's window, cracking it into a splayed web. The men in the truck jumped out, each backing away as they were pelted with stones and debris. Finally, they broke into a run toward the police barracks beyond the gates of Ballytara.

"Spot feckin' on!" Gina shouted.

Colin lowered the camera and turned to her, saw that her eyes were brimming with delight. "Your idea of a happy ending?" Colin said.

"They're just gettin' started," Gina said.

Colin turned back to the scene, raising the camera as the women and older children started climbing on to the lorry. They looked like pirates boarding a galleon. Crates of milk were hoisted onto the shoulders of skinny children, and the women filled their apron pockets and loaded their baby carriages with plastic milk bottles.

Bursting through the crowd came Luke Furey, the red-haired Elvis wannabe, accompanied by his crew of bomber-jacketed pals. Luke carried a toolbox and began distributing tools to his friends. The fat guy went to work on the big truck tires, unscrewing the lug nuts with a tire iron. Luke and the guy with the bad teeth popped the hood of the cab and tore out the battery and various other engine parts. They stripped the lorry with skilled professional dispatch as the giddy women and children carted away the milk.

"They're out of fucking control," Colin said.

"No, they're out of feckin' milk," Gina said. "Now they're taking control. Those greedy scabs are chargin' double and triple for the milk all over Dublin because of the strike. They're lucky they're not burnt at the stake. Would be, too, except it would be a terrible waste of good coal."

"Aye, but it'd be great feckin' crack watchin' a few a them sizzle," Paul said. "The Cup and the Darby in one, wha'?"

"Paul's nickname is the Unfriendly Match."

"Huh?" Colin said.

"He likes an oul fire, Paul does," Gina said.

"Nu'in' like it," Paul said, burning a hole in the upholstery of the driver's door with his lit cigarette. The smell of the ember on the synthetic fabric was nauseating. Colin stared at him in apprehensive horror.

"What the hell is everyone going to do if everything is on strike?" Colin asked.

"Och, it could be worse," said Paul, starting the car again and squealing up a narrow lane, passing more women who were rushing toward the milk truck. "Guinness is workin' and the pubs is open. Feck all else."

"Very sobering thought, there, Paul," Colin said.

He turned to Gina, shaking his head. She winked and smiled, rubbed her belly and pointed at herself and Colin in a "me and you" gesture, and pursed her lips. Paul screeched the car to a halt outside the house on Whiterock Road, where the piebald pony sniffed the barren ground for food and the nanny goat bayed and Granda stuck his head out of the covered wagon, scratching his ass. Granny appeared at the door of the house, surrounded by kids. Bridie, Philomena, and Susan also appeared behind the fat woman at the door.

"We're home," Gina said.

"Holy shit," said Colin.

eighteen

The house was a one-story cottage, with a bathroom to the left off the foyer. To the right was the master bedroom and straight ahead was a cozy living room. The living room was big enough for a settee, a small Danish lounge chair, a padded armchair that sat by the small coal fire, and a dining-room table surrounded by six wooden chairs. The smell of cooking meat and cabbage wafted from a small kitchenette next to the living room. The kitchenette was equipped with a small two-burner stove, a tiny sink, and a waist-high fridge, and was only big enough for two, maybe three, average-size adults, but when Granny was in it there was no room for anyone else. Another small bedroom faced the back garden.

Colin plopped in an overstuffed chair in the immaculate sitting room as Gina and the cousins crammed the couch with the children on their laps. The old man sat in the low-slung Danish chair next to Colin, pouring bottles of Guinness into sparkling glasses, handing them out. Gina took one.

"For the babby," the old man said. Colin reached in his sport jacket pocket and furtively pressed the record button on his small tape recorder. *Gotta get this shit down,* he thought. *Evidence of life on another galaxy.*

"Ta, Granda," Gina said, taking the glass of Guinness.

The old man then handed Colin a glass for himself and soon everyone in the sitting room had a glass of Guinness. Paul stood by the hearth, staring into the fire, which was beginning to expire.

"None of yiz thought to go borry some feckin' coal with a Yank coming into the house and all, wha'?" said Granny, stomping from the steam-shrouded kitchen. She bent and lifted the edge of the linoleum and tore a piece off matter-of-factly. None of the others reacted as she ripped up one linoleum hunk after another and tossed each hunk onto the fire.

"That poor Yank'll catch his death," the fat woman said, and made her way back into the kitchen as the flames roared.

Colin looked at the gaping hole left on the floor and thought, *You can't make this shit up. None of them thinks this is at all strange.*

Paul gleefully poked the torn linoleum into bright, blue flame. The smell of burning linoleum quickly overwhelmed the aroma of food.

"Magic, Granny," Paul said.

"We need a bit o' wood on that fire," Granny shouted.

Granda passed around a pack of cigarettes and each of the women took one—including Gina. Paul lifted out a piece of burning linoleum and lit Gina's cigarette.

"Gina, for chrissakes," Colin said.

"Go way outta dat," Gina said. "Next you'll be tellin' me to cut out me bottle of stout."

"Not a bad idea," Colin said.

"I will in me arse give up me fags and me bottle of stout because

I'm with child," Gina said, her voice dropping to a low register as she spoke through the puff of smoke. "Every mother I know drinks and smokes. All this worry is a bunch of shite yous Americans cooked up. Doctors in Ireland says the bottle of stout is good for the babbies, isn't that right, Granny?"

"Aye," Granny shouted, as she stirred several pots on a small stove. "'Tis true. Lots of yer iron and ministrels in porter. But I'd switch to a fag with a cork tip all the same, Gina."

"I can't smoke a filtered fag," Gina said. "And I'll not go nine feckin' months without an oul smoke all the same."

The old man flicked an ash behind his chair and threw his wooden match on the floor at his feet. Colin instinctively grabbed an ashtray from an end table, picked up the match, and placed it next to the assorted dead butts in the tray. He handed it to Granda. The old man shook his head and dumped the dead butts, matchsticks, and ashes onto the floor. Colin looked at the others for reactions. There were none. He saw Granda put the ashtray into his bathrobe pocket and flick another ash on the floor. *Could be a great bit of filmed business,* Colin thought. *Without a lick of dialogue.*

"Do yiz young wans have broken legs or do yiz want broken arms?" shouted Granny from the kitchen.

Gina and the cousins put their children down on the floor and sprung to action like soldiers responding to a command. Gina went directly into the kitchen, tying an apron around her waist and grabbing a serving platter. The other women began setting the table with delft, silverware, and condiments in preparation for a meal.

"See that there," the old man whispered to Colin, pointing to the butts and ashes he'd dumped on the floor. "That'll give the behemoth something to do later, so." Motioning to Granny standing outside the kitchen, he said, "And when the behemoth's busy with that, she stays off this," tapping himself on the back.

"How come I never thought of that?" Colin said.

"Wisdom comes with age, son," Granda said.

The room smelled faintly of shit and piss and burning linoleum and cabbage and Colin watched the saggy-diapered toddlers crisscross the floor in quest of their mothers.

"I hates a child what whinges," Granda said. *There's a word I have to have these people use,* Colin thought. *Whinge.*

Granda removed the pacifier from the mouth of the whinging baby, dipped it into his stout, and plugged it back in the child's mouth.

"Shut yeh up," he said. The child shut up.

"If yer gonna have a child with that young wan, Gina," Granda said to Colin, "yeh better learn a few rare oul rules of the road. Come outside wi' me a wee minute while the wimmins set the tay."

Colin followed the old man into the chilly hallway. Granda stopped in the bathroom on the way out and urinated loudly without closing the bathroom door. Colin noticed that he intentionally pissed all over the toilet seat.

"Never lift the seat," he said. "Don't make it comfortable for the wimmims in there or they'll stay in there hours, so."

He reached up and unscrewed the lightbulb from the overhead socket, placing it in his bathrobe pocket. "Same with them diabolical feckin' light bulbs, or else they'll read in the tub or on the bowl and you'll be paying the ESB until yer own lights is shut on Judgment Day."

He rapped on the mirrorless medicine cabinet. "Another t'ing, never keeps a feckin' looking glass in a jacks in a house of wimmins or you'll never get yer dinner or yer hole."

Colin laughed, thinking: *The man is a fucking genius in his own way.*

He followed the old man outside to the cluttered front garden, where the goat was napping and the horse stood idle. The cold Dublin sky was growing overcast.

"You're trouble, boyo," the old man said, now out of earshot of the women.

"Beg your pardon?" Colin said.

"Beggin's for the wimmins," he said. "So feck off wi' tha', righ'? But you, y'iv brought more trouble on this family, yeh have. Get somethin' straight. That young wan, Gina, is a traveler. Her mammy was a traveler, God rest her soul. And no matter what she did, Gina's one of us."

"I don't think I'm following you," Colin said.

"The babby in Gina's belly is also a traveler, no matter wha' yeh say or do," Granda said, jabbing a finger into Colin's chest. "But you, Yank, y'ill never be a traveler. Are we clear on tha'?"

"That part I get," Colin said, grabbing the old man's finger. "But my kid will always be *my* kid, too. No matter fuckin' what."

"See? Tha's trouble on the way already. Tha' babby will be a traveler. With cousins and uncles who'll see to tha'."

Colin had no intention of fighting a custody battle with a crazy old man here in Ballytara. He'd get Gina to the States, with an ocean between these lunatics and his unborn baby.

"What did you mean when you said that Gina was a traveler no matter what her mammy did?' What did her mother do?"

"Did Gina not tell you about her father?" the old man asked.

"She said her mother and father were killed," Colin said. "She didn't say how or why."

"Which father was she talkin' about?" the old man said as he made his move to go back inside. "The Irish one or the Eyetalian?"

"Italian? What Italian?" Colin asked.

"That bit o' business cost me a son to jail for life," said the old man. "His brothers are not too happy about it, either."

"Rory and Derek."

"Aye," the old man said. "They don't come in the house when Gina's around, except a course for the Furey Christmas hooley. Bad blood betwixt Gina and me sons, but they're still Fureys. And they won't mess with their mother."

"They talked about an Italian, too," Colin said. "What's with the Italian?"

"Time for our tay, sure," Granda said. "I'll say no more. My advice to you is, feck off to America and don't look back."

Inside, Granda plopped down in his chair and collapsed right through the cushion onto the floor. The women and the children laughed uproariously as he remained there in a comical heap. His great-grandchildren began climbing all over him and he tickled them until they writhed and squealed. Now the old man pointed to

the fire, where wooden slats, which until minutes ago had held up
the chair cushions, were burning.

"I knew I should have nailed them feckin' slats in," Granda
said. "If it isn't nailed, she burns it. That woman of mine would
burn the lid off my coffin and Christ's cross with Him on it."

"I needed the wood for the fire so that poor Yank won't catch
his death," Granny said as she carried out a plate of food piled high
with meat, vegetables, and potatoes and placed it at the head of the
table. Gina pushed Colin into a chair in front of the food.

"Eat up, Patrick," Granny said.

"His name is Colin, Granny," Gina corrected.

"I knew a Patrick once what looked like a Colin and that's why I
get confused," Granny said. "He was a bit mental, the poor crayture."

Colin noticed that Paul sat on the chair closest the fire, his dinner on his lap, feeding pieces of linoleum into the flames. He also
fed the fire with spoons full of sugar, which made the flames leap.

Colin looked down at his own plate—mashed potatoes and
roasted potatoes, lamb cooked until it was gray, brussels sprouts, cabbage, carrots, and peas. He waited for the others to sit. Then Granda
blessed himself and said, "Thanks for the oul grub, dear Lord."

The kids ate from bowls on the floor as the adults dug in at the
table. Colin made a mental note of how the Irish ate with both knife
and fork in either hand at the same time, using the blade of the knife
as a backstop for the fork.

Colin was swallowing a mouthful of meat and potato when he
began to gag. He reached in and pulled a long bright red hair
through his lips and it kept coming from his throat like a magician's
endless scarf. He looked across at the sweating fat granny, her
bright red hair exploding from under her greasy head scarf as she
leaned across Granda's plate and cut his meat into bite-size pieces.

"Eat it all, yeh rake-thin ghet, or I'll bleedin' clatter yeh," she
told him, as if he were a child.

"Feck off, and bu'er me bread," he said.

"Which teeth do yeh have in?" she asked. "I hope you're
wearin' your good ones with company in the house, wha'?"

"The good ones, aye," he said. "From the Galway dentist."

"Oh, aye, all right, then. Then use them for more than smilin' at your fancy women."

"Don't start," the old man said. "Leave it out, righ'?"

"Don't mind them, Colin," Gina said. "Mad as hatters but madly in love."

"I do not love this dirty oul chancer," Granny said. "There's a difference between love and a curse. God chose me to be cursed with this scrubber. Him and his fancy women. I'm wide to him . . ."

Granda looked at Colin, rolled his eyes as he chewed, and blew out a stream of air in frustration.

"Catch the next boat home, son," he said.

As Colin tried to settle his stomach, he looked more closely at his plate and saw other sprigs of bright red hair coiled in the butter of the potatoes, mired in a bog of shiny brown gravy, clashing with the green of the brussels sprouts. His stomach bucked and rolled as the others ate.

"'Scuse me," Colin mumbled, bolting for the bathroom. He groped in the dark, leaned over, and clutched the toilet seat that was slick with Granda's piss. And vomited.

After dinner, a loud knock came upon the door. Gina answered it and Luke Furey, covered in grease and coal dust, his Elvis hairdo in full collapse, walked in with a sack of coal on his shoulder and plopped it down in front of Colin.

"This is for you, cowboy, righ'," Luke said. "I traded three crates of milk for this. Payback for the pack of fags the last time. Someday I might come knockin' on yer door in America and I didn't want yeh to think I was inhospitable."

"Feck off outta dat, you," the old man said. "Brings us some milk as well."

"Me ma would kill me if she knew I brought yiz anythin' atall," said Luke.

"Tell me daughter Tesey to ask me arse," said Granny.

Paul snatched up the bag of coal and fed the fire as if it were a famished family pet.

Now the old man passed around glasses of poitin. He poured

one for Luke Furey, one for Paul, one for himself, and then one for Colin. Colin tossed it straight back, John Wayne style. It tasted like lighter fluid and he was certain it had melted his esophagus on the way down. "Holy fuck!" Colin shouted.

"Yeh know it's the best poitin when the rats go mad for it, so," Granda said. "They found six big dead ones in the vat at the still where this is from in Roscommon. Hungry feckers chews their way in, drinks it, and the oul rats gets so pissed drunk they drowns in it. When the rats die happy, yeh know it's proper poitin."

Colin said, "You're fuckin' kiddin' me, right?"

"Not atall," Granda said, swallowing another gulp.

Paul took tiny sips and spit it through his front teeth into the fire, watching the flames leap in a white-and-blue dance.

"The men always need a shot of poitin first to prepare themselves for what it does to the wimmins," Granda explained.

"Don't be fillin' that young lad's head with an old mon's shite," Granny shouted as the four granddaughters did the washing up in four separate ceramic washing basins—one for the dishes, one for the silverware, one for the glasses, and one to rinse.

The women finished the kitchen chores and the old man now poured shots of poitin for the women, who belted them back as if it were Ovaltine. Granny took three quick double shots with no initial visible effect.

"My Jaysus, we're in for a night of holy feckin' terror," the old man said. "Not to worry, music calms the married beast, wha'."

"I'll feckin' beast ya," Granny said.

The old man took a pennywhistle from his robe pocket and began to blow a lovely tune. Gina went into a bedroom and returned with a guitar and began to strum.

"A wee song called "The Emigrant's Letter," written by a bloke named Percy French in nineteen hundred and ten," Gina said to Colin. "Granda taught me it when I was about ten, didn't yeh, Granda?"

"Did, indeed," Granda said. "Sing it, lass."

Dear Daddy, I'm taking the pen in my hand,
To tell you we're just out of sight of the land,

On a grand ocean liner, we're sailing in style
And we're sailing away from the Emerald Isle.

And a queer sort of hush came over us all,
As the waves hid the last part of oul Donegal.
And it's well to be you that is taking your tay
Where they're cutting the corn in Creeshla today.

Several sad verses later, Gina was finished. No one clapped but everyone drank more poitin. Soon all the women were weeping and hugging each other, which made the babies begin to whinge. The children were put to bed in the back bedroom and more songs were sung. The cousins told some funny stories about life on the road, of weddings and fairs they'd attended all over the country as kids. More tears flowed. Feeling quite drunk, Colin realized he'd drunk six bottles of Guinness and three or four shots of poitin. By night's end, he was also sagging from all the travel. Gina was kissing her granny and telling her how much she was going to miss her, making her promise to come visit her in America.

Through it all, Granda sat nodding in a kitchen chair, watching the women embrace, nodding his head. Finally, the cousins pulled presents out for Gina. Granny went into the kitchen and stood looking out the window at a stucco wall, smoking a cigarette and crying, her big body heaving.

Colin went back to the bathroom, groping in the dark. As he stood relieving himself, he thought, *If Jack was here he'd throw a net over me and haul me off to a fucking asylum.*

He heard sudden screaming, breaking glass, and a loud commotion coming from the sitting room. He zipped up and hurried out. Granny, roaring drunk, was beating Granda over his head with a picture frame. Blood leaked from his scalp, down over his leathery, white-stubbled face, and splinters of glass covered the floor. Gina and the cousins were trying to restrain Granny, as Paul and Luke sat by the fire, laughing, sipping poitin, passing a blunt of hashish.

"You durty diabolical feckin' tomcat, yeh," Granny shouted, continuing to beat Granda, who cowered, covering his head from additional blows. "Showin' off a picture of yer fancy country woman.

I'm wide to yeh, yeh filthy bollocks, yeh. I'll cut if off yeh, I will, and burn it in the fire . . ."

"Granny, for Jaysus sakes," Bridie shouted. "I'm only after buyin' that frame in town today, for Gina, to send us back a picture of the new babby."

"Lamb of Jaysus, woman," shouted Granda, his arms covering his bloodied face. "Yer after drawing feckin' blood, yeh are. This time I'm sendin' yeh in for a good long rest in the mental."

"Don't threaten me with the feckin' mental," Granny bellowed, pointing to the bloodied commercial photograph in the shattered frame. "I'd know this fancy trollop anywhere."

"Jaysus, Granny, it's a picture of a model," Gina said. "The picture comes with the frame, for the love of God in heaven. She's about fifty year younger than me poor granda."

"He loves them young wans, so he does," Granny shouted. "That's why he stays with me."

Now all three women started laughing and were able to force Granny to sit in a kitchen chair. Luke and Paul were bent in half laughing in front of the fire as the old man dabbed at his skull and face with a snotty hankie, looking at the blood. Shaking his head. He took his teeth out of his mouth and put them in his bathrobe pocket, where they clanked against the ashtray, the lightbulb, and the pennywhistle. He looked up at Colin.

"I'm tellin yeh, boyo," Granda said, bleary with drink. "When yeh get to America, slam the feckin' gate."

The cousins' teary good-byes took half an hour. After they were gone, Colin felt exhausted, drunk, and ready for bed. Granda was asleep on the settee and Granny was snoring in the bedroom. Brianna was asleep in the small back bedroom.

"Your bags packed?" Colin whispered. Their flight was leaving at nine the next morning.

"Aye," Gina said. "I love a trip but this one is terrible sad. I'll miss them all, as mad as they are."

"Where do we sleep?" Colin asked.

"Granda is giving us his bed," Gina said.

"Which room?"

Gina took Colin by the hand and led him out the front door into the cold damp night, across the lawn, and climbed the back steps of the covered caravan.

"You're shitting me," Colin said.

"It's only pure lovely inside," she said, and he followed her in. "I'll light the oul Tilley lamp low and turn on his wireless for a bit o' music. These oul caravans is almost all gone. Hardly no one uses them anymore. All the families is borryin' money from the traveler kings in the Wards and Joyces and O'Briens clans to buy motor trailers like in America. But I love these oul caravans. I was born in this one."

He watched her light the small kerosene lamp, and it offered what little illumination they needed in the eight-by-five-foot living quarters. *This will look bizarre on film,* he thought. He had to bend to move around, but the barrel-top wagon was as neat as an army barracks during inspection. He imagined the camera doing a slow pan of the interior. The rear of the wagon provided a seating area and a small kitchen, filled with dangling pots, pans, and utensils. Canned provisions were stacked next to a hot plate. In the front of the wagon, closest to the driver's seat, was the sleeping area, where a full-size mattress lay on a platform like a captain's bed, with storage drawers underneath. All of Granda's clothes were tidily folded and stacked in a small press directly next to the bed. His shaving gear was on top of the press, next to mason jars filled with nuts, bolts, screws, nails, gizmos. Pieces of uilleann pipes clogged a small wooden barrel.

Framed pictures of the Sacred Heart and Mary with baby Jesus were jammed into the squares of the front wall of the wagon's circular wooden armature. Just over the headboard, a shotgun was wedged into a rack between a framed photo of the pope and a blue delft platter depicting the Last Supper. The overhead squares displayed reproductions of Michelangelo's Sistine Chapel. Many of the other squares on the walls of the wagon featured cracked and faded photographs of the family in different parts of the countryside over the years.

Several fishing poles and tackle boxes were stacked at the foot of the bed, along with some rabbit snares. Dozens of tin whistles, a few mandolins, a couple of fiddles, and three sets of uilleann pipes hung from an overhead beam.

"Neat," Colin said.

"Granny disinfects the wagon every day with bleach and Jeyes fluid," Gina said. "Cleanest sheets you ever seen, nary a flea or louse in here."

She pulled back the bedspread on the small bed to reveal snowy white sheets, stenciled with the legend TEMPLE BAR HOTEL. She sat for a moment, looked Colin in the eye.

"Are yeh ready for a babby, Colin Coyne?"

"It scares the shit out of me."

"At least you're honest."

It sounded funny coming from a thief. But he didn't laugh.

"I'll be the best father I can be," he said, shrugging.

"I want yeh to undress me like I was yer woman," she said. "Pretend we're out on the road in the west of Ireland, just us, alone. And then I want yeh in bed beside me and I want yeh to hold me in yer big arms."

Sometimes she spoke to him as if she were narrating a tale, another part of the fiction she created for herself. *She lives a fiction while I'm imagining one,* he thought.

Then, in the tinker's caravan, on the front lawn of a house in Ballytara, where no one acted normal, Colin made love to the real-life Gina Furey, who was carrying his soon-to-be-real-life child.

When he was with Gina, making love, he understood how a woman could make a man like Kieran feel more alive than he'd ever felt before in his life.

nineteen

March 7

"Come out, yeh Yank cunt, yeh," came the voice in the night.

Where am I? Colin thought, blinking his eyes, looking around. *Christ, I'm in a fucking tinker's caravan. I was dreaming of rats, a red-eyed rat with barbed-wire teeth looking up at me from the bottom of my poitin glass.*

His head pounded from jet lag, poitin, and Guinness, his empty stomach rumbling for want of food. He heard two more malevolent drunken voices. He sat up, felt Gina's bare breast against his chest, her nipple hardening from the cold as he lifted the blanket. He gathered his bearings in the dim, cramped enclosure. The Tilley-lamp light was low, casting a butterscotch hue. A reel was playing on the old transistor radio.

"Come out, yeh durty Yank," came the gruff voice from outside. "Come and see the new face I'm gown'a gives yeh. I'll send yeh back to New York with yeh dangler in your kit bag."

Colin cupped his balls with one hand and groped for his pants with the other. *Underwear,* he thought. He lifted the sheets and blanket, the odor of recent sex rising in the close air, the intoxicating smell of Gina. He found his underpants and pulled them on quickly, followed by his jeans.

Gina snapped up with a disoriented start. "Wha'?" she said.

"Another surprise visit from your genteel fucking family," he said, pulling on his heavy socks.

"Yeh fuckin' coward, yeh," came the drunken voice outside.

"Shite," Gina said. "It's Rory Furey, me uncle."

"Which one?"

"The poxy one," Gina said. "Hates me. A right evil swine."

"The one built like a fuckin' war memorial?"

"Aye," she said.

"Great."

"Come out here, yeh Yank poofter, yeh," Rory yelled. "Yeh

185

fuckin' homosexual, yeh. Just who the fuck do yeh think yeh are, a Yank in bed with one of us'ns, I'll tear off your bollocks and shoot snooker wi' 'em . . ."

Colin could hear two other drunks encouraging the loud one. "He's shitein' himself greener than a cow in Da's caravan, sure," said the second drunken voice, his laughter turning into a phlegmy coughing fit. "We'll bring him up to Garlic Hill for a moonlight serenade. When-a-the-moon-hits-a-your-eye-like-a-big-pizza-pie . . ."

Colin yanked on his cowboy boots, figuring he could crush a few gonads or kick out an eyeball or two with them.

"Righ' then," Gina said. "Keep out of the way of his grip. Once yer in his hands, Rory's like a human hay baler."

"Is this supposed to be a pep talk?"

"A bit o' advice, like," she said.

"You promised it would be a night I'd never forget."

"Yeh could just ignore them," she said, yawning.

"Until what?" Colin said. "Until they come in here after me? This is the second time these mutts have come after me. Where I come from, someone threatens you, you do something about it."

"I rather fancy this."

"Fancy what?"

"You fightin' for me honor," Gina said with a sleepy smile.

"I'm glad one of us does," he said.

Colin stepped out of the caravan into the cold night, his heart pounding. He spotted Derek, holding the hurling stick he'd brandished the last time they met. Luke, the red-haired Elvis, stood in the street, passing a big blunt back and forth with Derek. They were giggling like spectators at a comedy act. Colin concentrated on Rory, the muscle-bound guy, standing in the center of the lawn, his face snarling with whiskey. He was wearing the same green sweater he wore the last time Colin saw him. *Filthy fuck probably hasn't changed it since,* he thought.

"What's your fuckin' problem, apeman?" Colin said.

"Yer me problem, Yank," said Rory. "Yeh doin' the durty with the daughter of me dead sister is me feckin' problem."

"She's having my baby," Colin said.

"More the reason to kill him and dig 'im up and kill 'im again," said Derek, who had the hurling stick in his hand.

Luke just giggled.

"The babby'll be born fatherless, then," said Rory. "Better'n by a Yank buffer like yerself."

"You want me, asshole, you got me," Colin said. "You threaten me, I'll fuckin' kill you! Come on, one on one, tough guy. Tell your goon brothers to back the fuck off."

"I don't need them for the likes of you," Rory said.

Colin descended the stairs of the caravan and Rory charged him, head down, like a mad bull. Colin stepped to the side and shoved Rory as he passed. Rory's head slammed into the side of the wagon frame, shaking the whole caravan. He fell to his knees, blood trickling from his scalp. The horse whinnied and stomped in a demented circle, rearing at its tether by the fence. The goat ran in circles on its leash, baying, dinging the little bell around its neck.

Derek and Luke cheered for Rory. Lights came on in the houses along Whiterock Road, faces began appearing behind curtains, but no one ventured outside their homes.

"Break his Yank neck, Rory," shouted Derek. "Show him what we do to outsiders what meddle in Furey and Lynch family affairs."

Rory pushed himself to a standing position and he came at Colin with his arms apart. He charged Colin again, but Colin circled to his left, smashing a left jab into Rory's face. Rory chased him and Colin went flat-footed long enough to detonate a straight right off Rory's nose. He heard cartilage crunch and pop like dry twigs as Rory's hands instinctively cupped his face and tears filled his eyes, blood running through his dirty fingers. Colin immediately anchored himself and drove a ferocious left hook into Rory's right rib cage. Rory staggered, let out a loud animalistic war whoop, and stomped at Colin, swinging a wild left and an even more reckless right.

The right caught a backpedaling Colin high on the head; the force was momentarily numbing. Pinwheels spun in front of his eyes. *It was only an arm punch, without the full force of Rory's body behind it,* Colin thought. *This guy is right out of a fucking Marvel comic. Can't let him hit me again . . .*

Sensing he'd hurt Colin, Rory charged again, swinging a looping left. Colin bent at the knees, under the punch, and crushed a wicked right into Rory's left rib cage. He felt Rory begin to sag. Colin pivoted, springing his thighs, hips and shoulders into the right hand that he launched straight up, onto the tip of Rory's chin.

The perfect uppercut caused Colin's right hand to ignite in pain. He knew if he used the same hand again he'd break it. *I can't fight this baboon with one hand,* he thought. Colin stepped back and saw a bloodied, anguished Rory bend toward the left, clutching his shattered rib cage as the punch to the jaw finally rocked him in a delayed reaction, like a neurological echo, making his body jerk backward at the same time as he staggered left. Colin didn't take any chances. He circled again and exploded a short left hook into Rory's right temple, hoping it would send a bulletin directly to his brain. Rory fell twice, once to his left on his knees, then flat on his face, without breaking his own fall. Colin knew that, in boxing, if you landed on your face you usually didn't get up. Rory lay still.

Colin, in an adrenaline rush, considered kicking Rory in the other temple with his cowboy boot to make sure he stayed where he was, but he thought better of it. *I might kill this dirty cocksucker,* he thought. *And he ain't worth the paperwork.*

Now Derek came at Colin from the left with the hurling stick while a reluctant and frightened Luke circled from his left. Colin tried to decide which one to hit first.

"Here, now, that's not feckin' on," shouted Gina, who stood on the top step of the caravan, cocking the double-barreled shotgun. "Take yer moldy brudda home, Derek, and put him to bed. Leave off me fella or I'll fuckin' kill yiz."

Derek looked at her and nodded in relief. Luke giggled.

"She's a feckin' nutter," Luke whispered. "She'll do it."

"I feckin' will," Gina said.

"We're not finished with yeh, Yank," said Derek as he and Luke each took Rory under an arm. Rory came babbling to half-consciousness as they helped him to the High Ace Toyota.

"That Yank can bleedin' row," he mumbled.

Colin stood breathing for several seconds, thinking: *Perfect, the movie needed a good fight scene.*

Colin climbed back into the caravan and examined the shotgun. It was loaded. He looked Gina in the eye and she winked.

"Are you completely fucking crazy?" he said.

"Aye."

twenty

At daybreak, it took Gina ten full minutes to shake Paul from his slumber in the chair by the fire. When they finally left the house, Colin carried the two black canvas bags he'd seen Gina steal from the Pakistani dealer on Moore Street. His right hand pulsated and he had a lump on his head where Rory had punched him. Granda and Granny were still locked in poitin-induced sleep.

Paul drove the Opel Kadet through Ballytara, passing the stripped milk truck, now lying upside down and looking like a giant dead roach.

At the airport, Gina embraced Paul on the sidewalk outside the terminal.

"Bye-bye," Paul said, without a trace of melancholy. "If I don't see yeh through the week, I'll see yeh through the window."

"Remember what I told yeh," Gina said. "When you apply for the visa at the American Embassy, don't give them any agro, just nick some ID somewhere."

"No pro'lem," Paul said.

Jesus Christ, Colin thought. *Is she inviting this pyromaniac to New York?*

"Paul will love New York, won't he, Colin?" Gina said.

"A match made in heaven," Colin said. "I should warn you, arson is discouraged as a hobby."

"Is that supposed to be funny?" Gina asked.

"I'm not sure," Colin said, slinging Gina's two stolen canvas bags over his shoulders and lifting her two suitcases in his hands. Gina's eyes filled with tears as Paul hopped back into the stolen car and sped off toward Dublin.

She pushed Brianna in the pram, her two carry-on bags hanging from the handles. They checked in for the commuter flight to London and waited to go through the metal detectors. Gina immediately set off the metal detector. When she made it go off again, after emptying her pockets, the security guard went over her body with a scanner which blared intermittently.

"What are you carrying?" asked the airport security officer.

"Me life savin's," Gina said.

"Remove it," the suspicious security guard said.

Gina started removing necklaces, bangles, ankle bracelets, rings, earrings, and even a few strings of waist chains. The security people gathered around, staring at her jewelry, mostly gold, studded with small diamonds, rubies, emeralds, and opals, which made a sizable mound on the countertop. *Must be worth thousands,* Colin thought. *A tinker's 401-K.* His research had told him that tinkers carried around jewelry as a portable nest egg, so they wouldn't have to use banks.

"Elizabeth Taylor, wha'?" said the security guard.

They summoned a Dublin cop, who picked up his radio and spoke to an unseen comrade. "Dooley, Hallahan here, are we looking for any stolen jewelry?" he asked.

"Negative," came the crackling reply.

"That's her own jewelry," Colin said.

"She has more jewels than a gypo," said the cop.

"Who're yeh callin' a gypo, arse face?" Gina said.

Oh, Jesus, Colin thought. *Here we go.*

"Missus," the cop said, angrily, "I can charge you . . ."

"Charge her for what?" Colin said. "You just ethnically insulted this woman. In front of witnesses."

The cop looked around and saw the line of ticketed passengers behind them waiting to go through security.

"How do you figure I ethnically insulted her?" the cop asked.

"Because I'm a traveler, that's the why," Gina said.

The cop began to redden.

"I don't give a tinker's damn what you are," said the guard, realizing he'd just compounded his insult. "I can have you charged with harassment all the same."

"I bleedin' dare yeh," Gina said. "I'll be onto me solicitor and the traveler's organizations and I'll have yeh up on charges and wrote up in the papers so fast . . ."

"Look, we have a plane to catch," Colin interrupted.

A supervisor came over and inquired about the commotion. After taking the cop off to one side and hearing his version of the encounter, the supervisor walked back to Gina and Colin with an authoritative smile and a tip of his hat.

"Very sorry, missus," the supervisor said. "Carry on."

"What's his name?" Gina asked.

"The plane, Gina," Colin said, gathering up her jewelry. "We gotta catch the goddamned plane."

"I still say he's a pig-faced ghet," Gina said as Colin nudged her up the ramp toward the gate.

A professionally dressed woman in her thirties, holding an attaché case on her lap, sat at the window seat. Colin was crammed into the center seat. Gina sat on the aisle. Brianna ran up and down the aisle of the plane on the one-hour commuter hop to London.

"Shite, Mammy," yelled Brianna, standing frozen in the aisle.

"Och, Jaysus, Brianna," Gina said. "Not now, sure."

"Shite," Brianna said again, her face contorted.

"Is she saying what I think she's saying?" Colin asked.

"Why, didn't yeh ever shite in yer knickers when yeh were two?" Gina said defensively.

"I think I was toilet trained," Colin said.

"Aren't you the cat's arse, then," she said, fumbling in her carry-on bag for a disposable diaper and pre-moistened towelettes. "My wee girl is flyin' on an aeroplane for the first time in her little life and the poor flower couldn't contain her excitement."

Colin loved the way Gina could go from coarse hostility to sweetness like a blinding costume change. *Gotta write both personalities into her character,* he thought. *Make an index card for the cops and another one for the airplane.*

The professional-looking woman seated by the window glanced over. Gina smiled at her. A portly man seated across the aisle from Gina looked down from his peach-colored *Financial Times*.

"Shite, Mammy," Brianna said again.

Snickers came from a few seats behind. The portly man gruffly folded his *Financial Times* toward himself and leaned toward Gina. "Aren't you going to do something about that child?" he asked.

"Oh, aye," Gina said. "And I'm chargin' a pound a peek."

With that she pulled down her food tray, hoisted Brianna up onto it, pulled up her dress, and yanked her dark tights down over her diaper.

"Gina, the toilet," Colin whispered as the woman at the window glanced over, looking trapped.

"I get closetraphobia in cramped places," said Gina. "I was only on a plane the once't afore and got off when I seen the size of the jacks."

"You can't change her here, for chrissakes," Colin said.

"You take her into the toilets, then, Lord Mighty Shite?"

Colin closed his eyes, shut off his overhead light, reclined his seat, plugged headphones into his ears, and pretended he was asleep. He cracked one eye and through the parted lashes he could see Gina open the dirty diaper as Brianna lay on the food tray.

"Shite, Mammy."

"Good God!" shouted the man with the *Financial Times*.

"We know you were born without an arse," Gina said to him. "That's why yer so feckin' fat!"

"*Here,* now, I've just had my breakfast," the man declared.

"You could do losing a few meals," Gina said, opening the diaper and folding it over with practiced skill, wiping the child with the moist napkins.

The man pushed himself to his feet in a flustered rage, slamming his folded newspaper onto the seat.

"This is outrageous," the portly man growled.

"No, it's shite," Gina said. "Like yer wife serves yeh for tay."

The portly man stormed toward the front of the plane as some passengers laughed and a few made retching noises, but none complained.

Gina turned to the woman beyond Colin but she sat clutching her briefcase, staring out the window, never turning. Colin watched Gina fold the diaper, reach across the aisle, and grab the man's *Financial Times*. She folded the newspaper carefully around the dirty diaper, placed it back on the man's seat. *Close-up*, Colin thought.

Gina sprinkled talcum powder on Brianna, fastened a new diaper, and pulled up her tights.

"Dere, now, a gra," Gina said, rubbing her nose in the giggling child's belly. "A nice clean new nappy and if you shite again you'll need a bleedin' parachute."

Gina then sat Brianna on her lap, folded up the food tray, and bounced the child on her knee, singing:

Not last night but the night before,
Three little monkeys came to my door,
One with a fiddle, one with a drum,
One with a pancake tied to his bum.
Funny little monkey, funny little man,
Washed his face in a frying pan,
Combed his hair with the leg of a chair,
And scratched his belly with his big toenail . . .

"Madam, may I have a word with you?" said a uniformed steward, who now stood above Gina. Colin opened his eyes and sat straight up. The portly man from across the aisle was standing behind the steward. He was fuming.

"I'm trying to sing me child to sleep," Gina said.

"Madam, may I suggest that you use a lavatory the next time you change your child," the steward said in a pleasant British accent.

"My child is not a rat," she said.

The steward looked momentarily stumped for words. "The toilet," the steward said. "Maybe use the toilet."

"Did that tub of butcher's scrap complain about a frightened two-year-old durtyin' her diaper?" Gina said.

"I did indeed," the portly man said. "First your child is let to run loose. Then you change it at the *seat,* exposing everyone else to the odor."

"I think your nose is too close to your arse is what I think, fatty," Gina said.

"Madame," the steward said. "I can have the police meet this plane and have you taken off in chains. Is that what you want?"

Gina said, "I'll miscarriage here in the seat first."

The steward looked at her and swallowed. "Madame . . ."

"Charged with what?" Colin said, challenging the steward.

"Disturbing the flight," the steward said.

"This woman happens to be pregnant and suffers from claustrophobia," Colin said. "Her child needed to be changed. This was hardly a terrorist act."

"Pregnant . . . claustrophobic . . . I see," the steward said, raising his eyebrows. "Are you traveling with her, sir?"

"Yes," Colin said. "The child soiled herself and her mother changed the diaper as discreetly as possible. Where's the crime?"

The steward turned to the portly man, cleared his throat, and said, "Under the circumstances, sir, I can't say that anyone has actually behaved untoward."

"Untoward," the man said. "I've been flying this commuter plane for ten years and have never been exposed to the likes of this . . ."

The plane banked and the seat-belt lights popped on as the pilot announced the approach to London.

"I'm sorry for any inconvenience, sir," the steward said. "As unpleasant as it might have been, it was only a child. I suggest you sit down and fasten your belt for landing."

"I intend to write a letter," the man said.

"Fine."

The steward hurried toward the front of the plane. The portly businessman sat down in his seat, lifting the *Financial Times* and buckling his belt. He never looked over at Gina as he took his briefcase from under the seat in front of him, unsnapped the clasps, slammed his newspaper inside, snapped the briefcase shut, and fastened the clasps.

"Case closed," Gina said.

Colin and Gina broke up laughing as the plane made its approach to the runway.

twenty-one

Mercifully, Brianna slept on the flight from London to Mexico City.

Upon landing, Colin and Gina moved through immigration and customs with no problems, saying they were in Mexico on vacation. Colin had to lug their baggage. It was 1:05 P.M. and their connecting flight to Monterrey, Mexico, left at 1:30.

"My Jaysus, can't we camp for the night?" Gina asked. "Any oul kip will do. I'm banjaxed, and me child is wallfallen, the air is like a coal bin."

During the long walk through the crowded terminal, they passed bars, newsstands, souvenir shops, and a fast-food stand.

At one point, Gina steered Brianna's pram into an open-fronted bar and approached the brightly dressed Mexican bartender. "Give us a bottle of stout, luv, will yeh," she said.

"*De que?*"

"Guinness-o," said Gina.

"You won't get a Guinness at an airport bar in Mexico City," Colin said. To his amazement, he then saw the barman place a bottle of Guinness and a chilled glass in front of Gina.

"*Cerveza negra,*" the barman said, and then switched to English. "Gee-nees is good for you."

"Aye," Gina said.

"*Si,*" said the bartender.

"I said the magic word," she said. Colin paid the bartender with dollars as Gina poured the Guinness into the glass and took a deep long gulp, her face beaming as she swallowed. She bent and gave Brianna a big sip, the dark foamy stout running down the child's cheeks. The Mexicans at the bar exploded in laughter and approval as the baby smacked her lips and reached for more.

"I'd pitch tent for the night right here," Gina said.

Colin looked at his watch; they had seventeen minutes to catch their connecting plane.

"We're gonna miss the plane," Colin said.

"Och, could be worse," she said. "Least they serve Guinness."

Gina finished her Guinness, giving a last taste to the baby. *"Adios, amigos,"* Gina said.

"Adios, señora," said the smiling barman as they left the bar.

Gina sniffed the air as they moved into the terminal. "What in the name of God is it that smells so good?"

"Tacos," Colin said.

"Sounds like something you'd find in a nappy," Gina said. "But they smell like heaven's oven."

They stopped in front of a taco stand—it was thirteen minutes before their plane left.

"Tacos are like Mexican sandwiches," Colin said. "Made from ground corn, hammered flat, filled with pork or chicken or beef . . ."

"I'll have a chicken," she said.

"We don't have time," Colin said.

"G'wan, I'll catch up," she said.

Colin knew that if he allowed her to lag behind they would miss their flight, so he dropped his bags, approached the hawker, and bought her a chicken taco with mild sauce. As Gina bit into it, her eyes closed in delight.

"That's like nothin' I ever 'et," she said. "I'll have to send some of these back home."

Colin just looked at her and picked up the bags. Sometimes he didn't know if she was kidding or being serious; sometimes he confused her sarcasm for naivete and vice versa. Arriving with three minutes to spare they made the connecting flight to Monterrey.

Colin had carefully prepared for Gina's illegal crossing into the

United States. He had been warned by Irish friends in New York that real IRA lammisters and thousands of illegal Irish had raised red flags at the Canadian border. The same people said that if he crossed over from Mexico, they would be waved through like most people with gringo faces. So, three days earlier, Colin had flown from New York to San Antonio, where he'd rented a car from a small rental agency. Colin had crossed the border at Laredo and driven the rented Ford Taurus to Monterrey, where he parked it in an airport lot before catching a flight to London and then to Dublin.

Now he was retracing those circuitous steps.

Of course, if Gina Furey was like other people, he could have just sent her a ticket and met her in Monterrey. But Gina was different. Colin had been afraid that somewhere along the trip, her reckless mouth would have gotten her into trouble, the way it had when she applied for a visa at the American Embassy in Dublin. En route, her fuck-you behavior might have even gotten her locked up, and he'd end up trying to make bail in a foreign country.

Colin decided to go and get Gina himself. He'd personally smuggle her into the United States. Besides, later on, he was certain this adventure would all be grist for his movie mill.

"I'm bleedin' banjaxed," Gina said as they moved through the small Monterrey airport. "This child is delirious with travel. She has no idea where the hell we are, and neither do I. I feel like we should be halfways to Mars by now."

"We'll sleep on the plane back to New York," Colin said.

"Another bleedin' plane!"

"Hey, you're a traveler, no?"

"Aye, a traveler, not a feckin' astronaut."

Colin picked up his rental car and drove straight to the United States border. He crossed the bridge at Nuevo Laredo and pulled up to a sign reading UNITED STATES BORDER. There, trucks laden with manufactured goods were passing through the gates without being inspected. Most of the gringos in private cars were asked perfunctory questions and waved through. Several Mexicans were being detained, their vehicles searched by machine-gun-toting border patrol guards. A few young Mexicans were standing with their palms pressed against a wall as the guards searched them in the blistering sun.

"Remember to let me do all the talking," Colin said as he watched two uniformed United States border guards approach, one holding a German shepherd drug-sniffing dog.

Gina was staring silently out the window, looking ill and exhausted, her floppy hat pulled low over her face.

"I should never have left Ireland," she said with a deep sigh.

"Once we're settled, you'll be fine."

She glared at him, disgusted, and then glanced out the window.

Brianna was struggling against the straps of the child seat in the rear of the car, half-crying and rubbing her eyes. "Mammy, Mammy, Mammy," she moaned.

"Give her a bottle," Colin said. "We can't let anyone hear her Irish accent."

Gina reached into her carry-on bag and gave Brianna a bottle filled with apple juice. Brianna took it and sucked greedily.

"ID, please. Where you headed?" asked the border guard, a sun-leathered blond man in his thirties wearing aviator glasses and a short-sleeved shirt with half-moons of perspiration under the arms. His nameplate bore the name Hall.

"Home," Colin said.

He peeked in the passenger window as another guard circled the car with the German shepherd on a leash.

"New York," Colin said, reaching in his back pocket for his wallet.

"What were you doing in Mexico?" the guard asked.

"Looking at possible movie locations."

"Car was rented in San Antonio," the guard said.

"Yeah," Colin said, showing him his driver's license and his Directors Guild of America card. "I'm a filmmaker. We flew into San Antonio and rented a car. I'm thinking of shooting a border-town movie. Flew down with my wife and kid, figuring I'd look around while she can still travel."

The guard leaned in the window and looked at Gina, who tried a tired smile.

"Why, something wrong with her?" the guard asked.

"Pregnant," Colin said.

"You okay, ma'am?" the guard asked.

Gina didn't answer, looked at him, shook her head, covered her mouth, opened the passenger door, and vomited. The second guard backed away in revulsion as the drug-sniffing dog started barking and straining at the leash.

"Morning sickness," Colin explained.

"Shite, Mammy," Brianna said.

Colin's heart began to thump. His mouth went dry and his palms began to sweat. The guard looked at Brianna, who started to cry, "Shite, Maaammmeeee."

"What the hell kind of accent is that?" the guard said.

"Queens . . . baby talk," Colin said, hearing his own voice rise an octave.

"Only colored babies say 'mammy,'" the guard said.

"She has a Caribbean nanny in New York," Colin said.

"Never could understand that," the guard said, reaching in his pocket and handing Colin a business card. "You make enough money to get away from them people and then you hire them to raise your kids. Anyways, if you come back to make that movie, be sure you look me up. I'll give you stories enough to make ten movies."

"Thanks," Colin said.

"Hope you're feeling better, ma'am," the guard said to Gina.

"Ta-ra," Gina blurted, and Colin froze.

"What's that?" the guard said, curious.

"She said 'ba-ba' to the baby," Colin said.

"Better go, line's backing up," the guard said, waving Colin, Gina, and Brianna into the United States of America.

Part IV

New York

twenty-two

March 8

"I hate to interrupt, Colin," Jack shouted from the doorway of the bedroom. "But I think there's something you should see downstairs."

Colin awakened with a start, Jack's voice sounding like Gina's Uncle Rory in the fading echo of his dream. He looked around. *Am I in a tinker's wagon? On a plane? In London? Mexico? Arizona?* No, he realized. *Home. Back home, in Bayside, Queens, New York, U.S. of A. Jesus, sweet wonderful home.*

"This is no fuckin' joke, either," said Jack, holding the bedroom door open.

Gina now stirred to consciousness. "Who's tha'?" she asked Colin as Jack stormed away from the bedroom.

"My brother must have come back from Boston early this morning," he said.

Colin could hear Jack talking loudly to Brianna downstairs. "No, don't touch that, little girl," Jack scolded. "Go up to your mommy, she's calling you!"

Brianna started to cry and Colin heard her bare feet slapping on the hardwood floors as she climbed the stairs toward the bedroom. "Mammmmmeeee!"

"For fuck sake," Gina said, getting out of bed, wearing one of

Colin's T-shirts and a pair of panties, scooping Brianna, half-naked, into her arms, her ass dirty with caked feces. "What's goin' on?"

"I'll go see," Colin said.

"Fine way to greet someone, wha'?"

Colin looked at Gina and noticed the first swelling of pregnancy appearing over the top of her bikini panties. Gina took out the baby wipes and began cleaning Brianna. Colin tossed her a heavy flannel robe and pulled on a terrycloth robe and a pair of sneakers.

"Bold man," Brianna said, pointing toward the open bedroom door. They could hear Jack downstairs, mumbling curses under his breath as he swept up broken glass.

Colin walked downstairs and found Jack, broom in hand, sweeping up broken eggs, a shattered pickle jar, and a smashed jar of black olives. The kitchen floor was a mess of spilled milk, torn bread, overturned cereal, and mashed cookies.

"Sorry, man," Colin said.

"Not as sorry as I am," Jack said, without looking up.

"We traveled for almost twenty-four straight hours, Jack."

"Just to wreck my home. Thanks for going out of your way."

Colin grabbed the broom handle. "Gimme, I'll clean that."

"Maybe you can get started in there," Jack said, pointing to the living room. Colin saw that a set of Jack's blueprints were pulled from their cardboard tubes and spread on the coffee table, covered in ink and crayon scribbles. The couches and rugs were smeared with Chinese take-out leftovers, spilled milk, and blotches of mustard mixed in with fried rice and strings of lo mein.

"Christ," Colin said.

"Davey Grogan was on the fucking money," Jack said, walking into the dining area, pointing to Brianna's soiled diaper. "You traveled twenty thousand miles round trip to bring home shit."

"Hey . . ."

"Frankly, I can't smell the difference between imported and domestic," Jack said, "but then I'm not a connoisseur like you."

Gina, dressed in the flannel robe, walked briskly down the stairs and into the dining area, lifted and folded the diaper, and wrapped a newspaper around it. She held the diaper in her left hand behind her back, extended her right to Jack. "Gina Furey," she said. "Pleased to meetcha."

Jack took her hand and shook it limply.

"Jack," he said.

"Sorry about all this," she said. "Why don't yeh two fine fellas go out for a brotherly jar and I'll get stuck into this place and have it sparklin' in no time. Just leave out the Hoover and the sweepin' brush and the Jeyes fluid."

"You always let your kid run wild in the mornings?" Jack said.

"Och, no," said Gina. "The child slept on the plane, but we didn't, and so we overslept this mornin'. It's just the jet lag and me bein' preggos. That's the fat and skinny of it. Won't happen again, sure."

"I hope not," Jack said.

"Hey, Jack, she apologized," Colin said. "I apologized. Don't beat a dead horse."

"It smells like a horse did die in here," he said.

"Too bad you weren't the jockey," Gina said, no longer able to bite her tongue.

"Nice," Jack said. "Now I'm being insulted in my house, too."

"Jack I pay rent here, too," Colin said.

"Yeah, for one," Jack said, collecting his drawings, and carrying them toward the stairs. "Just remember, my name's on the lease."

Jack thudded up the stairs.

"Now I'm being insulted," Colin shouted after him. "This is bullshit, she said she'd clean up."

"Colin, didn't yeh say that if yeh got a certain call we might be moving to Los Angeles?" Gina said. "Is that right?"

"Yeah," Colin said. "If I get nominated for an Oscar, California, here we come."

"Yeh know that cup of Irish tea I made before we went to bed last night?" she said, carrying the trash barrel from the kitchen into the dining area, tossing in the diaper, and picking up the Chinese take-out boxes from the floor.

"Yeah," Colin said.

"I saw in me tea leaves yer gonna get that call about that Oscar business today," she said, scooping up the rice and lo mein from the couch and dumping it into the trash.

"Wait a minute," Colin said. "Today is the eighth. The nominations are announced today."

"Yeh told me that part," Gina said. "There was another bit a news in me cup about a wee bit a writin' that you did."

"My movie treatment," Colin said, dragging the vacuum cleaner from a wall closet.

"That's the yoke," she said. "You'll be gettin' that call soon as well. It'll be more good news."

"Wouldn't that be hot shit?" Colin said.

"One reads tea leaves and the other believes her," Jack said, walking downstairs. "Did your tea leaves tell you that when I walked in this morning after working in Boston all weekend I'd find my place looking like a bombed abortion clinic?"

"How far is Los Angeles?" Gina asked Colin, ignoring Jack.

"Three thousand miles," Colin said.

"Let's put that between us and himself, then," she said, picking up the largest pieces of debris from the kitchen floor. Colin turned on the vacuum and started cleaning the living room.

"Bold man, Mammy," Brianna said, pointing at Jack.

Jack grabbed his coat, looked at the three of them, and stormed out of the apartment.

Colin's first call came at noon. It was his agent, Bonnie Corbet, telling him that his film, *First Love, Last Love,* had been nominated for a best short feature Oscar. Apparently, the nomination had already caused a flurry of inquiries about his feature-film treatment called *Across the Pond,* an international Irish love story. Bonnie had faxed copies of it to six producers that morning. Three had already offered an option on the movie.

"What did I tell yeh," said Gina.

Colin ran out to the bank to withdraw money. His balance was down to less than five grand and the trip from Dublin had cost him at least another $2,500. The bill wouldn't be in for a month. *What the fuck,* he thought, as he withdrew five hundred dollars. *It isn't every day that you get nominated for an Oscar!* He ran to the liquor store and bought a bottle of Louis Roederer Cristal champagne before stopping to buy food and diapers. The regular checkout woman in the supermarket looked surprised.

"Colin Coyne . . . diapers? Gonna be an awful lot of broken hearts on Bell Boulevard."

"Visitors," he said.

When he got back home, the apartment was gleaming and freezing. The windows were thrown wide open.

"That central heatin' would kill a palm tree," Gina said when Colin commented on the temperature.

Colin looked around. He hadn't seen the place this spotless since he moved in. Gina had washed and ironed all the curtains and couch cushions, vacuumed and scrubbed the rug. She'd washed the windows, scoured the stove, sterilized the refrigerator and sinks. She had disinfected the bathroom and stripped and washed all the bedding.

Colin closed the windows, opened the champagne, and poured two glasses. Gina drank hers down like morning orange juice.

"Easy on the champagne," Colin said.

"Is it that dear?"

"It's a hundred bucks a bottle," Colin said. "But forget the price, I don't want our kid to stagger into the world."

Gina took out a pack of Dunhills, ripped a filter off one, dropping it into her tea saucer because she couldn't find an ashtray, and lit the smoke.

"Go way outta dat," she said. "If I don't have a drink and a smoke, I'll stop livin'. T'ink what *that* would mean to the baby."

"Booze can deform a baby," Colin said. "Smoking can give the baby respiratory problems and cause brain damage by cutting off its oxygen supply."

"Rubbish, we've been through all this before," she said. "It's bad enough I'm three thousand mile away from me family. Now yeh wants me to cut off me few fags and odd bottle of stout as well."

"Besides, this is a smoke-free apartment," Colin said. "Jack doesn't let anyone smoke in here."

"*Hear,* now," Gina said, blowing out her wooden match with a stream of smoke, while pouring herself another glass of bubbly. "Is this feckin' Jack yer brudda or yer warden? My Jaysus. He hates kids, he hates me, he hates fun. What's his nickname, Union Jack or Jack Boot?"

"We usually get along," Colin said, laughing. "He's just uptight these days. I dunno."

The phone rang and Colin snatched it up. It was Peggy Johnson, asking if she could see him. Colin said, "I'm kind of busy right now." He said he'd call her and hung up.

"Yer girlfriends have been leavin' messages all mornin.'"

"Jealous?"

"Not atall," she said, taking a gulp and a drag. "I like having a fella other women wish they had, because what's that make me but popular with the fella who's popular with them? And why wouldn't yeh be?"

He only had half an idea of what she'd just said, but he liked the way it sounded.

The phone rang again. It was Bonnie Corbet, saying that Global Screen Pictures, run by a powerhouse Hollywood player named James Thompson, had outbid the other two companies to option *Across the Pond.*

"It's a step deal," Bonnie said. "Twenty-five-thousand option on the treatment and then a hundred and fifty thou for two sets and a polish, a third and third and a third, with a quarter-mil bonus at the back end if you direct."

"What do you mean *if* I direct?"

"Well, you will direct, unless you completely fuck things up," she said. "They protect themselves by keeping control of the property in case you get sick, turn into a junkie, rape a nun, or die. You still get a one-percent budget bonus on first day of principal photography for the script even if you don't direct."

"When does all this happen?" Colin asked.

"They're faxing me a deal memo today," she said. "We'll work out the details later. You can start packing your bags; they want you out there at the first story meeting in two weeks. They'll be putting you up at the Chateau Marmont."

"Putting *us* up," he said.

"Us? As in who else?" Bonnie said.

"Me and Gina," he said. "She's pregnant with my baby."

There was a long, silent pause. "Are you out of your fucking mind?" Bonnie asked.

"What . . ."

"You're kick-starting your career with a knocked-up chick?"

"Well, yeah, and she has a kid of her own as well," Colin said, chuckling and putting on a proud face for Gina, who sat watching him, smoking and drinking.

"They won't pay for her," the agent said. "Bimbo and cocaine clauses are no longer negotiable. I might be able to haggle for a hit man for her or a fucking psychiatrist for you. Seriously, Colin, you can't do this to yourself. I can make you one of the hottest young directors in Hollywood; you can date your leading ladies, live in installments on *Entertainment Tonight,* bang your fan mail. Every hot starlet in town will be sending you pictures—nudes. Why the fuck are you doing this to me? To yourself? Who the hell is this person? Is her daddy rich and her mama good-looking? What?"

"I knew you'd understand," Colin said, pacing, sweat drooling from his armpits down his ribcage. "It's all in the treatment . . ."

There was a pause on the phone.

"Don't tell me the broad you're with is the one in the outline?" Bonnie said. "An Irish gypsy tinker in a covered wagon from County Dealbreaker?"

"Yes, it sure is exciting," Colin said, performing for Gina.

"She's there with you now? Okay. I can have two immigration cops there in a matter of hours with deportation papers . . ."

"She's dying to meet you, too," Colin said.

"I'll get a check to you as soon as possible," Bonnie said. "Two, maybe three weeks. Pay her off, send her home first class, buy her a thatched-roof cottage, forty Irish acres, and a mule."

"I'll leave as soon as the check arrives," Colin said.

"What a waste," she said and hung up.

"Thanks, I'll tell her, bye-bye," Colin said and hung up.

Colin turned to Gina and said, "She said . . ."

"That yeh were throwing yer life away on a durty tinker," Gina said, stubbing her cigarette out in the saucer. "Not to worry, any-time you want me to leave, I'm gone home like a rifle shot."

None of her verbal images are ever soft or warm; all of them are steeped in violence or rage, he thought.

"Stop being so defensive," he said. "We're leaving for L.A. in two weeks. Global Screen is buying my treatment."

"I told yeh it was in my teacup," she said. "I also went up to the local church this mornin', Sacred Heart, and said a wee prayer and lit a candle. If yeh see it in the leaves and folly it up with a prayer and a candle, it's a done deal. So, if we're goin' to the Academy Awards, I'll need a fancy dress. I want to see this store I hear about all the time in the movies. It was even on the telly this mornin'. 'Like no other store in the world.'"

"Bloomingdale's?"

"Aye, that's the yoke."

That night, Colin and Gina watched *Entertainment Tonight*'s cover-age of the Oscar nominations to see if Colin would be mentioned. He wasn't; his category didn't mean anything to the average viewer outside the industry.

Jack came home carrying a take-out meal from the local Italian restaurant. He took one look around the apartment and was amazed at the transformation.

"Congratulations, Col, I heard the great news," Jack said. "All your SoHo friends were calling Grogan's looking for you, wantin' to congratulate you. Lemme add mine."

"Thanks," Colin said coolly.

Gina looked at Jack, picked up Brianna, and walked toward the bedroom.

"I'm sorry about this morning, hon'," Jack said.

"Not to worry," Gina said. "We'll be long gone soon, sure."

Jack stood still, looking foolish and awkward, and said, "Your kid is beautiful."

"Thanks," Gina said. "She didn't lick it off the stones."

"Bold man," Brianna said, pointing at Jack.

"I shouldn't have raised my voice . . ."

"What's done's done," Gina said. "As long as she has me, she'll survive."

Gina climbed the stairs to Colin's bedroom and closed the door. Jack sat down on the couch and put his Italian take-out meal on the coffee table, the white bag soiled with tomato sauce and oil.

"I don't want to be accused of those grease stains," Colin said, clicking the remote to *Access Hollywood*.

"Look, Col," Jack said. "I was wrong. I wanna make it right."

"It's no big deal, bro," Colin said. "The place was a fucking disaster and I don't blame you for being pissed. But you had an attitude about Gina before she showed on the set. Whether or not you or Dad or Eddie like it, she's part of my life now. She's having my baby."

Jack leaned back on the couch and stared at the ceiling, exhaling deeply. "I was just worrying about you," he said. "Meanwhile, you get nominated for an Oscar . . ."

"I sold my treatment, too," Colin said.

Jack sat up, genuinely excited. "Jesus, that's fucking great, Col," he said. "With you directing?"

Colin nodded. "We're leaving for L.A. in two weeks. I'll give you a couple months of my share of the rent . . ."

"Not necessary," Jack said. "I got the gig in Boston. Good job and four month's work. I have to leave tomorrow so I can get started, hire a crew . . ."

"Red-letter day for the Coynes," Colin said.

"You tell the old man you're both leaving yet?"

"Afraid to," Colin said. "I don't wanna hurt him."

"Tell him you're marrying Gina and he'll be okay with it," Jack said. "It's the Catholic shit that bothers him."

"She doesn't want to get married," Colin said.

"Has to be the last pregnant babe alive who doesn't," Jack said. "Don't tell the old man that, give him something to hang his rosary beads on."

"Yeah," Colin said.

Jack looked at his kid brother, nodded, and sighed.

March 9

A little after noon Colin sat at a table in the coffee bar in Bloomingdale's. He had the *Daily News,* the *New York Post, The New York Times, Variety, Premiere, Entertainment Weekly,* and a coffee all in front of him on the bar.

Colin had given Gina four hundred dollars to buy a dress for the Oscars and was waiting for her to return.

Colin sipped his coffee, reading the daily papers, checking out the names of the megastar nominees who would be at the Oscar party with him. He'd be rubbing elbows and schmoozing with De Niro, Travolta, Sharon Stone, Julia Roberts, Mike Nichols, and Steven Spielberg, to name a few. He opened the *Times,* which had a complete list of the Oscar nominees, and stared at his name in the list. It was his childhood dream come true. *Colin Coyne, Academy Award nominee.* It made him feel accomplished, respected, talented, important, accepted.

He drained his coffee and ordered another one, still staring at his name in the *Times,* letting the pride bubble and tingle in his veins. He imagined Oscar night: limousines, tuxedos, gowns, movie legends, the world press, paparazzi, big-time investors, studio heads. *What a load of horseshit,* he thought. *But I want it all. A multi-pix deal, a house with a swimming pool in Los Angeles, where I'll teach Brianna and the new baby how to swim.* He thought about a life of directing movies, eating lunch in studio commissaries. He thought about the success, about seeing his name in bold letters in the gossip columns. *Imagine the ball-busting from the guys at Grogan's after reading my name on "Page Six" and "Rush and Malloy,"* he thought.

"Paging Mr. Colin Coyne," came a voice from the end of the coffee bar. In his reverie, it was his name being paged in Morton's, the exclusive West Hollywood restaurant he'd read about in so many articles, or announced at the Oscars. And then he heard it again. "Is there a Colin Coyne in the cafe?"

"I'm Colin Coyne," he said, waving to a man in a plain zippered jacket, soft-soled shoes, and dungarees. He had a walkie-talkie in his hand.

Right away, Colin knew it was about Gina.

"Do you know a Gina Furey?"

"Yeah?"

"Can you come with me, please?" the man asked.

"What's wrong?" said Colin, leaving a five-dollar bill on the table.

"We have Gina Furey in our security office upstairs," the man said as he led Colin out of the bar.

"Is she okay?"

"Depends what you mean by that," the guy said as they stepped out of the cafe. "I don't happen to think shoplifting is okay. Maybe you do. Maybe you wait here while your woman goes upstairs to boost for you, that how it works?"

Colin yanked his sleeve free from the man's grip.

"Who the hell are you, pal?" Colin asked.

The man showed him a Bloomingdale's Security ID card.

"You have a smart mouth for a dumb store dick," Colin said.

"The dumb one is the one who gets caught," the store dick said. "Gina Furey got caught red-handed. What's she to you?"

"My . . . friend," Colin said, embarrassed, as they stepped onto a freight elevator together.

"Your girlfriend had a big bag filled with stuff," the store dick said. "She was pushing her kid around like a prop."

"Christ," Colin said, following the guy down the corridor into an office with a steel door. Colin trailed him through the door and saw Gina sitting on a chair, rocking Brianna in her pram, as two female security guards sat on either side of her.

"I'll have these'ns up on charges, so I will," Gina said.

"She purchased some clothes in the women's department," the store dick said. "Then she moved onto the men's department and decided to outfit a man—about your size I'd say—from head to toe. Armani, Versace, Ralph Lauren."

The store dick went behind a plexiglass divider and came out with Gina's black canvas bag. He unzipped the bag and shook the contents out onto a large display table. There was a man's black suit, two men's sweaters, three shirts, three ties, socks, and underwear.

"I was gonna pay for them, a course," Gina said, "but I wanted to go find yeh first to make sure they fit."

"She walked past three security checkpoints," the store dick said. "We have her on video."

"Cheek of them puttin' alarms on clothes," she said. "Takin' me picture without me permission, and me hair like a porter's mop. Most untrustin' store I've ever met in me life."

"We could call the police right now and have her locked up," the store dick said.

"In my country yeh can't arrest a pregnant woman," Gina said.

Colin walked to her and whispered in her ear. "In this city, there are babies born in Rikers Island prison every single day. Be quiet, you could be deported. Let me do the talking, please."

"Pig's melts," she said, continuing to rock Brianna. "Body searchin' a pregnant woman pushing a child. State of him, toy copper that he is, with his buttons-ha'penny job, thinkin' he's that fella outta *NYPD Blue*."

"Okay, how do we square root this?" Colin asked.

"You purchase the merchandise," the store dick said. "Then she signs a document agreeing never to enter this store again."

"I wouldn't give you my good feckin' custom," she said.

"She always this sweet?" the store dick asked.

Colin handed the store detective his credit card and he ran it through a machine: $830. He asked Gina to sign a standard shoplifter's form, which she did.

"I'd pay cash money not to have to look at your miserable gob again," she said, pushing the form back, her signature the familiar child's printed scribble. Colin looked at it and then at Gina. He wondered if she could write in script, and then realized for the first time that he'd never seen her read.

The man put the clothes back in Gina's canvas bag, stuffing the credit card receipt on top of it. Colin grabbed the bag. The buzzer on the door sounded and Colin held the door open for Gina, who pushed Brianna out toward the elevators.

"I was only nickin' a few bits and pieces for yeh to wear for yer Oscar," she said, waiting for the elevator.

"No more stealing, Gina!"

"Listen to Mr. Law and Order," she said. "Didn't yeh just steal me out of my country and smuggle me into this one?"

"That's different," he said.

"Me, too," she said.

Colin sighed. She had a way of having the final word.

twenty-three

March 11

Colin awakened just after six on a chilly Tuesday morning and went quietly downstairs to make a cup of coffee as Gina and Brianna slept. It was only the three of them now, since Jack had gone back up to Boston. Colin stood in the kitchen, waiting for a cup of instant coffee to boil, when he heard the little feet behind him.

"Hungry, Daddy," Brianna said.

Colin turned and looked at the little girl in the Big Bird nightie, her red curly hair tousled, rubbing sleep from her right eye. This introverted kid had at first shied away from him, and been withdrawn and frightened in his company. Now she was calling him Daddy. It sounded like a judge giving a sentence. He half smiled at her and she smiled back, her tiny teeth perfect and white.

Colin shook her a bowl of Honey Nut Cheerios, popped an English muffin into the toaster, and poured her a glass of orange juice. He put two telephone books on a chair so she could reach the kitchen table. He poured himself a bowl of cereal and took a spoonful. Brianna watched him and then did the same, milk drooling down her face. He wiped it with a napkin.

"Good?" he asked.

"Grand."

Her Irish accent was broad, making her all the more adorable.

Colin added milk and sugar to his coffee and got up to retrieve his popped English muffin. As he buttered it, Brianna said, "Yang you, Daddy."

He turned to her again. At that moment, this kid who had been nothing more than part of Gina's excess baggage became a little person in Colin's life. An intricate, innocent, affectionate, mischievous parcel of emotions. Before this breakfast, Brianna had been a mere shit machine, a whinge in the day, a wail in the night, a regular pain in the ass, and a thirty-pound birth-control device that separated him from Gina in bed. But right now, as she sat eating with Colin, without Gina's presence, calling him Daddy and trying to say thank you, he realized that she was more than just some crazy tinker's kid. *Brianna is my kid's big sister,* he thought. *She always will be.*

"You're welcome, kiddo," he said, also realizing that this kid he'd never really listened to before was smart, precocious, funny, and good company. *She's Shirley Temple,* he thought. *But still a pain in the ass.*

He kissed her on the cheek and she scrunched up her face. "Yuck," she said, rubbing her face. "Wissirs."

After breakfast, as he shaved, Brianna sat on the sink and watched him rinse the whiskers down the drain.

"Where go?" she asked, shrugging her shoulders.

"Whiskers go down the drain, into a sewer, and out to sea," Colin said. "Maybe they go to Ireland."

Colin put a dab of shaving cream on her nose, chin, and both cheeks and she climbed on the sink to look at herself in the mirror, squealing with laughter.

He touched the razor to his throat, glancing down at her as she watched the soapy water swirl down the drain, her developing brain famished for new data.

Kieran first hears Gina's child call him Daddy and something magical happens inside him, Colin thought. *As if he's entering into a pact, or a special vow, he starts loving Gina's kid.*

As Brianna was claiming him as her father, Colin realized that he was avoiding visiting his own father. He told his father that he was too busy with work, which was partly true. All of this was work, in its own way. Each day a real-life first draft of Kieran's adventure.

In reality, he was trying to find the right time to introduce Gina and Brianna to his father. He was more afraid of his father insulting Gina than he was of upsetting him.

Colin rousted Gina from sleep at eight, ushering her and Brianna out of the house by nine. He played tour guide all day, imagining how he would shoot his New York City montage. Brianna grasped Colin's hand as the ferry rocked out to Liberty Island. "So that's the Statue of Liberty's face," Gina said, looking through the mounted pay telescope. "Poor crayture is gruesome-lookin'. What did she do exactly? For money, like?"

"She's just a symbol," Colin said. "Of freedom."

"Like me Granda's caravan," she said.

By 11 A.M., they were gazing at the city from the observation deck of the Empire State Building. Colin thought the majestic cityscape of New York looked even more enormous with Brianna sitting on his shoulders. "Which parts do the Eyetalians live in?" Gina asked.

"The parts that smell good," Colin said.

They ate lunch at the Hard Rock Cafe, where Gina asked for tacos and Guinness, neither of which they had. Afterward, they ice skated in Rockefeller Center, Brianna in the middle, holding Colin's and Gina's hands. Colin splurged on a Joe Tourist horse-and-buggy ride through Central Park. "Poor feckin' horse belongs on a pension," Gina told the driver.

Gina loved Greenwich Village and SoHo; she loved window-shopping and popping into bars, even though she thought every Irish pub they drank in was a fraud. "Too clean and there's no crack," she said.

Everywhere they went, Gina kept asking if Italians lived there. "Italians live everywhere in New York," Colin assured her, as they walked up Mulberry Street from Chinatown, stopping for a coffee in Cha Cha's Bocca al Lupo Cafe.

"Then he could be anywhere."

"Who, Gina? Who the hell are you looking for? Which Italian? Maybe I know him."

"How could you know him if I don't?"

Sometimes she asked questions that had no answers.

March 12

Colin had a lunch meeting with two executives from Global Screen Pictures who were in town on other business. The silver-haired man in his fifties was James Thompson, the studio president. His thirtysomething dark-haired assistant was a story executive named Syd Green. Thompson did most of the talking about the deal, budget, and casting, while Green made all the suggestions about the story. Both Thompson and Green said they loved the treatment for *Across the Pond.* There was one small thing: everyone thought it needed a new ending.

"I mean, there's no way you can expect an audience to believe that the protagonist would actually spend his whole life with this woman," Thompson said. "We don't want either of them to die, but the relationship has to end."

"We don't want the ending to be dark, either," said Greene. "It should be bittersweet, and funny. After all, it *is* a romantic comedy, if a dysfunctional one."

"You mean they break up and go their separate ways, laughing?" Colin asked, confused.

"If we had the exact answers we wouldn't be paying you so much dough to write it," said Thompson, chuckling darkly and checking his Rolex. "Would we, Colin?"

"Of course, you have no obligation to start doing rewrites until there's a signed contract," said Green. "But if you can crack this problem in the step outline, we'll be in a much better position to move to the next step and get this green-lighted."

"Global really wants to make this picture, Colin, but time is of the essence. Strike while you're hot, kid," Thompson prodded.

Colin knew this was a subtle way to tell him to get to work pronto on a pre-rewrite rewrite. Bonnie Corbet had warned him that the Global Screen guys would ask him to start rewriting before they went to contract. She'd advised him to get with the program, stay on agenda.

"By the way, are you married?" Thompson said.

"No," Colin said.

"Good," Thompson said. "My daughter flipped over your film. She's twenty-one and goes to UCLA. I told her I could get any director in town to give her some filmmaking pointers and she asked to meet you. I guess because you're more her age, just out of college yourself. She wants to make it on her own, without the old man's help, and wants to know how you did it. If you have time—no obligation here, Colin—maybe you can give her a few pointers."

Colin smiled, shrugged, said, "I'm not sure I'm in any position to teach anyone anything. But I'd be happy to help her in any way I can."

"She'll be happy to hear that," Thompson said.

March 15

Colin rewrote the ending to *Across the Pond* over the following two days, working mostly at night in Jack's room as Gina ate tacos, drank Guinness, and watched *Goodfellas, Vendetta I, II and III,* and *Casino* in the living room.

When he was finished, he wanted another opinion but felt awkward showing it to Gina. So he called Linda Parks and met her at her Clear Conscience office in SoHo. The office was a storefront floor-through, the walls covered in rap- and rock-video posters, with a beehive of cubicles where young NYU students and graduates were working on scripts and proposals. In the rear were two large video mixing rooms.

Dressed in tight jeans and a loose sweatshirt, her hair bundled under her beret, Linda invited Colin into her office, told her receptionist not to disturb them, and closed the door. Colin took a seat on a green leather couch and Linda walked around her glass-topped desk and took a seat in front of a bay window looking out on a flower garden.

"This is pretty fucking funny," she said, waving the treatment he'd faxed her. "Great chick character."

"Thanks," he said.

"Thank God it's only a movie."

"Whaddaya mean?"

"As a *movie* it's funny for two hours," she said. "As a *life* it's not funny that this Kieran guy gets so deep into a hole so young. What happens after the final credits ain't funny at all. This guy lets his own kid and another kid who calls him Daddy hit the road with this crazy Irish tinker girl?"

"It's not like he'll never see the kids again," Colin said defensively. "They make arrangements for the kids' housing, education, visitation, and like that."

"I guess it'll work for Hollywood," she said, "where happily ever after is determined by first-weekend grosses."

"It works as a film?"

"Yeah," she said. "You piss your pants laughing at first and then by the end there won't be a dry eye in the house. So, yeah, it works."

She walked around her desk, sat next to Colin on the couch, and leaned close to him. "How the fuck did you let this happen to you, Col?" she said.

He looked at her, so pretty, so smart, so much fun, and so young. Her eyes searched his, in a loving but pitying sort of way. *How did I ever let this one go,* he thought.

"It'll work out," he said.

"I thought I had it bad with a tattoo," she said. "I can use a laser to get you removed from my ass. But *kids*—and their mother—stay a lifetime, Col."

"What can I say? It's done."

"If the movie doesn't fly," she said, "call me. There's more work here than I can handle. The treatment is good. The picture'll be great. Now straighten out your fucking life."

He faxed the new pages to Thompson and Green that morning and had dinner with them at Elaine's on Second Avenue and Eighty-eighth Street that night.

"Oh, man, we're getting closer," said Thompson, rattling the new pages over his arugula salad. "You're a *pro,* kid."

"The end might still be just a tad *too* ambiguous," said Green, adding Romano cheese to his rigatoni. "But it's a big improvement. We have notes."

Colin was thrilled to take their notes, and over the next day and night, as Gina and Brianna slept, he incorporated them into the ending of the treatment. *I'm good at this shit,* he thought. *I can still work with a woman and a kid around. No problem. Like the man said, I'm a fucking pro.*

March 16

He faxed these changes out to L.A., his final installment before leaving for L.A. four days later.

Once he sent the pages off, he knew he could no longer avoid his father.

A little past 9 A.M., Colin heard his mother's silver bells as he held open the door to his father's house for Gina and Brianna. The father looked up from the *Daily News,* folded it, and nodded to his son. His face was a study in life's third act, wisdom creased into his brow above wary I've-seen-it-all eyes that always looked directly into the eyes of the person to whom he was speaking. His jaw was set like a spring trap and his thick, dark hair was layered with gray, each streak like a military ribbon with a story attached. He had the kind of workingman's face that told you he didn't owe anybody money and that there were no surprises left for him in the world.

He stared at Gina and half smiled when he saw Brianna climb out of her pram.

"Hey, Dad," Colin said. "This is Gina, Gina Furey, and this is her daughter, Brianna."

Liam Coyne stood and greeted Gina with a handshake. "Nice to meet you, Gina," he said. "I've heard lots about you. Colin, the kettle, son, it should still be warm."

"I'd love a wee cup," Gina said.

Colin strode into the kitchen, shook the half-full kettle, clanked it on the stove and clicked a light under it.

"So are you enjoying New York, Gina?" Liam asked.

"It's a grand city altogether, Mr. Coyne," Gina said. "Makes Dublin feel like a football pitch, wha'?"

"I still don't know the half of it myself after thirty-seven years," Liam said. "So, how long you over?"

Gina glanced at Colin, who rattled three cups and saucers onto the table.

"Actually, Dad, there's something we'd like to tell ya."

"There's cookies there above the fridge for the child," Liam said. "Let me give her one."

Colin carried a box of Social Tea biscuits over to his father and Liam offered one to Brianna, who glanced at Gina for permission before grabbing it.

"Yang you," Brianna said, bashfully.

"Ta-ta, yourself, darlin'," the father said, smiling broadly. "She's a stunner, all right. Smart as a fox with glasses."

Colin sat at the table and the father eased over and plopped into a chair, joined by Gina.

"So?" Liam said.

"I've been nominated for an Oscar."

"The whole world knows that," Liam said, waving his hand. "I guess that means the telephone company is out of the question altogether."

"Afraid so, Dad," Colin said.

"Anyway, I'm proud you done so well at what you want," Liam said. "That's what counts. Your mother would have been tickled. All the oul wans would have been over for tea, goin' on and on about it by now. Much cabbage involved?"

"Actually, that's why I'm here," Colin said. "I'm gonna sign a contract for a screenplay they want me to write and direct. Lotta cabbage."

"Great," the father said. "But is there a pension plan?"

"Actually, the Directors Guild and the Writers Guild both have health, life, and pension plans, Dad," Colin said.

"That's important, you know. Because one day, you'll wake up, and . . ." He snapped his fingers, loudly. Brianna tried to imitate him and they all laughed. "And you'll be my useless age and then you'll need a few bucks coming in."

"I'm moving to Los Angeles on the twentieth, Dad," Colin said.

Liam's long silence was broken by the whistle of the kettle.

Colin got up, poured the boiling water into the teapot, and placed it on the table with a container of milk.

"That soon, huh?" the father said.

"We'll need to find a place to live," Gina said.

The father looked from Gina to Colin, back to Gina, and then at Brianna. Colin poured the tea into the three cups.

"Dad," Colin said. "Gina is having my baby."

"Och, Jaysus," Liam said, pouring milk in his tea and stirring distractedly.

"It's done, Dad," Colin said.

"Are you getting married?"

"That's not in our plans," Colin said.

His father widened his eyes and took a deep breath, softening as he nodded at Brianna. "Ah, well, as your mother would have said, God's forgiven worse."

His father stirred a spoonful of sugar into his tea, staring into the memories in the steam. *Close-up, the tea cup,* Colin thought. Colin knew his father's whimsical eyebrow flick and the Irish nod of the head meant he was accepting this.

"I'll miss you, so," he said, lifting his teacup and looking at Colin through the steam.

I have to shoot the strong Irish father's face through the steam, Colin thought. *As if it were mist from the glens in the legendary west of Ireland.*

"I'll be back and forth all the time," Colin said. "A lot of the film will be shot here."

The father nodded and took another cookie out of the packet and showed it to Brianna. As she reached for it, Liam tapped his knee, inviting her to climb up. Brianna looked at Colin for approval this time. When he nodded, Brianna climbed up on the father's knee and took the cookie from his hand as he brushed her red curls from her face.

"She's a dazzler," he said and turned to Gina and Colin, lifting his cup in a toast. "Well, then, here's luck and God bless."

They all sipped.

• • •

At his agent's suggestion, Colin had started wearing a beeper. He had explained to Gina how it worked—all she had to do was put a quarter in any public phone, dial the beeper number, wait until she heard his message, then punch in the number of the phone she was dialing from followed by three number ones, which would be her private code, then push the pound symbol. He'd call her right back.

"You think I'm a feckin' thick, don't yeh," she said. "We have pagers in Ireland, yeh know. Every nun and drug dealer has a pager and a cell phone."

"Good, then you can reach me anytime," Colin said. "I have to go into the city to take care of some business."

"No problem," she said.

Jack was back from Boston but would be out all day meeting with new clients and Colin was going to his agent's office to sign some papers and to talk final strategy. He gave Gina one hundred dollars in cash and told her to spend it wisely. The two grand he had in the bank had to last them until the money for the treatment came in. He couldn't believe the price of Pampers. And paying for food for three, nine meals a day, was like shoveling coal into a locomotive.

He told her that if she wanted she could go up to Bell Boulevard and shop for dinner, catch a movie, or have lunch. She knew the number of the local car service in case she needed to go anywhere.

He kissed Gina good-bye and said he'd be home in time for dinner.

"I have a bit of business of me own to take care of," she said. "I've been waitin' years now for this chance."

"What business?"

"Mind your own nosy hole," she said.

"Gina, for chrissakes, no more shoplifting or the baby will be born with an inmate number."

"Not to worry," she said. "I won't nick anythin'."

Colin worried about Gina as he drove into Manhattan. In some ways, Gina was like a problem child. When he wasn't with her, he worried about what trouble she'd get herself into. When he was with her, he worried if she'd act out. It had been fine in Dublin, where she knew which buttons to push and how far she could go, but in New York she was playing by a different set of rules. If she gave a city cop lip, she'd be in handcuffs and on her way to Rikers. If she got into an argument with a streetwise New Yorker, she could wind up with her throat cut.

Colin and Bonnie Corbet spent more than an hour going over details of the contract. He was entranced, seeing his name listed as writer and director, and seeing the name of his treatment, *Across the Pond,* and the movie company, Global Screen, all in the same contract. When he saw the dollar amounts and percentages, he became fidgety and anxious, eager to sign his name before anyone changed his mind. He signed his name in twelve different places on three copies of the contract, the size of his signature growing larger each time. *I'm a pro,* he thought.

Before he left, Bonnie told him how he should behave at the Oscars, and warned him not to drink at any of the parties.

"Basically, Hollywood is a small town," she said. "You could invite all the people that matter to one moderately sized bar mitzvah. First impressions last a career out there, so behave. If you win, be humble and be brief, but remember to thank me. If you lose, be gracious to the winner at the party. Oh, and for chrissakes, leave the tinker broad home that night."

Colin was about to respond when his beeper sounded. He looked at the 212 area code. *Manhattan number,* he thought. He didn't recognize it, but saw Gina's 111 personal code, followed by a 911 emergency code, which he hadn't instructed Gina to use. *Ah, shit,* he thought.

His chest surged with adrenaline as he imagined Gina in handcuffs, or lost in a tough neighborhood, stranded with no money somewhere, or raped, hurt, or trapped, with Brianna in the stroller and his unborn baby in her belly. He didn't want Bonnie Corbet to know what was wrong, so he tried to contain his mild panic.

"Use the phone if you need it," she said.

He dialed the number on his beeper.

"Your dime," the voice said.

"I'm looking for Gina."

"Maybe you should come down here and explain a few things to us," the voice said. "Nobody here in the club can understand what this tomata's talking about."

The man on the phone gave Colin an address on Thompson Street and told him to come down and take this crazy Irish broad home before there was trouble.

"She's there right now?" Colin asked, incredulous.

"You better come get her," said the man on the other end of the line. "Ask for Rocco."

The man hung up and so did Colin.

"Is everything all right?" Bonnie Corbet asked.

"Fine," Colin said as he shook his agent's hand good-bye and headed for the door. "I gotta go. So much to do, so little time."

"Colin," Bonnie said softly, and he turned to her with his right hand on the doorknob. "You have a once-in-a-lifetime opportunity to have a terrific career here."

"I know," he said.

"Please don't fuck it up," she said.

Colin's heart was pounding as he drove downtown through the heavy traffic. He parked at a meter and searched for the address this Rocco character had given him. As he made his way down the block, he saw black windows bearing the image of a fiery volcano and realized he'd often seen guys in handcuffs led from the Vesuvius Soccer Club on the evening news. *Holy shit,* he thought.

A pleasant-faced white-haired man stood in the doorway, watching Colin approach.

"You the Colin guy knows the Irish girl?" he asked. Colin nodded.

"Inside," the guy said. "This broad a yours is some doozy, tellin' you."

He motioned for Colin to follow him into the building. The room had dropped ceilings, cheap wood paneling, an indoor-outdoor rug on the floor, a small Formica bar, and several card tables scattered around. *These gangsters risk jail to hang out in a dump like this,* he thought. *Like the waiting room in purgatory.* Posters of the Italian soccer team decorated the walls. Men played cards at one table and chess at another, some reading racing forms, most sipping espresso. The place stunk of cigars and cheap cologne.

"You mind?" the white-haired guy said as he held out his hands to pat Colin down. Colin nodded his approval and the guy checked his chest and back, waist and ankles.

"You ain't a cop, are you, or an FBI?" he asked. "As in Forever Bothering Italians?"

"DGA," Colin said, pulling out his wallet, showing him his Directors Guild of America card and giving him one of his business cards. "I make movies."

"I been in a lot of films," Rocco said, taking the card. "Surveillance."

The guys at the tables chuckled.

"You'd be good on film," Colin said, trying to ingratiate himself. "You have a great natural look."

"Think so?"

"Yeah," Colin said.

"Keep me in mind?"

"Absolutely."

Rocco took out a roll of bills wrapped with a rubber band and removed his own business card from the center of the cash. The card read: ROCCO—STREET LIAISON." It had a beeper number on it.

"I did technical advisor and location scoutin' on a few pitchers. I cut through red tape in certain neighborhoods."

Colin pocketed Rocco's card and said, "Where is she?"

"Lemme ask you a question first," Rocco said. "Can you unnerstand what this tomata says? *Mingya,* when it comes to English, I'm no mathematician myself, but she has one a them brogues. Plus she uses expressions no one knows what the fuck she means. Might as well be talking Apache. Even the FBIs, if they're listening, they'll figure we're talkin' in a new code."

"How'd she wind up in here?" Colin asked.

"I was just standing outside in the doorway, my usual lookin'-to-see-what-I-could-see routine," Rocco said. "This cute blond tomata comes walkin' down the block, pushin' a stroller, checkin' addresses.

She stops in front a here and alls a sudden she squats down, pulls up her long dress, pulls down her bloomers, and she's' ready to take a freakin' leak right in the snow between two parked cars, in fronna our store! Least I think it was a *leak*. I shouted, 'Wo, what the hell you doin,' lady?' She starts talkin' in the diddly-diddly-dee accent. I unnerstand one word. *Pregnant*. Needs a toilet. I remember my wife, pissin' like a reindeer every five feet when she was knocked up with my three. So I tell her come inside, use the toilet, don't make a leak in front of the club like a poodle. I mean, she got a gorgeous little kid in a stroller."

"So she came in to use the toilet?" Colin asked.

"Yeah, but when she comes out of the toilet, she starts makin' a racket, her kid is cryin', then she sits down, starts rantin' and ravin', asking about a guy name of Owl."

"Owl?" Colin said, baffled.

"Owl," Rocco said, shrugging. "So I gave her an espresso and gave the kid an anisette cookie to shut its trap. She says she wasn't goin' nowheres till she finds this guy name a Owl. How'm I gonna throw out a pregnant woman? How?"

"*Owl?* Like the bird?"

"Yeah, but first I think maybe she means Al. But she says no, 'Owl, Owl Fuller,'" Rocco said. "It's kind of funny, at first. Then she takes the broom and starts sweeping the place. Emptyin' ashtrays. Collecting dirty cups. Taking over like the lady of the house. Finally, she gave us your beeper number."

"I can't believe she's here," Colin said.

Rocco led Colin through another door into a back room, where Gina sat at a large round table between two soft-bellied, middle-aged guys with combed-back graying hair who were watching NY1, the all-news station. Brianna was asleep in the stroller. Gina was sipping a cup of espresso, replenishing it with a bottle of anisette. She looked up at him from under her floppy hat.

"What took yeh so long?" she asked.

"Gina," Colin said. "What the hell are you doing *here?*"

"Lookin' for me oulfulluh," she said.

"Here?" Colin asked, baffled.

"I showed them a pitcher, showed them me oulfulluh, but they just shrugged. They wouldn't listen to his name. Deaf and dummies, the lot."

"I tole her nobody's here name of Owl Fuller. She says to me something about a load of something called *shite.*"

"Load of shite that yeh don't know me oulfulluh," Gina said.

"See," Rocco said. "Owl Fuller. I had a Judge Fuller once, accused me of associatin' with organized crime. I says to him just because you know the president don't make you no senator. He gave me thirty days for contempt. But Owl Fuller I don't know from nothin'. Or this shit called shite."

"Shite means shit," Colin said.

"Wonderful," Rocco said, using his right index finger like a conductor's baton. "Lookit me, fellas, I'm speakin' Gaelic. Shite means shit."

"Oulfulluh means old fella," Colin said.

"She's watching too many Scorsese movies," Rocco said. "The old Mustache Petes are all dead, tell her."

"In this case, she's asking about her old fella, as in old man, father," Colin said.

"Her father?" Rocco said. "Her lookin' for her father in here is like me lookin' for my old man in the Saint Patrick's Day parade."

"Can I have a minute alone with her?" Colin asked.

Rocco nodded at the two guys and they got up and followed Rocco into the outer room, leaving the door open so they could keep an eye on them. "Let her finish her coffee, then yous gotta go," Rocco said at the door. Rocco walked out to the bar and watched them. Colin looked at Gina and said, "You can die walking into a place like this, Gina." She reached into her bag and took out an old *Time* magazine with a photograph of John Gotti on the cover. She opened it and turned to a series of surveillance photos of different hoods hanging around outside the Vesuvius Soccer Club.

"Says here this place is one of the Mafia headquarters of New York," Gina said. "Me da is one of them."

She can read, he thought.

"You better explain, fast," Colin said. "We gotta leave . . ."

"I ain't leavin' till they tell me where to find me oulfulluh," she said. "I told themn's his name's Gino Barilla."

"Gina, they can't understand your accent. I can't understand your thinking."

"Hold yeh on a wee minute, whilst I tell yeh somethin' for nothin', righ'?" Gina said. "Back before I was born, me ma was forced into a marriage with a right bastard, her third cousin, a traveler name of Gus Donohoe. He couldn't give her a baby, so instead he gave her beatin's as regular as the mornin' bus . . ."

"Gina, the goddamned family history can wait . . ."

"Shut yeh up, righ'? So, anyways, me ma wanted out of the marriage, away from the beatin's. Out of the clan. Out of the traveler's life and the country altogether. She decided to find herself a Yank who would take her off to America."

"And? Come on, keep going, Gina," Colin said, his eyes narrowing. "Tell me more."

"So me ma nicked herself some fancy clothes and made the rounds of the tourist hotels in Dublin," Gina said. "She met a few Yanks. Most were married or users or chancers. Then she met a Trinity student name of Gino Barilla. Well, me ma fell mad in love with this dark-haired Eyetalian Yank named Gino and together they made me. Did a good job, too, if I says so meself . . ."

Gina showed him a torn and faded snapshot of her mother with a handsome, dark-haired man wearing a white Aran turtleneck and a green tweed jacket. Gina's smiling mother wore a sleek black dress embroidered with brightly colored flowers, a black choker studded with pearls, and a floppy black hat with a peacock's feather.

Colin stared at the photograph. Gina was a delicate mix of her mother and father. *As delicate as nitro,* Colin thought.

"Your father is an American?" Colin asked, remembering the cryptic conversation he'd had with Granda about Gina's two fathers, one being Italian. "Italian? Your real father is an Italian-American? That's why you're always asking about Italians . . ."

It was starting to make sense to him.

"Aye," Gina said. "But then, with me ma up the pole with me, Gino Barilla took off back to America, somethin' about a death in the family. He promised he'd send for me ma after I was hatched, but the bollocks never did. The only thing he ever sent was a few bob, guilt money, care of—what else—a priest in Dublin. Just the once't. There was no return address, and he was never heard from after, I'm told."

"You were named after him?" Colin whispered. "Gino became . . . Gina."

"Aye," Gina said. "But me ma's husband didn't know anythin' about it. Until he found the one letter from Gino Barilla saying he was sorry and this picture they had taken at a Trinity dance. She'd held onto them because she loved him so. And because one day she wanted me to go and find him. I was three year of age when me ma's husband found the picture and the letter proving I wasn't his child. That night he came home with the devil drink on him and he bate me ma to death with a shovel, so he did. I was in the caravan when he did it. I'm not sure if I remember it or if I only think I do, but I dreams about it now and again. Anyway, then, me ma's oldest brudda, Billy Furey, sees what's happened and a week later he tracks Gus Donohoe down and kills him with the same shovel. The courts givved Billy Furey life, because they said it was pre-medicated. That's the why me other uncles Rory and Derek resent me, so. They figure it was all because of me, like, that their sister, me ma, was dead and their brother Billy is doing life. The Donohoes are related to us distant-like on me ma's side, the Lynch side of the family, and so there's always been a mule's hair up the arse of the Lynches and the Fureys over it all. Except for Paul Lynch, who is half Lynch and half Furey, and like a half-brother to both sides of a feudin' family, and that's the why he has two colored eyes. The feud between the Fureys and the Donohoes is always a match strike away from a trailer-burnin' and . . ."

Colin held up his hand for her to stop.

"You're giving me a fucking headache," Colin said.

She fell silent, took a sip of her espresso, and poured more anisette. He sat staring at her, then at the photograph, all the new data causing an overload in his head. He closed his eyes, rubbed them, pressed the heels of his hands against his temples. He opened his eyes and looked around the wood-paneled room, wondering if it was in fact bugged by the feds. In the outside room, there was a collection of low-level wise guys who didn't understand what the hell Gina was talking about. Gina was in front of him, telling him that she was part Italian-American, part Irish, looking for her possibly mobbed-up biological father.

He studied her mother's face, then Gino Barilla's, then Gina's Mediterranean features—the dark eyes and the red hair, the Romanesque nose. Her rage began to make sense. The clash of Irish and Italian blood almost certainly had something to do with Gina's temper and her aggressiveness. *Half Irish tinker, half Italian mobster,* he thought. *She's pure madness.*

"We gotta get the hell out of here," Colin said.

"Not until . . ."

"Gina, these people have been nice. But don't push it."

She sensed the urgency in his voice, got up, and took the last sip of her anisette-laced espresso. They stepped into the outer room where Rocco leaned patiently on the bar.

"Everything copacetic now?" Rocco asked, a warm smile on his face when he saw Gina pushing the stroller toward the front door.

"Yeah," Colin said.

"Good," Rocco said, following them to the door, waving Colin's business card. "I read the trades so I'm gonna call you about a job in your next movie."

"You do that," Colin said.

"Bye-bye, now, missus," Rocco said.

Gina turned to Rocco with a gleam in her eye that frightened Colin. "No one here knows me oulfulluh Gino Barilla," Gina said, showing Rocco the photograph. All the conversations at the card and chess tables stopped. Rocco's eyes narrowed as he studied the faded photograph.

"Never heard of him," Rocco said.

"Load of shite," Gina said, as Colin shoved her out the door.

twenty-four

March 17

Gina insisted on going to the Saint Patrick's Day parade. Colin hadn't gone in years. He found it too crowded and filled with once-a-year stage Irishmen who lurched in from the suburbs to puke green beer on each other in the name of Celtic pride.

But Gina was hell-bent on going. "How could I travel to New York and not see the famous Patrick's Day parade?" she said. "Not going would be like missing the hanging of a judge. Besides, Patrick's Day was when we'd pack up the caravan after kippin' in a winter house and head for the road, for spring and summer. Granda always said that on Patrick's Day the stones in the streams rolled over, which meant the winter was also over and it was time for the travelin' and the sellin' swag and the horse fairs and apples. On the road, after leavin' every halting site, we'd put three sods of grass in the road, in the form of an arrow to point which way we'd gone. The sods was too heavy to be blownt away by the wind and all the cars did was flatten them. Three sods let other travelers know we'd been there and left our blessin', because they symbolized the Father, Son, and the Holy Ghost. And here it is Patrick's Day and sure enough we'll be travelin' now that the stones have turned in our stream."

Gina wore yellow.

Almost everyone else at the Saint Patrick's Day parade was dressed in green, but Gina wore a yellow hat, yellow down jacket, yellow turtleneck, skin-tight black pants, and yellow designer sneakers. *It's like a costume designer had dressed her in yellow to make the leading lady pop out of the background of extras,* Colin thought.

As they stood on Fifth Avenue and Forty-ninth Street, they saw countless numbers of cops work the parade route, arresting drunks, confiscating beer, keeping rowdies in order. There were hundreds more in the dress uniforms of the NYPD Emerald Society strutting the green line painted down the center of Fifth Avenue. Pipers played and school bands performed. Firemen, politicians, Irish-American celebrities, religious and civic leaders, and all of the cultural Irish-American groups of New York marched on the crisp and sunny seventeenth of March, passing the cheering mobs of onlookers, ninety-nine percent of whom were dressed in green.

Colin carried Brianna on his shoulders as Gina pushed the folded pram through the dense crowd. *I'll use a hand-held camera here,* he thought. *Swish-panning. Jittering. Lurching. Staggering. Like the crowd. Wild track sound, the bands, the crowd, the hawkers. All while the camera is following Gina in yellow.*

They passed a half-drunk businessman in his fifties, dressed in a neat Brooks Brothers suit, carrying a clear plastic cup of green beer and wearing a KISS ME, I'M IRISH button. A fortyish bottle-blond woman, pretty in an effusive, big-smiley-mouthed kind of way, sashayed directly up to the businessman and kissed him wetly on the lips with a histrionic lip-popping sound. She grabbed his beer and took a sip as he grabbed her around the waist. "Now you kiss me," she said, and he did, pushing his tongue in her mouth.

The businessman bought the woman her own KISS ME, I'M IRISH button from a Pakistani hawker who was charging five bucks each. The businessman removed his wallet from his inside jacket pocket, chose a ten-dollar bill from a thick wad, and handed it to the dealer.

"Keep the change, Gunga Din," the businessman said.

"Jaysus, a tenner for a tuppence button," Gina commented.

Colin and Gina watched the man pin the button over the woman's left breast, copping a cheap feel and planting another wet kiss on her red-glossed lips.

"What's your name?" the man asked the woman.

"Ima," the woman said, taking another drink of the man's beer and leaving a lipstick imprint on the glass.

"Ima what?"

"Ima gonna kiss you where the sun don't shine," the woman said, and kissed the businessman once more as the people in the mob around them laughed, hooted, and clapped.

Colin laughed, too, and Gina said, "Gobshites. Anybody's, her."

"They're harmless," Colin said. "Just drunks having fun."

"I never seen a mob like this in me life," Gina said. Suddenly she was pushed and swayed in the crowd as a group of step dancers paused on the corner of Fiftieth Street and began to dance in front of Saint Patrick's Cathedral. A shiver went through the multitude as a clique of drunken young rowdies surged forward to get a better view of the show.

"Check out the ass on the redhead," yelled an ossified teenage guy wearing a green plastic derby. Five different redheads in the vicinity turned. But he was referring to a parading step dancer.

"My jaysus," Gina said, swept away in the surging tide of young beefy drunken teens angling for a better look at the dancing girls. Colin sidestepped to protect Brianna and kept his eye on Gina's broad-brimmed yellow hat as she bobbed in the tide of people. Gina clutched the drunken businessman for support but was abruptly pushed away by the stampede of teenagers. Colin was quickly spun around by another pack of rowdy kids who came shoving through the crowd. Brianna grabbed his hair and held on tight, squeezing her thighs around his neck. "Mammy, Daddy," she said.

"That's them," shouted one dark-haired guy, pointing to the first group of young men. "Scumbag with the green plastic derby said they were from Brooklyn. They're the ones jacked up Benny and grabbed Angie's ass."

"Show 'em what Yonkers does to Brooklyn," said a big blond guy in this second crew. They split the crowd in a raging wedge, elbowing and shoving people out of the way, angling toward the first group of malevolent young drunks. Women screamed and men shoved back, many protecting their small children.

Uniformed cops immediately waded into the commotion as a Yonkers thug smashed a beer bottle across the face of the Brooklyn guy with the green plastic derby. Colin held on to Brianna's wrists as he searched for Gina, but his film-trained eye kept cutting perversely back to the violence. Then he cut away again, again, and again, searching for Gina's yellow hat in the crowd.

Spraying blood from the wounded kid's face whipped Colin's focus back to the action. More blood lashed the screaming onlookers as the kid was smashed with a second bottle. *Faces freckled with blood,* he thought. *Red splats on green people. A metaphor for the history of Ireland. Nah, that's too corny. Just leave it as a fleeting visual image; less is more.*

The wounded teenager's green derby fell from his head as a half-full bottle of vodka smashed down on it, followed by a double jab from the jagged bottle neck, tearing open a wound at the base of his neck. Colin spun around, like a horse with rider, not wanting Brianna to witness more of the carnage. People scrambled away. Two arm-locked women in platform shoes stumbled, and were trampled by the clashing teens.

"Mammy," Brianna shouted, cowering on Colin's shoulders. "I want Mammy."

Colin searched again for Gina's yellow hat in the crowd, but all he could see was red-splattered green and a frenzy of wild punches, sailing beer cans, shattering bottles, and violent curses. The crowd whirlpooled as riot cops burst through the crowd, flailing batons and collaring a half-dozen warring punks, as old people hugged lampposts and the ground, panicked women screamed, and fathers elbowed and shouted for the safety of their kids.

Colin backpedaled with Brianna on his shoulders, still trying to spot Gina. *Overhead shot,* he thought. And realized immediately how perverse it was to be thinking of his movie as people were being maimed. Adrenaline carbonated his veins as he searched for Gina's yellow floppy hat, and still there was no sign of her.

He watched the cops drag the drunken kids under the wooden police barriers in the gutter of East Forty-ninth Street, where they laid them like fish on ice, roughly handcuffing them behind their backs and whacking them with batons in the shadow of Saint Patrick's Cathedral.

The guy with the green derby lay in the gutter, deep purple arterial blood pumping from his neck. Three ambulances arrived in a wail of sirens. Citizens with head wounds or badly trampled by the crowd were quickly treated by paramedics. The bleeding kid now gasped for breath, his body in a spasm. An oxygen mask was placed over his face as he was lifted onto a gurney and rolled into the back of an ambulance. The doors slammed. *He's going to die,* Colin thought.

On Fifth Avenue, the parade continued. The brawl was over and the paddy wagons had taken the rioters away. The ambulances had collected the wounded in a matter of minutes. *Paddy wagons on Paddy's Day,* Colin thought. *Like a fucking parody of itself.*

Colin shouldered Brianna, still scanning the crowd for Gina, when he spotted the expensively dressed businessman with the KISS ME, I'M IRISH button leaning on a lamppost, frantically patting his jacket pockets. He saw the bottle blond woman kissing one fireman after another. Still no Gina, anywhere.

"My wallet!" shouted the businessman, his voice slurry with booze. "My fucking wallet!"

He searched the ground as harried people stepped out of the way. The bottle-blonde lurched at strangers, lingering for deep, wet, drunken kisses with men half her age, gulping greedily from their beer bottles, then winking and kissing the next available drunk. *She looks a little older after each gulp,* Colin thought. *After each kiss.*

"My fucking wallet," shouted the businessman, grabbing the blond. "All my fuckin' money, bitch. My fucking credit cards . . ."

"Hey, moron, there's kids here," shouted a furious father.

"I don't have your friggin' wallet, asshole," shouted the blond woman. "What the frig I look like to you, huh? My husband earns more in a day than you do in a friggin' year, so I don't need your chump change."

Colin searched for Gina. Then from behind him he heard her say, "The crack is ninety, wha'?"

"I was worried about you," he said, after spinning to see Gina standing there, beaming under the yellow hat.

"Mammy!" shouted Brianna.

"Did yeh see the half-kilt fella taken away in ambulance?" she said. There was a scary gleam in her eye, like someone juiced by a major sporting event.

"Awful," Colin said.

"Big Nancy, yeh," she said. "If yeh were a turnip you'd moan of livin' in dirt." She pinched Brianna's cheeks. "Best parade I was ever at, isn't it darlin'? Except the music is only melojin."

"Let's get outta here before it gets nuttier," Colin said. "The later you stay, the drunker people get."

"Can we try that Saks Fifth Avenue yoke?" she asked.

"Can't afford it. I don't get the check till next week."

"Och, I've saved a few bob from the wages yeh gived me."

He looked at her as the frantic businessman stumbled by searching the ground for his wallet. Now he remembered her clutching the drunk in the crowd. *She's still at it,* he thought.

That night on the six o'clock news Colin and Gina learned that the kid who had been stabbed had bled to death on the way to Bellevue Hospital.

"I've heard a lot about that Bellevue place," she said. "In all the fil-ums, and on *Law & Order.* Why'd yeh never take us there?"

"They're still preparing my bed," Colin said. "Gina, they're talking about a dead kid here and you're talking sightseeing."

"Not all parades is meant to be happy," she said, carefully folding Brianna's clothes that she had just taken from the dryer in the kitchen. "I've watched re-lay-tives die every year at horse fairs. No one weeps for a dead traveler. It rarely makes the telly news unless he kills a buffer. There was no telly or newspaper writin's about me ma after she was kilt. At least this fella's people have him on telly and more than likely in the newspapers with smiley pictures and all, sure."

Sometimes her heart is as cold as her logic, he thought. *I'll do it just like this. Have the Gina character folding her baby's clothes with motherly loving care as she coldly compares the murder of a stranger with her own mother's. A visual clue to her complicated soul. Just hold a beat on her face before cutting.*

The newscaster said the kid from Yonkers who did the stabbing had tearfully confessed; his lawyer was negotiating a plea bargain.

"All it takes is one moment of madness," Colin said.

"Aye, but what moment isn't?" Gina said.

twenty-five

March 19

The night before Colin, Gina, and Brianna were to leave for Los Angeles, Colin's father agreed to mind Brianna, as Jack and Eddie had organized what they called "a small gathering" at Grogan's pub.

The "small gathering" was a mob scene. Grogan's was packed. Jack and Eddie had invited the entire neighborhood. Two big banners hung in the barroom—CONGRATULATIONS COLIN! and OSCAR WIENER. The second banner was illustrated with a drawing of an Oscar statuette clutching its crotch in one hand and its other hand over its head with an upended middle finger.

Colin laughed as he entered with Gina on his arm. She turned heads in a tapered gray wool double-breasted pinstripe suit with a matching broad-brimmed fedora. She hardly looked three months pregnant. Neighborhood friends greeted Colin one at a time, shaking his hand, embracing him, handing him beers, and lining up shots. Their wives and girlfriends kissed him. A few of his own ex-girlfriends gave him congratulations cards. Colin introduced each person to Gina, who beamed and nodded and said, "Howayeh."

Jack passed a glass of Guinness from Davey Grogan to Gina and she took it and winked. "Och, you're too kind," Gina said, closing her eyes dreamily as she sipped. She licked the foam from her upper lip, took a deeper slug. A few people laughed and applauded.

"She drinks like a true Paddy," someone yelled, bringing a round of applause.

Colin saw that Gina was embarrassed.

Somehow, through her eyes, I have to show the difference between the Irish and the Irish-Americans, he thought. *Most Dubs think we're all horse's asses. The Irish in Dublin pubs speak in hushed conspiratorial knots. The micks here in Queens taverns shout in all capital letters and exclamation points. This is a culture shock to the Gina character. Shoot it all from the Gina character's stunned point of view. She's used to being the only loud one. In New York, she's overwhelmed.*

Jack and Eddie hugged Colin. Davey Grogan leaned across the bar, grabbed his ears and kissed his nose. Colin finally wiggled in a space at the bar and raised a mug of beer to his mouth.

Then he saw Peggy Johnson appear through the crowd of faces.

Zipped into a snug leather bomber jacket, jeans so tight they visibly split her vagina, her eyes glinting with drink. His heart thumped, his face flushed. *Trouble,* he thought. He looked for Gina, who caught his eye and then saw the source of his discomfort.

"Congratulations, Colin," Peggy Johnson said, her voice low, seething.

"Thanks, Peggy," Colin said, shifting his eyes to Gina.

"I hope you're very *happy* out there," Peggy said. "Out in Holly-*woody*. With the big shots."

Gina stepped in between them, saying, "Aye, luv, no better woman for the job, wha'? Me fella'll be very happy indeed. He's bringin' a big shot wi' him who goes by the name of *me.*"

"And you must be . . ."

"I must be, all right, because I'm not anyone else," Gina said, smiling, her voice never rising, her stare like a laser. "Gina Furey, the one and only."

Gina's fist tightened on the handle of the beer mug.

Colin panned to see who else was watching this face-off. No one was. They were all roaring along with Billy Joel.

"Charmed," Peggy Johnson said.

"Are yeh now?" Gina said, still smiling, still looking Peggy deep in the eye. "That's grand, brilliant."

"And baby makes four, I hear," Peggy said, staring back, trying to hold her own.

"So, ladies," Colin said with a laugh. "What do you think should be done about the future of Social Security?"

"Yer the one who calls mornin', noon, and night, aren't yeh, luv?" Gina said, chuckling. "Must be great to have so much time on yer hands. Maybe yeh should start a family of yer own. Is yer problem biological or diabolical? Or a combo, like?"

"I've known Colin a lot longer than you," Peggy said, standing defiantly in front of Gina. "Long before he scooped you off the back roads of Ireland."

"Hey, Peggy, maybe you should take a hike," Colin said.

Gina placed her glass on the bar, looked Peggy in the eyes, and said, "Better, why don't we both get a bit o' air?"

"Gina, no," Colin said, grabbing her by the sleeve. Gina smiled, pulled herself free. Peggy hesitated, nervously evaluating the smaller Gina.

"S'matter, luv?"

"I'm not afraid of you," Peggy Johnson said.

"Good girl," Gina said. "Then we'll go for a wee stroll."

Gina pushed through the crowd, smiling, grabbed the door handle. Peggy hesitated. Several people watched as Colin moved toward the door.

"Leave us wimmins be, a gra," Gina said.

"Gina, the baby, for chrissakes," Colin said.

"The babby'll be just fine," she said.

Peggy Johnson now walked out the door, taking her hands out of a leather bomber jacket. When she stepped out onto the sidewalk, Gina raised her arm. Peggy took a quick step to the side, flinching. But Gina just put her arm around Peggy's shoulder, leading her toward the corner, talking animatedly. Colin watched through the frosted window as the two women began walking slowly down the boulevard, talking, and as they turned the corner, Colin could have sworn he saw Peggy Johnson begin to laugh.

He was tempted to go after them. Instead he went back to the bar, drank, and joked with his pals. Some guys seemed genuinely proud of him, others bled envy all over him. "I thought about being an actor until I found out everyone in that business, man and woman, has to suck at least one cock," said a cop named Kroker.

"Yeah, but the second one gets easier," Colin said.

The music pounded from the jukebox. People told dirty jokes. Davey Grogan told Colin to make sure to write and tell him which movie stars had real tits and which had plastic.

"How long's Gina been gone?" Colin asked after several beers.

"Jeez, must be over an hour," said Davey Grogan.

Colin checked his watch. He'd promised his father he'd pick up Brianna no later than eleven. He shrugged, ordered another beer, felt the booze working in his shoulders, loosening him up, making his tongue wag and his head loll.

The good-bye party should all be shot in silence, he thought. *Let the faces and the actions say it all. Pick a good song to play over it. It's important to avoid sentimentality. Remember, he's not leaving home, he's leaving his fuckin' senses when he takes off with Gina.*

His brother Eddie finally draped an arm around Colin's shoulder, while Jack sidled up on the other side. Davey Grogan served them fresh foamy mugs of beer.

"I'll miss you, big brother," Eddie sang, his head tilted sideways like a sniper's dream. It was a family trait—the neck muscles weren't strong enough to support such big Irish heads when they were heavy with booze.

"I'll miss you, too, Eduardo," Colin said, his head slightly tilted in kind. "But these days the flight to L.A. is a shuttle."

"Crime there's worse than New York now," Eddie said.

"Come visit," Colin said. "I'll protect ya."

"I was sort of looking forward to carpooling with ya," Eddie said. "I'll leave your name in the local Century 21, in case it don't work out in L.A."

"Great fuckin' vote of confidence," Jack said.

"He didn't mean it that way," Colin said, laughing, headlocking Eddie. "I don't know how the fuck it all happened so fast."

"You jumped in with both feet, bro," Jack said.

"I know," Colin said, shaking his head. "You don't know half of it. Where the hell is Gina, anyway?"

He looked at his watch; it was 11:33. The floor was sticky under his feet, the barroom was choked with smoke, body heat, and booze breath. Drunks were standing at odd angles, groping the bar rail like drowning men.

In the morning, he'd be leaving this place, where he was born and raised. He felt an alcohol-fueled surge of emotion rise in him. He controlled himself. *Bargain-basement nostalgia,* he thought.

"Hey, you're going to the Oscars!" Jack said, and then raised his mug and shouted. "MY LITTLE BROTHER IS GOING TO THE FUCKING OSCARS!"

The barroom broke into applause, whistles, and war whoops again. When the commotion ended, Davey Grogan handed Colin the phone. It was his father. Brianna was awake, and screaming for her mother.

"Be right there, Dad," he said. He placed the phone on the bar and wordlessly left without saying good-bye to anyone.

Colin picked up Brianna from his father, lying that Gina was home packing for the morning flight. Colin shook his father's hand good-bye.

"I'll call soon," Colin said.

"Good luck, son," Liam Coyne said.

Colin lifted the sobbing Brianna into his arms and left.

twenty-six

March 20

In the morning, he wasn't sure what awakened him—his blaring beeper or Brianna crying. Probably both. He sat up in the bed, fully clothed, his head banging with a headache. Brianna sat in the bed, the telephone off the hook on her lap, sobbing, "Mammy, Daddy, I want Mammy . . ."

His beeper blared again. He looked at the time—6:15 A.M. Their plane was leaving JFK at nine. He looked at the phone number on the beeper; it looked oddly familiar, but he could not place it in his hungover haze. He saw Gina's three ones following the number. He dialed the number and jammed the phone between his shoulder and his ear. His head pounded. He lifted Brianna onto his lap and tried to soothe her as the phone rang on the other end. He handed Brianna a baby bottle, which she put in her mouth and sucked briefly before spitting out. "Shite, daddy," she said. "Shite." He could smell her dirty diaper. *No wonder the poor thing is moaning,* he thought.

He reached in the carry-on bag and took out a disposable diaper and a tub of baby wipes. He lay Brianna on her back on the bed, wiped her nose, and unsnapped the dirty diaper. The smell hit him like a kick in the balls. *What the fuck have I done to myself,* he thought.

"Good morning," Peggy Johnson said after answering the phone on the other end.

Colin stood in a half-crouch over the smelly toddler, his head combusting, confused beyond dexterity. Had he dialed the wrong number? *Did I dial Peggy Johnson by mistake?* He checked the beeper. *Peggy's number,* he thought. *Gina's code. What the fuck?*

"Peggy?"

"Colin, that you?" she asked cheerfully.

"Yeah . . . is . . . um . . . Gina there?"

He realized how deeply weird this was.

"She sure is," said Peggy. "Oh, and Colin, in case I don't see you, good luck and congratulations. You have a great woman."

"Um . . . thanks," he said, as Brianna stopped crying after he wiped her clean, his hand now covered in the mess.

"Mornin', luv," Gina said. "How's me child?"

Colin was furious with her. He wanted to rant into the phone, to tell her off for disappearing all night, for leaving him with her kid, and now for asking how the kid was and never asking how he was feeling.

"I'm wiping her ass right now. Our plane boards in two hours."

"Fair play to yeh, yeh big Nancy, yeh," she said and laughed as he heard her talking to Peggy. "He's changing the child for breakfast. That's how yeh want 'em, luv."

As he heard the two of them laughing, his anger mounted and he fought for control. Fighting with Gina before boarding a plane was a losing proposition. Invulnerable to public shame, she'd stage another scene and keep him mortified for five hours on a crowded jet. He realized that he might actually be afraid of Gina Furey. He was afraid because she'd think nothing of boarding a different plane back to Dublin, with his unborn kid, afraid because she wasn't afraid of anything. Especially him.

"I'm glad someone is having fun," he said.

"Some father you'll be, one shitey nappy and yer already Joan of Arc," she said. "Freshen me little flower and collect me on the way to the airport."

Colin put a clean outfit on Brianna, strapped her into the stroller, gave her a bottle of apple juice, showered quickly, dressed, and loaded the four suitcases into the waiting hired car. He had sold his Explorer to Jack. He left the registration, title and car keys on the kitchen table. Jack had told him to keep the key to the apartment—just in case. He didn't leave a note. Notes were too final. He peeked into Jack's bedroom, heard him snoring loudly, and looked one last time around the apartment where he would breathe his last deep breath as a bachelor. He exhaled slowly, thinking of all the great times, all the wild nights with beautiful girls, all the long days at the computer chasing his dream. Now, at age twenty-five, with a third of his life gone, Colin was off to the life of the domesticated male.

Nightmare, he thought.

Colin watched Peggy Johnson hug Gina on the sidewalk in front of her house before Gina hurried down the walkway, wearing the same clothes she wore the night before, smoking a cigarette. She climbed into the backseat of the car. Peggy waved good-bye. Colin looked at Peggy and blinked. *Bizarre,* he thought.

"That cigarette will make me throw up," Colin said when Gina got in the back.

Without a comment, she tossed it out the window and hoisted Brianna onto her lap. "Mammy," Brianna said.

"I know, darlin'," Gina said, turning to wave to Peggy as the car pulled out.

"With a lovely girl like her here at home why'd yeh go to Ireland looking for a woman, yeh greedy swine, yeh?" Gina asked, without looking at Colin.

"The hell are you talking about?"

"Yeh have that poor young wan's heart broke, yeh do," Gina said. "And I don't appreciate yeh using me to do the breakin'.'"

Colin noticed the driver looking at him in the rearview mirror, rolling his eyes.

"What the hell are you talking about, Gina?" Colin said. "First you almost came to blows with her . . ."

"Don't flatter yerself," Gina said. "Probably at home having a wank over two birds fightin' over the likes of yerself."

"As a matter of fact, I was home taking care of the baby that you neglected all night," Colin said.

"Don't you ever accuse me of neglectin' my child," she said. "If yeh can't mind one child for one night what kind of father will you be atall? And I'll tell you what I was doin' all night . . ."

She opened her pocketbook and removed a bottle of Xanax and a razor blade and brandished both. "I was keepin' that poor jilted bird from killin' herself over you! Where do yeh get the bottle to parade a foreign girl, with child, in front of an emotionally disturbed poor critter like that lovely wee Peggy Johnson? Were yeh doin' it just to feed yer feckin' ego? To watch the two of us claw each other to death over the privilege to get into yer bed? Or did you really want to see that poor girl hurt herself? Die?"

"This is ridiculous," Colin said. "My brothers wanted to meet me in Grogan's."

"You knew she'd be there. You wanted to parade me in front of her."

"Bullshit," Colin said. "She was never my girlfriend."

"Yeh did the durty with her, yeh durty randy tomcat, yeh."

"Casual sex . . ."

"Baby in car," the Russian driver said.

"Yeh knew how she felt about yeh, though, didn't yeh?"

"She initiated it."

"But yeh knew she was in love with yeh," she said. "And so when you gonkied her, yeh knew she was making love to yeh, righ'?

"That's twisted logic."

"Then yeh flew off to Ireland, met me, sent me right up the pole,

American flags wavin', snuck me into this godforsaken country, paraded me in front of that poor emotional wreck of a t'ing, broke her little heart, and hoped the two of us would kill each other over the likes of you."

"None of that was my intention," Colin said.

"I'm of a good mind to go right to the Aer Lingus terminal and take the next flight back to Dublin," Gina said. "I could be in a nice pub having a glass of stout with me cousins in a few hours . . ."

Go, he thought, seething quietly. *Go back to your covered fucking wagon. Back to your goat and your psychotic granny and your screwball granda and your thieving, conniving, useless relatives. Not with my baby in your belly, you won't.*

"You're wrong," he said. "But I'm in no mood for arguing."

"Good," said the driver.

"He's gas," Gina said, nodding toward the driver. "Doesn't have a tooth in his head, can't speak three words of English, but he's worried about me child."

Gina's mood changed instantly, as if all were forgiven, because she had had the last word. Again.

"I hear the weather is lovely and warm out there in California," she said. "Maybe the shift'll do us good."

Less than an hour before the plane landed at LAX, Colin had three Bloody Marys in him and his hangover was disappearing. His anger had subsided. Every time he'd tried to ask Gina what she and Peggy had talked about, she told him to mind his business. Instead, she talked almost all the way across the country about finding her father. She asked if there was a Mafia in Los Angeles. He told her there was one in almost every major American city. She said she'd continue her search for Gino Barilla in Los Angeles. "Maybe he's here on his holliers," she said.

With the booze lifting his spirits, Colin told her that when he could afford it, he might even hire a private investigator to help track down Gino Barilla. This gave her hope. She kissed him, deep, wet, with passion.

He realized he hadn't made love to her in two weeks, because

Brianna always slept in the same bed. *You pay for a wife and kid and you don't even get laid,* he thought.

"Brianna needs her own bed," Gina said. "I'm randy for yeh."

That morning she was accusing him of bringing Peggy Johnson to the brink of suicide; now she was being lovey-dovey and sexy.

Schizoid, he thought, as they descended into Los Angeles.

Part V

Los Angeles

twenty-seven

Global Screen Films had a Ford Mustang rental car waiting at the airport. Colin knew the town. He'd been to L.A. several times. He drove directly to the Chateau Marmont hotel, a Spanish-style hacienda overlooking Sunset Boulevard, where they checked into a small prepaid suite, with a bedroom and a living room and a foldout couch.

After unpacking, they ate lunch, and Gina asked Colin to give her a tabloid tour of the city. She wanted to see where the riots following the Rodney King beating had erupted. "I remember watchin' them fil-ums when I was just in pruberty," she said. "Especially the ones where the cops bate that poor blackie bloke senseless and then the black fulluhs batin' the shiverin' shite outta the white fulluh. I can't wait to tell me cousins I seen it in the flesh. More blacks than Brixton, wha'?"

Gina bought a disposable camera and insisted on posing for snapshots with Brianna in front of the Brentwood condo where Nicole Simpson and Ron Goldman had been murdered. They moved on to the site of O.J. Simpson's former mansion and Gina posed for more pictures, sitting behind the wheel of the Mustang, wearing shades. "Mark my words," she said. "These'll be worth money in Dublin."

Colin showed her Malibu, where the mud slides and the brush fires had ravaged the gorgeous coastline. He drove her over the

Santa Monica Freeway, which had collapsed during the last earth-quake.

"If this is a city, then me arse is me face," Gina said. "Might as well be filled with gamey-legged cripples. No one walks here. How do you bump into friends? Which way's the crack?"

"You'll have to learn to drive," Colin said.

"What do yeh do then?" she asked. "Crash into them?"

"Only if you drink and drive," he said, "which you simply cannot do here because they will put you in jail, where they'll find out you're an illegal and deport you."

"Then there's only one thing to do," she said. "I won't drive. Period. I'll tell yeh what I will do. I'm letting me hair grow out to its natural red. I will not be a blondie in Los Angeles. It's like being a redhead in Dublin. Me red hair is the one bit of Irishness I'll be able to see in the mirror every day."

He knew life in L.A. with Gina wasn't going to be easy.

When he got back to the hotel, an envelope was waiting for him at the hotel desk, containing six single-spaced pages of detailed notes from James Thompson and Syd Green on his treatment. They expected the changes to be incorporated before the Academy Awards ceremony on April 3, just thirty-three days away.

March 27

Colin and Gina moved out of the Chateau Marmont after a week. She'd had the room-service waiters running up and down with bottles of Guinness and shrimp cocktails. The local Mexican restaurant was delivering tacos three or four times a day as he tried to work on the treatment.

Colin wasn't getting much work done and the Global Screen business-affairs people said his hotel bill was becoming ridiculous. Colin had to admit he was there with his girlfriend and her child. They pointed out that his contract said they would only pay for him, so a flustered Bonnie Corbet worked out a flat per-diem expense deal for Colin. "Don't blow this deal with arrogance," Bonnie warned him. "Remember, you're the new kid on the block."

The two-hundred-dollar-a-day expense money allowed them to move into a seventy-five-dollar-a-day efficiency apartment in North Hollywood.

March 30
High noon.

"You could roast pigs in this heat, wha'?" Gina said, sitting pool-side at the Esplanade Apartments complex, which was filled with vaguely recognizable, semi-regular episodic TV actors, studies in familiar anonymity, many sitting on beach-chairs and moving their lips as they read scripts. Everywhere Colin went in L.A. people had screenplays in their hands—gas station attendants, bartenders, restaurant hostesses, 7-Eleven countermen, hotel clerks, pool cleaners. Everybody was either a writer or an actor making a living doing something else. "I have a personal trainer who also does script doctoring," Colin heard a fortyish woman sitting poolside tell an older woman. "His card says, EVERYTHING FROM CELLULITE TO CELLULOID, LEANER HIPS AND TIGHTER SCRIPTS. This guy is a freaking genius. He edits flab out of your ass and your scripts. If he was straight I'd marry him."

Because he had to entertain or drive Gina everywhere, Colin rose at 5:00 A.M. every day and worked for four hours on script rewrites before Gina and Brianna awakened around nine. If he was lucky, he grabbed an hour's nap in the afternoon and was in bed by by 11 P.M.

Gina found Los Angeles curiously interesting for the first week, but by the second week, living in the Valley, Gina was on the phone every day, calling her cousins in the pubs of Dublin, yakking about how she hated L.A. She complained that she didn't know how to swim or drive. That the heat was "hotter than the hearth of hell," and that very few stores or bars sold Guinness. "And finding a pack of Dunhills is like finding a shopkeeper who doesn't t'ink he's the new Bruce Willis," he heard her tell her cousin Philomena. "Buyin' fags in this city is like commitin' bleedin' murder. Feckin' sirens go off. You can't smoke in feckin' pubs or restaurants or shops. No wonder they have feckin' earthquakes. Everyone here who smokes is shiverin' with feckin' fear."

April 9

By his third week in L.A., Colin was spending a third of his time telling Gina how expensive it was to call Dublin from L.A., a third fighting with her about her smoking and drinking while pregnant, and still another third driving around finding stores that sold Dunhills and Guinness.

If he didn't get these daily poisons for Gina, she became angry and moody, drinking regular American beer and smoking American cigarettes. She cursed L.A., calling it fake and boring. She said she already missed her family and friends, and couldn't believe she was six thousand miles from home. "If my grannies visited by caravan I'd be their age by the time they reached here," she said.

Colin realized that what she hated most about L.A. was her immobility and her dependence on him. "I can't even walk out to get a few messages," she said, sitting poolside and wearing a floppy straw hat and a loose white dress that covered her swelling belly. "The nearest pub is over two mile away and they won't even let yeh in with kids. And I'm sick and tired sitting around this feckin' pool lookin' at all these decaying muttons dressed as lamb. Do they do face-lifts in barber shops here? By Jaysus, the state a them, oulfulluhs me granda's age tryin' to look like action heroes, wha'? Faces on the oul wans tighter than Mary Magdalene's ghee, God forgive me."

Several of the actors at poolside looked over their scripts at Gina, who gaped back at them.

"To be or not to be," she shouted at no one in particular, and took a long gulp of Guinness. "Me ghee or not me ghee, that is the question, wha'?"

She broke into guffaws, and only Brianna laughed along. Colin sat looking at her as a few people gathered their sunblock, towels, and scripts and headed for the lobby and their efficiencies.

"The pre-Oscar lunch is tomorrow," Colin said, softly. "I have to go. I'd like you to come too, but we can't bring Brianna."

He hadn't mentioned the lunch since New York and he purposely waited until this late date to remind Gina of it. He was hoping circumstances would force her to stay home while he went alone. He didn't want to be embarrassed by her antics at the lunch, smoking and drinking while pregnant, cursing and being blunt with movie stars, directors, producers, and Academy people. It had all the promise of a fiasco. Bonnie Corbet had warned him not to fuck up his whole life for this tinker girl.

Gina's homesickness was growing and she was hinting of going home to Dublin. Sometimes, when she acted out, part of him wished she'd get on the next Aer Lingus flight, but another part of him said he had a responsibility to his unborn kid.

Besides I made the fucking promise to Mom, he thought. *Anyway, every day Gina does or says something new that I might use in this script.*

"Why aren't kids allowed?" she asked. "Why does everyone in this city hate kids so much? I was looking in the newspaper the other day and all these beautiful-sounding flats and houses were for let, three and four bedrooms, swimmin' pools and gymnasiums and tennis and basketball courts, and then at the bottom it says NO KIDS. What the bloody hell do they put in all them spare bedrooms? Mistresses? Butlers and maids? Their cash? There was one great-soundin' house in a place called Chatsworth, where it said NO KIDS, HORSE OKAY. What kind of a place hates kids so much that they'd rather have a feckin' horse than a child? Even on the back roads of Ireland, me granny always made sure the kids were fed and warm before she thought about the feckin' pony."

She tore the filter off a Dunhill, lit it, and took a sip of Guinness. Behind her, Colin could see some of the actors and actresses talking in a knot at the lobby doorway, looking over at Gina and shaking their heads. He was glad she couldn't see them, or a confrontation would erupt.

He reminded her again of the Oscar lunch the next day.

"Well, I have no one to mind Brianna," Gina said. "Go to your precious feckin' lunch without me, so."

"Gina, this is important," Colin said.

"Bunch of grown-ups sittin' around makin' plans to win little fake gold statues and thinkin' they're important," she said. "I think it's comical meself. I can't wait until the big night so I can laugh at the losers. Millionaires cryin' because a different millionaire won the wee statue when kids are starvin' all over the world. Tell me that isn't the height of hypocrisy."

She has a point, Colin thought. *Maybe I'll use that speech . . .*

"It's important to those of us who get nominated," he said.

"Then go, Mr. Colin-Oscar-Feckin'-Nomination-Coyne," she said. "By all means go to your lunch. We're too busy, anyway, aren't we, Brianna? We don't want to go to his durty lunch, do we, darlin'? With all the make-believe people from their little make-believe-we're-important-Oscar-world. We'll stay at home and play make-believe ourselves. We'll make believe we're back in Dublin, where we belong, havin' the crack."

"You wanna come, you find a goddamned baby-sitter," Colin said.

"You must be *jokin',*" she said. "I won't leave my child with a complete Yank stranger, so I won't. Even the cats in this country is quare."

"Then I'll go alone," Colin said.

"I was doin' grand *alone* before I met yeh," she said. "I'm certain we can manage one afternoon without yer lordshite's company."

She got up from her chair, pushed her cigarette into the Guinness bottle, and dropped it into a trash barrel. Then she took Brianna by the hand. "C'mon Brianna, I have to write a letter home," she said. "My God, darlin', what has yer mammy done?"

Colin saw her walk toward the lobby, noticing the first waddle of pregnancy in her gait.

April 10

On his way to the Oscar luncheon, Colin carried Gina's letter, which she had asked him to send by Express Mail. It was addressed in her childish spidery scrawl to her cousin Bridie in Ballytara. *Another universe,* Colin thought. *The letter is probably a scam to get her back home, with my kid.* Colin considered opening and reading the letter, but thought that would be something Gina would do, so he didn't. The postal clerk in Beverly Hills station said delivery would take three days.

The Oscar lunch was a dose of reality. Taylor Hackford, the noted director, hosted the ceremony, which was held at Morton's on Melrose Avenue, an exclusive restaurant where, Bonnie Corbet had said, only those on the Hollywood A-list were guaranteed a table and where fans, tourists, paparazzi, autograph hounds, and other riffraff were kept away by beefy staffers who kept an ever-updated Rolodex of Hollywood's who's who in their heads. The valet-parking ritual at Morton's was intimidating, almost as if the make and model of your automobile was a prerequisite for a meal. *It's like getting proofed for income instead of age,* Colin thought. *They should hang a sign: "No One Under Twenty Mil Per Picture Will Be Served."* Colin was too self-conscious of his RentAWreck Chevy Lumina to bring it to the valet parking attendant, who was being handed the keys to Porsches, Mercedeses, Lexuses, Rolls-Royces. So Colin circled the block, parked on a side street, and walked to the restaurant.

Inside, three gorgeous actressy hostesses gave him his Oscar sweatshirt, a nominee certificate, and a name tag. In the large, palm-filled room, he chatted self-consciously with some of the other short-film nominees and met a smooth-mannered director named Frank Burston, a rich Beverly Hills real estate baron's son and UCLA film school graduate, dressed in a beige linen suit and black Ralph Lauren polo shirt with the top button fastened. Burston had directed a short called *Green Eyes,* which Bonnie Corbet had told him was generating a whole lot of buzz and was the picture to beat. He was Colin's main competition.

"I don't care if I win," Burston told Colin, drinking Perrier with no ice. "I'm just happy to be nominated. To be in the game."

Fucking liar, Colin thought.

He'd seen *Green Eyes,* on the Sundance channel, thought it was brilliantly mounted, great to look at, but ultimately a pretentious, emotionally empty film about being a young filmmaker and what a great privilege it was to follow in the footsteps of Hitchcock, Welles, Ford, Hawks, and Spielberg, all of whom made Burston green with envy. *A fucking job application,* Colin thought of Burston's film. *His brown nose goes good with his beige suit.*

At first Colin felt small, comparing the elaborate, slick production values of *Green Eyes,* with his little ragtag street film about a kid from Queens losing his first love, which he is convinced will be his last love. Now, in Morton's, he believed his picture had more human heart than Burston's.

After Taylor Hackford finished his humorous speech, Colin quickly confirmed his suspicions that the short film director nominees were about as important in this room as the busboys.

But Burston knew how to work a room. To begin with, his film was a cinematic asskiss to Hollywood gods, and he was here to worship.

As Colin stood in a corner, alone, beer in hand, he watched Burston schmooze with the big shots. *They must give a class in advanced asskissing at UCLA,* he thought. Burston dressed as the stars do, wore a gold Rolex watch like the ones the stars wear, and boasted a big cigar with Havana band in his breast pocket. *A fucking prop,* Colin thought. Burston drank his designer water with no ice with one hand while the other hand rested in his pleated trousers pocket. A pair of Ray-Bans were perched on top of his blond head. He looked as if a chemical food additive had never passed his lips. With his deep tan, white teeth, supple complexion, and tennis-toned body, Burston looked like he had been picked out of central casting to play an Oscar winner.

Colin felt fidgety, uneasy, and sweaty. He thought people could see the booze and the junk food oozing from his skin, the way they heard Bell Boulevard rattle out of his mouth. He turned away from Burston and glanced around the room at the celebrities positioned every two feet; short actors with big names, surgically beautiful starlets with their publicists squiring them around like pimps, brand-name directors bored silly by the proceedings, pedigree producers touting their next pictures while being nominated for their last, powerful agents like Jeff Berg, Jim Wiatt, Ed Limato, Mike Ovitz, and Morton Janklow.

Colin was damp with stage fright, but he forced himself to mix, and soon found himself chatting with some of the celebrities— Robert Redford, Warren Beatty, Quentin Tarantino, Mel Gibson, Tom Hanks, Michelle Pfeiffer, Alec Baldwin, Goldie Hawn.

"Colin Coyne, hey, I liked your film," Baldwin said. "Loved the Queens neighborhood sensibility. It's tough and sweet. Good stuff. Stay in touch."

"Thanks," Colin said. "I could use some advice."

"Us New York guys should always remember," Baldwin said with that low menacing charm, "that instead of thinking *tougher,* it's always better to think *smarter.*"

"Good luck, Colin," said Tom Hanks, startling Colin as he read his name tag. "But be prepared for luck. It's easy to squander if you're not prepared for it. And luck rarely comes twice."

"What do you mean by being prepared for luck?"

"I was on unemployment when I got offered a picture everyone else had turned down called *Splash,* and . . ."

Hanks didn't get to finish the line. Flashbulbs popped rudely in his eyes and bodies separated them. Colin wanted to ask him for more advice, but Hanks and the rest of the celebs were quickly surrounded by an obnoxious herd of paparazzi, most from the wire services and European press but also from CNN, E! channel, *Entertainment Tonight,* and *Access Hollywood.* Hanks and the others were soon trapped into posing and giving sound bites. That's what the lunch was all about, a promo for the big Oscar night. The whole celebrity life was a sort of performance.

Colin watched Burston glide into the galaxy of stars, into the spotlight, putting his arm around a surprised Quentin Tarantino as the photographers snapped. As Colin stood watching all these people on the make, bullshitting one another, studio publicists trying to make each star outshine the other for the press in the heated Oscar campaign, he suddenly wished Gina were there. As irrational as that idea was, Gina would have figured out how to get some attention, how to mix it up with the big shots. She would have made herself the center of attention. He was oddly surprised at himself that he missed her.

"I saw you talking to Tom Hanks," said a photographer with a French accent. "Are you somebody?"

"Any day now," Colin said.

The photographer drifted away. Colin noticed Burston watching him. They nodded to one another. "Good line," Burston said, striding into the crowd like a man who belonged there.

Colin felt suddenly guilty that he hadn't tried harder to arrange for Gina to attend the luncheon.

Fuck all these people, he thought. *I'd rather be home eating a taco with loony Gina. Listening to my baby in her belly. Working on the script.*

The second he had the chance, he slipped out of Morton's and headed home. Well aware that no one had noticed.

twenty-eight

April 11

Just before seven the next morning, while Colin tried to work, Gina made a few calls to Dublin from the kitchen wall phone. She located Bridie Lynch, told her she needed some American ID, from a girl about her age, same physical kind of look, from anywhere but California.

Colin called the phone company and learned that Gina had already racked up a $478 phone bill in ten days. He was spending more than his two-hundred-dollar per diem on rent, take-out Mexican food, Guinness, Dunhills, gas, phone bills, and Pampers.

"I'm looking for an Irish baby-sitter," she assured Colin. "So we can go out and have a bit of crack."

"Gina, we don't need a baby-sitter. We need an accountant. We're spending more than I'm earning."

"Then get a proper man's job with hammers and nails. Instead of a schoolboy's paper and pen job."

"Maybe I should rob a fuckin' bank like your ex," he said.

"At least he had the balls."

"But no fucking brains to hang them from," Colin said.

"What are yer brains getting' us? Bills and moans. You sound like an oul settled woman. I never in me life heard me granda moan about bills when we was on the road."

"When you rob and fuckin' cheat people for a living, what's there to complain about? The world's the Garden of Eden—pick from any tree and live off other people's toil."

"Buy us our feckin' tickets home outta this kip and I'll mail yeh yer money plus VAT," she said.

"I'm not letting you go back to raise my kid as a . . ."

"As a what? Go ahead, say it, as a *knacker*."

"As a kid without a father," he said.

"I was raised without one."

"I rest my case."

She glared at him. For the first time, his words wounded her. But she maintained her composure.

"I think I turned out grand," she said, looking him straight in the eyes, her own watering. She walked into the bedroom and gently closed the door behind her.

Fuck you, he thought. And then felt immediately sad for her.

April 15

A COD Federal Express envelope arrived at the house. Colin paid the sixty dollars due while Gina grabbed the envelope and tore it open. Inside was a Rhode Island driver's license, an American passport, and a Trinity College ID card in the name of Priscilla McCarthy, age twenty-four, five-foot-three, blond hair, dark eyes.

Gina started her first driving lesson the very next day under the name Priscilla McCarthy. She made repeated calls to Dublin, searching from pub to pub, until she found her cousins drinking in a place called McMurphy's. She thanked them for the ID and told each of the three cousins the same fifteen-minute story about her driving in America, "on the left-hand side of the road, mind yeh." The cost, Colin figured, was about a buck a word.

Colin tended to Brianna during the day as Gina took her driving lessons. He continued to work on his movie treatment from five to nine in the mornings, the only time he could get any kind of peace.

After ten days of lessons, Gina took her road test. To Colin's astonishment, the driving test went without incident. While at the department of motor vehicles getting her license, Gina bumped into a plump, middle-aged, gray-haired Irish woman from Galway named Moira O'Keefe who had been living in North Hollywood for nine years and who waited tables in an Irish bar and restaurant called Ireland's Eye. She told Gina about a house for rent on Klump Avenue with a lovely backyard and three bedrooms.

April 25

The day after Gina received her driver's license, Colin found himself signing a $1,300-a-month lease on a house two blocks from Moira O'Keefe's rented home. He had to dip into his eight-thousand-dollar savings to shell out one month's rent, along with a month's security, but the house saved him about one grand a month compared to the $75 per night for the efficiency apartment.

Gina bought five gallons of bleach, tied a babushka around her head, threw open all the windows, and proceeded to sterilize every square inch of the rented house.

"I wouldn't bring childer into this house until I kilt every one of them DNAs of the scrubbers what lived here afore us," she said. Moira O'Keefe brought her teenage daughter, Caitlin, to help Gina drape the windows. Caitlin was a gawky fifteen-year-old teenager wearing braces on her teeth. Gina decided she was the ideal baby-sitter.

"I have me Irish baby-sitter," Gina told Colin. "I have me license, now all I need is a car of me own."

Gina was preparing her nest for the new baby and grudgingly settling into life in L.A. Colin leased a second car, a Ford Taurus, the same day Gina rented furniture—a living room set, a master bedroom set, a children's room set, and a desk and bookcases for his small office—from Abbey Furniture Rentals. Added to the rent, his monthly nut was now more than $2,500. Before basic food, Pampers, Guinness, Dunhills, and tacos.

After he had set up a home, with furniture and two rented cars, he had four thousand dollars left in the bank. But Colin was proud of his new home. It had a bedroom for Brianna, one for him and Gina, and a small room overlooking a backyard blooming with palm trees and rosebushes that was ideal for his long-awaited office. Colin could close and lock the door and be wondrously alone. He set up his laptop and rented a laser printer. Once he had his books shipped, he'd be in business.

More money, money, fucking money, he thought. *But at least my little office will give me a place to work to earn the bread to pay the bills.*

Gina bought lace and satin and velour fabric and made her own curtains and drapes for the windows. She began knitting clothes, blankets, and shawls for the baby. Everything she made was blue.

With five days before the Academy Awards, and an office with a door, Colin was now able to get back onto a daytime schedule, working on the treatment in a final eighteen-hour marathon.

Every day, Gina took Brianna in the Taurus to the playground nearby, where she would meet Moira O'Keefe. They would share a few bottles of Guinness and Gina would eat her tacos.

Gina, who was now visibly four months pregnant, still hated Los Angeles, but Colin hoped that a friend and her newfound freedom would alleviate her isolation. Having an Irish friend also gave her a chance to have the "crack." Three nights before the Oscars, Colin even minded Brianna while Gina went out with Moira to Ireland's Eye.

April 28

Two days before the Academy Awards, Gina arranged for Caitlin, Moira's teenage daughter, to baby-sit Brianna while Colin took Gina for her first trip to Rodeo Drive in search of something for her to wear to the Oscars. Colin went with Gina into every shop, claiming he'd have to sign the credit-card slip if she found something she wanted. He was figuring the gown alone would cost him a grand and there would be another couple hundred for shoes, and then accessories. He really shadowed Gina for fear that she would steal an Armani or Anne Klein original. His palms dampened as Gina rummaged through the ostentatious stores on one of the most expensive shopping streets in the world.

"I wouldn't give yeh the pennies off a dead cop's eyes for this dishrag," she told one saleslady in a maternity shop called Neuf Mois, fingering a sequined gown with a price tag of $1,800. For once, Colin applauded Gina's opinion.

"But, Madam, this was designed by . . ."

"I wouldn't care if it was designed by the Mona Lisa," Gina said. "For eighteen hundred I could dress all of Dolphin's Barn."

The woman looked at her in baffled, speechless amazement.

Gina browsed almost every single store on Rodeo Drive, from Wilshire to Santa Monica Boulevard. Pretending he was doing an over-the-shoulder shot, Colin's filmic eye followed Gina's point of view to security guards, alarm systems, and surveillance cameras. He was certain she spent more time looking at the security systems than at the clothes.

She's casing Rodeo Drive, Colin decided as Gina checked the emergency exits in one store, triggering an alarm. She set off another alarm in a second store when she opened the window of the ladies' room. In a third store she asked a security guard for a light. When he said he didn't smoke, she asked if his partner had a light. The guard replied he didn't have a partner. "And besides, ma'am, there is no smoking."

"I wouldn't waste yer good money here, Colin," she said in yet another store after pushing a piece of chewing gum into the lens of a security video camera. "I have this place sussed."

"Gina, I hope you're not thinking of doing anything stupid," Colin said.

She laughed and asked to be taken to an ordinary department store. At JC Penney in the Santa Monica Mall Gina bought herself a plain white cotton maternity dress. She bought herself some embroidery needles and silk threads in a fabric shop, plus a pair of low-heeled white sandals and a brand new white floppy hat and a pair of long white cotton gloves.

The entire outfit came to $220.

"I asked meself if I'd ever spend me last penny dressin' for a fella named Oscar," she said. "Me answer was 'never.'"

That evening, Colin polished his treatment, occasionally looking out the window at Brianna, who played with her toys in a splash pool in the backyard as Gina sat sunning herself and sewing bright silk flowers onto her plain white dress. He had no idea how the dress would look and felt almost sorry for her that she would be the only woman at the Oscars without a designer gown.

The next morning, Gina went to the beauty parlor and had her hair dyed to her natural red color.

April 30

Oscar night.

As Colin buttoned his rented tux, Gina waltzed out of the bedroom wearing the white cotton dress that now bloomed with almost as much life as the belly that swelled proudly beneath it. A bouquet of silk Easter lilies exploded above her left breast and a chain of daisies embroidered the hems and seams of the dress. She'd sewn matching floral designs on her plain white floppy hat, white cloth clutch bag, and long white gloves. Her supple Italian olive skin was freshly tanned, offsetting her brilliant white teeth and her gold necklaces and the emeralds that glittered from her ears. With her big, sparkling dark eyes and her shimmering wavy red hair, Colin thought Gina looked more like a movie star than most of today's movie stars.

"You're beyond beautiful," he said, smoothing his tux.

Global Screen had rented Colin the tux and a small Lincoln Town Car with a driver for the big night. In his inside jacket pocket, Colin had his invitations to the Shrine Auditorium and the governor's ball, the fancy raised script on the invitations indicating that for at least one night they were members of Hollywood royalty.

Before departing, Moira O'Keefe took Polaroid pictures of Colin and Gina as Caitlin held a stupefied Brianna by the hand.

"Shite, Mammy," Brianna said.

"Shite on yer shite," Gina said.

"I'll take care of her," Moira said. "G'wan, the both of yeh."

They waved good-bye as they climbed into the Town Car. Gina had made certain there were bottles of Guinness stocked in the refrigerated side panels of the backseat. Using a bottle opener on a long gold chain, Gina popped the lid off one as soon as she got in the car. Colin looked at her anxiously. She looked back at him and winked.

"Here's health," she said, taking a sip.

Good luck would be nice, too, he thought.

Colin opened a Heineken for himself. He took a deep drink.

"Yer nervous, aren't yeh?" she said.

"A little," he said.

"It's only a statue of a wee mon, for chrissakes," she said. "It couldn't buy you a handshake with a leper."

"It could mean a career. It could mean the difference between a life of struggle and a life of luxury."

"Luxury is a bore," she said. "Unless you nick it."

"Or earn it," he said.

"Aye," she said. "Yeh could do it that way, too, I suppose. But people who work the hardest are usually worked hardest against. So, in this life, yeh need a plan. Nick what they won't let yeh earn and the good life is somewhere in the middle."

He looked at her and swallowed some beer. Her philosophy of life forever astounded him. *She lives her life in the present tense,* he thought. *Never regretting things she did yesterday, never worrying about tomorrow.* She took another swig of the Guinness as the car whispered south on the Hollywood Freeway.

"Don't worry, boyo," she said. "So long as you have me you'll never go home empty-handed."

He smiled and said, "Gina, one thing I have to ask you. For chrissakes, don't curse anyone out in public tonight. I'm begging you to be . . . fucking *nice.*"

She looked at him and nodded, her dark eyes churning with danger, alluringly treacherous. *She can hold a stare like hammer-head shark,* he thought.

"Yer asking me for an Oscar performance, then," she said.

"Something like that," he said.

"Okay," she said. "For our childer's sake I'll swally me tongue, but I won't put up with any guff, either."

"Fair enough," he said, clinking his bottle against hers.

"Good luck, Colin," she said. "If it means so much to yeh, I hope to God yeh win. If yeh don't, get drunk, get up tomorrow mornin', and go back to work. A real loser is someone who gets lost in the not winnin'. That's the why mostly the rich commit suicide."

"I didn't even write an acceptance speech," he said.

"Then it won't go unused."

The Town Car bearing a street kid from Queens and a tinker girl from Dublin sped toward the Academy Awards.

twenty-nine

Jesus Christ, Colin thought as the Town car pulled up outside the Shrine Auditorium in Downtown Los Angeles. *I'm in one of the cars pulling up to the fucking Oscars! I've seen this on TV a dozen times but never from this point of view. I have to remember how this looks from the inside out, instead of the outside in. Get that onto film.*

He'd never seen so many photographers before in his life. *The spectacle looks like one huge glittering diamond,* he thought. *Gotta get that Arctic glare into the shot. Like the blinding light coming through the door in* Close Encounters.

Crowds were cordoned behind wooden police barricades, hundreds of cops in riot gear keeping the paparazzi from stampeding the stars who paraded the red carpet to the front lobby.

"I told you not to tell anyone I was comin', wha'?" Gina said as Colin helped her out of the car. She laughed at her own joke. Colin smiled, offered his arm, and escorted Gina up the red carpet, following John Travolta and his wife, Kelly Preston. The flashbulbs exploded like a tropical lightning storm. TV reporters crushed around the star while cops tried to clear a path for the famous couple.

"I hope the Dublin warrant squad isn't watching," Gina said.

Colin looked at her and said, "Why?"

"I'm wearin' the evidence from a half-dozen open cases," she said, flicking her earrings and shaking her bracelets and bangles. She began to guffaw, catching the attention of several foreign photographers. Gina pushed out her swollen belly, crossed her eyes, and laughed wildly.

A crazed female autograph hound burst through the police barricade, groping at Travolta. Three cops grabbed her, wrestling her to the ground, briefly blocking Colin's and Gina's path.

"Who are you, luv?" asked a swarthy photographer with an Indian accent, leaning toward Gina.

"Rumor has it I'm me mother's daughter," she said. "Gina Furey, the one and only. But don't spread it around. And this is me fella, Colin Coyne, and he's nominated for best director."

The photographer snapped four quick pictures of Colin. His flash grabbed the attention of more shutterbugs. A dozen flashes popped in Colin's face, reporters asking the name of his film.

"It's a short film called *First Love, Last Love,*" Colin said.

The flashbulbs abruptly ceased.

"Why you waste my time?" the Indian photographer asked, turning and pushing his way back into the crowd. "Short film . . ."

"Feck off, yeh durty Arab, yeh," Gina said.

Colin grabbed Gina's hand and led her past the crowd surrounding Travolta and now Tom Hanks and Harvey Keitel and Michelle Pfeiffer.

"Hold on a wee minute," Gina said. "Bridie loves that Hanksie fella. Och, ever since the poor crayture turned mental her heart's gone out to 'im."

"Tom Hanks isn't *retarded,* Gina. Forrest Gump was a *role.* He was playing a character. We're guests here, nominees can't go around asking for autographs."

"Why not?" she said. "He can have mine, if he asks nice."

"Let's find our seats," he said.

"Och, it's great crack out here," Gina said, pulling herself free from Colin's hand.

Finally, a woman reporter broke from the herd, notebook in hand, approaching Gina. "Excuse me, ma'am," the reporter said. "Mind if I ask your name, a few questions?"

"I'm Gina Tinker," Gina said, smiling. "No autographs . . ."

"Any relation to Grant or Mark Tinker?"

"Ask them," she said. "Whoever they are, they prolly come from the scrubber side of the family, wha'?"

"I'm Alana Polk from W. A bunch of us were marveling at your dress," she said. "Can you tell us who the designer is?"

Colin smiled and looked at the hot sky, shaking his head.

"Actually, it was designed by a famous Irish designer named Granny Furey of Ballytara Designs," Gina said.

"Is there a name for the dress?" the reporter asked. "It's one of the most beautiful maternity dresses I've seen in years."

"Aye," Gina said. "This one is called Ask Me Ghee from the Up the Pole collection."

"Ask Magee?" the reporter intoned, scribbling notes as her photographer took pictures. "Updapole? Is that Gaelic?"

"Aye, it's Irish all right," Gina said. "And this is me fella, Colin Coyne, who's only bleedin' gorgeous and brilliant. He has a wee fil-um nominated this year but he's in the process of directing his first big picture house fil-um for Global Screen Pictures . . ."

Now there was a gathering of print reporters around Colin, a woman from *The Hollywood Reporter* and another from *Variety* and a couple of gossipmongers taking notes.

"What's the new film about?" asked *Variety*.

"A sort of dysfunctional Irish love story," Colin said. Gina looked at him, hand on her hip, leaning backwards.

"It better have a happy endin'," Gina said. "Or I'll bleedin' kill him."

The reporters laughed. Colin was impressed at how easily Gina worked the press.

"He was gonna cast me to play meself," she said. "But I was cheaper to keep barefoot and preggos in the kitchen."

Pens scribbled, tape recorders unspooled, cameras flashed. After the cops shuffled away the sobbing autograph hound, and checked credentials and cleared the way, a crew from *Entertainment Tonight* followed Colin and Gina into the lobby, asking how they met.

"Well, the clumsy sod lost his wallet," she said, inventing a scenario out of the smoggy air. "I found it. Inside was a receipt for the Shelbourne hotel, where he was stayin'. I felt sorry for the poor lad, it being Christmas week and all. I also saw his picture on the driving license and thought, 'Hmm, not bad, fer a Yank.' So I takes the wallet over to the Shelbourne to return it and it was love at first sight, or so he says."

The press laughed. Colin noticed James Thompson from Global Screen Pictures clocking the minor commotion. Thompson moved their way. *Oh, shit,* Colin thought. *Gina's on a fucking roll and here comes moneybags.* Thompson drifted by with his daughter on his arm. She was a beautiful, blond, blue-eyed Californian in a tight, shiny designer gown that made her hard body look like sculpted marble. Colin shook Thompson's hand and introduced him to Gina. She ignored his daughter, grabbed Thompson's arm, and dragged him in front of the TV camera.

"Are you the fella that signs the checks?" she asked.

"Well," said an amused Thompson, "I signed Colin Coyne to a contract."

"Then I'll have to have yeh over for a proper sheep's-head stew," she said, patting his flat belly. "They don't feed yeh movie chaps enough in this city. Everyone looks like they're cast for a film about Somalia. Instead of Oscars they should be giving out baked potatoes."

The press was having a ball with Gina. She was an earthy breath of fresh air amid the rehearsed casualness and hype. Most of her little performance would never be aired or see print, but the reporters enjoyed her.

Finally, as Colin and Gina made their way into the Auditorium, two foreign fashion reporters asked Gina about her dress while Thompson took Colin by the arm. "She's intriguing," he said. "Keep plugged into her, she's like the chick in your script. We might need her as a technical advisor. By the way, this is my daughter, Melissa. Melissa, this is Colin Coyne, *First Love, Last Love.*"

Colin extended his hand and took Melissa's soft warm hand in his. She looked in his eyes and smiled. "If you don't win tonight, there's no justice," she said, still holding his hand, longer than necessary. "I've watched your film at least fifty times. I'd love to know how you blocked and lit some of the shots. Maybe we can go over it some time, shot by shot."

"Anytime," Colin said, stealing a glance at Gina, who was still joking with the press.

"She with you?" Melissa asked.

"Yeah," Colin said.

"Your wife?" she asked.

"No," he said. "No, I'm not married."

"Ditto," she said.

"We better get to our seats," Thompson said.

"We'll talk later," Melissa said, looking back at Colin. Colin nodded and watched her walk up the aisle.

"Good luck, Colin," Thompson said. "Your Oscar could make the stockholders relax."

"What if I don't win?" Colin asked.

"What kind of attitude is that?" the executive asked, slapping Colin on the back before re-joining his daughter.

Colin watched Thompson approach a uniformed usher, who led them down the center aisle. *He looks like he's walking on a cushion of money,* Colin thought. *It's amazing the things people say when they have more money than you do.*

An usher now led Colin and Gina up to their seats, twenty rows back in the second tier of the plush auditorium. *The fuckin' cheap seats,* Colin thought. *In Madison Square Garden, this would be where hockey fans with no teeth would sit.* Colin looked around, unsure whether or not he was supposed to tip the usher. The only times he was ever escorted to a seat, he always tipped—at a Broadway show or a fight at the Garden. But at the Oscars? James Thompson hadn't tipped his usher. He watched the rest of the stars being seated and none of them tipped.

Cheap fucks, Colin thought. *Ask any waitress and she'll tell you the rich are stingy pricks. The usher is probably another struggling screenwriter still waiting for his fucking option check to arrive, like me. That's the other thing about these rich cocksuckers; they think everyone has so much money they ain't waiting for the check. Meanwhile, we're spending half the day waiting for the mailman, who usually has more loot in his pocket than most screenwriters in this town. Unless the mailman is also a struggling screenwriter, and spends all his disposable income on printer cartridges, computer repairs, reams of paper, Xeroxing, and stamps.*

He thanked the usher and pressed a five-dollar bill into his gloved hand. The usher looked at him and the five in amazement. "Thanks, dude," he said, and bounded away.

Their seats were smack in the middle of the row. The rows were wide with ample leg and passing room, but when they saw that Gina was pregnant five couples politely stood to let Gina and Colin pass to their seats.

As soon as they sat down, Gina said, "I have to have a slash."

"Christ," Colin said.

"I'm sure His mother had to piss when she was carrying Him, too," Gina said. "Even if He was but a skinny little Jew lad."

Colin's eyes popped open wide as an uneasy silence befell the people in the surrounding rows. *Holy fuck,* he thought.

The five couples rose again as Colin escorted Gina out of the long row, up the aisle, to where the toilets were located.

"Gina, I'm gonna tell you this once," Colin whispered. "Don't you ever, ever, *never* fucking *ever* talk disrespectfully about the Jews. Especially in Hollywood, where it's suicide."

"I never said anythin' disrespectful about the Jewish people," she said. "Me granda told us from we'uns that the Jews was fellow travelers. And don't tell me Jesus wasn't skinny. He couldn't've 'et much at his last supper to look that thin on the cross, could He?"

"Just keep your theological opinions to yourself tonight."

The non-televised categories of the Oscars, which included short film dramas, were starting to be announced from the stage. The technical awards came first and there was polite, distracted applause as each winner was announced. Colin led Gina up the corridor, searching for the ladies' room.

Feeling nervous, Colin slipped into the men's room to relieve himself. Walking out of a toilet stall was Frank Burston, his eyes bloodshot, taking short, desperate breaths. The smell of vomit wafted from the stall and Colin saw small speckles of puke on his patent-leather shoes. Burston walked toward the sinks and was startled to see Colin standing at the urinal.

"Hey, guy," Burston said, snapping into a casual California style.

"Hiya, Frank," Colin said.

Burston turned on the faucets and washed his face, scooping water into his mouth, gargling, and spitting it into the sink. He dried his face with paper towels, sprayed some breath freshener into his mouth, and combed his hair back.

"Jitters, huh?" Colin said.

"Not me," Burston said defensively. "Like I said, I don't care if I win or lose. It's already an honor to be here."

"That why you wore your speckled shoes?" Colin asked, zipping up and laughing.

"Fuck you, Coyne," Burston said, wiping his shoes with a wet towel.

"Hey, take a tranq, Frank," Colin said, rinsing his hands and drying them. "I wasn't goofing on you, we're all nervous."

"I finally saw your . . . *home* movie," Burston said. "If anyone should be nervous, it's you."

Colin shook his head, smiled and said, "Good luck, pally."

He slapped Burston on his shoulder and walked out into the corridor. Gina was standing with a woman, a Sharon Stone look alike, both bent in half having a good laugh. As Colin approached, the woman checked her watch and hurried back down the ramp to the lower tiers.

"Everybody loves me dress," Gina said.

Colin nodded and thought, *Kieran would say, "I love the lady who's wearing it."*

"Let's hope it brings you luck, so," she said.

"Who was that woman?" Colin asked, leading Gina toward the aisle. "She looked like . . ."

"Aye, that was Sharon Stone," Gina said matter of factly. "Great crack."

• • •

The five couples rose again as Colin and Gina made their way back to their seats. A man in the middle groaned as Gina passed, clearly annoyed at having to repeatedly pop up and down.

"Maybe you'd like to carry around a lump this large for an hour and see how many times yeh piss in yer pants, poxo," Gina said, staring directly into the man's face. He turned away, unable to hold her glare. His date looked at the floor, abashed. A few heads turned in the audience as the best special effects award was announced.

Colin urged Gina to her seat, but she wasn't finished with the man who'd groaned. "Yous test-tube babies is all alike," she said and then she was finished. She opened her handbag and took out a bottle of Guinness and popped the lid with a bottle opener.

Colin dropped his head into his right hand and sagged as Billy Crystal, the emcee, announced the short-film category.

"Here's luck and looking up yer hole," Gina said, gulping the Guinness. More heads turned, watching Gina drink the black beer. Colin's palms dampened, his mouth parching over Gina's behavior. And over the upcoming award, which Thompson had made seem so vital.

"Have you ever heard of fetal alcohol syndrome?" said a tight-faced middle-aged woman sitting in a row in front of them.

"Is that what happened to yeh?" Gina said, wiping her mouth. "Poor t'ing, that explains it. Born with your nose in yer arse. Pity all them face-lifts couldn't get it out."

The reddening woman blinked twice, made a motion to speak, but no words formed. She turned around, astonished, as a murmur spread through the section like a small tremor. Colin snatched Gina's arm and asked her to please be quiet.

"I told yeh I'd take no guff from any of these'ns," Gina said. "Mice posing as minks, turnips dressed like tulips."

Billy Crystal named the five nominated short films and the directors, mentioning Colin Coyne last. Gina stuffed the bottle between her legs and applauded loudly, stuck her fingers in her mouth, and whistled, the way she always had for her pony or her dog.

"That's me fella!" Gina shouted through megaphoned hands,

and snickering broke out in the audience. Colin sat with his forehead in both hands, shielding his face from view.

"Holy shit," he mumbled.

"Sober up, Saint Patrick's Day was last month, lass," Billy Crystal quipped. The crowd laughed again.

There was a brief pause at the presenter's pulpit, where the actor Jeff Goldblum, a former short-film Oscar nominee, awaited the envelope. It finally came. Goldblum cracked open the envelope.

"And the winner for best short film is," he said, removing the card from the envelope, "Frank Burston, for *Green Eyes.*"

The applause was restrained. Frank Burston paraded down the aisle, beaming as he climbed the steps.

"Fix," Gina said loud enough for those around her to hear.

Colin sat with his head in his hands as Frank Burston read a five-minute speech thanking everyone from D. W. Griffith to Spielberg, with stops in between for his mother and father, his agent, his UCLA teachers, his fiancée Nancy, and finally the other talented directors he'd beaten out.

In those five agonizingly long minutes, as Frank Burston spoke, Colin felt the sweat drool down his arms and chest. His head pounded. His stomach flopped. He felt dirty under the nails. His breath was short and his palms grew spongy. *I'm a fucking loser,* he thought. *It's official now. All the years of dreaming, my great ambitions, my magic moment in the spotlight, all vanished with the loss to a pompous rich kid. All the guys back in Grogan's will be disappointed. My brothers will be sad for me, or getting their balls busted by the humps who always root against neighborhood guys who dare to be different, who try to break through the green ceiling. My agent, Bonnie Corbet, will put on a brave face. The old man will ask what it means "cabbage-wise." Thompson and the Global Screen people will probably patronize me, say it doesn't matter. But it will matter. Burston'll be the flavor of the fuckin' month. And a month in Hollywood is a long time.*

"Gina, let's go home," Colin whispered as Billy Crystal announced the best short documentary category.

"Home my ghee, we have tickets to a ball."

"I can't sit through this whole show," he said.

"Stop acting like a loser and start acting like a man," she said. "I didn't win anythin' either and I'm not complaining."

She passed him the bottle of Guinness and he sat up. No one was looking at him. He took a long gulp, hoping to wash down the metallic taste of losing. He spotted the three other losers in his category sitting in the crowd, putting on phony smile-button faces. Then he spotted Burston, sitting with his gleaming Oscar, his fiancée next to him, kissing his face and then the Oscar.

"I'll be right back," Colin said, handing her the Guinness.

"Aye," Gina said as Colin made the five couples rise again while he moved out of the row and down the aisle. He went up to Frank Burston and held out his hand.

"Congratulations, Frank," Colin said.

Burston shook his hand vigorously, holding the Oscar in his left hand. "Thanks, Colin," he said. "If it means anything to you, yours was the film I was so terrified of. I'm sorry for what I said upstairs. Jitters."

"It's okay," Colin said.

They both laughed and Colin returned to his seat.

The Governor's ball was one giant audition. A live band played soft rock under a bright April moon. Celebrities danced. Oscar winners sauntered through the crowd, carrying their statuettes, drinking champagne, hugging and kissing and talking deals. Gina dragged Colin onto the dance floor for two dances, and even in her swollen condition could outdance half the crowd.

Colin watched Frank Burston shooting the breeze with a bunch of producers and writers near the bar. His fiancée, Nancy, a slim redhead wearing a big diamond engagement ring, grabbed his Oscar and moved through the crowd like a mother showing off a newborn baby. Gina lit a cigarette and took a sip of champagne, watching Nancy network in the crowd.

"State of her, and the price of buh'er," Gina said, watching Nancy pose for pictures with her boyfriend's Oscar. "Water dressed up."

"An Oscar gives you bragging rights," Colin said, sipping a beer. "I wish I was bringing one home."

"Yeh should mingle," Gina said. "Mix and match, meet some of these gobshites."

"I don't want to leave you here alone," he said.

"Och, g'wan," she said. "I'll be all right. I have to go to the loo to freshen up. I'm not feeling the best. But you go and meet people, push yer face and yer arse will folly."

Gina rose, grabbing her shoulder bag and waddling off toward the ladies' room. Colin approached Burston again, who introduced him to a few of the producers he was speaking to. They told him they hadn't seen his film yet, but had it on their list. A producer named Mark Johnson asked what he was doing and Colin told him about his deal with Global Screen.

"Really?" said Burston, who nodded and scoured the crowd.

Colin saw a pair of other nominees from his category and he excused himself to go and commiserate. *Use a hand-held camera in a scene like this,* Colin thought, thinking of his movie again. *Moving through the crowd of celebs seeing faces, cameos, ad-libs, Oscars in fists.*

Colin yakked with two young directors who said they loved his movie. He told them how much he liked theirs; they compared notes on new projects.

Colin spotted James Thompson, standing with his daughter, Melissa. *What a fucking body,* he thought. *What a prick I am gaping at her while Gina's in the bathroom. Fuck it, there's nothing wrong with looking. Observing is what I do.*

He drifted away from the two young directors, zigzagging through the crowd, imagining himself with a hand-held camera. By the time Colin reached him, Thompson was deep in discussion with Frank Burston. Melissa was standing at his side, half-listening, sipping a glass of champagne. Melissa broke away from her father when she spotted Colin and walked to him, her luxuriant perfume preceding her.

"Sorry you didn't win," she said.

"No big deal," he said.

She pushed a slip of paper into his breast pocket. "Call me," she said. He nodded.

"Hey, Colin, how's it going?" Thompson said, shaking Colin's hand and checking his watch on his left wrist for the time. "Wait'll next year, huh? Listen, I was just discussing something with Frank here and then I have to run to Dani Jansen's house. Call the office in the morning."

Colin nodded, knowing if he'd won he would have been invited to Jansen's party, the hottest A-list Oscar bash in town.

"You won't miss much," Melissa said. Colin nodded as he watched Thompson hand Burston a business card.

"Load of horseshit artists standing around congratulating each other," she said.

Thompson took Melissa by the arm. "We better go, honey," he said, leading her away.

Colin watched them leave the ballroom and then turned to find Gina at his side, a brilliant white apparition in a dark moment. She took Colin by the arm. "I'm not feeling the best," she said. "Would yeh mind terrible if we went home?"

"Love to," Colin said.

As they left the governor's ball, Colin's eye focused on faces in the crowd. *Look at them,* he thought. *From Kieran's POV I'll shoot adoring fans, grubby photographers, assorted creeps, bored cops, steroidian bodyguards, chain-smoking limo drivers, bims on the make. I'll get all of it into my film. Then, like Arnold says, I'll be back. This time as a winner.*

Colin's reverie was snapped as he heard a commotion behind them. A hysterical woman was yelling at the top of her lungs from inside the ladies' room.

"Some of these young wans can't hold their drink atall," Gina said as they descended the steps and climbed into the backseat of their hired Town Car, which slowly pulled away.

"I told yeh as long as yeh have me, you'll never go home empty-handed," Gina said. He kissed her.

I'll be back, he thought.

thirty

May 1

Colin awoke early the next morning and walked through the dining room toward the kitchen to get a drink of ice water. He stopped at the front door and grabbed the *Los Angeles Times* from the doorstep. His eyes were still sticky with sleep so he thought he'd only imagined what he'd seen standing on the dining-room table. After lifting the paper, he turned and stood as still as the golden statue on the table, the morning sun angling through a window glinting off its shiny face.

"Holy shit," he whispered.

He walked slowly across the living room, rubbed his eyes, and shook his head.

He dropped the newspaper on the tabletop and lifted the Oscar. He hefted its glorious weight and rubbed his fingers over the smooth, polished contours. His heart started pounding.

"Gina," he said in a low voice, slowly sitting in a chair at the table. Then he noticed a small story on the front page of the *Times*: OSCAR STOLEN AT GOVERNOR'S BALL.

"GINA!"

He grabbed the Oscar and hurried through the bedroom door.

"Wha'?" came Gina's muffled voice.

"You stole Burston's Oscar," he said, too astonished for anger.

"Aye."

"This is a fucking disaster, Gina," he said.

"I promised yeh wouldn't go home empty-handed."

"They'll suspect me right away."

"So wha'? *You* didn't nick it, *I* did. That Frank fella's gobshite girlfriend was showing it off to everyone in the ladies' jacks like she'd just given birth to the Christ child," she said. "She put it down on the sink to have a slash. And I figured you deserved it more than the other gobshite, so I put it under me dress. There was tons of room. Thought it'd go good on yer desk, like."

"You *win* Oscars, Gina," Colin shouted, finally losing his cool. "You don't *steal* them!"

Brianna began to cry from her bedroom and Gina got up.

"Yeh ungrateful swine, yeh," she said, waddling past Colin to Brianna's room. "I took it for you, not meself, now yer rearin' and shoutin' and scarin' me child. Some thanks."

"Gina, you don't seem to understand . . ."

"No, I feckin' don't understand all the fascination with a little toy statue that grown-ups make such a fuss about," she said, lifting Brianna into her arms with a grunt. "It's all a bunch of shite. Nuthin' to do with the price of bread and buh'er. Nothin' to do with nobody else but a few pig's melts what thinks they're important because they all gets together to make believe they're somebody else on a big screen. 'Hi, what do you do for a livin'?' 'Me, oh, I spend me life pretending I'm not me.' 'That's great, here's a feckin' award, a statue to go along wit' yer millions for not bein' you and for pretendin' to be somebody else. There yeh are, now, here's an Oscar for yeh.' Jaysus, Colin Coyne, where's the meat-and-potatoes, the hammer-and-nail, in that?"

"It's how your peers acknowledge their appreciation for your *work*," Colin said.

"I have no patience for all this shite. I have one child to raise and another to hatch. Real-life little childer, more important than some puny fake statue named feckin' Oscar. Talk about believin' in little people and fairies. Cop on, man. Yer in this fairy-tale city less than a month and already yer livin' in a dream world. Fine for you, maybe. But I've got me eyes wide open. Every mornin' I keep lookin' at that front door and I think about walkin' out and shiftin' straight to the airport and never turnin' back. So don't tell me about a silly statue named Oscar."

Colin sat staring at her. There was nothing left to say.

Later that day, Colin wiped the Oscar clean of fingerprints, wrapped it in newspaper, packed it in a box, and mailed it anonymously to the Academy. They'd return it to Frank Burston.

thirty-one

Over the next week, Colin tried to get James Thompson on the phone five times, but he was repeatedly told the Global Screen executive was on another call, in a meeting, or out of the office. Colin was not surprised. *If I'd won the Oscar,* he thought, *Thompson would have taken my call. He'd be calling me. I didn't win, so now I have to prove I'm not a loser.*

He Federal Expressed his completed treatment to Bonnie Corbet, who forwarded it to Thompson. Global Screen told Bonnie the treatment was great and gave Colin the green light to go to the next step, a first-draft screenplay.

May 10

Colin received another fifteen thousand dollars from Global, minus ten percent for his agent, opened a Los Angeles bank account with the $13,500, and began work on the script as Gina entered her fifth month of pregnancy.

The booze and the nicotine are no longer a joke, he thought. *Instead of going to a doctor, she visits Saint Bonaventure's church, lights a candle every morning, leaves a folded dollar bill in the collection box, and takes a candle home. Like she did that day at Saint Brendan's in Dublin.*

"I'm not knocking you going to church," Colin said as he ate a bowl of raisin bran after bringing in the mail on the seventeenth straight sunny day, without a drop of rain. "Lighting candles, doing the abracadabra with the saints, but don't you think it's about time you saw a goddamned obstetrician? A baby doctor?"

"What's he gonna do?" she asked. "Tell me I'm pregnant? Or that the sun is shining? I'm up the pole and the sun shines every feckin' day in this monotonous penal colony. I'd give my left diddy for a day of Dublin rain."

"You need to make sure you and the baby are okay," he said.

"Save yer money," she said, squirming on the couch. "Lightin'
candles is cheaper and more reliable than doctors."

"I'm covered by the Writers Guild health plan and the Directors
Guild now."

"I don't want their charity," she said.

"It isn't charity," he said, as he opened the phone bill and plopped
into a chair.

"Maybe I should ask for some," he said, in a low, restrained voice.
"Gina, here's the new phone bill. It's twelve hundred and thirty-six
dollars and . . ."

"And so?"

"And so, that's fucking ridiculous," Colin said. "Dozens of collect calls from Ireland! Some *two hours* long . . ."

"I need a bit of feckin' crack," she said. "I'm locked up here like
a zoo animal. Everywhere yeh go you have to drive. My only friend,
Moira, bless her soul, is sufferin' from emphysema, which she's convinced she got from the L.A. smog. She had to quit her job and can't
even go out for a jar. Yer locked up in that room, doin' yer bit a
scribblin' by day and by night. I'm out here gapin' at the hopeless
Yank telly, watchin' meself get fatter than a parson's pig, the sweat
comin' out of me like a harvest mule. And now you want to cut off
me one connection to the life I love . . ."

"Jesus Christ, a few minutes on the line is fine. Hi, how are ya,
how's the fuckin' goat, small talk. But Gina, twelve hun . . ."

He stopped as he saw a tear leak from Gina's left eye, cutting
down her tanned cheek like a silver wound. She quickly wiped it off,
her strong face fractured in sadness, turning away from him.

"I'm the one should be crying here," he said. "I have to pay this
bill, for chrissakes."

"I'm a very unhappy girl," she said, weeping.

Brianna walked out of her room, saw her mother crying, and she
started to bawl. *Jesus Christ,* he thought. *Crying in fucking stereo.*

"Come on, huh," Colin said. "Don't say that. Don't cry."

He sat next to her on the couch, wrapping his arms around her.
Brianna climbed on her lap. *Like a godamned wake here,* he
thought. Gina felt warm and soft in his embrace, so much gentler

than her usually tough demeanor. He wiped her tears. Kissed her eyes, her cheekbones, her lips.

"I'm sorry," she said. "I'm acting the schoolgirl . . ."

"No," he said. "You're just pregnant and a little nuts. You're entitled to a tear or two, but Jesus Christ, go easy on the phone."

"Aye, I'll cut down," she said.

"And please see a damn doctor?" he asked, softly.

"Back home, we almost never see a doctor," Gina said. "But I'll give it a try."

May 12

The first thing the doctor said was, "You must stop smoking. Immediately."

"But I only smoke English fags, not these American yokes," Gina explained. "I rip off the cork tip to avoid the chemicals."

The doctor, a woman in her fifties named Gagliardi, turned to Colin and said, "Is she from another country or another dimension?"

Colin shrugged. "Both."

The second thing the doctor said was, "You also must stop drinking alcohol, immediately."

"Och, I just have me bottle of stout," Gina said. "Doctors in Ireland prescribe it for pregnant women."

"Except for one glass of beer after an amniocentesis, Dr. Frankenstein wouldn't prescribe alcohol to a pregnant woman," Dr. Gagliardi said. "That's a demented wives' tale."

She reached into a bookcase, took out a medical magazine, and opened it to some gruesome pictures of deformed children born with fetal alcohol syndrome. Cyclopses, monsters, babies without mouths, missing ears, with shortened or missing limbs.

"Ireland has one of the highest rates of FAS in western Europe," Dr. Gagliardi said. "I don't care if you're drinking French vanilla extract, Russian vodka, Japanese sake, or Guinness stout. Alcohol is alcohol. It's a ferocious drug, can turn fetuses into monsters. And smoking can cause the baby to be born with emphysema or heart problems. Is that clear, Gina? You are threatening the life of your baby. Am I getting through?"

"Aye, but tell us, luv, what sort of a name is Gagliardi?" Gina asked.

"Italian," the doctor said, looking to Colin for help. He just raised his eyebrows.

"Do you know a fella name of Gino Barilla?" Gina asked. "He's in the Mafia. He's me da."

Dr. Gagliardi took a deep inhale and let it out slowly.

"Amazingly, as far as I can tell, without an amnio, you and the baby are doing fine," she said. "And I don't know anyone in the Mafia. No."

They left the doctor's office and walked to the car parked on Ventura Boulevard. "I told you she'd be useless," Gina said, pulling a pack of Dunhills from her pocketbook. Colin snatched the cigarettes away from her, and crumpled them in his hands.

"What the feck do yeh think yer doin'?" she said.

"That child in your womb is as much mine as it is yours," he said. "I won't let you destroy its little heart and lungs."

"Is that a fact?" she said. "Well, if it's as much yours as mine, then let's see yeh carry the big lump of shite for the next four months."

Colin broke up laughing, but Gina was fuming, clutching her swollen belly.

"What's so funny?" she demanded, finally smiling herself.

"You're convinced it's a boy, aren't you?"

"'Course it's a boy," she said. "What makes you say that?"

"You wouldn't have called a little girl a lump of shite."

"Aye," she said. "Yer right."

"If you give up the smokes and the drink, I'll stop drinking."

"Christ, I don't know if I can live without me bottle of stout and a fag. I haven't got anything else to remind me of home."

"As soon as I'm done with the script it'll get better," Colin said. "Keep in mind, part of this film will be shot in Ireland."

"Och, bless the day," she said.

Over the next three weeks, Colin enlisted Caitlin to baby-sit at least one night during the weekend so that he could take Gina out to a movie or a Mexican meal. The waiters in El Caramba, a local Mexican restaurant, loved watching Gina eat chicken tacos; even the cook came out to watch. These nights out cheered Gina up, gave her a chance to get dressed up and to see new faces. But her craving for cigarettes and beer made her eat all the more.

By the beginning of June, Gina was depressed by her weight. Colin was enraged by the size of the phone bill, which had climbed to fourteen hundred dollars, mostly from collect calls from her cousins in the pubs of Dublin.

The script was half written and there were only three weeks until the deadline.

June 10

Colin's brother Jack passed through Los Angeles and came out to Colin and Gina's for dinner. Jack arrived with two bottles of wine and a date named Barb. Barb was an attorney for the California Brew-and-Moo franchise association. She was a pretty but professional-looking dark-haired woman from Marin County.

Dinner went fine until Jack opened the wine and poured glasses for everyone but Gina.

"I'm not drinking either, Jack," Colin said.

"Jeez, that's too bad, this is a lovely burgundy," Jack said. "You on the wagon until the script's finished?"

"Until the baby's finished," Gina said, sipping club soda.

Jack told them that Barb's parents had several hundred acres of land up in northern California and that they were going to visit the spread together before he went back to New York.

"Hundreds of acres," Gina said. "God, they must have a big herd."

"Herd?" Barb said.

"Cattle," Gina said. "Surely they have cattle."

"No," Barb laughed. "My father doesn't even drink milk, never mind own a cow."

"What's he do with all that land?" Gina asked.

Barb shrugged, looked to Jack. "He just . . . owns it."

"And he doesn't do anythin' with it?" Gina asked.

"It's a good investment," Barb said.

"Does it have water on it?" Gina asked.

"Absolutely," Barb said, beaming. "A marvelous river runs through the land and . . ."

"The river has fish, I take it," Gina said.

"Lots, I hear, but my father's too busy to fish," Barb said.

"When you go up there next," Gina said, waving a fork with a square of lamb on the end of it, "tell your father for me that his river would die without fish. The same goes for his land without cattle, because cattle are the salmon of the field."

Barb blinked and Jack and Colin looked at each other.

"I like that," Jack said.

"I'll tell my father that," Barb said.

"I'm stealing that line," Colin said, writing it down on scrap of paper.

Jack and Barb finished the first bottle of wine and Jack opened the second bottle when dinner was almost over.

"Sure you won't have even one glass, Col?" Jack asked.

"Nah," Colin said, although he'd have loved one. "We're pregnant, bro."

"Jesus, that's what I call solidarity," Jack said. "Very California, and very new-century of you."

"I'll have yeh know it was his idea, not mine," Gina said, waving her fork for emphasis. "If I had my way, I'd be having a bottle of stout right now."

"Yeah, and there'd be a pony, a goat, and a covered wagon on the lawn," Jack said.

Barb broke up laughing. Colin knew this touched a raw nerve in Gina, but remained silent. Gina looked at them all, nodded, and took a sip of club soda.

"You must love all the luxuries of L.A. after a life like that, Gina," Barb said, swallowing some lamb and sipping her wine.

"Actually, the lamb yer eatin' was raised right in that back garden," Gina said, taking a mouthful of lamb and chewing. "Wee thing's name was Jodie, after Jodie Foster. Lovely baby spring lamb, she was, too, but there was company comin' and I wanted somethin' special for yer tay. Baby lamb's the best eatin' yeh can get 'cause they haven't been walkin' the earth long enough to get muscles in their wee, wobbly legs. Still suckling the mammy, milk-fed, and that's why that lamb is so tender, all juicy baby flesh. Back home we calls it leg o' lamb of Jaysus."

She cut her knife through a medallion of lamb and lifted it; the juices dripped out of it. Barb watched Gina, her face frozen in horror as Colin sat back and Jack blinked silently.

"Matter of fact, Gina used that same steak knife you're using, Barb," Colin said, joining the riff.

"Aye, that's right but this wee baby lamb wasn't silent atall," Gina said, looking at the meat on her fork. "It made an awful screamin' racket when I cut its throat yesterday afternoon. They know when they're 'bout to be slaughtered, yeh know, and they scream for their mammies. Its mother was tethered on a rope by the tree in the rear of the garden, screamin' and kickin' and cryin' bloody murder as well as I kilt her babby. I severed its head and put it in the freezer for a proper stew during the week. Then I hung up the carcass and let it bleed itself dry overnight afore I skinned the wee crayture this mornin'. Yeh can always tell when it'll be tender when the flies flock to it in swarms. Nothing like a fresh bit a baby lamb. Every bite makes you want to say baaaahhh . . ."

Barb looked at Jack and down at her plate. Jack cocked his head and gazed at Colin in mid-chew. Colin cut another piece of lamb, nodded, and shrugged.

Barb excused herself and hurried into the bathroom and Colin heard the faucets turn on and the bowl flush at the same time.

"Time for dessert," Gina said.

She walked splay-footed into the kitchen to prepare the dessert, standing at the kitchen counter within earshot of the dining room.

"How goes life out here, bro?" Jack asked, sipping his wine.

"Not bad," Colin said. "But I always seem to be pinching pennies. Rent on a whole house, two cars, phone, baby-sitters."

"That's married life, babes," Jack said. "I warned ya . . ."

"Yeah, when you have to put food in the mouths and shoes on the feet of two more people, it adds up," Colin said.

Gina stormed out of the kitchen carrying a bowl of fresh fruit salad and tossed it over Colin's head. Colin jumped up. Shocked. Jack leaped from his chair in astonishment, backing away. Barb came out of the bathroom looking a paler shade of white than when she'd entered. She froze when she saw Colin dripping with watermelon and pineapple and cantaloupe sections, his hair matted with fruit and juice.

"What the fuck's your problem?" Colin asked, embarrassed and angered, grabbing a handful of the fruit from his head and flinging it at Gina. It spattered on her face and against the far wall of the dining room.

Gina stalked the room, brandishing the knife she'd been using to cut up the fruit salad, her eyes dilated in fury. "No one ever put food in the mouth or shoes on the feet of Gina Furey!" she screamed, seething, wiping her face with the back of her knife hand. "Do yeh feckin' hear me? Not me or me child, righ'? When I met yeh I had all the feckin' food I could eat and all the shoes I could ever wear. My problem was I didn't feckin' use a pair of them to run the other way when I saw yeh comin'."

"Calm the fuck down, Gina," Colin said. "Jesus Christ. It was a figure of speech. Put the goddamned knife down."

Gina jabbed the air in front of her as Colin circled the table to avoid her. Jack backed away and Barb rushed toward the door.

"I'm so outta here I'm already gone," Barb shouted.

"No one ever put feckin' shoes on Gina Furey's feet!" she screamed.

Barb clutched her pocketbook and Jack's arm. "Jack, please," she said in a panic.

"You gonna be okay, Col?" Jack asked.

"Fine, Jack," Colin said, waving him out. "Go ahead. I'll talk to you later."

"Who the feck do yeh t'ink yeh are, tellin' people yeh put shoes on my feckin' feet?" Gina demanded, pointing at her feet with the point of the knife.

"You need serious fucking help," Colin said, embarrassed, as he kept the table between him and Gina.

Barb was yanking Jack out the door, terrified.

"I'm goin', Col," Jack said. "Sure you're okay?"

"Fuck off," Gina snapped at Jack, jamming the knife into the tabletop, watching it twang and vibrate back and forth.

Colin grabbed the handle of the knife. "I'll call you at the hotel later."

Jack left with Barb and Colin stood staring at Gina.

"You're a sick fuck, know that?" Colin said.

"Who the feck do you and your high and mighty brother think yiz are?" she asked. "Makin' fun of me and my family. Where and what I came from. I'll tell yeh what I had before I met yeh that I don't have now! A feckin' *life!* Living with you is like a slow feckin' poison. I die a little more every single day in this country, trapped under the same roof with you, listenin' to yeh typin' your silly make-believe stories, which is what yeh have instead of a real life."

"I'm sick and tired of you always running me down," Colin said. "I work my balls off every day. I'm trying to write us a future and trying to keep you fucking happy at the same time. I'm not an entertainment director or your court jester, you know. My job isn't to juggle balls to make you laugh. You're always knocking what I do for a living. Well, what the fuck do *you* do? I met you picking my fucking pocket. Everyone in your family is a cheap thief or a two-bit hustler. You have talent, you can sing, you have a flair for fashion design, but you shit on those gifts because it takes hard, honest work to nurture talent and turn it into a career. Instead, your full-time job is to feel sorry for yourself and break my fucking balls. Well, I'm not taking it anymore. Go ahead. Try to leave. I'll go into family court and stop you from leaving this country while you're carrying my baby."

Gina ran from the dining area to the kitchen, a deep, savage wail coming from a dungeon within. She yanked the knife drawer open. The drawer came off its rollers, crashed to the floor, spilling the various knifes in a clattering racket. She bent among the assorted cutlery and chose a small boning knife and rushed back into the dining area. This time, Colin defiantly stood his ground and without compunction she jabbed the point of the knife into his shoulder, a small, nasty little puncture. She thrust her jaw out, awaiting retaliation.

"I'll feckin' kill yeh if yeh try to hold me prisoner," she screamed, holding the bloodied knife in front of her swollen belly, instinctively protecting the unborn child. "I'll feckin' kill yeh, I will."

Colin strode to the bathroom and tore his shirt off and saw the deep purplish puncture on his right shoulder, pulsing blood.

"Fuckin' sicko," he screamed. Now Brianna was awake and frantically running around Gina's legs. Colin poured peroxide over the bleeding wound and pressed a towel against it.

Gina threw her shoulder into the door to Colin's office, popping the lock and falling into the room with the forward motion. Brianna held her own ears, screaming and stamping her bare feet. Gina pushed herself to her feet, gripped the knife with two hands, and plunged the blade into the top of the closed laptop computer. "Yeh feckin' pathetic little word farmer, yeh," she screamed.

She rocked the blade out of the gouge in the plastic lid of the computer and stabbed it again and again. She lifted the small machine over her head as Colin rushed in, bare chested, holding the bloody towel to his shoulder. "Gina, no!" he pleaded.

"Shoes on me feckin' feet," she screamed as she smashed the laptop onto the floor. "Food in me feckin' mouth! No one, not me mammy, not me feckin' da I never knew, not me granny, not the courts or the Borstal or the governesses in the orphanages, no one ever put shoes on my fuckin' feet, food in my mouth! Gina Furey fends for herself and her child. I need no one! Hear me? I feckin' need no one!"

Neighbors were banging on the door now as Gina plopped onto her butt on the floor, sobbing, picking up an hysterical Brianna and rocking her in her arms, smothering her against her swollen breasts.

After assuring neighbors that everything was all right, Colin drove to North Hollywood Hospital for five stitches in his shoulder. *This is how a man is driven to murder,* he thought, as he drove down Ventura Boulevard. *Maybe Kieran thinks about killing this crazy bitch. Shit, I could kill her tonight and not lose sleep. But, of course, that was insanity, that would make Kieran worse than her. Besides, he'd be killing the mother of his own kid. I gotta write this fucking knife scene into the script.*

He'd finally finished a first draft of the script. He was supposed to turn it in the next day. Luckily, he had copied all his work onto computer disks as he went along, always keeping one disk in the glove compartment of his car in case the house ever caught fire.

He spent all night in the emergency room waiting to be stitched up. He took a notebook, which he always kept in the car, and sketched out the stabbing scene as a close to the second act. *It's like it was destined to happen because it was missing from the script,* he thought. *The blade is mightier than the pen.* He would rent a new laptop and plug the scene into the script in the morning. He also knew that this scene would mean the third and final act would eventually have to change again. He was almost certain those changes would present themselves from the dynamics of real life.

On the drive back from the hospital in the early morning, he was still furious. All night, he had tried to see the situation from Gina's point of view.

For three months, he'd thought about nothing but how hard he had it. How hard it was to work at home with a screaming toddler and a pregnant woman in the house. How hard it was to take on all this sudden responsibility. How hard the future looked, saddled with two kids at age twenty-five.

He'd never stopped to think how life looked while standing in Gina's shoes, the shoes he'd told Jack he'd put on her feet. She was an illegal in what might be the strangest of all the big cities of a vast foreign country. She'd left behind an entirely different life and was looking ahead to years of separation from her family. *I have my work,* he thought, *my career, and I'm living in my own country.*

Gina was more than a fish out of water. She was like a live lobster, with claws bound, sitting in a tank, waiting her turn in the pot of boiling water.

If she'd really wanted to kill me, he reasoned, *she easily could have.* Instead, she wounded him. She wanted to draw blood to let him know how wounded she was. She took it out on the thing she believed he cared about more than her—his work. The computer, a symbol of his livelihood. Jack would say that it was an attack by the untalented on the talented. That was probably also true.

Whatever the shrinks might call it, Colin knew it was the act of a scared, trapped woman unleashing all her frustrations.

Her alienation was enough to make anyone crack, he thought.

But as he got closer to home, to the scene of the crime, he decided that was all rationalization. *Bullshit,* he thought. *You're a fucking fool. The woman is a screwball. Dangerous. Scary. If she's capable of stabbing me, what could she do to Brianna? Or the new baby? I should call the cops and have her arrested. But then who takes care of Brianna? My kid will be born in an INS lockup. Gina will be deported as an undesirable, and my kid, a baby I swore to my mother I'd never abandon, will go back with her and be lost forever in a fucking covered wagon on the back roads of Ireland. Like it or not, I gotta stick this out until the baby is born. Then, if necessary, I can drag Gina into court and have a custody hearing.*

When he walked into the quiet house, Gina was sitting on the bed, fully clothed, her suitcases packed. Brianna was asleep beside her, her breathing fitful from the earlier hysteria.

"I shouldn't have hurt you," she said in a very soft voice.

"The doctor gives me five, maybe six decades to live."

"I hope so," she said. "I want our boy to have his father. A good man yeh are, too. You've been very good to me and Brianna, so. I had no right smashing your typin' machine up like that. Can't even blame it on the divil drink."

He stood silently.

"I never felt so small in my life till I come here," she said. "I stood down on the beach in Santa Monica last week, surrounded by strangers, looking out at the ocean, a different ocean than the one in Ireland, and I just felt like a little insignificant jot in a big huge bewk. I don't want to be a wee jot, Colin. I want to be me, *alive,* the way I was back home. Here, I feel dead. It's why I lashed out, I suppose."

She's incapable of saying the word "sorry," he thought. *Fuck it, let her go.*

"When are you leaving?"

"Today . . . but I want you to stop me," she said. "And I don't want you to stop me at the same time. I'll go home now, two kids, no man, on the dole. It's the wrong thing to do to the kids, an unhappy mother is awful for them as well. I'd miss you madly, as well. I didn't think I would until I closed the suitcase and snapped the locks. It sounded like a cell door closing. The thought of life without yeh made me shiver with the cold. Wantin' yeh that much also scares me. Jaysus, I don't know what I want. I'd love to see me cousins here in Los Angeles."

Jesus Christ, he thought. *What an insane but fresh idea. It's the third act. Fuck her, she stabbed me. Now I'll get even by putting her under the microscope with one of her cousins. Exploit the shit out of this, like a laboratory experiment. Truffaut's* The Wild Child *times two. Imagine the twisted possibilities in the next draft. You really couldn't make this shit up. The current draft ends with Kieran and Gina parting but agreeing to share the upbringing of the kids. It's a Hollywood cop-out. Why not roll the dice and see how this really plays out? That's what Kieran would do, wouldn't he? See how it really ends? Let art imitate life.*

"I'm turning in my first-draft script today," he said. "I'll have a few weeks free while they read it, make their notes, before I have to do the rewrite. With the few extra bucks, I was thinking, how about you fly over one of your cousins?"

"You'd do that?" Gina said, looking at him oddly.

"The airfare'll probably be cheaper than the phone bill."

"Yer as daft as me."

"Aye," he said.

thirty-two

July 2

"I can't understand why she would fly a charter flight on Sphere Airlines instead of using the Aer Lingus ticket I bought for her," Colin said as they waited in the grubby charter terminal of LAX for Bridie to arrive from Ireland.

"She said she was bringing a surprise," Gina said. "It's probably too large to carry on an ordinary plane."

"That doesn't make any sense," Colin said. "Unless she's bringing the pony and the goat." He figured Bridie took the Aer Lingus ticket, cashed it in, bought a cheapo charter ticket, and pocketed the difference.

The flight was two hours late and had been on the ground for more than ninety minutes as passengers cleared immigration and customs. In the charter terminal, the steerage of air travel, the poor, mostly non-Caucasian tourists were all treated like refugees.

It was another blistering Los Angeles day of drought. Gina was in her seventh month of pregnancy. Mercifully, Bridie was coming without her own toddler because it was only a two-week trip and she said she wanted to spend the time helping Gina, who, at 160 pounds, thirty of them pure chicken taco, was having a hard time doing anything in the southern California heat. Bridie could help with Brianna, the house chores, and, most important, could keep Gina happy. Dr. Gagliardi had told Colin that an expectant mother's moods greatly affect the health of the unborn child.

Global Screen Pictures acknowledged receipt of Colin's finished first draft and, three weeks later, an eighteen-thousand-dollar check arrived. His accountant warned him that since he was being paid through his private corporation, there was no withholding tax, so he should put at least six thousand in the bank for the IRS.

Colin was brand new to large sums of money and what he saw in the bank he tended to spend. He didn't have anything left from the first check.

"It's as close as a priest to an altar boy in here," Gina said, fanning herself with a Taco Bell carton.

The charter terminal was not air-conditioned and Gina was sagging with the heat. Mobs of Third World people packed the waiting area, most awaiting relatives from South America and Asia. Brianna refused to sit in her stroller any longer. "Daddy, sit on your shoulders, ple-uz," she asked. "I big girl now."

Colin and Brianna had grown very close over the months. He proudly looked over at her, dressed in her beautiful yellow sundress, which Gina had embroidered in silk thread with the design of a family of Irish travelers in a covered wagon and a piebald pony. Her red hair hung in cylindrical curls and Gina had placed real emerald earrings on her pierced ears. He hoisted her onto his sweaty neck. *Kid's gaining weight,* he thought. *It's her American diet.*

Brianna leaned down and kissed Colin on the top of his head and started putting her sticky hands over his eyes, leaning down to see him in a clammy game of peekaboo.

"Daddy, I want a Coke," Brianna said.

He felt a thrill every time she called him Daddy.

"You got it, kiddo," he said.

Colin put her down, led her across the crowded terminal to a coin-operated machine, and bought the kid a soda. He bent down, wiped her runny nose, opened the soda, and handed it to Brianna. He kissed her on the cheek.

"Thank you, Daddy," Brianna said, now mastering her "th's."

"You're welcome, cutie pie," he said.

"I love you, Daddy," she said, taking a long sip of the cold Coke.

Jesus Christ, he thought. *This little kid gives me all her trust and unconditional love. I better be careful here.*

Colin remained there in the crouch for a long moment, the words from the little girl's mouth melting through him.

"I love you, too," he said, "stealing" her nose and showing her his thumb tucked between his middle and index finger.

"Put it back," she said with a squealing laugh. She spoke with a combination of American TV twang, a jagged edge of Queensese, and a lilt of Dublin.

He pushed his thumb back onto her nose. She giggled and held up her hand for him to lead her through the terminal. The pure trust she put in him made Colin feel privileged. There was a place inside him where this kid would always live, no mater what else happened. *This kid deserves better than Bally-fucking-tara,* he thought. *I read about a father winning custody of his stepkid once. Stop, this is Gina's kid. Try taking Brianna away from her and she'll put a knife through your heart, in your sleep. Just love the kid while she's with you and leave it at that.*

When he made his way through the crowd, he saw Gina rushing for the doors where passengers were appearing. She embraced her cousin Bridie.

Holy shit, Colin thought. *She has a stroller.*

In the stroller was Bridie's two-year-old kid, Finbar.

Christ, Colin thought, *standing to the side. She said she was coming alone, now we'll have two terrible twos in the house.*

Gina and Bridie turned toward the swinging doors, as if awaiting someone else. Colin froze. *No way there's more,* he thought.

Through the doors came Philomena, also pushing a pram, with her eighteen-month-old toddler, Huey, who was crying and clutching his ears. "Och, Philo," Gina shrieked. "And yeh brought little Huey!"

Four of them, Colin thought, *including a real-life Baby fucking Huey.*

Now came the suitcases, six in all, battered and mismatched, tied with ropes and nylon stockings, covered in crayon scribbles.

"Shanty Airways," Colin whispered to himself.

Brianna shyly clutched Colin's leg, watching Gina and Bridie and Philomena all embrace. Bridie's sleeping kid awoke with a wail and the three women did a campfire dance around the luggage as the kids in the strollers looked up at them, bewildered, both of them crying intermittently and rubbing their ears from airplane decompression.

"I told yeh I was bringin' a surprise," Bridie shouted. "We cashed in the Aer Lingus ticket and got two seats on the charter for the same price as one on bloody Aer Lingus. But by Jaysus we had to keep the kids on our laps all across the universe. How feckin' far are we from home? Four shitey nappies long, anyway. Well, laicin, yer lookin' smashin', wha'?"

"This doesn't look like Beverly Hills nine-oh-two-one-oh atall," said Philomena, looking around at the Third World people who packed the terminal. "If I see a swimmin' pool or a movie star, I'm jumpin' into one or the other before dark."

"Banjaxed we are," said Bridie. "Wallfallen for a jar."

"Aye," said Philomena. "We've got duty-free Jameson and Bacardi and Granda sent pots of poitin. The airport security thought it was a petrol bomb. By Jaysus, the crack'll be ninety tonight, girl."

Colin stood gaping at the women and the kids. There would now be three women, all Irish travelers, and three kids living in his house for the next two weeks. *The goat and the pony would have been better,* he thought.

Gina made a fuss over the two kids in the strollers and Bridie looked around the crowded terminal, searching for Brianna.

"Where's yer little darlin' and the Yank fella?" Bridie asked.

Colin nodded, trying to shield his shock and anger. He lifted Brianna up in his arms, and Bridie's eyes widened.

"Dere's the little flower," she squealed. "Feckin' gorgeous."

She grabbed Brianna and started kissing her face and Brianna started to cry. "Daddy," she said, holding out her arms for Colin.

Bridie and Philomena exchanged what Colin thought were disapproving looks. Bridie handed Brianna to Gina.

"Howayeh, Colin," Bridie said, shaking his hand.

"What about yeh?" said Philomena, also shaking hands.

"Well, ladies, this is a surprise," Colin said. "Welcome to the City of Angels. So where are all you guys staying?"

The women looked at him, aghast, and then at Gina.

"Don't mind him," Gina said.

"Feckin' devil's horns would melt in this heat, wha'?" said Philomena.

"Let's get out of this kip, anyway," said Gina. "We'll need one of them wee carts for the luggage, Colin."

"We'll need more than that," Colin said. "There isn't enough room in the car for all the luggage and all the people."

"Then we'll get a taxi as well," she said. "You can take the luggage home in the taxi and I'll drive the lot of us home."

Colin looked at her and nodded.

"Get me out of this heat," said Bridie.

Colin gave Gina his car keys, rented a luggage cart, kissed Brianna, and went in search of a taxi. The cab driver took one look at the mismatched, rope-and-pantyhose-bound luggage, and said, "Lemme see your money first."

Embarrassed, Colin showed him the cash and the driver opened his trunk and helped Colin load it. Colin climbed in the backseat with two of the bags.

He gave the driver his address in the Valley and the driver pressed his computerized meter.

"Mind if I ask you a question?" the driver said as he took the ramp to the San Diego Freeway north.

"What?"

"You didn't escape from someplace or something, did you?"

"No," Colin said, "but it's not a bad idea."

Two hours and fifteen minutes later, after loading the suitcases into the house, Colin was still waiting for Gina, the two cousins, and the three kids to get home. He was starting to worry that Gina had gotten into a car accident or gone into premature labor on the road home. He listened to the radio, tuning in to the all-news station and listening to traffic reports. There were no reports of an accident on the freeway. He called a few hospitals to see if a woman in premature labor had checked in, but none had.

For the first time since he went on the wagon, he truly craved a beer. He was stewing in anger. His home was being invaded. He was being taken for granted. He could throw them all out on their asses, but the cousins would convince Gina to go home with them and his baby would be born six thousand miles away, in the equivalent of a manger.

I'm doomed, he thought, looking at the six suitcases in the center of his living room, amid the new velour couches and the gleaming teak furniture.

I gotta let this play out, he thought. *Gotta think smarter. Think of this as work, as R and D. Kieran is in love with Gina, so he'd put up with this for a while. Let's see the cousins in action here in L.A. for the third act. Even Kieran will have a limit.*

He drew a glass of water from the water cooler and drank it slowly, hydrating his parched body.

He sat down and listened to the news about the upcoming Independence Day festivities, including the fireworks show on the Santa Monica pier.

A little more than three hours after he had arrived home, the women and children burst through the front door of his house. The three cousins were singing:

I'm a rambler, I'm a gambler,
I'm a long way from home,
And if you don't like it
Then leave me alone.
I'll eat when I'm hungry,
I'll drink when I'm dry,
And if the moonshine don't kill me,
Then I'll live till I die . . .

Philomena grabbed the unlabeled bottle of poitin from Gina, took a short sip, and the three of them stumbled into the living room, roaring and red-faced with laughter.

The three children were smeared with chocolate, the two just off the plane totally dazed and disoriented. Brianna ran across the room to Colin, her arms outstretched. He lifted her up as Gina bent in a squat, fitfully laughing, clutching herself between the legs.

"Stop, Jaysus, please stop, I'm gonna wet on the feckin' floor," Gina said between rattles of laughter.

"Mommy drunk," Brianna said, pointing.

Bridie collapsed onto the couch, convulsed in laughter, holding a Guinness bottle in one hand and a lit cigarette in the other. The agitated Guinness bubbled up out of the neck of the bottle, the foam running over Bridie's fist onto the forest-green couch cushion. She sat up with a start, sucked the rushing foam off the head of the bottle. Then she took a long drag of her cigarette, the ash falling on the living-room rug.

"Finish the story about the Yank in the hotel before yeh left," said Gina.

"Where was I . . . oh, aye, so yer mon says to me, 'You're a Trinity College student?'" Bridie shouted. "'I am indeed,' says I. 'Irish lit'rature.' So he invites me upstairs from the bar to his hotel room. A suite, mind yeh. He starts readin' me poetry by that Yeatsie fella."

Philomena helped Gina to the bathroom, stumbling and lurching, both of them still laughing. Gina sat on the bowl and urinated loudly with the door wide open.

"G'wan, I'm list'nin," she yelled. Her speech was slurred, the hee-haw in her laughter was loud and obnoxious. She hadn't even said hello, none of them had.

"So he t'inks he's gonna feckin' love-poem the knickers offa me, righ'?" Bridie said. "And there's nothin' worse than a Yank readin' them Yeatsie love poems with a feckin' fake gobshite Irish accent. I asks him if he minds do I call room service for a jar. Fine, says he, order anythin' yeh want. That's all I needs to hear. Well, by Jaysus, six bottles of Moet chambo later, he's feckin' paralyzed drunk, legless as a scarecrow, and still readin' the Yeatsie poems with one eye closed, only now he's usin' a feckin' French accent. I t'ink he thinks we were in Paris instead of Jurys Hotel in Dublin, righ'? So I gives him two shots of Granda's poitin and he was out like a corpse. His head fell forward and his feckin' toupee falls half way off his baldie Yank head. I almost wet meself writin' 'T'anks for a swell time' on his feckin' baldie head. Then I just helped meself to a few bob to spend over here. Didn't even have to go to currency exchange."

Gina continued to laugh from the bathroom, pulling her maternity panties up over her swollen belly as she came back into the living room, a lit cigarette dangling from her lips. She looked at Colin and stopped laughing.

"Feck off," she said in a preemptive strike, taking a drag, inhaling, and blowing a long stream at him. Colin said nothing, just looked at her evenly, holding Brianna in his arms.

"Mommy's drunk," Brianna said.

"That's right, darlin'," Gina said. "I'm stinkin' filthy durty fallin'-down drunk as a lord's bastard. And so wha'? Me family is here and I needed a bit a crack. So I don't give a monkey's bollocks what some lady doctor has to say. I feel great, like I just pulled a stake outta me heart and climbed out of a feckin' coffin to join the livin'."

Philomena was still laughing at the story Bridie had told. Finally, Bridie was finished laughing and gasping for breath. She sat up, looking for an ashtray, and couldn't find one, so she stood the filtered cigarette upright on the coffee table, the ash suspended in the act of collapse.

"Well, I don't know about you girls," Bridie said. "But I've had my fill of gargle and I need a good feed of sleep. Those childer needs to ate. Is there a chipper open nearby?"

"Chipper?" Gina said. "You need to get back on the plane to find a proper chip shop, there's nothin' of the sort here."

"What do yeh feed a child, then?"

"Get them a taco," Gina said

"A wha'?" Bridie asked.

"A taco."

"Sounds like the name for a dog," said Philomena.

"Get some sleep," Colin said. "I'll take the kids for something to eat."

"Saint Colin the bleedin' martyr," Gina said.

"Och, leave it out," Philomena said. "The poor fella's offerin' to take care of the kids while we get some sleep. Fair play to him, all the same."

"Aye, Grace," Philomena said. "Leave him alone, he's grand."

Gina looked at him and winked. "He is a fine fella," Gina said. "But I know when he's not happy and he's not happy right now, are yeh, luv?'

"I'd be happier if you got some sleep," Colin said, unwilling to argue with her in her drunken state.

Think smarter, he thought. *It's work . . .*

thirty-three

July 3

Bridie barged into Colin and Gina's bedroom in the morning. "I can't find a fork or a knife in the house," she said.

Colin sat up, wiped the sleep from his eyes.

"Use your feet," Colin said.

Gina groaned with the pillow over her face. Colin looked at the clock radio next to the bed. It was 5:18.

"We haven't caught up with the new century yet," he said.

Bridie stood in the doorway looking at him, waiting for him to get up from the bed. Now Brianna and the other two children gathered around her legs.

"Well . . ." Bridie said.

"Close the door and I'll get some clothes on," Colin said.

"Is it naked yeh sleep?" she asked. "With Gina preggos?"

"Close the door," Colin asked.

"These kids are atein' the fists off themselves," Bridie said, and slammed the door.

Colin stood up, his head pounding, pulled on a pair of pants, and walked out into the kitchen, bare-chested and barefoot. He opened the kitchen pantry and took out a large toolbox with a combination lock. Bridie watched him spin the dial and open the toolbox and take out a single butter knife and a half-dozen forks.

"Feckin' Mother of Mary," Bridie said, and now Philomena stumbled into the kitchen, her pretty face distorted with a hangover and sleep wrinkles, her hair spiky and frayed.

"Wha'?" said Philomena.

"He has the feckin' silverware under lock and key," Bridie said. "Do yeh not trust us, so?"

"I only have things with sharp points under lock and key," he said, showing them the carving knives, steak knives, butter knives, dinner forks, skewers, corkscrew, can opener, and three screwdrivers. He even had the little yellow corncob holders under lock and key.

"For wha'?" asked Philomena, drinking milk from the container, standing in front of the fridge.

"Ask Gina," Colin said, scratching the still-raw area around the shoulder wound.

"Och, a bit of a row," Bridie laughed. "Left her mark. That's a sign of true love."

"Aye," said Philomena, with a laugh. "Gina wouldn't take sass from a screw, never mind her fella."

"Surely you'll not keep all them locked up," Bridie said.

"I will," he said. "We've been eating mostly with spoons around here, and our fingers."

"Yous is mad," said Bridie. "For feck sake, it isn't civilized not to have knives and forks."

"I know," Colin said. "But when in Rome . . ."

He walked back toward the living room. *Maybe I can starve them out of the house,* he thought.

"What the hell does Rome hafta do with it?" Philomena asked. "This is Los Angeles, i'nit?"

Colin drove to the bank to deposit his check and withdraw some money for the Fourth of July weekend. He wanted to make Gina and Brianna's first American holiday special. He also knew the cousins wouldn't have much spending money, so he took out five hundred dollars in cash. *Research and development,* he reminded himself. They'd see the fireworks on the Santa Monica pier, have a barbecue in the backyard, and make sure the kids had a great day. He hoped he'd be able to get Gina to refrain from booze and cigarettes.

In order to let the cousins have time to get properly unpacked and settled into the house, Colin went to Westwood to see the new John Woo action flick. He enjoyed the film and the time alone in the dark.

When he got home, five hours after leaving, he stopped at the threshold—all the furniture in the living room was rearranged. The couches were in different positions, the tables were all placed at different angles, even the rectangular rug was turned sideways. The most startling difference was that his desk and his computer had been moved from his office into the living room.

Stepping into the house, he saw that the lock to his office had been popped open and there was now a folding bed in his special sanctuary. The books from his office bookcase had been piled high against a wall in a corner of the room and the bookcase was now stacked with a woman's and a child's clothes.

Anger bubbled in him as he heard women's voices coming from the backyard. He walked into the kitchen and looked through the screen door into the yard, which was draped with drying laundry. Bridie was washing clothes by hand in a lobster pot, wringing the soapy water onto the lush green lawn, shaking them out, and hanging them on the line. Philomena was scrubbing breakfast dishes in a plastic basin, rinsing them in a spaghetti pot, and stacking them on top of each other. The kids were all naked and splashing in a big plastic pool.

The yard was separated from the house next door by a simple hurricane fence. An elderly couple stood sentry inside their screen door, silently looking out at the women and the naked kids. The old man appeared frozen in disbelief, his wife's fingers strapped across her mouth, her head bobbing with a mild palsy.

Colin heard the toilet flush, turned and saw Gina walking out of the bathroom, clutching her stomach and wiping her mouth.

"Booze is really great fuckin' stuff isn't it?" Colin said.

"Feck off, you," she said. She belched, plopping down in a dining-room chair and gasping with a terrible attack of heartburn. "Jaysus, see what goin' off the gargle does to yeh? It makes yeh as sick as a distempered dog the minute you go back on it."

"Your body is telling you the booze is poison," he said. "For you and our kid."

"If that witch doctor hadn't made me stop in the first place, I'd be laughing," she said.

He drew her a glass of clear water from the dispenser.

"Gina, about my office . . ."

"Och, it's only temporary," she said. "Besides, yer done with yer script."

"I still write every day," he said. "I'll have to do the next draft soon."

"Well, we couldn't have five of them in the one room," she said. "The kids were keeping each other awake. Besides, we'll all be out most of the time during the day. Bridie and Philomena are starting driving lessons this afternoon."

"Driving lessons?" Colin said. "They'll only be here two weeks. Besides, they don't give out licenses if they aren't legal residents."

"Well, they aren't getting them in their own names," she said. "They're gonna do what I did."

"What names are they getting them in?" Colin felt a sinking feeling in his guts; they were liable to get him in deep trouble.

"They met a few American students at Trinity who sort of lent them their IDs," Gina said.

Colin knew this meant they had pickpocketed a few wallets from American exchange students who vaguely resembled them.

"You know how this L.A. is," she said. "Yeh need a drivin' license in order to open a checkin' account."

"Why the hell do they need checking accounts?" Colin asked.

"Everyone here has one," she said. "They take checks like they were cash as long as you have a license."

"Gina, you can go to jail for bouncing checks in this state . . ."

Colin was interrupted by the doorbell. At the door was Gina's old driving instructor asking for *Anne McCarthy* and *Julie Brady*. Gina shouted to Bridie and Philomena.

The two cousins ran into separate bedrooms to change, and twenty minutes later the instructor was still sitting on the couch.

"I'm sorry about this," Colin said.

"No problem," the instructor said. "I'll prorate it the hourly rate—fifty an hour per student."

Finally, after forty minutes, the two cousins appeared, dressed in evening wear, high heels, and jewelry, with their hair done and ready to roll.

"Thank you," Philomena said, kissing Colin on the cheek. "Yer too kind."

"Very generous of yeh," Bridie said, also kissing his cheek.

Colin seemed baffled by their display of affection until the instructor said, "I'll need the check before we begin."

Gina now waddled from the kitchen and gave Colin his checkbook. He gaped at Gina in astonishment. She winked at him.

He then took the pen from Gina and wrote the check out to the Valley Driving School, repeating a silent mantra: *It's R and D, R and D, R and D.* The instructor took the check and left with Philomena and Bridie.

Gina wished them luck at the door and then turned and clapped her hands and rubbed them together.

"I think they're startin' to like yeh," she said.

"Thrilled," Colin said.

July 4

Fireworks exploded over the dark Pacific as the women from the far side of the Atlantic moved through the dense crowd on the Santa Monica pier. Philomena and Bridie, dressed in tight denim shorts, tube tops, and sandals, pushed their kids in their prams, eyes shifting for marks. Colin had Brianna, who squealed at each exploding man-made star, on his shoulders. Gina sagged in the night heat, her belly protruding under the loose white dress, her feet swollen in the flat sandals, sweat matting her usually impeccable hair. A black man on a bench got up and gave her his chair.

"Rest your tired bones, ma'am," said the middle-aged guy with the flattened nose of an ex-pug.

"I'd vote you pope," she said to the man, who moved off into the night, away from the festivities, alone.

Bridie and Philomena angled deeper into the crowd, furtively whispering to one another. Gina fanned herself with her hand.

As the fireworks burst in a half-moon sky, illuminating the Malibu hills and the ships at sea, Colin saw a commotion shudder through the crowd. Three sweaty uniformed cops barged into the mob, hands on their batons. The crowd knotted around two people, one a man shouting in a flat American accent. He grasped a woman by the wrist, who shouted even louder in an unmistakable Irish accent.

"Get yer filthy hands off me privates, yeh durty pig, yeh," Bridie shouted.

"Oh, Jesus," Colin said, shivering with déjà vu, realizing exactly what was happening. It was the same routine Gina had pulled on him in the Shelbourne hotel, six thousand miles and seven months ago.

"Relax," Gina said.

Now a policewoman pried into the tangle of onlookers as the brilliant fireworks drooled in the inky sky.

"This woman picked my pocket," the man shouted. "I demand to have her searched. You'll find my wallet!"

"This bollocks tried to touch me privates," Bridie hollered. "I'm a woman alone with me child, a tourist in this country, and he has the audacity to try to touch me up."

"That's a goddamned lie!" the man shouted. "I happen to be *gay* for chrissakes."

The crowd laughed, parting for the approaching cops, who got between Bridie and her accuser. The police woman removed the man's hand from Bridie's wrist and led her off to the side. The male cops escorted the man to the railing, talking to him.

"I'm not getting involved in this one," Colin said.

"Not to worry," Gina said.

Through the crowd came Philomena, with a cat that ate the canary smile spreading on her face. He knew Bridie had probably done the dip and then passed the wallet to Philomena.

"Great," Colin said. "They come to America and steal the Fourth of July from a hard-working citizen with a Statue of Liberty pass. Gina, this is wrong."

"Will yeh ever blow it out yer hole?" Gina snapped.

The female cop asked Bridie's permission to search her bag. Bridie told her to search all she wanted. The policewoman did but found no trace of the missing wallet. She looked in the child's stroller, found nothing and turned to the male cops and shrugged, indicating she hadn't found anything.

"She must have it," the gay man said. "All my credit cards, my ID, driver's license, medical cards."

"He's only trying to cover up for touchin' me up," snapped Bridie.

One of the male cops produced a pair of handcuffs, pulled the man's right arm behind his back, and shackled his wrist.

"You have the right to remain silent," the cop said.

"I won't let them arrest this guy, Gina," Colin whispered.

"Not to worry," Gina said, fanning herself, yawning.

Suddenly, Bridie shouted, "I don't want to press charges. As far as I'm concerned this was all a big mistake. Maybe he touched me by accident."

The cop let go of the man's arm and said, "Are you sure, lady?"

"Och, it's the Fourth of July," she said. "No real harm done."

"What about my goddamned wallet?" the man shouted. "That bitch stole my wallet and . . ."

The cop unlocked the handcuffs and led the man down the pier, away from Bridie. "You should be thanking that lady," the cop said. "And if you don't shut up, I'll arrest you for verbal abuse and trying to file a false claim."

The cop nudged the man to the ocean end of the pier and Gina put out her hand for Colin to help her to her feet.

"I'm hungry," Gina said.

"I'm buyin'," said Bridie.

"I'll baby-sit," Colin said, angry, as he stormed ahead of them up the ramp to the parking lot.

Later, when she was showering back at the house, Colin searched Philomena's bag, found the man's stolen wallet, sans cash, and the next day anonymously mailed it back to him.

thirty-four

Over the next two weeks, Colin quickly learned that the cousins planned to stay a lot longer than two weeks. He also learned, too late, that the Sphere Airlines charter flight tickets became invalid when they missed the return date. Meaning that eventually Colin would have to buy the cousins new tickets back to Ireland. *Or feed them for life,* he tought.

The cousins got their driver's licenses under the names of Anne McCarthy and Julie Brady, opened personal checking accounts, did some creative shopping, and started dating, all while using their pseudonyms.

At least three nights a week, Colin watched an auto show of Mercedeses, Porsches and Lexuses pull up outside his rented house. The cars were driven by guys aged anywhere from twenty-five to fifty, who arrived to collect either Bridie or Philomena for nights out on the town in Hollywood, Westwood, Beverly Hills, Santa Monica, and all over Los Angeles. Sometimes they double-dated, but more often than not they went out separately. Bridie and Philomena began competing, one usually bragging that her date had a more expensive car than the other's.

Philomena even spent a weekend in Catalina gambling with a guy she met the week before on line in the local bank. "He was making a ten-grand deposit," she said. "That was him for me."

July 20

As they awaited the arrival of their dates, Colin asked the Cousins, as he had come to call them, how and where they met most of these guys.

"When the one I'm with goes to the jacks, another one slips me his phone number," said Philomena. "Men is sneaky bastards."

"In this city, the fellas at a pick-up pub usually puts their keys up on the bar in front of them to show off the make of the car with a little brand-name emblemy t'ing," Bridie said. "They have Mercedes symbols or Lexus, or Porsche or even RR for Rolls-Royce. If yeh spot a set of keys yeh really like and the fella is halfway decent-lookin', yeh wait for him to go to the toilets and yeh excuse yourself from yer date and follow the new fella and ask if he has a change for the pay phone and then yeh ask him how a phone works in this country. Yeh act stewpid while he shows yeh how and as soon as he hears the mad Irish accent he asks yeh out the next night. Fellas with lolly is like pickin' wild berries here if yeh have an accent."

"You make dates on dates?" Colin asked.

"Aye," Philomena said. "Datin's a great way to meet new fellas. Even yer date's friends slip yeh their numbers because they know yer only here on holliers."

I'll need to have a scene in a singles bar with the cousins, he thought.

Every night, Gina watched her cousins dress in new, ridiculously expensive Rodeo Drive fashions, dripping with jewelry and fragrant with expensive perfume, and go to trendy clubs and hot restaurants.

Colin detected an agonizing envy in Gina's eyes as she grew larger and seemed to eat chicken tacos every hour. She ached for the carefree single life; longed for late nights of drink, song, dancing, and whatever else came with the maniacal pull of the moon.

July 25

In the humid morning—sitting at his computer in the living room, using a Q-tip to clean peanut butter and jelly, which had attracted a colony of ants, out of the keyboard—Colin overheard Bridie telling Gina about her most recent date.

"I 'et in a place called Ago last night," said Bridie. "And doesn't only Robert feckin' De Niro own it and isn't he only sittin' there in the gorgeous flesh. The man is only *beautiful.* I asked him for an autograph and a phone number, as a lark. The gobshite fella I was with got so jealous he stormed off and left me stranded with the bill and no motor. I had to wind up signing me own autograph on a wee check for the meal. It was great gas, all the same. The manager was this sweet fella named Paul. Or was it Herman? Can't remember. Anyway, he drove me home after closing. I'm supposed to go out with him tonight but the problem is he t'inks me name is the one on the check and the license and the check I wrote him is gonna bounce like a football unless I cover it."

Without hesitation, Gina wrote her one of Colin's checks to cover the bad check and handed it to Colin to sign. He looked at it and tore it up.

"Get a fucking job," Colin said.

"The feckin' cheek of him," Bridie said, astonished.

Gina said, "Don't yeh dare be talkin' to me re-lay-tives like she was common."

"She's fuckin' *un*common, all right," Colin said. "Common people work for a living; she mooches. She thinks my money's hers. Well, it isn't. I work my ass off for it. If she wrote a bad check, let her go out and shake her fuckin' moneymaker to cover it."

Gina led her cousin into the backyard, where the two of them whispered between themselves.

He knew Gina would write Bridie another check and forge his signature. He could have called the bank and stopped payment but he didn't because he knew a bad check would bring a cop to his door, which could lead to a disaster for the unborn kid if they contacted INS.

I leveled my protest, he thought. *I'll put up with this shit for a while longer. One day soon I'll announce the last stop on the gravy train.*

Gina wrote another check. Colin sat there realizing that he was now paying for the cousins' nights out in addition to the daily food bill for seven, gas for the three women, baby-sitting, and twenty-four-hour air-conditioning.

August 1

The direct calls to and collect calls from Dublin had Colin on the edge of insanity. Most were from the fathers of the cousins' kids, who called to keep tabs on the children they didn't bother to visit or support when they were home in Ireland.

"I wouldn't reverse the call, mate," said one collect caller. "But I'm skint at the moment and I haven't talked to me son's mum in ages."

"Why don't you call her when she's home in Ireland?"

"Well, she has no phone at home," the guy said. "And I live on the other side of Dublin."

"Oh, I get it," Colin said. "Now that she's six thousand miles away it's easier for you keep in touch with her by calling collect on my bill?"

"Aye."

"Eat dog shit, pal," Colin said as he slammed down the phone.

August 5

Colin thought it was odd that morning when he brought in the mail and there were three birthday cards addressed to Bridie's two-year-old son. Each card had a different return address. A few days later, he saw the cards again, after they had been opened. Each one said, "Happy Birthday Huey, Love, Dad." Bridie had three men convinced they were the father of the child, each one sending her money.

Meanwhile, Colin watched his own bank account steadily decline. He'd already spent nine thousand of the eighteen thousand. His accountant also told him that his corporate tax was now due and Colin had to sit down and write a check for six thousand dollars to the IRS, leaving him with three grand to support seven people.

August 15

Nearly broke, Colin finally heard from James Thompson of Global Screen and took a story meeting on the first-draft screenplay. The company liked the first draft but had ten pages of notes that they wanted incorporated into the second draft of the script. Colin would be receiving another check for commencement of second draft.

"Oh," Thompson said before Colin left his office. "My daughter, Melissa, said to say hello. She's still waiting to go through your short movie with you, shot by shot. The one that lost . . ."

He snapped his fingers, trying to think of the title.

"First Love, Last Love," Colin said, certain now that it was considered a film that had *lost* as opposed to a film that had been *nominated*.

"Right," Thompson said. "That can wait until after you finish the script. On Labor Day weekend, I'm having a twenty-first birthday party for Melissa at my place in Malibu Colony. Get the address from my secretary, and why don't you bring the tinker girl with you? I want some people to meet her."

"She's eight months pregnant," Colin said.

"Perfect!" he said and laughed.

"I'll be there," Colin said. He knew Gina was an oddball but he resented Thompson referring to the woman who was carrying his baby as the tinker girl, as if she were a curiosity for his amusement and display, like the elephant man.

"Bring some sides," Thompson said, meaning rewritten script pages. "I'd like to read the new draft as it comes out of the computer."

"Sure," Colin said, immediately feeling the pressure. The problem was there was nowhere to write at home.

The house was in tumult by day, with kids running in and out of the backyard, the screen door banging, telephones ringing, women using hair dryers, radios blaring, cartoons exploding from the TV.

There wasn't much more peace at night, as the cousins would come home at all hours, usually drunk and singing, making french fries and egg sandwiches with a side of beans, laughing, waking up the kids.

August 25

To get cracking on the script, Colin rented a motel room a few blocks away in a place called the Valley Villa, asking for a room with no phone service. Even as he went to work there, he was interrupted several times a day by one of the cousins, asking Colin to sign checks for Gina or to mind all three kids in the motel pool while the women went out for "messages," which always included a stop in Ireland's Eye for a pint.

When he received his bank statement in the mail, he learned that Gina had signed three of his checks to cover bad checks her cousins had written. He gathered all the loose checkbooks in the house and locked them in the toolbox with the carving knives.

"When are they going home?" Colin asked Gina, as they lay in bed together, Brianna asleep at their feet.

"After the babby is born," Gina said.

"Very thoughtful of them to wait, but I can't afford them anymore."

Their two-week visit was stretching to at least ten weeks and maybe twelve, since they'd probably stay to help Gina in her first month after the birth.

"They're working on payin' yeh back," Gina assured him.

Colin knew this meant they were scheming a Big Score and he wanted no part of their scam.

He also was very careful not to blow his top at Gina, now that she was nearing her ninth and critical month of pregnancy. Her already volatile temper was even more hair-trigger with the added weight, the heat, and general discomfort.

"Tell them not to do me any favors," Colin said.

thirty-five

August 31

The party at James Thompson's Malibu Colony house began with a viewing of a rough cut of a new Global Screen picture in his private screening room. At the end, the thirty-odd guests applauded, shook Thompson's hand, and told him it was wonderful. Colin clapped and nudged a still and uncomfortable Gina to join in. She didn't and Thompson noticed.

"Well, Gina, what did you think of the film?" he asked.

"Load of shite," Gina said.

You could have heard a hair turn gray in the silent room. The guests looked at each other in awkward discomfort. Colin swallowed and looked at Melissa, who put her hand to her mouth to stifle a snicker. He made eye contact with Thompson and shrugged in an embarrassed way.

"Tell me why you think it's a load of shit," Thompson said.

"Everything was goin' great guns until the malarkey endin'," she said. "There's just no way that fella would take her back after she cheated on him like that."

"But the film is about forgiveness," Thompson said. "About how love is more powerful than anger."

"Hollywood shite," she said. "No woman in the audience will ever fantasize about a fella who would take back a cheater. Say what you want about the old pictures, but when Clark Gable tells Scarlett O'Hara that he doesn't give a damn, every woman in the picture house wanted him. No one wants a jellyfish for a man. Not where I come from, anyway. You asked, so there yeh are, now, the endin' is a load of shite."

An intrigued Thompson looked around the room at the other women. He could see that Gina had unearthed a buried truth.

He asked the other women in the audience if they thought the guy looked weak and wimpy when he took the woman back. There was hesitation, but, finally, one after another, the women agreed they wouldn't be attracted by a man who could so easily forgive a woman for her infidelities.

"Thank you, Gina," Thompson said. "We might have some reshooting to do."

The party spread from the air-conditioned living room to the back deck and spilled onto the beach in front of Thompson's two-story house. Gina insisted on sitting in the living room, where a group of women thanked her for her candor.

"Och, it's only a bit of make-believe anyway," Gina said. "Whoever heard of a movie at a party? To me a party isn't a proper hoolie until there's an oul sing-song."

As the party broke into small, chattering knots, everyone was suddenly startled by Gina, who sat on the edge of the sofa, spine straight, shoulders back, big belly out, and broke into song.

> *I remember the mad March moon*
> *drip blood from it's cold dark eye*
> *Saw the bloody blade, of a rusty spade*
> *Swipe down from the starry sky*
> *It cracked the sweet lovin' life*
> *Right out of the demented night*
> *And it left me, a travelin' lass of three*
> *With no milk in me hungry mouth*

James Thompson watched her intently, the others gaping in fascinated silence. Her voice was strong, confident, beautiful. She transported herself out of this room, away from the Pacific, high across the Rockies, the plains, and the Atlantic. Colin was both proud and sad as he watched her.

> *I was reared on four squeaky wheels*
> *With spokes instead of bones*
> *With thoughts of you, and a Joey Gray stew*
> *The road became me home*

Now Gina's voice rose even higher, growing more powerful, her fist clenching. Colin surveyed the room, saw that Melissa Thompson was watching him watching Gina. He held her stare for a long moment, then broke it, turning back to Gina.

> *I wish I could tell yeh all*
> *That me life's been one long death*
> *But yeh learn to brave, fears of the grave*
> *If life buries yeh from yer first breath*

When she was finished, Gina opened her eyes, smiled, and said, "Dere, now, that was stuck in me throat and I had to cough it out." The people in the room broke into applause.

"It's a wee song called 'Mad Moon,' writ by a girl what seen her ma kilt by her da after learnin' he weren't her da atall," Gina said.

Colin brought her a glass of water rimmed with a piece of lime and she drank it down in one long gulp. A few women gathered around her, asking if she had ever recorded an album. Colin left Gina sitting on the couch and drifted outside to gab with some of Thompson's other writers, actors, and directors.

Melissa Thompson sidled up to Colin by the railing on the deck, handing him a fresh, cold Heineken, dripping with ice.

"Happy Birthday," he said, clinking her mimosa.

"How are you going to manage it?" she asked, looking him deep in the eye and then out to sea. He squinted at her. She was young, tanned, rich, beautiful, single, and interested in him. She was also James Thompson's daughter; she scared the shit out of him.

"Manage what?" Colin said.

"Having your baby raised in another country."

"What makes you think that's gonna happen?" he asked.

"No way that lady is going to spend her life in America," Melissa said. "She's interesting, kind of cute, an oddity. But there's no way your relationship will last."

"What makes you so certain?"

"You love her?"

"I'll love my kid."

"I bet she never tells you she loves you, either."

"We don't have a conventional relationship," he said.

"I don't date attached men. When she hits the road, which she will, give me a call."

She walked off toward the beach, where more people tossed Frisbees, played volleyball, and gathered in knots. He watched her for a long moment as she trudged the sand, dressed in tight little tennis shorts and low white sneakers, her blond hair glistening in the California sun.

Colin walked back into the living room and Gina was sitting on the edge of the couch. "I'm bored, I'm tired, and I want to go home," she said for all to hear.

Colin helped her up. James Thompson kissed her hand and

thanked her for her honesty and the beautiful song. Before he left, Colin gave Thompson twenty-five pages of the second-draft script.

On the way home in the car, Gina said, "The party was a load of shite, too. That Thompson fella's shite. Mark my words, he'll give you trouble. I'd lance a boil with a gravedigger's spade before I'd trust him."

thirty-six

September 14

Colin nodded on the living-room couch, a copy of James Lee Burke's newest novel on his lap, as Brianna started shaking him.

"Daddy, look, Mommy on TV," she shouted.

Colin awoke with a start as Gina and the cousins hurried in from the kitchen.

Colin rolled on his side and saw that the local news was on, featuring a segment called "Crime Stoppers: Caught On Tape!" And there on the screen was Gina, lying on the floor of a Rodeo Drive boutique, as Bridie tended to her. The newscaster's voice said, "Now watch as this scam is CAUGHT ON TAPE!"

The tape was rewound and played again in slow motion, as Gina and Bridie walked in together. Philomena entered about thirty seconds later.

"Three women enter the store," the newscaster narrated. "The pregnant one lies down on the floor. Pretends to go into labor. The other one tends to her. Now watch the store clerk and the security guard also come to her aid, like good, concerned citizens. Now watch this one in the background, in slow motion."

The camera highlighted Philomena in the background, grabbing gowns, blouses, underwear, dresses, skirts, and pantsuits and stuffing them into her large shoulder bag, the same black shoulder bag he'd watched Gina rob on Moore Street in Dublin.

"Now watch her as she joins the store clerks, the guard, her partners in crime, and other customers who have gathered around the pregnant woman," the newscaster said. "Then she slowly slinks out the door, and out of range of the camera. Now watch as the pregnant woman sits up, belches, laughs, and she tells the people who are concerned for her that it was a false labor, just a gas attack. Everyone seems relieved and begins laughing. Her other crime partner gets her to her feet. They thank everyone and they leave, heading in the same direction as the one with the bag. The Rodeo Maternity Gang strikes again!"

"Mommy on TV," shouted Brianna, jumping up and down. "Auntie Bridie and Auntie Phillo on TV, too."

Colin sat up ever so slowly as Bridie and Philomena giggled uncontrollably. Gina looked at Colin, trying to hold a straight face, and said, "Wha'?"

"The one and only," Colin said.

The newscaster said, "If you have any information about these three women, who have reportedly ripped off more than a halfdozen Rodeo Drive stores for upwards of ten thousand dollars, please call 'Crime Stoppers: Caught on Tape' immediately."

"The whole city saw you," Colin said. "James Thompson. The neighbors. Dr. Gagliardi."

"Feck 'em all but six and leave dem for pallbearers, righ', Gina?" Bridie said.

"State of my hair in that film," Philomena said. "Jaysus, I looked like a scrubber."

"I had me hat and sunglasses on," Gina said to Colin. "And I really did think I was going into labor."

"Gina, you promised me," he said.

"Don't be annoyin' me. A few bits and pieces is all we took."

"Hardly bits and pieces," Colin said. "It's a felony!"

"They overcharge," said Philomena. "It's their own fault we stole that much."

"They have the insurance as well," said Bridie.

"You people are incredible," Colin said. "The kids just watched their mothers rob a store blind, using my unborn kid as a prop! This your idea of *Sesame Street*? *R* is for rob, *S* is for steal, *T* is for thief. You people . . ."

"That's the second time yeh said *you people*," Gina said. "And just what the hell do you mean by *you people?*"

"Knackers is what he means," said Bridie.

"Durty tinkers," said Philomena. "Pavies, wha'?"

"Bullshit," Colin said, pointing a finger at each one of them. "I mean you, you, and you. Individually, and as a trio, you people, you gang of petty thieves. You can't come to this country, this city, with no money, paint the town red, and rob it blind. This is not the Irish countryside, where the berries grow wild all around the blooming heather. This is not a covered wagon. This is my home, in Los Angeles, U.S. of Fucking A., my country, where I live and work my balls off."

"He does a bit a scribblin' and he moans that his muscles is achin'," Gina said.

"And I've been paying for seven of us for the past ten weeks, covering your bad checks, food, gas, electric, your baby-sitters, the whole deal," he said. "That ain't enough. No, you gotta humiliate me by getting caught on tape looting a store."

"So put it in yer script for a few laughs, write it off on your taxes as research, and shut up yer gob," Gina said.

"I wouldn't put up with the cheeky likes of you," Bridie said.

"We'll be gone as soon as the babby's born," said Philomena. "We'll be having a nice cool pint in Dublin. We're only here out of the kindness of our hearts for our cousin, who you shanghaied to this pathetic place. So wha' if we nick a few odd sorts to wear when we're goin' out?"

Colin was about to answer her but saw Gina weeping on the couch, tears streaming down her face.

"Yeh insensitive bollocks, yeh," Bridie said, shooting Colin a fierce scowl. "Yer after upsettin' her."

"I don't want yiz to leave after the babby is born," Gina said. "I've got no one here."

"We'll be here awhile, gra," Philomena said.

"What you need is a proper night out, luv," Bridie said.

"Aye," Philomena said. "And Colin will mind the kids, won't yeh?"

He looked at them comforting Gina. "Go, I need to work," Colin said, and walked out into the backyard, ready to explode.

He stood watching the palm fronds clatter in the limp valley breeze and thought about what Melissa Thompson had told him.

thirty-seven

Colin put the cousins' kids, Finbar and Huey, to bed and sat up teaching Brianna to read from a child's first reader he'd picked up in a bookstore in Westwood. Gina and the cousins were gone only about an hour when the doorbell rang. He opened the door and two men in cheap suits stood on the small stoop. Both of them displayed the gold shields of the Los Angeles police department. The hair on Colin's arms stood out. His mouth went dry and his palms dampened.

"Help you?" Colin asked, realizing his voice had risen.

"We're looking for two women," one cop said. "Anne McCarthy and Julie Brady. It has to do with several bad checks."

Fucking disaster, Colin thought. *Cops at my door.*

"Never heard of them," Colin said.

"They're using this address," the second cop said.

Colin assured the two detectives that no one named McCarthy or Brady lived here. They asked to see his lease, saw his name on it, and left. He knew they were skeptical.

Now he was starting to get nervous. First, Gina and her cousins had been caught on tape stealing; now cops were coming to the door.

"What the hell's next?" he shouted rhetorically.

"How about a kiss, Daddy?" Brianna said, pouting her lips. Colin smiled and kissed her. He took her to bed, taught her a few new words, and turned off the light. As she was going to sleep, he told her a story about a magic dog named Sticky who could smell when people were telling a lie. He told her how Sticky went around the world solving crimes and catching bad people in lies. Colin had intended to work all night, but before he got to the end of the never-ending Sticky story, both he and Brianna were fast asleep.

A ringing phone awakened him a little after midnight. He answered it and a Beverly Hills cop told him that Gina and her cousins were in custody after a bar brawl.

"Christ," Colin said. "Is Gina okay?"

"Yeah, but you better get over here," he said. "I think she might be going into labor."

"Oh, man," he said. "Oh, man."

He thanked the cop, hung up, and dialed Moira O'Keefe.

Moira O'Keefe rang the doorbell seven minutes later, her sleepy daughter Caitlin in tow.

Colin arrived at the police station to learn that Gina had just been taken from the police station in an ambulance to the hospital. She was having contractions. Dr. Gagliardi had been notified and was meeting her at the hospital.

"Now about the other two screwballs in the back," said the young, handsome arresting officer, whose nameplate read MILLER. "The older one, McCarthy, has a mouth on her filthier than Eddie Murphy. But the younger one, Julie Brady, man, she's a knockout. I like me a full-bodied woman. And she's funny."

"A regular riot," Colin said.

"I told her that if she agrees to go out with me, ya know, I can give her a ROR ticket," he said. "Then at trial, I can make this meatball rap go away by not showing up."

"What happened, anyway?" Colin asked.

"Some guy claimed one of the girls stole his wallet," he said. "He couldn't prove it. Then the bartender refused to serve your wife any liquor because she was pregnant. Which is only right. So she ordered a glass of water. He gave it to her and she threw it on him. He ordered them out and the older one, McCarthy, threw her drink on him. The bartender grabbed your wife by the arm to escort her to the door. The minute he touched her, the young one, Brady, the one I like, clocked him with a lollapalooza of a right hand. She knocked him on his ass, I hear. Nice big shiner he got, too."

The cop laughed. Colin didn't.

"So they're charged with assault?" Colin said.

"Nah," the cop said. "Dis con and resisting arrest. The bartender didn't want to press charges; he's too embarrassed to get on a stand and admit he got decked by a babe."

"So if there's no felony, they release on own recognizance tickets anyway, don't they?" Colin asked.

"Yeah," he said. "But, see, I watch the TV news. These are the three broads known as the Rodeo Maternity Gang. Bunco is also looking for them for Air Jordan checks."

Miller smiled. Colin looked at him glumly.

"Fact is, I don't care about the other shit," he said. "I just want to take the young one out to dinner."

"You have no idea what you're getting yourself into."

"I took this job to live dangerously," he said.

"What did she say when you offered her the deal?"

"Said she doesn't date shades," Miller said. "What's a shade?"

"An Irish nickname for cops," Colin said. "Among a certain kind of people known as travelers. Irish gypsies."

Miller's eyes widened. "An Irish gypsy," he whispered. "Jesus Christ, you don't get any more exotic than that. I'm so sick and tired of hard-bodied blond beach babes and wannabe actresses. . ."

Colin asked the cop to let him talk to the cousins and was led to the holding cells in the rear of the police station, where the hookers and the drug dealers were packed into the cages.

Colin told them about the warrants that were out on them, and that detectives were looking for them for bad checks. That this cop knew they were the ones in the videotape. It didn't take Colin long to convince Philomena to accept a date with the cop. Within ten minutes, Miller had issued both of them desk appearance tickets.

"By the way, Coyne, your wife was brought to UCLA Medical Center," he said.

thirty-eight

September 15

When the nurse placed his son in his arms, Colin Coyne was suddenly a different man.

He'd been a changed man since Gina and Brianna entered his life. But this was different. He was holding an actual extension of his life, the bloodlines of his beloved deceased mother and cherished father pumping through the tiny heart of the red-headed baby boy in his arms.

He knew that everything he did from that day on would be different. *There's a new life in my life,* he thought. *It's like having a second shadow. I am now more than just me. I am me and this child, for as long as we both shall live. I will never let you disappear from my life.*

Colin loved Brianna as his own, but knew that no matter how much he loved her, she would always be Gina Furey's child. But this little boy, this six-pound, fifteen-ounce parcel of life, was his. *For always,* he thought.

Colin held him for a delicate, possessive few minutes until the nurse took the baby from Colin and handed him to Gina, who lay in the hospital bed, beaming with pride. She placed a bottle in the baby's mouth and Colin watched her feed him.

"After this hungry t'ing finishes atein' I'm outta here," Gina said. "I'm ready for me well-deserved bottle of stout. I'm not even breast-feedin', to shut that doctor's trap about the gargle."

"Doctor says you should go home tomorrow," Colin said.

"Ask me arse," she said. "So, what have we decided to call the weefulluh?"

"I told you I like Seamus. Like the poet Seamus Heaney."

"I fancy Gino," she said. "Like me Mafia da."

"I'm not naming my kid Gino, after some gangster lam artist."

"Seamus it is, then. But you change half the shitey nappies."

"Deal, but only if you agree to spend the night here."

"Will yeh bring me a few bottles of stout?"

He took a six-pack out of a bag and opened two. They clinked the bottles together and kissed, deeply.

"Thank you for giving me a beautiful baby boy," he said.

Kieran would say, "I love you, Gina."

"After what I've been through, I deserve thanks," she said, and took a long guzzle of the bitter black beer.

Over the course of the next week, Colin became obsessed with little Seamus. He cradled him, rocked him, burped him, changed him, fed him, and sang him songs his mother had sung to him. He imagined Seamus growing up and playing Little League. He envisioned helping Seamus with his homework, walking him to the school bus, taking him to boxing matches and ball games.

Colin's father was delighted he had a grandson with a proper Irish name, and couldn't wait to see him.

Miller the cop called incessantly. Philomena made a date with him, then broke it. They made another and she stood him up. They arranged for a third date, and she called at the last minute to say she was sick. "Let him handcuff himself to his willie," she said. Finally, Philomena called the cop and made arrangements to go out with him on the twenty-ninth. She didn't tell Miller she was returning to Dublin the next day.

September 25

As the Cousins' departure day approached, Gina's bubbly mood turned dark. Homesickness consumed her. She began cursing Los Angeles, and America.

Gina drank heavily and started smoking again. When Colin asked her to smoke out in the yard, away from the baby, she threw a fit.

"You care about the baby but yeh don't give a monkey's fuck

how I feel," she said. "Me cousins is goin' away and I'll be all alone, with no family."

"Gina," he said. "*We're* family—me, you, Brianna, and Seamus."

"This is nothing more than a halting site, Colin Coyne," she said. "This is a place to park my caravan until I'm ready to move on. Yer just a fella I met at a fork in the road. You go your way and I'll go mine. I want you to understand that."

"Not with Seamus," he said. "You won't go anywhere with my kid."

"I'm young, I'm pretty, and there's no weddin' ring on my finger, and I'll feckin' move on when I say I shift."

Colin felt a twist in his stomach. *I should grab Seamus, fly to New York, and call the INS,* he thought. *I could have her deported. Seamus is an American. I could get custody of him but that would mean a trial. They'd put Brianna in an INS lockup with Gina while they scheduled the trial. That little girl calls me Daddy, she loves me, and, goddamn it, I love her, too. She'd be traumatized, emotionally scarred for life. She'd never forgive me. I'd never forgive myself. I have to try to settle this amiably. First I need to get rid of the cousins. Then I need to get a lawyer. I should make contingency plans. Don't do anything rash. Think smarter. I need to calm down, calm Gina down. This ain't about Kieran, this is about me and my son. This ain't a fucking Hollywood movie, it's the real deal.*

Gina made a few idle threats—"I'll kill yeh in yer sleep and they won't find yeh till I'm having a pint on in me local back home in County Nowhere," she said.

But Colin chose not to argue with her, especially with her cousins still around to help her get away.

September 27

Three days before the cousins were to leave, Gina sat with them around a roaring campfire they had built in the backyard. As they sipped Granda's poitin, Colin overheard them talking when they thought he was asleep.

"Christ, Gina, at some point you have to tell him about the other fella," Bridie said.

"I will not," said Gina. "That's over."

"Whadda ya mean, over?" said Philomena. "'Tisn't over atall."

Colin felt lava rising from his guts, a painful burning surge of dread, followed by anger, hurt, betrayal. *Am I feeling jealous?* he wondered. *Nah, Kieran would be jealous. Not me. Why do I feel violated? Why do I feel the dick-shriveling, hollow-gutted, heart-aching bile of jealousy rising in me? What the fuck is this shit? I can't feel jealousy for someone I don't love.*

"Daddy . . ."

He turned to see Brianna behind him in her Goldilocks nightie, rubbing her eyes, with her arms outstretched to him.

"Who's dere?" Gina shouted.

Colin lifted Brianna into his arms as Gina stumbled in from the yard, carrying her cup of poitin.

"Are yeh all right, gra?" Gina asked, bleary-eyed and slurry.

"I'm fine," Colin said.

"I was asking me daughter. Yer always flippin' fine. You, yerself and yer big career."

"Maybe you talk to *'the other fella'* like that," he said in a low, flat tone, looking Gina square in the eyes. "But in my house, where I pay the rent, and where I feed your family, you talk to me with respect, especially in front of the kid."

She glared at him, the moonshine fueling a wicked anger, but before she could say a word, sirens pierced the quiet of the street. Flashing lights licked across the front windows of the house. Soon the loud voices of firemen and the squawking of walkie-talkies were audible. The firefighters pounded on the windows and one kicked open the front door.

"Jesus Christ," Colin shouted, rushing toward the front door.

Two firemen pushed past Colin, carrying big water cans with small attached hoses. A fire lieutenant followed them in.

"Arseholes," Gina shouted.

"You're lucky we don't have you all arrested," said the fire lieutenant as he brushed by Colin and hurried through the living room toward the backyard, shaking his head. "You can be charged with a felony for lighting a goddamned fire like that during a drought. One spark can take out a whole county. Do you want to see that baby burned to a crisp?"

"Och, g'wan," Gina said. "It's only a wee campfire, sure."

Colin followed the lieutenant into the yard and saw the firemen dousing the campfire. The angry lieutenant wrote him a summons. The elderly couple next door peeked through their back window. Other neighbors looked on, shaking their heads.

"I don't know where you're from, lady," the lieutenant said, "but we don't allow open campfires in Los Angeles. If we have to come back, we'll bring the police."

Colin looked at the $500 ticket, watched the firemen leave and bowed toward the nosy neighbors. "Thank you and good evening," he shouted, and walked back inside, holding the summons in his hand.

Gina and the cousins were sitting around the kitchen table, still drinking, unfazed.

"All dat was uncalled for," said Bridie.

"The one with the ax was only gorgeous," said Philomena.

"First cops come banging on my door," Colin said, waving the summons at Gina. "Now firemen kick my door down. Why don't we just invite the bomb squad over for dinner?"

"Aye, and why don't I poison yeh while we're at it?" she said, bouncing Brianna on her knee.

Over the next two days, *the other fella* stayed in Colin's head like a hot-and-cold-flashing low-grade fever. But he didn't mention him to Gina again. He wanted the cousins to leave with as little added angst or melodrama as possible.

September 29

Philomena finally made good on her promise to Miller the cop and dressed in her purloined Rodeo Drive finest to go out with him.

Miller pulled up in a new Explorer, looking even more like a movie star, dressed in a perfectly tailored Versace suit with a black T-shirt accentuating his muscular chest and expensive imported loafers with no socks. *He dresses like a dirty cop,* Colin thought.

"I'll be home early," Philomena said with a wink in the doorway of the house as Miller stood at the curb holding open the passenger door to his Explorer. "I made sure to pick an expensive restaurant that doesn't take credit cards."

"Brilliant," said Bridie.

"Cash and carry," Gina said.

Colin was unsure what the scam was, but he knew Philomena had every intention of taking some of Miller's cash back to Dublin.

She walked with an exaggerated gait and climbed into the Explorer. Miller closed the door, got in, and glided away.

Philomena was home before midnight, in record time.

The three women whispered covertly and laughed uproariously in the bedrooms as the cousins packed. Colin kept imagining that they were talking about *the other fella*.

Then, as heartily as they rocked with laughter, they all began to rattle with sobs when the metal locks on the suitcases were fastened and the ropes and nylons were bound around the old bags.

They sat at the dining-room table, drinking stout and Jameson whiskey while Colin went wordlessly to bed.

He lay awake for a long time, listening to Brianna and Seamus breathing softly beside him. He stared at the ceiling, thinking about the future of his son, Seamus, how the kid was born into a family that could never stay together. He worried about Brianna, over whom he had no authority. He did not think about his film.

There's big trouble coming, he thought. After a while, he drifted off to fitful sleep.

thirty-nine

September 30

The good-bye at the airport was predictably messy, loud, drunken, sobby, and sloppy. The cousins were the last to board the Aer

Lingus 747. As they embraced Gina at the gate, Colin stood to the side with Brianna holding onto his pants leg as he also cradled a blanket-wrapped Seamus in his arms. The infant stared up at him with dark, mesmerized eyes.

"I'll be home for Christmas, so," Gina promised. "Tell Granny and everyone I send me love."

"Throw caution to the wind, girl," Bridie said. "Just come with us now. Leave outta this kip."

"Och, you know I can't," Gina said. "Yet . . ."

Colin listened with dread. Every day, the words Melissa Thompson spoke to him became louder in his head.

"Why is Mommy crying?" Brianna asked.

"Because her cousins are going away," Colin said.

"You're not going away, are you, Daddy?"

"No, angel face," Colin said. "Daddy isn't going anywhere."

"Now I can have my own room again, right?"

"That's right," Colin said.

Gina, Bridie, and Philomena locked arms in a triangle of tears and then the Aer Lingus stewards firmly told them they had to get on board. The cousins moved down the walkway to the plane, Gina running down after them, a caged wail escaping.

"Noooo . . . I don't want yiz to leave me here a-lo-un," Gina shouted. A sky marshal now stopped her, leading her back behind the retaining ropes. The cousins waved once more before disappearing onto the plane.

Gina stood sobbing and finally turned to Colin.

"Why don't yeh just feckin' bury me," she said, taking Seamus from Colin's arms as they walked to the parking lot.

On the ride home, Gina sat in the backseat with Seamus. Brianna curled into the front passenger seat, chattering all the way home to a Barbie doll. The talkative kid peppered Colin with questions about why trees were green and how cars eat and why Seamus had a willie and she didn't.

"Boys use them to break girls' hearts," Gina said.

Colin ignored Gina, playfully answering each of Brianna's questions as clearly as he could. He stole glances at Gina all the way home, as she stared out the window with red-rimmed eyes, feeding the baby his bottle. She was a portrait of despair, a still life of sadness.

"How ya feeling, Gina?" Colin asked, exiting the freeway.

"I don't," she said.

When he neared his house, he saw a familiar face on the stoop. Police officer Miller was wearing jeans, sneakers, a T-shirt and a very angry face. Colin drove past the house, made a right at the corner, and pulled to the curb.

"Go park in the alley and come in through the yard," Colin told Gina. "Miller doesn't look like he's here bearing thank-you gifts."

"Tell him to die in sections," Gina said, climbing out of the backseat and then behind the wheel. Colin looped back around the corner to confront Miller on his front stoop.

"Where is that motherfucking cunt?" Miller said, yanking off his sunglasses, his eyes glowing with anger.

"Gone," Colin said.

"That little cuntrag is going to pussy prison, where some big jigaboo bulldagger is gonna dog-collar her," he said.

"What's the problem?" Colin said as Miller stepped down from the stoop, jabbing a finger into Colin's chest. Colin peered down at the finger, noticing that both of Miller's wrists were bandaged.

"I'll tell you what's the fuckin' problem," Miller said, poking Colin again. "Before we went to dinner, this Irish whore says she wants to see my pad. So I take her, and she starts cockteasing me like a pro, rubbing my dick, tongue in the ear, undressing me. I let her handcuff me to my fucking headboard with my own cuffs."

He poked Colin again.

"Whatever turns you on, pal," Colin said. "Stop poking me in the fucking chest."

"Then this dirty bitch put my underpants in my mouth," Miller said. "And proceeded to rob eight hundred dollars cash, my shield, police ID card, my gold watch, and some other jewelry. Then the fucking bitch takes a red ribbon out of her hair and ties a bow around my fucking dick. She ties it so tight my dick is throbbing! And then she leaves! Just fucking leaves me there, naked, both hands around the brass headboard, underpants in my mouth, and a red bow tied around my dick. And fucking splits!"

"Jesus Christ," Colin said. "I'm sorry, pal, but . . ."

"Sorry? Not as fucking sorry as this broad is gonna be. You'll think that spade in Brooklyn with the plunger up his ass got off easy when I get through with her. Where the fuck is she?"

"On her way to Ireland."

The cop stood rock still for a long, trembling moment. Then he began shaking, ran his fingers through his hair, walked in a circle, mumbling to himself.

"When I didn't report to work this morning my partner came and found me there," he said. "You know how humiliating that is?"

"I can imagine," Colin said.

"No you can't fucking imagine!" Miller whispered through tight lips. "My partner is a *woman!* And she finds me lying there, balls ass naked, my dick all shriveled, tied in a bow, my underpants in my mouth. When she untied the bow I pissed all over myself and the bed. She laughed so hard she couldn't catch her breath. Everyone in the station will know the story. Plus I have to explain to my commanding officer how I lost my shield and ID."

"I tried to warn you," Colin said, knowing he'd write this scene into the next draft of his script.

"Yeah, well, maybe I'll bust your fuckin' wife," Miller said, poking Colin again. "She's in that security video."

Colin grabbed Miller's finger this time and bent it. "All she's doing in that video is lying on the floor, going through a false labor," Colin said, talking deliberately and bending the finger while looking in Miller's eyes. "Without the other two, especially the one actually stealing, you know as well as I know that it's a bullshit arrest. Besides, you do that and I'll talk—to your commanding officer, to internal affairs, to the press. I'll say you had them all in custody, knew who they were, and cut them loose in exchange for a date. For a piece of ass who wound up handcuffing you to a fucking bed. I bet you made some of the calls to this house from your home phone. There'll be a record that you were in touch with someone here in your off hours. I don't think you wanna pursue this, Miller, I really don't. And if you poke me one more time I'm gonna break your fucking finger and tie my own fuckin' bow around it. Honey."

Miller looked at him, his mouth moving but no words coming out. For one brief moment, he looked as if he might even cry. Colin let go of his finger and Miller started walking toward his Explorer, then turned and said, "Let me tell you, pal, these broads, they're no good. One of these days they're gonna mess with the wrong guy, pick the wrong pocket, and they're gonna get themselves or you killed. Mark my fuckin' words."

forty

December 25

Seamus's eyes reflected the Christmas lights when Gina plugged in the tree. The three-month-old baby bounced in his Johnny Jumper swinging harness suspended from a hook in the archway between the dining room and living room, awestruck and excited. Gina was trying her best to make the house cheerful and Christmassy in the Los Angeles sunshine.

"I seen a Santy on Rodeo yesterday who was only wearin' sandals, shorts, and sunglasses," she said. "Christmas in L.A. is like mittins in July, i'nit? All the underfed, redundant actors linin' up to play Santy. Terrible sad, really."

Brianna unwrapped her gifts and Seamus's gifts in a dizzy fit. She got a big-wheel tricycle, three new Barbies, and a dozen other toys. Seamus got stuffed animals and plastic baby blocks. Gina put a turkey and a ham on the table, as Nat King Cole's Christmas album echoed through the house.

Gina had not gone home for Christmas and her severe homesickness following the departure of the Cousins had slowly ebbed. She was too concerned with losing all the weight she'd gained while pregnant to concentrate on anything else. She went to the gym daily, doing aerobics, taking step classes, working out on the Stairmaster, the stationary bike, the crunch machine, the butt buster, and all the other toning machines. She also used free weights. After the Cousins left, Gina voluntarily stopped booze and cigarettes.

Colin had also convinced Gina to see an eye doctor. She was fitted for reading glasses and started to read incessantly. "The words all looked like crawling ants before," she said. "I was afraid people would take the mickey out of me if I wore glasses. Plus I can't read the curly squiggly writin'."

Now it made sense—she couldn't read or write script and so she printed. Fancy menus written in script were a mystery to her. Colin said, "Why don't you enroll in a high-school equivalency course?"

"I'd feel funny in a school in America," she said. "Someday, maybe . . ."

Instead, Gina took cooking lessons and prepared healthful, low-fat meals, swearing she'd never eat another taco in her life.

Most days Gina took the children with her to the gym and put them in the day care center while she worked out. Colin reestablished his office and did draft after draft of *Across the Pond* for Global Screen while meeting with stars. When a star would pass, the studio would suggest a new star and send it to the star's agent or manager, who would suggest changes to suit his client. Then when the star finally read it, he or she would pass.

"They are not going to give a first-time director a green light until there is a star attached who can open the picture," Bonnie Corbet explained when he complained of the endless rewrites. He'd already drained the project of every dime in the writing budget and was barely treading water to support his new family.

But Colin kept at it, starting yet another draft in January for the hottest new female star in Hollywood.

January 16

The *Los Angeles Times* ran a story called "The Mob in Movie Land," about attempts by organized crime to infiltrate the film industry. Gina studied the names and faces of several of the "mob moguls." Some were from Philadelphia, a few were from Chicago and Florida, but most were wise guys from New York who were now trying to launder mob money through Hollywood.

Gina started visiting a pizza parlor in Beverly Hills, a comedy club on Sunset, and a restaurant on Melrose, all fingered by the story as regular movie-mobster hangouts.

Colin agreed to accompany Gina on her search for her biological father, Gino Barilla, figuring it would be better if he went with her than if he left her on her own, as he did in New York. In each place, with Colin at her side, Gina discreetly asked to see the mob guy cited in the story. Guys with names like Uptown Richie Agrillo, JoJo Ramble, Handsome Sammy Rinaldi.

The only one they were able to speak to was Uptown Richie, who, inexplicably, was from downtown Brooklyn. Colin told him who he was, showed him his DGA card, and he took Colin for a walk-and-talk around the block from the Beverly Hills pizzeria. He said, "I knew a guy named Gino Barilla in the old days, but he got whacked. He had a son they called Junior but if it's him she's lookin' for, I don't think he ever got made. He went legit with the old man's money. Probably changed his name. I'm out here trying to go legit myself. Get a few movies made so my own kid can get into the business. I married a Jew broad so I made him use his mother's maiden name, Stein. I figure he has a Yid name out here, he has a shot, know what I mean? This thing my family always did, it's over. It's become La Squealer Nostra. RICO laws, rats, book deals, witness programs. We went from *omerta* to Oprah. Sammy the Bull on Diane Sawyer. It's not for my kid. I want him to be like you. The new Coppola instead of a capo. Maybe I could see what I could find out about this Barilla, and you could put my son to work on your flick as an assistant director, and maybe I could invest a few balloons in your movie, too."

Just what I need, Colin thought. Mortgage my career to the wiseos on my first film. Be indentured for life. Colin told him he didn't even have a movie set up yet, but took Uptown's card and put it in his wallet next to Rocco's card. *The whole mob wants to be in the movie business,* he thought.

Colin assured Gina that the only trace of Gino Barilla was still back in New York.

February 8

For her twenty-third birthday, Colin bought Gina a Martin acoustic guitar. She seemed pleased with it at first, a big smile spreading across her face, and instinctively began to tune it.

"I remember the day I turned seven," she said, strumming the guitar. "We were in the caravan at a halting sight near Ballybunion in Kerry in the glorious west of Ireland. There was a place called Doneen Point and it was only gorgeous. Me granny gave me pair of tiny emerald earring studs. They're the very ones in Brianna's ears now. Me granda took out a penny whistle and played me a tune called 'The Cliffs of Doneen,' which gave me the air. He showed me the chords on an oul guitar, and taught me the words. Went somethin' like this."

> *Oh, you may travel far from your own native home,*
> *Far a-way o'er the mountains, far away o'er the foam,*
> *But of all the fine places, that I've ever seen*
> *There's none can compare with the cliffs of Doneen.*

Her small manicured fingers slid skillfully over the strings. This woman, who was capable of so much anger and coarseness, gently picked out the soft melody as if from some secret golden mother lode of tenderness.

Colin watched Seamus, who at five months was just learning to sit up on his own, staring up at his mother singing in her strong, beautiful voice, her eyes closed, her mind traveling back in time and in place to Ireland.

> *Oh, it's a nice place to be on a fine summer's day*
> *Watching all the wild flowers that ne'er do decay*
> *Oh, the hare and the pheasant are plain to be seen*
> *Making homes for their young 'round the Cliffs of Doneen*

Gina put the guitar down when the last words lumped in her throat. She said nothing.

"That was beautiful," Colin said, clapping along with Brianna. Seamus imitated them clapping, making Brianna laugh giddily. Gina silently laced on her sneakers and went out for a three-mile run.

When she returned, invigorated, soaked in sweat, her young body progressively slimming to her pre-pregnancy dimensions, she put the guitar in the back of the hall closet.

February 27

The story about the cliffs of Doneen intrigued Colin. He wanted to know more about Gina's life on the road. *I need her back story,* he thought. *I could tell it in voice-over in a black-and-white flashback.* In bed at night, after they made love or as they lay awake watching TV or reading, he would pick her brains about her childhood.

Hers was a life of cold nights in strange towns in near-constant rain. Of nights sleeping jammed between her uncles and cousins in the covered wagon or a lean-to, shivering, dreaming of the campfire in the morning. A life of rats in the night, of other traveler kids dying of pneumonia, rabies, meningitis, exposure, consumption, convulsions, drownings. A life of being chased by cops and angry farmers or "buffers" or townies. A life of big tinker campsites, where the clan would gather for a wedding or a funeral and where women in other caravans were routinely beaten in the night by their drunken men for feeding all the food to the children while the men were in town drinking the money the women and children had begged on street corners during the day.

"You could hear the fists hitting the women's faces, the knuckles on the bone, and the men raging, whipping the women with their belts or the sally rod when their hands hurt from hitting too much," Gina said, one night, shivering in the air-conditioning as she lay on his shoulder. "The women bit the cloth with black teeth as they were batein', so the neighbors or the childer wouldn't know how bad it was. No one would dare interfere with a man batein' his mot, or else it would lead to clan feuds, knifin's, shootin's, dogs, and killin's. The next day, there was always wimmins walkin' around with huge black eyes and swollen horse's lips, like birthmarks. No one ever made talk on it."

She told of a past as bleak as anything Dickens ever rendered in fiction. Colin listened in silent horror, sometimes feeling sorry for Gina. He never once detected a droplet of self-pity in Gina's recollections. They were just facts, passages, events, details as they happened. She told them the way an accountant ticked off numbers.

"In some families, as soon as the young wans was in puberty, a little pair of diddies and a bit o' crinkly hair down there, a bit of a grab in her bum, they was offered up to the durty oulfulluhs for a price and turned into babby factories, for the dole. The wimmins were always preggo from their early teens into their thirties, usually dead in their forties. I promised meself that when I was old enough I would never be out on the road if I didn't want to be."

She paused and blinked at the ceiling, her big eyes like mini-movie screens on which Colin could almost see her life.

"Don't get me wrong, mind yeh, because in the spring or the summer it was grand. There was fishin' and swimmin' and apples and berries and sugar and a biscuit for your tay and you were never cold and there was tourists in the towns who gave yeh money when you begged or sold yer swag. But when winter came and you were on the muddy road with holey shoes, and the pickin' and the beggin' and the swag sellin' was thin, listenin' to the drunken frustrated men beat the women like it was sport, it was awful. I don't mind a good row now and again meself, but I promised meself I'd never let a man bate me like some farm animal. Never . . ."

Gina also told of a half-dozen times when she was placed in orphanages when the family couldn't feed her. Because she had no mother or father of her own, she was always the first hungry mouth in the family to be sent to a state facility. "I was the family *bastard*," she said. "Worse, me real father, my biological father, wasn't even a traveler, he was Eyetalian, and a Yank, and gone missing into the bargain. It's a very feckin' cruel word, that word 'bastard,' so it is."

Gina said that at the age of nine she began her life as a thief after hearing her granda and granny talking of putting her in an orphanage because times were so grim. "I figured if they had a few bob they'd keep me with them rather than put me in that feckin' place, where the governess always locked me in a broom closet with the rats if I refused to call her 'Mum,'" Gina said. "So, anyway, we were at a manky halting site near the city of Waterford where all the expensive glass is made and all the tourists wearing the Bing Crosby golf pants and tam-o'-shams come to buy the glass.

"I walks into a glass shop sellin' shoelaces and needles and thread and other swag to the tourists. I was chased out, called a durty knacker. On the way out the door I puts a Waterford glass crucifix under my cardigan, praying to the wee glass Jesus on the Waterford glass cross I won't get caught. I figures granda can sell it to one of the Americans for a good few bob and that will keep me with them instead of at the orphan girls' home. But the storekeeper grabs me at the door and as I wrestles to get away the crucifix only demolishes on the ground. I looked down at poor dear Jesus smashed in bits on the floor and I thought I would go straight to hell, never you mind Borstal or an orphanage.

"The guards was called. I was brought up in the courts. The social workers went and visited me grannies who said they couldn't afford to keep me, never mind make good for the price of the Waterford crucifix. So the social workers figured I was better in a state Borstal. They kept me the better part of a year that time, until Granny got a corporation house in Galway. The whole town protested a'gin' us moving in. But the guards moved us in. Month later, we was burnt out by the townies, who didn't want knackers in their town. Paul Lynch lost his wee dog, who was stayin' wi' us, in that fire. No one was ever charged. Granda said no one gave a tinker's damn."

Explains Paul Lynch's pyromania, Colin thought. *Vengeance.*

"They burned the family out just because you were travelers?"

"Oh, aye," she said. "Me one and only dollie went up in flames as well. Its name was Brianna."

Later she had a daughter to replace the burnt doll, he thought. *Freud would need a shrink after listening to this.*

"What happened in Borstal?" he asked.

"In nick they tried to teach me the religion, but I had a hard time accepting it because I'd prayed to that glass Jesus not to let me get caught and I wound up in nick anyway on account he shattered.

I told that to the priest and he said it was Jesus who wanted me caught so I could get a warm bed and a hot meal and a bit of the education. The priest told me Jesus sacrificed Himself for me on the cross as he had two thousand year ago. I learned to read and print a bit, all right, that much I got from nick, fair play to them. And at least me uncles weren't rubbing their hard willies up agin' me bum in the night in the caravan, pretending they were trying to keep me warm. So I forgave Jesus, even though the governess called me a little bastard every day. Maybe it was for the best. I dunno. But all them nights I was there I dreamt of one day comin' to America to find me American da, the rich Mafia gangster, and he'd give me everything I never had. Gas, i'nit?"

"Who taught you to pickpocket?" Colin asked, mining her while she was feeling loquacious.

"When I was thirteen, me uncle Rory agreed to teach me how to dip if I let him demonstrate on me," she said. "He made me promise not to tell anyone else. For months he was always inside me jacket, showing me how to get a wallet from a man's inside pocket, but a course he was always feeling me little diddies as he did it, grinding his willie agin' me from behind. When he went into me back pockets he was always touchin' up me bum. Or makin' me go in his back pockets to feel his bum. One time he said he'd show me how to get money out of man's front pocket and when I reached in to grab what I thought was a roll of money, he had a hole in his pocket and I grabbed his big stiff willie. He held me there while the durty wanker jollied all over me hand. The thought of one them big ugly sticky t'ings inside me body made me vomity. But I learnt what I needed to know about dippin'—and men. It made me a good earner and kept me out of orphanages and kept me from beggin' while I looked for me da. And Jaysus . . . now look where's it got me . . ."

She stared at the ceiling. Blinking. Colin didn't know whether to feel pity or rage. He just felt numb. The way Gina did.

March 6

Colin was awakened in the middle of the night as he heard Seamus and Brianna being led, half-asleep, out into the backyard.

"I'm tired, Mammy," he heard Brianna say. He worried for a moment that Gina was absconding with the kids.

"I want yeh to see something," he heard Gina whisper.

Colin sat up with a start, lightning flashing behind the blinds, rain pelting the windows. He jumped out of bed, pulled on a pair of shorts, and ran after Gina and the kids.

He found them in the backyard, holding hands, dancing in a circle in the pouring night rain as if celebrating some primordial pagan rite. Lightning sizzled in the spooky sky. The kids were laughing and Gina held her head to sky, her mouth open, catching the drops, letting the rain drench her.

Colin noticed the neighbors watching from their upstairs bedroom window, literally thunderstruck as a deafening clap resounded across the night.

Colin stood smiling at Gina and the kids for half a minute and then Brianna called to him and Gina held out her hand. Colin joined the rain dance. *At times like this, I know why Kieran loves her,* he thought.

March 16

He wrote the rain dance scene while he waited for news on his film. After fighting insomnia, Colin was again awakened in the middle of the night by Gina. This time she sat in a chair in the bedroom, her back to him, staring out at the full moon in a starry sky, playing her guitar softly, singing a song like a nursery rhyme.

> *Yer daddy's in Americay*
> *and yer mammy's in her grave,*
> *"So if you ever want to see yer da*
> *Yeh better beg and save . . ."*
>
> *They say he's a right rich Yank*
> *and lives in a fancy home . . .*
> *And if yeh want to live with him*
> *you'll have to travel o'er the foam . . .*

But what makes yeh think he'll want yeh
If he didn't love yer ma?
I'll have to go see for meself,
no matter how so far. . .

"That's very sad," Colin said, sitting up in the bed. "Who wrote that?"

"Just some wee bastard," she said.

As she made love to him that night, Gina held him as tightly as a frightened child.

"Make me feel safe," she whispered into his wet ear. He wrapped his arms around her, squeezed her, which also made him feel oddly secure.

As winter became spring and then summer returned to Los Angeles, Seamus took his first steps and was teething madly. The family lived frugally as Colin tried to get his first feature film on the boards in the slow, agonizing grind of the studio system. He had a little more than seven thousand bucks in the bank.

Colin and Gina's social life consisted of an occasional movie and dinner, then home early to save on the six-dollar an hour baby-sitting costs. Seamus usually slept between them, so sex became less frequent. When they did have sex, it was satisfying, but Colin still compared it to those first passionate days in Dublin, in the Wavefront by the sea, and it didn't measure up.

Still, life with Gina after Seamus arrived was better than he had anticipated. When she was busy with the house and the children, Gina almost seemed happy. If she was not a reliable companion, she was certainly an interesting one.

When you live in fear of someone running away with your kid at any moment, without explanation or reason, you keep your guard up.

So Colin tolerated Gina rearranging the furniture once a week, which she said gave her the illusion of "shifting," or traveling to new surroundings. He endured the constant, overwhelming stench of bleach as she "de-germed" the kitchen and bathrooms daily. He put up with her teaching Brianna old wives' tales about tea leaves, or rubbing match heads on warts to make them disappear, brushing their teeth with ashes from a fire to make them pearly white. When Brianna developed a sore throat, Gina placed a packet of salt soaked in hot water into a nylon stocking and wrapped it around the child's neck. By the time Colin could get an appointment with the pediatrician the next morning, the throat had cleared up.

After living with Gina for more than a year, after siring a son with her, loving her daughter as his own, somewhere in the sweaty haze of that smoggy summer he slowly began to wrestle with the reality that it was he—and not only the fictitious Kieran—who'd contracted some infectious strain of demented love for Gina Furey. *I have fallen in love with my own character,* he thought. *I have invented my own doom. This is sick, scary shit.*

The night he'd overheard Gina and the Cousins discussing "the other fella," he had felt the first rising bile of jealousy. He never mentioned that nameless man again but thought about him all the time, trying to put a face on a phantom. Ever since she gave birth to his son, he had to admit that envisioning Gina with another man, naked, sharing herself completely with him, the way she did with him, tied his guts in crazy knots. *I have fallen in love with this mad woman. How the hell did this happen? Knocking her up was reckless; falling in love with her is reckless times ten.*

The irrational love he felt for Gina only made him feel worse about his situation. For he knew there was no way this relationship could ever last.

July 8

"I read this great line by a writer today," Colin told Gina as she lay on his shoulder after making love. "He wrote, 'I have two children. One of them is adopted. I can't remember which one.'"

"I'd like to have whatever he's drinkin'," she said.

"I want you to promise me something," he said.

"Maybe, and even that's dodgy."

"If we ever go our separate ways," he said. "I always want to be able to visit Brianna as well as Seamus."

She was silent a long time, staring at the ceiling.

"If she wants to see you," she said.

She'd had the opportunity right there to say that the relationship wasn't going to end. She didn't take it. She knew, like he knew, that their relationship was cursed.

He thought of telling her he loved her but figured it was better left unsaid. It didn't matter. He stroked her hair and looked in her eyes. She smiled.

"You won't stand in her way?"

"Only if I'm randy for yeh," she said, and climbed on top of him as the children slept.

The next week, when he turned in his seventh draft of the *Across the Pond* script, Global Screen got a pass from yet another star. Colin went into a deep depression for a week. He and Gina bickered over silly things, mostly to do with dwindling money.

Then he picked up *Variety* on a hot Monday in August and read that James Thompson had been fired from Global Screen Pictures. The story said most of the projects he had in development would either be shelved or put in turnaround, which meant the rights would revert back to the authors. In his case, it also meant that before any new studio made the film, they would have to reimburse Global Screen for every penny they had paid Colin. When a script has that kind of baggage, it is always hard to set up. Especially if it comes attached to a first-time director whose single claim to fame was a short film that "lost" at the Oscars.

Bonnie Corbet told him to sit tight, be patient, and see how it all shook out. Colin knew that meant he better live on what he had in the bank, which wasn't going to last very long for a family of four.

August 19

Colin began writing a treatment for a new script called *Diamond in the Rough,* loosely based on a jewel thief he knew from Queens who used to pull scores to raise the money to launch his son's political career. The scores got bigger as the son's career escalated from the school board to the city council to the state assembly to the Congress to the U.S. Senate. Finally, the father had to pull the score of a lifetime to finance his son's run for the presidency of the United States.

Colin worked with his index cards, making calls to old friends back home for details, reading books on precious stones and the jewel business and politics. But mostly he moped around the house, played with the kids, and waited for the phone to ring. Seamus was walking now, saying his first word, which sounded like "mada." Gina swore it was "mama," but Colin decided it was a combination of "ma" and "da."

August 25

As Seamus's first birthday approached, Gina received an urgent call from Bridie in Dublin. Granny was sick and she wanted to see Gina. Once again, Gina began to drown in tidal waves of homesickness.

"I've been in this country for almost two years now," she told Colin. "You've been a great fella to all of us, so yeh have. But I'm dyin' inside, Colin Coyne. I need a trip home. Me granny is sick. She's never laid eyes on me new child. Brianna doesn't even remember her. I know how much the kids mean to yeh, and I'll never keep them from yeh, but I need to go home soon. I need to feel rain on me face and cobblestones under me feet. I need to hear music and have a pint with me granda and have the crack with me cousins. I need back the life I had before I went the wrong way when me and you met at the fork in the road."

This time, Gina's appeal came in soft, reasonable tones. He saw the sincerity in her eyes. He felt like the head of the parole board hearing a plea from a prisoner who had put in a lot of good time. He knew the call from Bridie about Granny could have been a hoax, a lie contrived to get Gina home. *That fat woman is no health resort,* he thought. *She could kick the bucket any minute of any day.*

"This relationship was never gonna work out, was it?" he said.

"We're stuck in Fiddler's Green, Colin, the place where fishermen go when they don't go to hell."

"Let's see what happens," he said.

September 1

With two grand left in the bank, Colin received a call from Bonnie Corbet. She said that James Thompson was just appointed head of

Crusade Pictures, a new mini-studio production company with a big influx of European and Asian money. "One of the first things he wants to do is reoption your script," Bonnie said.

"Great," Colin said, itchy with excitement.

"Only this time there's going to be a clause," Bonnie said, "that gives him the right to replace you as director if you can't attract a star after the first new draft."

Colin's heart sank. "What are my options?" he asked.

"There aren't any," she said. "Take the deal, you can use the money. It's your only shot."

She sent the deal memo the next day and Colin signed it.

When he told Gina about it, she quietly walked into the bedroom and closed the door. When he followed her in, she was lying face down, her head in a pillow, crying. He went to her and stroked her hair. She turned to him, her strong face collapsed in sobs. "I'm happy for yeh, because I want yeh to be successful at what yeh do," she said. "But it's not good news for me. It means you'll be staying here in Los Angeles. I told you, Colin, I'm at the end of me rope. Me granny's sick, I have to go home. At least for a while. I'll petrify to stone here."

For the next week, Colin agonized over his decision, spending time alone walking the surf at Santa Monica, staring into the deep sea and the big sky, imagining life without Gina and the kids. He remembered her saying she had walked these same shores, feeling like an insignificant jot in a big book. He could hear Brianna reading sentences from *Pippi Longstocking* to him, hear her reading the cereal-box copy to him, hear her call him Daddy and telling him that she loved him. He didn't want Brianna and Seamus raised in Ballytara with a goat on the lawn and people stuck two centuries behind Western civilization.

But, rather than parting after another stabbing, or something equally disastrous and ugly, it would be better to make their inevitable parting an amiable one.

Besides, I don't want to be in love with Gina Furey, he thought. *She was just supposed to be a model for a character in a script. But life is not a movie. In movies you can leave out the boring parts. You can edit the parts that don't make sense. You can assign motivations and psychological coherence. But life is too erratic and surprising and heartbreakingly complicated to fix with a story conference. You can't live a movie. Gina is a wild and wacky broad I met when she was robbing me. A great piece of ass but a terrible choice for a soul mate. I have to learn to live without her; it's the only way I can fall out of love with her. If that means living without the kids, it's better now than later, when the parting will be more painful. I have to concentrate on my career. I'll send money and visit the kids. I have to take my chances. I have to get back to my life.*

He also knew that to make Gina stay was a selfish and cruel sentence on a woman like her. He could tie custody of Seamus up in the courts; maybe even win, but he cared for Gina too much to take the baby from her. Maybe all she needed was some time away, a short time to recharge her batteries. Then maybe they could alternate. He could fly over there, she and the kids could visit him. He'd have a roll in the sack with Gina a couple of times a year.

He also gave lots of thought to the *other fella,* whoever that might be. He decided that if there was another man, he'd have to deal with that reality. He hoped he was a good guy. *If he ever lifts a finger to either of the kids,* he thought, *I'll catch the next plane over and put him in a fucking wheelchair. This love affair is now over. Cut. That's a wrap.*

September 15

After Seamus blew out the candle on his first birthday cake, Gina put the kids in the tub together to wash off the chocolate and the ice cream. Colin placed an American passport bearing Seamus's picture on the kitchen table. Inside the passport were three Aer Lingus tickets.

"This is the saddest gift I've ever given to anyone," he said.

Gina sat down, picked up the tickets, and looked suddenly frightened. "Just like that," she said with a snap of her fingers.

"It's what you wanted," he said.

She was silent for a long time.

"What'll yeh do?" she asked, very softly.

"I'll work," he said.

"I hate meself for doing this to yeh," she said, so quietly it was hard to believe it was her voice. "I feckin' hate meself."

"Stop it," he said, putting his arm around her. "If you ever want to come back for a while, I'll come get ya and we'll go through Mexico again."

"What if I don't wanna?" she said.

"Then I'll visit them over there," he said. "I'll love the kids no matter what. We'll work out the details. But this last week I decided that I can't let you live in a state of constant unhappiness. If you're unhappy, I'll be unhappy. And the kids will grow up unhappy with two unhappy parents. Something has to give."

"Terrible sad," she said, clutching the passport and tickets.

September 21

The fracturing family stood at the same airport gate where the Lynch cousins had passed a year before. Colin held both kids in his arms, kissing one, then the other, repeatedly, making them giggle, trying to keep himself composed.

"I'll go back home with yeh," Gina said. "Right now if yeh want."

"The pain won't go away," he said. "You'll be worse tomorrow than yesterday if you did that."

"Aye," she said, biting her lower lip.

He'd insisted that neither of them drink before the farewell; he didn't want a sloppy, drunken display in front of the kids.

"Why aren't you coming on vacation, Daddy?" Brianna said.

"Daddy has to work," Colin said.

"Then you'll come to Ireland to meet us?"

"Maybe," Colin said. "But you'll call me, right?"

"Every day," Brianna said.

"Dada, more," Seamus insisted, and Colin kissed him again, puffing his cheeks and blowing it out against his son's face, making loud rude noises. Seamus squealed with laughter.

Colin looked at Gina; she had to turn away. He watched Gina walk in a small circle, her red hair thick under her floppy hat, dressed in tight jeans, cowboy boots, and a denim jacket tight around her narrow waist. *God, she's so beautiful,* Colin thought. *Even knowing what I know about her, how fucking crazy she is, I'd chase her again.*

The last call for boarding was announced over the PA system. Colin kissed Seamus and Brianna one more time. And now Brianna began to cry.

"I don't wanna go," she said, reaching for Colin. "I want you to come, too, Daddy."

"Daddy has to work," Colin said.

"Throw caution to the wind, Col, come with us."

Colin looked up from his crouch, where he was kissing Seamus good-bye. "You know I can't," he said.

The Aer Lingus steward urged Gina to get on board.

"Well, this is it, then, so," she said.

"Have fun," Colin said.

She put her arms around him, grabbed him by the back of the hair and whispered in his ear. "You're better off without me," she said. "Kiss me, yeh big bollocks."

He kissed her deeply.

Then she turned, unable to look at him, grabbed the handles of the pram, and pushed Seamus down the ramp to the plane. Brianna held on to the handle and cried as she waved good-bye to Colin and then the steward closed the door and they were gone.

forty-one

November 15

In the private screening room of James Thompson's Malibu Colony house, Melissa Thompson ran through *First Love, Last Love,* for a third time. Colin explained that in order to light the final shot he'd climbed over a fence into someone's backyard, jerryrigged the electric power box, and ran the cable into the Queens street.

"It looks like it was shot by Gordon Willis," she said, referring to one of the great cinematographers of modern film, a man who had shot all the *Godfather* movies, and who loved to probe the netherworld of shadow and low light.

Colin laughed and said, "Don't ever let *him* hear you say that."

Gina had been gone for more than a month and had called him exactly twice. He'd given her five thousand dollars and asked her to rent a decent flat or small cottage. Of course, she'd let him know she was staying with the grannies out on Whiterock Road in Ballytara, where there was no phone and no way for him to reach her. "Feck off if you t'ink I'm paying for a cell phone out of me children's allowance wages," she said.

Communication with her or the kids was totally dependent on her whim. One call came two weeks earlier, at four in the morning L.A. time, when she was out in a Dublin pub with the kids, having a noon pint with her cousins. The second call came the night before, at 8:30 P.M. L.A. time, which meant it was 4:30 A.M. in Dublin. Gina was drunk. She said she was at a friend's house, refused to say which friend, and said she couldn't find a decent flat to rent and that the money was running out fast because she gave away most of it to her cousins, all of whom were broke.

"Not to worry," she said, slurring her words and laughing. "There's no shortage of rich Yank wankers in the hotels. I'll call yeh when there's somethin' to say or when yer child needs a few bob. Other than that, enjoy the feckin' sun and the blond ghees of California."

Then, in the background, he heard a man's voice say, "That call is costing me a fortune, Gina."

The other fella, he thought.

When Colin asked who the man was, Gina grew defensive. "Mind yer own nosy hole," she'd said. "Do I ask where you've been? I just called out of the goodness of me heart to say the kids is fine, at home with their grannies, right as rain. Wee Seamus asks for his dada all the time. If you truly gave a donkey's shite, you'd be here with them. Wee Brianna sent you a card. Anyway, yer there, I'm here, and tha's the that and I'm gloriously drunk and tha's me for now, bye-bye."

As Gina drunkenly tried to cradle the phone, Colin heard the man laughing in the background. "You're pissed," he said. "I've got the fire roaring now, luv, and there's plenty to drink."

The man laughed and Colin heard Gina laughing as the phone was finally hung up, leaving him with the big hollow transatlantic echo and a dial tone.

After that call, he sat in his chair in the living room, looking around the house. He walked to the kids' bedroom and gently closed the door. He couldn't stand looking at the emptiness. Then, in need of human comfort, he'd picked up the phone and called Melissa Thompson. He told her he finally had a free day to go over his short film. She invited him out to Malibu the next day.

After watching the film three times, Melissa made them dinner, serving a pair of barbecued yellowfin tuna steaks and a large green salad, and pouring two glasses of California chablis. They ate on the rear deck, overlooking the Pacific, listening to the gulls and the waves. In the distance, he could see pelicans divebomb the sea.

"How long has she been gone?" Melissa asked as she squeezed lemon over her salad and fish.

"Over a month," he said.

"Do you miss her?"

"You want the answer I should give you or the truth?"

"Do you love her?" she asked.

"I wish I didn't," he said.

"Don't let your love for your kid confuse how you feel about the kid's mother," Melissa said. "My father stayed with my mother a lot longer than he should have. For me. If he'd left her when he should have, after the first time he caught her fucking around, I might not have grown up thinking she was a slut. A promiscuous divorcée mother is more palatable for a kid than a married cheater. When I was seventeen, I was dating this twenty-five-year-old guy who took me to a pool party at a Beverly Hills mansion. I went to the pool house to change. The door was locked and I heard two people getting it on inside. So I waited till they were done. Amused. And ten minutes later, out walks my mother, in a string bikini, with a boy toy in a Speedo beside her. I wound up hating her for what she was doing to my dad. If they were divorced, I wouldn't have minded so much. Finally, I had to convince my dad to get rid of the bitch."

"You still talk to her?"

"We get along a lot better now," she said, watching a gull nose-dive into the rolling surf and rise with small fish in its mouth. "She doesn't run around as much anymore, either. I think it was more of a can-I-get-away-with-it sport when she was married. Now that it's allowed, it doesn't interest her as much. The cloak-and-dagger was sexier than the sex."

"I miss the kids," Colin said.

"If you didn't, I wouldn't talk to you," she said, lifting her glass and holding it out to clink with his. "To cuckolded fathers."

Colin lifted his glass, clinked hers, and they both sipped.

Sex with a new partner was always more sensation than emotion, and Melissa Thompson was sensational in bed. She was a natural blonde, athletically toned, southern Californian, with tiny string-bikini tan lines. She was adventurous and generous in bed, and afterward she talked knowledgeably and intelligently about movies and actors and the latest draft of his script.

Day turned to evening, with more wine and more sex and chicken-and-shrimp kabobs on the grill. By the time night fell, they lay on her big bed in her massive bedroom staring through the unobstructed cathedral windows at the moon and the starry sky over the Pacific. Melissa stretched naked next to him, a blond and tanned offering to the gods. She sucked the thumb of his left hand and whispered, "I have some information to tell you. But you didn't hear it from me. My father read your latest draft and . . ."

Melissa kept talking, intermittently sucking his thumb, but her words became muted as all Colin could think about was Gina in bed with *the other fella,* sucking him. Another man, in another city, with his dick in Gina's mouth, and he let out a loud, frustrated, sickened growl.

"Ahhhhhhrrrrg!" He slammed his fist into the bed.

"What?" Melissa said, sitting up with a start.

Abashed, he cleared his throat and shook his head. "Sorry."

"Here I am telling you that my father liked your last draft so much he's thinking of green-lighting it with or without a star and you act like you're ready to vomit on me," she said. "You are *weird.*"

"My mind drifted," he said. "Did your father really say that?"

She looked at him and nodded. "You were thinking of *her* doing what we're doing," she said. "Weren't you? It's eating you alive that she might be fucking some other guy."

His silence told her she was right.

"It's okay," she said.

"No it's not," he said.

"The reason I loved your short movie so much is because my first love, my high-school sweetheart, broke my heart so badly I thought I'd never love anyone again," she said. "Your little film expressed those sentiments so well that it gave me hope that I wasn't alone. Now I see that you are able to love again. You love this odd-ball Irish girl. It won't last long, but at least it tells me that you're still capable of love. That gives me faith."

"Yeah?" he said. He wished he was half as mature as Melissa.

"Yeah," she said. "I have a confession to make, too. Just now, as we made love, I thought about my first love. I compared everything you did to how he did it."

He looked at her, propped himself up on an elbow. "You fantasized about him as you fucked me?"

"I've done that with every guy since him," she said.

"How many?"

"Obviously not enough," she said with a laugh, kissing his lips, his face, his neck, his nipples, his belly, as she made her way lower. "If you can get over the first one, you'll get over the second one. But I'm warning you, Coyne, three strikes and you're out."

Now she couldn't talk any more and as she loved him there on the edge of the warm Pacific, he wondered if Gina was doing the same to the other fella in some chilly Dublin flat.

forty-two

November 16

Just as Melissa had said, James Thompson called Colin to say that he was putting *Across the Pond* into pre-production for Crusade Pictures.

"We're counting on ya, guy," Thompson said.

"I won't let you down," Colin said before saying good-bye and hanging up.

He stood motionless in the living room, closed his eyes, imagining the whole opening sequence of following the Gina character through Dublin. "Yes," he whispered.

Finally, Colin thought as he paced the room, picking up one of Seamus's teething rings. *I'm gonna make a movie! A real Hollywood movie. No little student film. Professional actors, a seasoned crew, location permits, a caterer. Christ, Mom would have been so proud. It's a long way from her ten grand hidden in the statue of the Infant of Prague for the short film. Gotta call Dad, Jack, Eddie. I'll call Linda Parks, too. Nah, let her and all my NYU and SoHo film friends read about it in* Variety. *I wish Gina was here to celebrate this with me. No, better that she's not because she would only find the negatives in the good news.*

Then, as quickly as the euphoria surged in him, dread consumed him. *God Almighty, if I screw it up, I'll never work again. It's like getting a title shot. I already lost at the Oscars. Two strikes in this town is a lifetime banishment for a new director. I can do this, I know these characters. I know the performances I must get from my actors. I know my script. All I need is a good cameraman, a good sound man, a good editor all working for me—no, with me, as part-ners—and I can pull this off. I can't let anything distract me. Not Gina, not the kids, not anyone.*

In his excitement, Colin chomped on Seamus's teething ring.

Even in his house, alone, it made him feel foolish. A wave of loss and separation washed through him. *Don't let cheap emotion overtake you,* he thought. *There's too much work to be done.*

An hour later, a fax came from Thompson that stated that even though he couldn't find an A-list star, any one of the actresses from the approved B-list would be acceptable to the studio as long as he could do it within a seven-million-dollar budget.

Then a messenger arrived at the door with a letter on studio stationery that gave him full authority to negotiate with the Irish Film Board to secure locations and hire actors and crew members in Ireland. Any casting he needed to do in the United States would be handled by the Crusade Pictures business affairs office.

Colin waited all day for Gina to call. He wanted to tell her he would be in Dublin after the New Year to scout locations, open a production office.

Gina didn't call.

When Colin arrived at Thompson's beach house, Melissa popped a bottle of Louis Roederer Cristal champagne. She toasted his green-lighted movie and they drank one glass each before falling into bed.

He never thought of Gina or "the other fella."

When they were finished, Melissa poured Colin another glass of champagne, and toasted him again. "To a simply great piece of ass," she said, clinking his glass.

"I'm supposed to say that to you," he said.

"I'm feeling victorious," she said.

"Why's that?"

"This time all I thought about was you," she said.

"I'm flattered," he said with a laugh.

"It's like, suddenly, my first love doesn't even *compare* to you. Like you screwed him right out of my system, into history."

"Was it an orgasm or an exorcism?"

"Both," she said.

Yeah, sure, he thought, *and how much did my relationship with you influence your old man green-lighting my script?*

"Ya know, if I thought your script sucked I would have told my father that, too," she said, lifting a glass of champagne from the night table. "No matter how good you are in bed."

She reads my mind, he thought.

"I don't want you to take this the wrong way," she said. "I'm not husband shopping. But I think you've helped me believe I'm capable—if I wanted to—of falling in love again. I didn't know if that was possible before I met you. Like I said, this is not a spiel for a serious relationship. Just a thank you."

She smiled nervously and he lifted her chin and kissed her, hoping the gesture would substitute for words. *She wants me to tell her I love her,* Colin thought. *But I don't love this girl. I don't feel it. So don't bullshit her by saying it. I feel for Melissa what Gina probably feels for me—I like her, care about her, enjoy sex with her. But I don't love her.*

He loved Gina Furey. *That goddamned selfish bitch,* he thought. And it made him feel lousy.

The green-lighting of *Across the Pond* was announced in *Variety* and *The Hollywood Reporter.* Colin began interviewing crew members and had actors reading together for him during the day. At night, he and Melissa went together to screenings, ate in Ago's, Morton's, The Palm, Spago, Dan Tana's. Melissa introduced Colin to various celebrities, agents, and executives who all congratulated him on his "go" picture.

Colin and Melissa danced in the Sky Bar, hung out in the Viper Room, and laughed out loud in the Comedy Store. They sipped champagne, kissed, and groped each other in the hot tub of James Thompson's Beverly Hills mansion or walked at midnight along the Malibu surf. They made love in her Mercedes, on the beach, in the pool house, in his production office, on her father's desk.

November 20

At a movie premiere party at Spago in Beverly Hills, Melissa introduced Colin to Nicolas Cage and several other top Hollywood actors and directors. With the daughter of James Thompson as arm candy, people handed Colin their cards, asked to do lunch or dinner, or to get a chance to see his script.

Melissa excused herself to go to the ladies' room, and when Colin walked to the bar to get a club soda he bumped into Frank Burston, the young director who'd won the best short film Oscar that Gina had robbed. Burston seemed a little high and Colin could smell the scotch on his breath.

"Hey, Frank," Colin said.

"Congrats to the Melissa Thompson flavor of the month," Burston said. "I see you've graduated Schmooze U., cum-in-my-mouth laude."

"Not enough fish with the wine, Frank, huh?"

"Melissa sure is Daddy's little girl," Burston said, and took another sip. "She flashes her blond bush on first dates. On second dates, she flashes daddy's green light on your script."

"That what you think?"

"That's what everybody says," Burston says. "But, hey, look, I can think of worse ways to get a picture made. Doing Melissa isn't exactly rough duty. I should have called her back for seconds myself. But, silly old-fashioned me, I wanted to get my picture made on the merits."

"I think Johnnie Walker is your ventriloquist tonight, Frank," Colin said.

"At least she beats that shanty pregnoid you were dragging around like something from a fossil dig," Burston said. "The one who stole my fucking Oscar."

"Hey, Frank, how'd you like me to break your fucking nose?"

"Nice," he said. "I win the fucking Oscar, you fuck your way into a go picture, and she attaches herself to the film as an AD or coproducer as Daddy's plant. And now you want to hit me for warning you? What do they call male bimbos, anyway, Coyne? Bambos? Bimballs? In your Celtic case, O'Bimbang?"

"First, I'm gonna call *you* an ambulette. That way, asshole, by the time I snap your fucking neck like a number-two pencil they'll be ready to take you to the hospital."

Burston slugged the rest of the drink, turned to the bartender, and ordered another. "Good line," he said. "Melissa write it? No, that might have been the shanty one."

Colin was ready to drop him there in the middle of the party, but he restrained himself. *It's what Burston wants,* he thought. *He wants to make me look like a hothead asshole, a Queens street hitter, and make himself look like a victim. Think smarter.*

Colin took a deep breath, anger tingling his skin like a flesh-eating disease. Melissa made her way through the crowd and hooked her arm through one of his, felt the tension.

"Hello, Frank," she said. "Any nibbles yet?"

"Any day now," Burston said, using Colin's line from an earlier conversation.

Melissa led Colin back through the crowd.

"How well do you know Burston?" Colin asked.

"Not as well as he'd like me to," she said. "His fiancée, Nancy, dumped him for some hotshot Hong Kong director. Ever since, Frank calls me all the time. It's kind of sad. Technically, he can direct, but he has no original ideas, can't write, doesn't have the emotional maturity for dramatic irony, and doesn't know how to take criticism in developing a script. But if he was handed a shooting script in perfect shape he could probably make a technically competent movie."

"It's none of my business," he said, "but did you ever . . ."

"No," she said. "I'm not saying there aren't others, maybe even a few in this room. But certainly not Frank Burston, who always seemed to have the idea that if he bedded me, I could get my father to green-light a picture for him."

Colin *wanted* to believe her, so he did.

November 25

Colin awoke in a sweat.

In Gina's absence, Colin was becoming very fond of Melissa. He valued her opinions, respected her intelligence, listened to her advice. She was the kind of woman with whom any man could easily fall in love. But for some reason, probably his working-class Queens inferiority complex, he felt like an outsider. Whenever he left his rented Valley home and drove over Laurel Canyon to Melissa's father's Beverly Hills estate or out to the Malibu Colony sand castle, he felt like he should use the servants' entrance. He felt like an employee, a pool boy.

Whenever he awoke like this next to Melissa in the night, from anxiety or heartache, he would lie there in the dark and think of Gina, Seamus, and Brianna. Wondering whose bed Gina was in. She hadn't called in more than a month, even after he'd sent two telegrams to the Whiterock Road address. He was terrified Seamus would forget him; angst-ridden that Brianna would think he'd abandoned her.

"You're thinking of her again, aren't you?" Melissa said two nights before Thanksgiving, as she sensed him lying awake in the night. He stared out the cathedral windows at the cloudy night sky, listening to the lap of the sea.

"I feel like half a man without my kids," he said.

"You'll see them when we go location scouting," she said.

"We?" he said, remembering what Burston had said about her attaching herself to his movie to keep an eye on it for her father.

"Oh," she said. "Sorry for being presumptuous. I thought maybe you wanted me to work on the film."

"I hadn't thought about it," Colin said.

"My mistake."

They said no more about it.

That night, Colin missed a phone call from Gina.

"I don't know, nor do I care, where yeh are but I thought you'd want to talk to yer kids," Gina said on tape. "Brianna drives me mad askin' about her daddy. Wee Seamus is gas altogether, learnin' Irish sayin's, callin' everybody a bollocks and a gobshite in his mad American accent. Anyway, I better jet, I have to get Seamus a cough bottle and raise a few bob for Christmas. Ta-ra."

"Fucking selfish bitch," he said aloud, slamming his hand down on the tabletop. He'd sent Gina three telegrams asking her to always call him at 8 A.M. Los Angeles time, which was 4 P.M. in Dublin, when he was sure to always be home. Instead, she called at indiscriminate hours, whenever it occurred to her, whenever there was a phone free in a pub.

He walked to the children's room and for the first time since they'd left he opened the door. He looked around at their small beds, the scattered toys, the tricycle. The room was like a mausoleum. *I should put all this stuff in storage,* he thought. *It's like a wake in here.*

Colin had the phone company equip him with call forwarding service, so that if Gina called him at home it would be redirected to his cell phone.

Gina never called.

Melissa did. She invited him to eat Thanksgiving dinner at her family's chalet in Aspen. Colin declined, saying he wanted to spend the weekend polishing the script, looking at actors' head shots and reels, making casting notes.

"I'll spend Thanksgiving here with you if you want," she said.

"Nah, I'll be all right," he said.

"I'll see you when I get back, then?"

"Absolutely."

He didn't mention her working on his film. Neither did she. On Thanksgiving, he ate in Ireland's Eye. Alone.

Colin had auditioned some very good Irish actresses, but the studio wanted someone with some American recognition. By the end of the holiday weekend, Colin reduced the casting of the leading lady down to three actresses: one Brit, one Irish-American, and the front runner, a beautiful redhead named Amanda Jones, the Welsh-born star of a Warner Brothers hit youth-TV series. The Irish-American actress's agent called Colin to say, "Julia doesn't play psychopathic villains."

Amanda Jones wanted the part and the studio was high on her as long as the chemistry worked with the as-yet-uncast leading man.

"The chemistry should be oil and water," Colin told the executives.

"Yeah, but we want heat coming off the screen," Thompson said. "Make sure the actor is not a fucking wimp. We want a real guy who stands up to this crazy-ass chick."

Colin continued to read some of the best young actors in

Hollywood for the role, trying to get the right combination of friction and humor. As he read Amanda Jones in the role of Gina, he began to see Gina in a new, hard, cold light. He realized he missed Gina less and less. Seeing some of the scenes based on real life performed at readings made him see how insane his life with Gina had been.

"Don't get me wrong, I think the script is great," Amanda Jones said, after one reading. "I love the part of Gina. She's funny and wicked and complicated. But I'm having a hard time understanding why this Yank would fall in love with me after I treat him so badly."

Colin was silent for a long beat and nodded. "So is he," Colin explained. "He falls in love with her early in the story and then his arc, his mission, is to fall madly out of love with her."

"But with the child in the middle, two children, actually, it makes it very sad," Amanda Jones said.

"It ain't a fairy tale, Mandy," Colin said.

"Yeah," she said. "They do have to part ways, as they would in real life."

She's definitely right for the part, he thought. *Thank God she's married or else I'd probably chase her, too.*

Colin only saw Melissa twice in the two weeks after the long Thanksgiving weekend. He busied himself hiring a production manager, production designer, cinematographer. He slept at home, alone, hoping that Gina would call. She didn't.

December 17

Colin checked his mailbox and found an envelope with an Irish postmark. He tore it open and found a handmade card from Brianna inside with a crude Santa carrying his sack. Her printing was childish and her spelling was obviously supervised by Gina.

"Deer Dady, Al I wunt for Christmis is you. An lots of prestens. Ha ha. I miss you. I miss Stiky storys. Luv, Brianna."

Underneath that note there was a big explosive scribble in black crayon with a P.S. from Brianna next to it. *"This is Seamis saying he mises you, to. Ha ha."*

There was no note from Gina.

Colin went inside and called his travel agent.

"You're going to see her," Melissa said that afternoon, as they sat at a window booth in Gladstone's 4 Fish on the Pacific Coast Highway, cracking crabs and drinking cold Corona beers with lime.

"I miss the kids," he said. "While I'm there, I'll do some scouting, I'll talk to the film board, and do some preliminary local casting."

"My father won't be happy you're leaving in the middle of casting the male lead," she said, issuing a friendly warning.

"It'll be just one week."

"You don't want me to go?"

"It's complicated."

"I won't be seeing you for Christmas, then?" she said.

"Christmas is for kids, Melissa. It's sentimental horseshit."

She smiled, nodded, took a sip of a cold beer, and excused herself to go to the ladies' room. He watched Melissa walk tall and proud in the tight blue jeans and white high heels, noticing several other men at various tables turn as she passed.

Colin was still sitting there alone a half-hour later when he finally asked the waitress for a check.

Part VI

Dublin, Ireland

forty-three

December 19

The pony was gone but the goat was still tethered to a rope, lying in the mud of the bald lawn. A cold drizzle pattered on the canvas of the covered wagon. At a little past 8:00 A.M., Granny opened the door, squinted at Colin, and erupted into a phlegmy coughing fit.

The plane had landed at 7:00 A.M. Dublin time and Colin had told the nervous taxi driver to wait at the curb on Whiterock Road. His suitcase was in the backseat.

"Don't leave me here long," the driver had said. "Or I'll be feckin' 'et."

Granny recovered from her coughing fit long enough to be uncivil. "Fine feckin' fella you are, off and leavin' them childer here for months without a farthin' to their name," she said, coughing deeply again, her whole body rattling. "Me useless husband is even after selling his pony to feed yer young wans."

"Where's Gina?" Colin asked.

"Fat man's arse on Moore Street," she said, launching into another phlegmy fit of coughing. She lit a cigarette.

Colin knew she wasn't going to divulge anything resembling intelligent information. He looked past Granny as Brianna approached from inside the house.

"Daddy?" she whispered and then she saw him and came running with her arms outstretched. "Daaadeeee . . ."

Colin scooped her up in his arms and kissed her as Seamus appeared. He was naked, waddling down the corridor, a baby bottle filled with tea and milk in one hand, his face glazed with dried snot, his hair sooty and matted, and his dirty feet bare. He stared up at Colin with big, tired eyes. His right eye was half closed from an inflamed sty.

"I'm tired of that wee wan pissin' me bed," Granny said. "I've known sheep what pisses less."

Brianna was kissing Colin's face and holding him tightly as he bent and held out his left hand for Seamus. The baby just stood staring, stuck his bottle in his mouth, looked up at Granny, and then back at Colin. A stream of urine fired out of Seamus's penis like a fountain, causing Brianna to laugh. "In one end, out the udder," she said, with a touch of a Dublin accent.

"One of Brown's cows, he is," Granny said.

Colin moved past Granny into the house, which smelled like urine, bleach, coal, and tobacco smoke, and lifted Seamus in his free arm. The baby kept staring him in the eyes, sucking on his bottle, his nostrils sealed with membranes of green mucus, the right eye a purple sore.

"Brianna, get me a clean nappy and something to clean Seamus with," Colin said, and she ran off into the bedroom and returned with a box of baby wipes. Colin scoured Seamus's face, peeling the dried mucus like old glue, wiping his genitals and his behind. Colin fastened the clean diaper on the baby, who stared up at him, bewildered.

"It's Daddy, Seamo," Brianna said. "He's come to take us back to America—hot water and pizza and a car."

Colin kissed Seamus on the face, tickled his belly, and the baby boy finally smiled, a glimmer of recognition bubbling to the surface.

"Say Dada, you gobshite," Brianna said.

"Gobshi'," said Seamus. "Dada . . ."

Brianna laughed. "Granny says he should work for the RTE . . ."

Now Granda came in from the austere master bedroom, blinking and frowning, his teeth out, clothes wrinkled from sleep. "Howayeh," he said. "Bit of a chill, wha'?"

"Where's Gina?" Colin asked.

"The answer to that is in the Letter of Fatima," he said. "She's in Mountjoy for all I know. Probably in one of her cousins's kips."

Colin put Brianna down, told her to get dressed, and to find some clothes for Seamus. Brianna rushed into the back bedroom, dragging her little brother behind her by the hand. Seamus held the bottle in his teeth and turned his head to reach for Colin.

Granda barked at Granny: "*You*, a feckin' cup of tea, wha'?"

Granny didn't even look at him, just turned, ripped a piece of peeling wallpaper from the wall, stuck the edge of it into the embers in the small coal fire until it burst to flame, carried it, burning, into the kitchen, turned on the gas, lit the fire under a scorched kettle, and dropped the burning paper into the sink. She stood in the kitchen, alone, coughing so hard the delft on the racks in the living room rattled.

Jesus Christ, Colin thought. *This shit ends here and now. I hate Gina for leaving the kids like this.*

None of the cousins had phones, so he got their addresses from Granda and loaded the kids into the back of the waiting taxi. He told the nervous driver he had a few stops to make.

"Do I get combat pay?" the driver asked.

"I'll make it worth your while," Colin said.

Philomena answered her door holding her pink polyester robe closed and wiping sleep from hungover eyes.

"My Jaysus, Colin. What about yeh?" she asked.

"See Gina?"

She looked like a witness evoking the Fifth Amendment.

"Was I supposed to?"

"Never mind," Colin said and walked back to the taxi.

"You can stay for a wee cup whilst I go find her for yeh," she said.

"I better go," Colin said.

By the time he got to Susan's house, the rain had stopped and a dim bulb of sun shone through the gray sky. Susan was in her front yard, hanging wash on a line, as her two-year-old son, Sammy, handed her clothespins.

"Lamb of Jaysus, what're you doin' home?" she asked Colin.

"Looking for Gina," he said.

"Haven't seen her for a few days. Where yeh takin' them childer?"

"To a hotel with some heat and hot water," Colin said.

"Central heatin' will make them catch their death," Susan said. "Are you staying for a wee cup?"

"No thanks, but tell Gina I'm at the Westbury Hotel."

He was going to use his hotel suite as a home base for secondary casting and for setting up location scouting while he was in Dublin. It was going to be hard getting any work done with two kids around, but he wasn't sending them back to Whiterock Road.

Bridie seemed the most nervous of the three cousins. She was the only one who didn't invite him in for a cup of tea. She kept looking down the road, nervously.

"Och, she can't be far," Bridie said. "Come back after."

Colin told her where he would be staying and turned to walk back to the taxi. Then he saw a Mercedes pull up at the curb of the intersecting street. A man was driving and Gina kissed him good-bye and climbed out. Her hair was platinum again and she was stunned to see Colin standing in the pathway, hearing Brianna and Seamus calling to her from the taxi window.

"Howayeh," Gina said, staring at Colin.

"Merry Christmas," Colin said.

She looked over at the Mercedes, where the driver rolled down the window to lean out.

"Are yeh all right, Grace?" the man asked, eyeing Colin, who stood staring at her, hands jammed in his jacket pockets. The man had a long ponytail and a hardened, sun-starved face like a gray stone in a prison wall.

"Grand," Gina said. "G'wan."

"Sure, luv?" the man asked, looking from her to Colin. Gina nodded to him and the wary man drove slowly away.

"I'll put on the kettle," said a nervous Bridie, disappearing inside the house.

"He's just a fella I know for years what give me a lift," she said. "I slept at Philomena's and . . ."

Colin nodded. "I just came from Philomena's."

Gina took a breath and said, "Feck off outta dat. There's no weddin' ring on my fingers. I don't need alibis or lullabies. And don't tell me you weren't with your own fancy women in L.A."

"You wanted to leave," he said. "And I don't give a shit where you were or who you were with. But when I found them, the kids were cold and dirty and sick. I'm taking them to my hotel to feed them, bathe them, and spend some time with them."

"I'll go with yeh."

"You can go to hell."

He climbed in the taxi, which roared off, leaving Gina alone on the street.

forty-four

In the hotel suite, Colin gave the kids a bath and ordered room service for all three of them. They ate mashed potatoes, peas, carrots, chicken, bread, and ice cream. After dinner, they all climbed under the covers of the king-size bed, one on each side.

"I want a Sticky story, Daddy," Brianna said.

He told them a new story about Sticky. The dog swam all the way across the Atlantic Ocean to find Brianna and Seamus. He had to fight lots of sea monsters along the way.

"Does Sticky take us back to America?" Brianna asked.

"Yeah, he does, but this time he takes a plane," Colin said.

"Does Sticky fly the plane?"

"Absolutely," Colin said, telling them about the plane ride and how they got lost and wound up in a jungle. Before he could ad-lib an ending, both kids were sleeping.

December 20

Gina knocked on the hotel door at 7:00 A.M. Colin said nothing but left the door open. She looked like she hadn't slept. Gina was quiet and reserved when she came into the room and poured herself a cup of tea from the room-service cart and proceeded to dress the kids in clean clothes she took from her large carry-bag.

"They have their breakies?"

"Yep," Colin said.

"We had cornflakes, eggs, bacon, jam, toast, tea, and orange juice," Brianna said. "Daddy's taking us to the Green to feed the ducks."

As they were leaving, Colin said, "Leave the silverware."

"Fuck off," she said.

Gina didn't talk much during the morning as the kids demanded Colin's undivided attention. They fed the swans and ducks in St. Stephen's Green.

"Daddy, why do ducks go quack?" Brianna asked.

"They tried barking but it was too ruff, ruff, ruff."

"Yeh silly goose," she said, giggling.

Seamus sat on Colin's shoulders, throwing pieces of bread into the water, pointing at the ducks and shouting, "Duh, duh, duh."

Gina sat on a bench, smoking, distracted, withdrawn, and preoccupied. When she caught Colin's attention briefly, she asked, "How's yer fil-um comin' along?"

"Fine," he said.

They ate lunch in the hotel. Brianna told Colin all about her new Dublin friends. She also said that she missed Los Angeles. "I don't want you to go back without us," she said.

"Your mom and I are going to talk about that," Colin told her.

Gina listened but said nothing.

That afternoon, at Colin's request, a young, earnest, baby-faced doctor, Dr. Terrence Maloney, arrived to check out the kids. He said he was from Clare and was trying to establish himself in Dublin. He thought the best way to build a practice was to make himself available for house calls twenty-four hours a day.

Dr. Maloney said both kids had heavy colds and he gave them antibiotic drops and cough syrup and an eyewash for Seamus's sty.

Colin paid him in cash and Doctor Maloney handed Colin his card and told him to call him anytime, any hour, anywhere.

After the doctor left, Colin placed his first long-distance call to James Thompson at Crusade Pictures. Colin told Thompson's secretary he was calling from Dublin and she told him to hold on. Colin waited for a good ten minutes and then the secretary told him that Thompson was in a meeting, and couldn't be disturbed.

He called every half an hour after that, and each time Thompson was either at a meeting, on the phone, or had gone to lunch.

Am I blowing my career, here? he wondered. *Did Melissa sabotage me because I wouldn't hire her? What the fuck am I doing here instead of casting the movie back in L.A.?*

The family spent the night in the hotel, all of them sitting on the big bed, eating chicken and chips from room service and watching an animated movie on the hotel pay-per-view channel. Colin and Gina hardly spoke.

Colin could sense a mounting anxiety in Gina as she repeatedly rose from the bed, walked to the window, and looked out into the Dublin street. It was as if she were missing something, or someone, rudely sighing. She sipped a Guinness. Colin swirled a club soda, weary with jet lag and sickened by the thought of booze. Before the film ended, the two kids were fast asleep. They were spotlessly clean, in warm pajamas, their breathing deep and clear. Colin stared at them as Gina stood looking aimlessly out the window, her blond hair tumbling down her back in big curls that looked like gold bracelets.

Colin walked out to the sitting room of the suite. Gina followed, closing the door to the bedroom.

"Yer disappointed in me, aren't yeh?"

"Yes," he said. "I won't have the kids living like that, dirty, cold, and sick. There's nothing romantic or noble about poverty. Poverty sucks, period. This was worse than just poverty, this was neglect. That's worse."

"It was good enough for me . . ."

"No it fucking wasn't, Gina," he said. "You have a murdered mother, a lam-artist father, degenerate uncles who molested you as a kid. You lived in fucking orphanages and Borstal and on the road. You steal, you're on the dole, you're half illiterate. That's not good enough for you or any kid anywhere on the goddamned planet. Certainly not *my* kids, or at least the one I have a say about."

"Yer right," she said. "I wanted the better for them. That's the why I went to America in the first place. But America wasn't what I expected. There was no crack."

"Fuck you and the motherfucking *crack*, Gina," he said. "You're a mother, an adult, not a teenage party animal. Ireland is a great country. It's going through an economic revolution, but you choose to raise the kids as travelers here. And America's what you make of it. It has a lot to offer the kids. I'm glad my parents emigrated when they did, tell you that."

"You'd want me back?"

He was about to shout no, but instead he let the simple question hover in mid-air. *If this was my film, the answer would be to hold for a double beat and then cut,* he thought. *Let the pictures give the answer. But there are no jump cuts in real life. You have to live through the transitions.*

"I want my kids around me," he said, knowing he would use that ambiguous, noncommittal line in the film. *Avoid the question about Kieran and Gina's relationship. Focus on the kids.*

"Can yeh stay here through Christmas?" she asked softly.

"I'll see if I can be away that long," he said. "I can't get this guy Thompson on the phone. I'm sure he's pissed off. I don't blame him. Maybe I can tell him I'm scouting locations while I'm here, talking to some film board people. I should be home casting. I have a leading lady to rehearse and a leading man to cast. I have a picture to get on the boards. Then I'll be coming back here anyway. My plans were to rent a house, where we could all stay until shooting finishes, separate bedrooms if you want."

"Feck tha'. If I'm with yeh, I'm with yeh."

"I was thinking about getting you back into the States, this time on a motion-picture visa. If I cast you in the film I can legally bring you into the States to shoot scenes."

"I thought it was kinda fun the Mexico way," she said.

That seems so long ago, he thought.

There was a long silence and then she turned from the window.

"Who's your fancy woman?"

"That's finished," he said.

"I bet it was that producer fella's daughter," she said. "The one who smelt herself. She probably carries baby pictures of herself."

He looked at her, wondering how she knew it was Melissa.

"You mean the one who acted like a normal human being?"

"She had the gonkey eyes for yeh the night of the Oscars and that day in her father's house," Gina said. "Any woman who goes after a pregnant woman's man deserves a life without kids."

"It wasn't like that," he said.

"That's the curse I wished on her but I kept me gob shut for your sake, so yeh could get yer movie made."

"The movie getting made has nothing to do with me and her."

"Yer so gullible it's a right laugh," she said.

"Must be to be involved with you."

"She knows yer here with me?"

"Yes," he said.

"She must think I'm a right eejit," she said.

"No, she thinks I'm sick to give a rat's ass about you," he said. "You split. You cut off communication between me and my kids. I come back and find them living like fucking stray dogs, sick, dirty, covered in snot, shit, and piss, living in that hell-hole while you were out getting your hole plugged by 'the other fella.'"

"What other fella?" she demanded.

"Gina, let's not be fucking ridiculous, okay?" Colin said. "For chrissakes, you pulled up yesterday morning, after being out all night, with a complete scuz bucket who looked like he'd still be carrying ten diseases after he was boiled in bleach."

"I told yeh he was nuthin'," she said. "He bought drink. I slept on his couch. He gave me a lift . . ."

"Bullshit," Colin said. "All those phone calls from some guy's house in the middle of the night, laughing and drunk . . ."

"That makes me a durty whore like you? Rolling around with your Beverly Hills nine-oh-two-one-oh bimbo?"

Colin remained calm. "This time I'm not buying your lying tinker scams, baby," he said.

"Suit yerself," she said, moving toward the door, grabbing her coat as she went.

"I've crossed a continent and an ocean to see my kids," Colin said. "I won't chase you another fucking step."

She stood by the door with her coat in her hand. Colin lay staring at the ceiling. *One Mississippi, two Mississippi,* he thought.

"Be back later," she said, and left.

fortζ-five

December 21

Colin slept fitfully, comforted only by the nearness of the kids. When he popped awake in the night, his throat was parched and he felt slightly nauseated.

He'd tried calling James Thompson every hour until four A.M. Dublin time. The secretary kept telling him to hold on, and as the minutes ticked by, he knew Thompson wouldn't be getting on the phone.

Colin was worried. He wondered if Melissa had told her father that Colin had rebuffed her proposal to work on the picture, and to travel with him to Dublin.

Nah, he thought. *She wasn't that vindictive. Not that immature.*

He dialed Melissa's number. It rang four times before she picked it up. "Hello," she said, a little exasperated.

"Melissa, it's Colin," he said. "I've been trying to . . ."

"Um, it's sort of a bad time," she said.

"Sorry."

"Me, too. Bye."

She hung up.

She's getting laid, he thought. *While I'm over here fucking myself out of a picture and a career.*

He showered early, washed and dressed the kids, and took them down for breakfast in the hotel dining room.

They were all just digging into their sausages and eggs when Gina swept into the room with a flourish, a big smile exploding from her festive face.

"How's me gorgeous darlin's," she said with a singsongy exaggeration, loudly kissing both of the excited kids before kissing a startled Colin on the lips. "Good mornin', handsome, and how's me love-a-ly little family?"

She was dressed in snug black wool slacks and a green turtleneck Aran sweater and a black Italian leather jacket that covered her hips and tied around her slim waist. The green floppy hat on her head was pinned with a sprig of Christmas pine. "Morning," Colin said.

Gina lifted the teapot, felt the bottom for warmth, took a piece of dry toast, smeared it with jam, and took a bite before carrying the teapot into the hotel kitchen. About a minute later, she came out through the flapping doors, followed by the shuffling culchie waitress carrying a larger, fresher pot.

"You're ruining my breakfast acting like that," Colin said.

She sat down at the table and took a portion of egg from each plate and made a sandwich for herself. She poured everyone a fresh cup of tea. "Now, wasn't I up all the night dug into me granny's kip, fixin' it up for the Christmas hoolie?"

"You on something?" Colin asked.

"Me an me cousins went up and only fumigated the place with bleach, ammonia, and Jeyes fluid," she said. "Poor feckin' Granny is coughing like a volcano, poor t'ing. She can't lift a finger. She doesn't eat, all she does is smoke. Bridie got her new lino for the living-room floor and Paul Lynch did a lovely job laying it down and puttin' up new wallpaper on the walls. Me and Philomena got a wee tree and some decorations. We put a wreath on the front door, Father Christmases, angels, and snowmen on the walls. The windows is all washed, there's a load of coal in the chute, drink and food in the press. Susan washed all the beddin'. Yeh wouldn't know the place. We have the back bedroom lovely and warm and cozy for us."

"Us?" Colin said. "I'm not staying out there, and I don't want the kids out there, either. The doctor said we have to keep these kids warm and dry. Besides, there's no phone, and I'm here to do a j-o-b."

"You don't spend Christmas week in a hotel with kids," Gina said, reaching into her bag and taking out a cell phone and handing it to him. "How is Father Christmas supposed to climb down the chimney of the Westbury Hotel, right, me darlin's?"

"Santa comes to Granny's house, down the chimney, and burns his bum on the hot coals," Brianna said, giggling.

"Gobshi'," said Seamus, holding a fork with a speared sausage.

"Where'd you get this?" Colin asked, perusing the cell phone.

"I rented it for yeh," she said. "It's all legal, like."

"Thanks, but I'm still not sleeping in Ballytara."

"I want to stay with Daddy," Brianna said.

"Gobshi', Dada," said Seamus.

Gina walked to Colin, pulled his chair away from the table, sat on his lap, and covered his face with kisses, the kids squealing with delighted laughter.

"Gina, knock it off."

"There's a big hoolie tonight in Ballytara," she said. "The families in the clan is coming from all over for the Furey Christmas hoolie. They're comin' in their caravans and trailers from the west, from the north, some from England and Scotland, from all over the place. There'll be songs and gargle and the crack. I'd say a few oul babbies will be made, a few weddin's planned, stories and fights and killin's galore. The halting site at the crossroads outside the estate will be filled. Should be mad altogether, wha'? You'll be the token buffer."

"Great," he said. "Everyone can take turns kicking the shit out of me."

I should see this for the movie, he thought. *Probably a great scene. I better go see this. I'll tell Thompson it's the reason I came.*

Gina laughed and took a gulp of tea as she ran her ringed fingers through his hair.

"No one will bother yeh if I'm around, sure they won't," she said, reaching into her pocketbook and taking out three passports, two Irish one American. "Tell yeh what, though, if yeh do come, I promise that the day after Saint Stevens's Day, I'll be ready to shift anywhere you want. All of us, and here's the passports as a guarantee."

Colin took the passports from Gina.

Maybe I can let them have the house back in L.A. and I'll rent a studio apartment, he thought. *At least the kids will be nearby. It'll be a fucking nightmare no matter what, but it has to be better for the kids than this shit.*

He shoved the passports into his jacket pocket.

Colin gave the kids their medicine and by the time breakfast was finished, Gina had convinced Colin to travel back out to Ballytara for the big Christmas hoolie.

"The first asshole that gives me a hard time, I'm breaking his jaw," Colin said.

"If yer feckin' able."

"First I have some things to do in Dublin to justify this trip," he said. "Plus, I have to apply for your emergency motion-picture visa."

"Grand," Gina said. "I'll take these'ns down to see Father Christmas on Grafton Street. Same fat rubber man as last year, moldy drunk again this year, I hear. I have to get a wagon full of messages, as well. We'll meet back here about five and head out to Granny's."

Gina took the kids off as Colin walked directly to the American embassy and made the initial applications for Gina and Brianna's motion-picture visas. He'd had the forethought to bring along the letter of authorization from Crusade Pictures. He told the clerk that he would be casting both of them in the film and that part of it would be shot here in Dublin and part of it in the United States and that for continuity he would need both of them to come to America.

The clerk checked Gina's file and the paperwork from the last time she applied for a visa. The clerk said that the visas should be no problem but they might require a ten-thousand-dollar security bond to ensure that Gina and Brianna would return to Ireland. Colin said that could be arranged if necessary. They told him to check back the next day, bringing Gina and Brianna with him.

Filled with mounting dread about his picture and the idea of bringing Gina back to America, Colin walked around the city alone, looking at some locations. He felt damp and sweaty under the collar and cold in the toes. His stomach grumbled. He'd had diarrhea during the night and was clogged with Immodium, making him feel both bloated and dehydrated. He popped into a few pubs, had a shandy in the first one, a glass of Harp in the second, and a pint of Guinness in the third.

At three o'clock, he walked through St. Stephen's Green and took a seat on an empty bench facing the statue of James Joyce. A pigeon sat on the head of the great Irish writer. *Even the great ones get shit on,* he thought. He dialed James Thompson's home number in Beverly Hills. "Hello," Melissa said, sounding a little dreamy.

His heart thumped when he heard her voice again, and imagined her naked and beautiful in the big bed.

"Melissa, it's Colin," he said. "I really need to speak . . ."

"Sorry, you have the wrong number," she said.

He heard her gently hang up the phone. "Shit!" he shouted, and the pigeon took flight from Joyce's head.

He quickly dialed Bonnie Corbet to see if she had heard anything from Thompson. A recording told him that Bonnie Corbet was out of the office and wouldn't be back until after the New Year. At 5:00 P.M., he tried James Thompson at his Crusade Pictures office. The secretary said he was tied up in an emergency meeting, and that it would probably last all day. Colin asked if she'd given Thompson all his messages. She said she had. He left the cell phone number.

Something is definitely wrong, he thought. *My picture is going down in flames.* He wanted to puke. *But that would be another movie cliché.*

They arrived at Granny's in a taxi at a little after 6:00 p.m. The street was lined with rusty trailers and shabby campers, like a low-budget independent movie location. Oil-barrel fires crackled near each trailer, casting long shadows and taking the chill off the clear night. The three-quarter moon washed the vast housing tract with a lunar glow. A few old-timers were parked in covered wagons, their ponies snorting into pails of oats. Women and girls hauled buckets of water from Granny's house and a dozen unleashed dogs sniffed each other's asses, familiarizing or reacquainting themselves. Kids of every age, in tattered and grimy clothes, worn in bulky layers, ran haphazardly in the gutters and through the front gardens of the Ballytara houses.

Some of the older teenagers led a half-dozen pubescent girls off on a firewood-gathering mission toward the cemetery behind the tract. Colin felt sorry for them. Colin figured a few of those girls would come back deflowered and pregnant, ready for the dole and the children's allowance before the next Christmas hoolie.

It's like a National Geographic *documentary,* he thought, staring through the back window of the taxi.

Colin lifted his camera to his eye and in the light of the white winter moon he scanned the dozens of young, hard men with high, angular cheekbones and leathery faces the color of strong tea. Some had different-colored eyes, like huskies, and wore flat caps or tweed walking hats. Most wore well-worn tweed sport jackets, wrinkled white shirts with stained ties and diamond tie pins, and unpolished blocky shoes or Wellington boots with the pants tucked in. They leaned on their motorized trailers and High Ace Toyotas parked at the curbside, drinking stout from bottles and smoking unfiltered cigarettes. When they saw Gina climb out of a taxi with the two kids, followed by Colin, the men gaped and spoke in the gammon traveler language.

As Colin paid the jittery cabbie, he could pick out "Yank" and "buffer" and knew they were referring to him. Gina stopped, handed the kids to Colin, and faced the men, tearing into them in a tirade of gammon. Colin held Seamus on his hip and had Brianna by the hand. *I'll superimpose English subtitles over the gammon,* he thought.

After Gina was finished, the men said nothing, just kept staring at Colin. "Uck-fay ou-yay," Colin said in pig latin, which seemed to baffle the travelers.

A Garda patrol car slithered by, scrutinizing the men leaning on the vehicles. *"Shadogs,"* shouted one in one direction, through cupped hands.

"Shades," shouted another in the opposite direction.

The cop car made a right at the corner. Colin followed Gina up the path to the house, where a parade of traveler women and girls did a bucket brigade to the trailers, hauling fresh water for cooking, washing, and giving to the animals while the men stood smoking, drinking, talking, and farting, some pissing against the trailers.

Inside the house, Granny sat in her master bedroom smoking and coughing in the half-gloom. "She's drownin' in phlegm," Gina said to Colin. "Do us a favor, luv, she'll never go see a doctor or a hospital. Call that wee freckly-faced doctor yoke from yesterday. He won't come all the way out here on my account, but he will if you ask him to in your dollar-bill accent."

Colin was in a bad mood, preoccupied with James Thompson. "Hey, I'm not the fucking welfare department," Colin said. "What would you do if I wasn't here? Let her die? That old hag compared my son to a sheep."

He called Dr. Terrence Maloney and asked him to come out to examine his "mother-in-law" in Ballytara, who was suffering from some kind of severe respiratory ailment. The good and earnest doctor took the address and said he would be there within an hour.

"Is a real doctor really coming here?" asked Paul Lynch in astonishment.

"Yeah," Colin said as he dialed Los Angeles again.

Paul Lynch ran out the front door and shouted to some of the other cousins who were standing around barrel fires. "Feckin' doctor coming to see Granny!"

"Go way," said a woman's voice. "Heeere?"

"A witch doctor, maybe," said a male voice. "Voodoo, wha'?"

As the murmur grew outside the house, Colin walked into the back bedroom to make his phone call in silence.

"It's Colin Coyne again," he said into the phone.

"Yes, Colin," Thompson's secretary said, sounding exasperated. "Is he free yet?"

"I told you he was in an emergency meeting all day," she said.

"Does this emergency meeting have anything to do with me?"

There was a long silence, three full Mississippi's. *She's giving me a triple beat,* he thought. *In a movie that would mean "Yes."* "I'm not at liberty to discuss what goes on in Mr. Thompson's meetings, Colin."

"It's about my picture, isn't it?"

"You'd have to discuss that with Mr. Thompson," she said.

"Who else is in this meeting, Evelyn?"

"I'm not at liberty to discuss that, Colin," she said. "I'm sorry, really I am. I have other calls coming in. I'll tell him you called again."

As the travelers prepared for their Christmas hoolie on the other side of the door—strumming banjos, pouring beer, and cooking food—Colin tried to reach Bonnie Corbet. He wrote down her "emergency-only" number and called her. It was at a hotel in Saint Bart's in the Caribbean. A man with a French accent answered the phone, and Colin asked for Bonnie Corbet. He was put on hold for what seemed like fifteen minutes.

Waiting, he could hear the growing commotion outside the bedroom door as more and more travelers arrived, their voices laced with whiskey. Brianna and Seamus were banging on the door to get in to see him. Gina popped her head in and asked how long he was going to stay locked up in there. He asked her to keep the kids out until he finished his call.

"The doctor has arrived," she said. "Poor lad looks ready to shite his knickers, so he does."

"Tell him to check out Granny and I'll be with him soon."

Finally, Bonnie Corbet came on the phone. "Colin, I'm on vacation," she said, clearly pissed off. "This better be good."

He told her he was Ireland and that he had been unable to reach James Thompson for two days, and that the studio head was at an emergency meeting all day today. She told him that Crusade had more than one film in development and that he should relax.

"But I haven't signed a full contract yet," he said.

"You signed a deal memo," she said. "Stop worrying. Look, I'll call him tomorrow. I don't have time to get into it right now."

When Colin stepped out of the back bedroom, the sitting room was mobbed with travelers, standing on a queue that stretched from the master-bedroom door down the hallway, through the foyer, and out into the front garden. Old ladies, children, teenage mothers with babies, and stooped old men were impatiently waiting. Colin looked at Gina, who shrugged and then he saw Dr. Terrence Maloney appear at the bedroom door, looking harried and frightened, his stethoscope dangling from his neck.

"Doctor, me t'roat, and I have a terrible durty pain in me oul chest, like," said an old woman with a head scarf, her three black lower teeth jabbing her toothless upper lip and gums.

"Look at me babby first, doctor, plea-uz," said a teenage mother with her baby in a dirty beggar's blanket. "The rats is only after atein' at her." She looked like the beggar girl Gina had chased off O'Connell Bridge two years ago. She had the two-year-old at her side, and a screaming infant in her arms who madly rubbed at its left ear.

"You need to get to Children's Hospital for a rat bite in case of rabies or meningitis," Dr. Maloney said. "Plus, I have other calls to make."

"Yer not leaving here till us'ns is seen to first, righ'," said Derek Furey, taking a sip of poitin from a Coke bottle.

"We could all use a bit of a Christmas check-up," said Rory.

The women in the crowd assured him he wasn't going anywhere without checking on every one of them.

Dr. Maloney spotted Colin in the crowd and looked at him with desperation. "Mr. Coyne, thank God, can you please explain to these people . . ."

"We don't need no Yank to explain us nothin,' righ'?" said Derek.

"My medical bag is missing," Dr. Maloney said. "All my medicines. My chemist pads."

"What about Granny?" asked Gina.

"She needs to be in hospital immediately," he said. "My guess is emphysema. She needs respiratory tests."

"No feckin' hospitals, righ'!" said Granda, pointing a finger into the doctor's face, backing him up. "Don't for Jaysus sake be puttin' hospitals in an oul wan's diabolical head. Everybody is always rushin' to use hospitals and French dry cleaners in this country today. Worst t'ing ever happened to this country was dry cleaners. The money the wimmins do be spendin' on dry cleaners is what's killin' us all."

Dr. Maloney looked at Granda, swallowed, then glanced over at Colin, his eyes pleading for help.

Colin and Gina followed Dr. Maloney into the master bedroom, where Granny sat on the edge of the bed smoking a cigarette, the ash falling on her stained gray dress.

"She won't even take off her top and let me examine her properly," said Dr. Maloney. "She won't tell me her correct age."

"I'm forty-eight," she said. "And I never took off me clothes for any man beside me husband in me life. I'd rather die."

"See what I mean?" the doctor said, looking at Colin. "This is what I'm up against." He turned back to Granny and said, "Missus, we need to take tests."

"How much do I owe you?" Colin asked.

"Forget the money," he said. "Just get me out of here. And get her into hospital."

"I think I can get yeh out but you'll have to at least look at the oul wans and the babbies," Gina said.

Dr. Maloney looked at Colin for advice.

"Doc, after seeing what these people can do to a milk truck," he said, "I wouldn't want to imagine what they might do to you."

"Fine," Dr. Maloney said. "It'll be my Christmas deed. But old people and children only, and I need my black bag back."

His black bag reappeared through the crowd and three hours later the doctor had finished examining the last child on Whiterock

Road. When he finally placed his stethoscope into his black bag, Gina handed Dr. Maloney a jar with two inches of clear poitín.

Colin raised identical glasses and the two of them belted down the moonshine and chased it with Guinness. Granda started the hoolie off with the uilleann pipes, pressing melodic notes through the bellows under his arm. Gina picked at her guitar and Paul Lynch played a harmonica. Derek blew into a pennywhistle, Rory raked a pair of spoons over his fingers, and Philomena beat a tattoo on a bodhran, an Irish hand-held drum. The doctor who was so eager to leave only minutes before stood his ground as Bridie poured him another glass of poitín and Gina began to sing a song called "The Spanish Lady."

As I went down to Dublin City
At the hour of twelve at night,
Who should I see but a Spanish lady
Washing her feet by candlelight?
First she washed them, then she dried them
Over a fire of amber coal;
in all me life I ne'er did see
A maid so sweet about the sole . . .

The whole room joined the chorus:

Whack fol the too ra loo-ra lady,
Whack fol the too ra loo-ra lay.

Colin sat in an armchair with both his kids on his lap as the other children ran from room to room, squealing, stealing biscuits, and nipping sips of Guinness from the glasses of various adults, who thought it cute for kids to be imbibing alcohol so young.

The table was set with smoked salmon and cold Christmas ham and cheese, bread, chutney, mustards, fruit, and biscuits. The Fureys and the Lynches filed in and out of the house, eating and drinking and joining the song.

The doctor, his tie askew, his hair tousled, stains of perspiration under his armpits, belted back the second glass of moonshine and held out his glass for more.

The two kids crawled off Colin's lap and ran into the back bedroom to jump up and down on the bed with the other kids. Gina walked to Colin as she plucked the guitar strings and sang, "A Jug of Punch." She sat on Colin's lap as she sang a stanza to him, smiling and looking him directly in the eyes.

The doctor fails with all his art
To cure an impression on the heart.
But if life was gone, within an inch,
What would bring it back but a jug of punch?

The doctor laughed heartily and Colin saw a mangy dog enter the living room, furtively snaking through the crowd. It was the dog named Cat, the same dog that had greeted him with a growl on the very first day he'd set foot in Ballytara. Owned, as Colin remembered, by one Patsy Donohoe, brother of Gus Donohoe, who had murdered Gina's mother, and who was killed in return by Billy Furey, who was doing life for that act of revenge.

Colin was amazed that the dog had lived this long, its bones still showing through its bald coat. He watched the dog make a beeline for the table of meats and cheeses, brazenly climbing up and grabbing a big slice of ham in its mouth.

Derek Furey whacked it on its snout with his pennywhistle and then kicked it square in its pronounced hind-leg bone. The dog yelped in pain and dropped the ham and limped out the door.

"For fuck sake, Derek," shouted Susan. "The wee mutt is hungry. Jaysus, it's Christmas. Didn't animals keep baby Jaysus Himself warm of a feckin' Christmas night, wha'?"

Derek picked the ham up from the floor and tossed it onto the fire. "That's Patsy Donohoe's mongrel and I won't have it robbin' food in Granny's kip, right'?" Derek said. "No Donohoe, not even a feckin' dog Donohoe, steps foot in a Furey house, never mind steals in one."

"Och, but there's no need hurting the poor critter," said Granda. "I don't give a monkey's if you kick Patsy Donohoe in his bollocks. But his oul dog knows no better, sure; not enough hair on the poor hound to knit a cat's mitten."

"Feck it, anyway," Derek added. "It's done, now. Give us another song, Grace."

Colin and Gina exchanged a glance. Gina winked at him and started a new song called "I Am Me Mammy," which she said was written by a girl to her dead mother.

With me babby in me belly
And her father in me bed
I wake up in the mornin'
With me ma inside me head
They say she belongs to the ages
Never more for to return
But with me babby at me breast now
Me mammy's lantern ever burns

Now the other women in the room joined the chorus, holding hands and swaying as they sang.

For I have become me mammy
And me daughter will soon be me
And when I'm dead and buried
I'll bounce her babby on me knee

The hoolie ended when the cops came at about 4:00 A.M. A big, six-foot-six Garda named Sergeant Carey told the travelers the party was over. He advised them to pack up their trailers and caravans and shift them to a proper halting site on the outskirts of Ballytara Estates. "No more singing and music," said Sergeant Carey, who was forceful but pleasant enough. He didn't hesitate to pour himself a shot of poitin and help himself to a few slices of Christmas ham.

Dr. Terrence Maloney awakened from a drunken stupor in the armchair near the fire, his poitin glass clenched in one hand, his doctor's bag in the other. He looked around like he was still dreaming and then realized where he was. He stood in disbelief, wobbled, and hurried out the door to his car.

"You're no traveler," Sergeant Carey said to Colin.

"Tourist," said Colin. "From New York."

"Don't know what feckin' guide book yer after reading but the night's done," the big guard said, leading Colin off to the side and motioning toward Paul Lynch, who was poking the fire. "Did yeh know that bollocks Paul Lynch over there once torched a newspaper office for reporting that he was convicted of arson? Terrible fella for a match, that one. He's determined to see hell burn on earth. He's totally mental but he's not even the worst in the lot. Now, I don't know what yer doin' with these people, but my advice, go back to safe New York."

Colin slept fully clothed in the bed with Gina, with the kids asleep between them. At six in the morning, the door burst open and Paul Lynch stood there weeping. The kids awakened and Gina sat bolt upright with a start. Colin was getting used to expecting the unexpected in this family.

"Wha'?" Gina said.

"Derek . . ." Paul Lynch said, dissolving in sobs.

"What about him?" Gina asked.

"Mammy," said Brianna.

"They kilt him," Paul said. "They found him halfway between here and the halting site, beaten and stabbed."

"Oh, sweet Jesus, Mary, and Joseph the Carpenter," Gina said.

She rose from the bed and took Paul in her arms and now Colin got out of bed, already dressed, his head beginning to pound from the moonshine and the Guinness. He pulled on a hooded sweatshirt, searched Gina's black canvas bag for socks for the kids, and found two wallets. As Gina hugged Paul in the doorway, and as more shrill voices came to life in the house, Colin flipped open the wallets in the dull glow of the dawn light spilling through the door and saw that they belonged to two American men with Italian last names.

It never fucking ends, he thought, grabbing the kids' clothes.

Now Sergeant Carey was back in the living room, sterner now, standing with a dumpy detective from the murder squad, asking if there had been an incident concerning Derek Lynch and a dog owned by one Patsy Donohoe. Colin looked at Gina, who now held a whinging, sleepy Seamus against her shoulder. Paul Lynch sat on the chair near the fire, which was covered with a layer of slag to keep the embers smoldering until dawn.

"There was no dog in here," said Gina.

"No dog atall," said Granda, who poured himself a shot of moonshine and offered some to the cops, who declined. "Never let a dog in a house or you'll have him roont."

"Did Derek Lynch leave here in good humor?" the detective asked.

"Oh, aye," said Granda.

"Singin'," said Gina.

"Was Patsy Donohoe here?" asked Sergeant Carey.

"Not in this house," said Granda.

"Och, Jaysus, bigfulluh," Gina said. "Give us the space to grieve in peace, wha'?"

"No dog here atall, lads," said Granda again.

The cops left, promising to return later.

"There'll be killin's at this funeral, boyo," said Granda. Paul Lynch got up from the chair and bolted out the door, a wail escaping from inside him.

Colin whispered into Gina's ear, "Time to go."

forty-six

December 22

Colin had kept the room at the Westbury because he knew he'd never spend two nights out in Ballytara.

After dropping all the luggage at the hotel, Colin piled Gina and the kids into a cab and went straight to the American embassy, where Gina signed visa applications. After receiving the ten-thousand-dollar wire transfer from Colin's Los Angeles bank, the clerk approved the applications.

"Jaysus, I hope yeh get that back," Gina said.

He knew he'd never see the money again because he wasn't going to let Gina take his kids back to this life. Ever.

Outside, on the clean streets of Ballsbridge, Colin said, "There's going to be no Christmas here after Derek."

"Today's what, the twenty-third?" she asked. "That means they'll have to bury poor Derek tomorrow. There won't be any burials again till the twenty-seventh."

"Your grandfather says there'll be bloody murder at that funeral," Colin said. "We're not going."

He booked a flight to New York leaving the next morning.

December 23

At the Dublin Airport, while Gina was in the ladies' room changing Seamus's wet diaper, Colin sat in the airport bar, reading *The Irish Times* and watching a TV breakfast chat show. The broadcast was interrupted by a bulletin about a riot at a funeral in Ballytara that morning, leaving one man murdered and another critically wounded. The announcer said it all stemmed from an incident two nights earlier involving a dog that had stolen a slice of Christmas ham.

"At this morning's funeral, the family of the previously murdered traveler apparently urinated on a grave of the matriarch of the rival traveler family and, as a high-ranking Garda spokesman said, 'All hell broke loose on hallowed ground.'"

Rory, Colin thought.

When Gina returned, he whisked her and the kids out of the bar and through the security checkpoint gates to the boarding area, where there were no TVs. He never mentioned the news of the deadly riot on the uneventful flight across the Atlantic.

Part VII

New York

forty-seven

December 25

Colin, Gina, and the kids went to Eddie's house on Long Island for Christmas day. They had a wonderful time with his father, Jack and Eddie, and Eddie's wife and kids. Brianna was the hit of the afternoon, chattering away, opening gifts, and singing Irish songs. Gina remained uncharacteristically quiet, sober, and reserved. The Coyne family tried very hard to make her feel welcome.

Jack told Colin he and Gina and the kids could stay in his apartment until they left for Los Angeles.

That night, in Colin's old bed in Bayside, Gina said, "I want to stay here in New York."

"My job is in Los Angeles," he said.

"I won't live there again."

"Why the fuck didn't you tell me that in Dublin?"

"I thought you were smart enough to know it," she said. "I hate that city, I won't go back."

"I have a rented house out there."

"Rent a place here," she said, "and I'll stay with the kids. Otherwise, I'm shifting off home."

"I'll stop you in the courts."

"Don't make me laugh."

He lay still for a while and thought about keeping her in a place here in New York while he eventually rented himself a small efficiency apartment in L.A., and flew back and forth. He'd be shooting most of his movie in New York anyway.

"We'll see," he said.

December 26

Colin tried calling James Thompson in Los Angeles and got a recording saying the studio was closed until January 2. He called Bonnie Corbet in Saint Bart's again. She told him to relax and enjoy the holidays in New York with his family. She wished him a Happy New Year and told him that they'd speak on January 2.

December 31

On New Year's Eve, the guys in Grogan's toasted Colin on the upcoming start of his new movie.

January 2

On the second day of the new year, Colin received a call from Bonnie Corbet.

"Crusade Pictures has fired you as director," she said.

"How the hell can they do that?" he asked, feeling adrenaline rise in him like steam, his heart suddenly pumping like an overworked motor.

"They exercised their option to assign a new director to your script," she said. "The silver lining is that they owe you another one hundred and fifty thousand dollars immediately."

"I knew it," Colin said, the words gluey in his dry mouth. "Jesus Christ, I'm ruined. Did Thompson give a reason?"

Shame seemed to soil him, a clammy, itchy sensation that made him feel second-rate, mired in laughing-stock Queens as one phone call turned him into a Hollywood has-been before he'd even had a chance to succeed.

"He wasn't thrilled that you ran off to Ireland without his approval, before you cast the male lead," she said. "He says he liked the pitch he got from another director on where to take the script."

"Who's replacing me?" he asked, realizing he was almost whispering, his voice growing smaller with his esteem.

"Frank Burston," said Bonnie.

A double fuck, Colin thought.

If Burston was replacing him as director, Colin was certain it also meant that Burston had replaced him in Melissa Thompson's bed. Colin felt nauseated. *Burston is fucking Melissa and me at the same time,* he thought. *Burston is going to make my movie. I have no one to blame but myself; I chased Gina when I should have been casting my picture in L.A.*

"Burston is having a page-one rewrite done on it," Corbet said. "Instead of an Irish tinker they're going to make the girl lead a member of British royalty, à la Princess Di. She catches a working-class Yank pickpocketing her at Oxford, they wind up in bed, she gets knocked up by the Yank, who is on scholarship at Oxford, and eventually she comes to live with him and the baby in Queens. The story is about a princess as a soccer mom in blue-collar Queens."

"Oh, Jesus," Colin said. "Why don't they call it 'Nothing Hill?'"

"Sorry, kid," Bonnie said. "That's show biz. I warned you about being distracted by that tinker girl."

"Bonnie, what does all this mean? For my, um, career?"

"Square one," she said. "However, getting fired before you start is better than being canned in the middle of production. You can claim creative differences. To reestablish your directing cachet, I think you're gonna have to try to do an independent film, or maybe a cable movie. It isn't going to be easy. Spend what you get wisely and pay your taxes on it right away. For better or worse, you got a kid now. Get yourself a place to live, a house. Go back to work right away. You're young, you're talented, and you'll be back. Start writing another movie, one you can make for a dollar and a half. I should have a check from Crusade for you tomorrow. It's not a bad way to start a new year."

Colin sheepishly broke the news to his family, who were supportive but embarrassed for him. "Not to worry, as long as there's some cabbage involved," his father said. "I didn't make a hundred and fifty thousand dollars in my first ten years with the phone company."

Gina tried to reassure Colin that he would be back doing another movie in no time. Secretly he knew the momentum of his two-year-old Oscar nomination had come to a grinding halt. *Variety* had a story about Burston, the Oscar winner, replacing Colin Coyne on his first feature. The headline on the news brief read: COYNE CANNED, BURSTON BAGGED ON CRUSADE COMEDY. Burston's quotes made it sound like nothing of Coyne's script would ever make it to the screen.

Colin was crushed.

January 5

"How could you be so fucking stupid?" Jack asked as they sat in his apartment that night while Gina gave the kids a bath upstairs.

"I don't know how it all happened, Jack," Colin said. "It's like when you're writing a script. Sometimes the characters take over, they tell you what they want you to do and the script starts writing you. I got my characters and my life jumbled together. Did my character, Kieran, love Gina or did I? In the end, it didn't really matter because both of us knocked her up. The end came when I got her pregnant and Seamus showed on the set."

"What are you gonna do?"

"I'm gonna take what money I have and put it down on a house," he said. "I figure I'll put a roof over my kids' heads, and their mother's head, and then I'll go back to work on my career."

"Where you gonna buy this house?"

"In New York," he said. "Gina won't live out in L.A. I'll buy anywhere but around here; I couldn't take the snickering of the neighborhood humps who resented me for daring to 'go Hollywood' in the first place."

"Fuck them," Jack said. "Where the fuck you gonna buy? Manhattan? I hope you have two million dollars for two bedrooms. Plus in Manhattan a kid can't just go out and play like in Queens. The yuppies arrange fucking play dates!"

"I was thinking maybe Brooklyn, Park Slope."

"Forget it," Jack said. "I did work there on some brownstones.

The fucking Wall Street yuppies and doctors and lawyers have bought all of brownstone Brooklyn like it was a land grab. Even neighborhoods like Williamsburg have been annexed by bohemian Manhattan real-estate barons, like SoHo."

"Well, I won't live on Long Island," Colin said. "That would be like waving two white flags. I might as well join the cops or the phone company, which is noble work, but not for me. And Jersey is where people from Queens go to die."

"You made yourself a real shit sandwich, bro," Jack said.

"I can't let Gina take the kids back to Dublin, Jack," he said. "You have no fuckin' idea. If I fight this shit in court, even if I win, some lawyer will wind up with all my dough, and where will that leave me?"

Jack leaned closer to Colin, his eyes casting upward toward the bathroom, where Gina was singing to the kids in the tub.

"Look, you didn't make your first million," Jack said. "So it's time to start trying for your second mil. And when you're trapped, the way you are right now, sometimes the old cliché is the only answer, Col."

"What's that?" Colin asked.

"It's cheaper to keep her. Live under the same roof, coexist. Get yourself a home base and fly to where the work is. But at least your kid will be in one place."

Gina came walking down the stairs carrying Seamus, who was wrapped in a towel.

"Time to make these'ns a bit o' dinner and off to beddy-byes," she said.

Colin looked at Jack and nodded.

January 6

Colin picked up the severance check—$135,000, after the agent's ten-percent fee. With Jack and Eddie's help, they located a Queens banker friend who would give Colin a thirty-year mortgage on a house as long as he put a third of the price down.

Over the next two weeks, Gina and Colin looked at more than forty houses in Brooklyn and Queens. None of them were right.

January 17

As Colin drove down Thirty-eighth Avenue in Bayside to visit his father, Gina shouted, "Stop."

Colin stopped in front of a two-story Dutch colonial single-family house on a corner lot, semi-attached, all white with hunter-green shutters, and just five short blocks from his father's house. There was a "For Sale by Owner" sign on the front lawn.

"I said I didn't want to live in Bayside."

"That's the house for these childer," she said. "I know it, you know it. Stop thinking of yerself. It's walking distance to the train, pubs, and shoppin' of Bell Boulevard."

The house was a three-bedroom fixer-upper for $240,000. It had a thirty-by-fifty-foot backyard, a grass lawn, a big blue spruce sagging with snow, and an elegant Chinese maple, and was blocked from the next yard by a six-foot wooden slatted fence.

The next day, Jack checked the place out. "Structurally sound and a good buy," he said.

"We'll take it," Gina told the seller.

Colin led Gina to the side in the backyard.

"Get it straight, Gina," Colin said. "This is *my* house. I'm buying it for the kids."

"I don't want to be strapped to a piece of feckin' land like some settled buffer," she said. "I want our son's name on the deed saying he owns a piece of America."

Colin agreed. He put eighty thousand dollars down on the house, and after closing fees he had about forty-five thousand dollars left in the bank. He would probably owe that much in income taxes, but he wasn't worried about the IRS right now. They could always put a lien on the house until he got another movie deal, if he ever got another movie deal.

After the closing, he grabbed the deed and drove to the new house. He stood on the sidewalk and looked at it, sitting there like a giant tomb. *I should be happy but I feel like shit,* he thought. *I get nominated for an Oscar and wind up living five blocks from where I was raised. What the hell. Faulkner lived in Mississippi, didn't he?*

Dickens lived in London. Balzac lived in Paris. Norman Mailer lives in Brooklyn. I might be rationalizing, but, after all, this place, Bayside, Queens, is part of who I am. Living in Hollywood certainly doesn't make you see the world better because your point of reference is other movies instead of real life. I can work here. See things clearly from here. The anchor is dropped. This is where I raise my kids. This is where I work, where I rebuild. This is home.

Before he flew out to Los Angeles to close up the rented house, Colin wanted to get some initial repairs done on the new house. He borrowed two big toolboxes from his father, filled with prized tools he'd collected over a lifetime of hard work as a lineman for the telephone company. The tools were cherished as family treasures. He also borrowed a power saw, an electric drill and an electric sander.

"Don't let anything happen to my tools," his father warned. "Those tools kept this family alive all these years, paid for every summer vacation, every Christmas, every dime of tuition . . ."

Eddie and Jack and a crew of Grogan's regulars helped him fix up the new house—painting, sanding the floor, and repairing the roof. A local carpenter named Maz dropped the ceiling and created a work area and a small bathroom in the raw cellar so that Colin would have a private place to work on his new script.

Colin and Gina enrolled Brianna into a private preschool on the next block.

As a housewarming gift, Jack gave Colin a gorgeous deep-pile Persian rug, with ruby-red, royal-blue, and monarch-gold patterns.

"For that big dining room," Jack said. "There's lots of red in the design in case Gina decides to do another Benihana demonstration on your other shoulder."

"Fuck you, Jack," Colin said, laughing and admiring the rug. "Looks like it could be in a museum."

"Actually, it was meant for a Wall Street law-firm office I was designing," he said. "The partnership was dissolved when the senior partner died of a heart attack—probably over the price of the fuckin' rug. Anyway, they were selling off all the office furniture and they let me have it for a third of the price. Just don't let the kids finger-paint on it. It's a four-thousand-dollar rug, bro. Happy house."

"Jesus, thanks, Jack."

They shook hands. Colin had a four-thousand-dollar rug and now all his brood needed was their furniture from the rented house in Los Angeles.

"For what it's worth," Jack said, "you're doing the right thing. Making the best of a complicated situation."

"I hope so," Colin said.

February 10

The house was ready.

Before they moved in, Colin finally met their new neighbor. Lipinski was a heavyset city tax assessor who looked like he was in his early forties. Colin and Lipinski exchanged hellos, names, and a few pleasantries.

"Me and the missus just wanted to say welcome," Lipinski said.

"Thanks," Colin said.

"It's a nice, quiet block," Lipinski said.

"Sure is," Colin said.

"I'm the president of the block association," Lipinski said.

"Congratulations."

"I'm sure that, like the rest of us on this nice, quiet block you'll want to keep it that way," Lipinski said. "I told the missus and a few of the concerned neighbors that the racket you guys have been making this week is to be expected, just moving in and all. The music, the six-packs, the Grogan's crowd. But it'll be just you and the wife and two kids, that right?"

Trouble, Colin thought. *This guy and his wife are gonna be pains in the fucking ass. Might as well back him off a few steps, right now.*

"Actually, my wife is a musician and we're thinking of having a big family and starting a band," Colin said. "My daughter wants to be a drummer, and my son likes the cowbell. I'm thinking of tuba lessons."

Lipinski stood nodding, looking Colin in the eye.

"Kind of a small house for a big family," Lipinski said.

"Bunk beds," Colin said, smiling.

"Me and the missus, we don't have any kids," Lipinski said. "We both work all week. We like to sleep late on weekends. We cherish our privacy, that's why I put up a six-foot fence."

"Look, I don't want to get off on the wrong foot here," Colin said, "but I don't live my life by other people's schedules. Mutual respect always seems to work. I'll respect that you don't have kids if you respect that I do."

"Fine," Lipinski said. "I just wanted to say welcome to this nice, quiet block. One we'd all like to keep that way."

"Thanks," Colin said.

He watched Lipinski walk back to his attached house.

Trouble, Colin thought.

Jack spent the month in Chicago, refurbishing more restaurants so he had no problem letting Colin and Gina and the kids stay in his apartment until Colin moved into the new house.

February 22

Colin flew to Los Angeles to pack up the rented house, to close out his lease, and drive his Lumina back to New York. He knew that if he didn't give Gina some spending money she'd steal some and bail and lawyers would cost him more than her allowance. So he opened a joint household checking account with a five-thousand-dollar deposit and left Gina a checkbook. The local supermarket would take checks for food, and she had an ATM card in case she needed cash. She could start buying brooms, mops, plants, garden tools, and other odds and ends for the new house while he was away.

Colin was in Los Angeles for three days. He was tempted to call Melissa Thompson to tell her what a piece of shit he thought she was for sabotaging him with her father, but he restrained himself. He was too embarrassed by recent events to call anyone in the movie business.

He simply packed all the books, dishes, clothes, paintings, and knickknacks and left.

He drove his Lumina across the country back to New York. He stayed in cheap motels in tank towns all the way across America, calling Gina occasionally, asking how she was doing and joking with the kids.

"We have a surprise for yeh when you get home," Gina said.

"What is it?" he asked.

"Then it wouldn't be a surprise, would it?" she said.

He hoped it wasn't a dog, some yapping little shit factory that would keep him and the new neighbors up all night. On the other hand, a dog helped give a house with kids a sense of completeness. He smiled at the thought of the kids playing with the puppy.

He reveled in the time spent lost in the belly of the nation, out on the open highways, passing through squalid little hamlets, where unemployed men stood around rusting trailers scratching and belching their lives away. It made him feel like less of a failure when he saw people of true struggle in small company towns where the factory had closed down or moved. Watching cross-country truckers pick up hitchhiking teenage runaway chicks, rednecks tricking with cheap whores outside honky-tonk saloons, weary farmers riding on rusting tractors, divorced middle-aged waitresses serving pie in desperate little diners, fat county cops cuffing out-of-staters at sneaky speed traps, anonymous night managers in shit-hole motels, Colin was able to put his own life in perspective. *You ain't doing so fucking bad, pally,* he thought.

As he took copious notes, on his tape recorder and in his notebook, an idea for a new script started to form in his head. *A wrongly accused widow is being chased for the murder of her cheating husband when she meets a busted-valise lawyer who was just dumped by his wife,* he thought. *One is fleeing east, the other west, and they meet in middle America. They fall in love and together they try to clear her of her husband's murder. I could set it against all this and call it* Middle America.

The drive across the United States gave him time to think and plan and launder his aching brain.

He decided that once he settled in the new house, with his family safe and secure around him, he would repair to the basement seven nights a week and work until he had a new script. It would be so good that he could raise the financing himself. *I'll direct the little road movie,* he thought. *And write the commercial caper* Diamond in the Rough, *as a script for sale, to make some money.*

As he drove east, he used the tape recorder to sketch out the characters and plots of both script ideas.

March 2

He arrived back in New York eight days after he'd left, a full day ahead of schedule. When he walked into Jack's apartment, the first thing that hit him was the smell of marijuana. The second thing he noticed was Peggy Johnson sitting on Paul Lynch's lap, making out. The third thing was Gina's other cousin, Susan, chasing her naked two-year-old son, Sammy, through the living room and into Jack's bedroom.

"Howayeh, Colin," Susan said as she dashed past, dressed in a pair of Jack's shorts and a Global Screen T-shirt. "C'mere, Sambo, yeh little bollocks, yeh, whilst I dress yeh for the scratcher. Mammy has a date and I wants you in beddy-byes by the time me fella arrives."

She grabbed the kid and carried him upstairs. "Shhh, Brianna and Seamus are sleeping," she said to squirming Sammy.

"Hey, there, Colin," Paul said, coming up for air from Peggy Johnson's lips. "What about yeh?"

Paul Lynch took another toke on the blunt, scratching his groin. *This dirty fuck must have crabs,* Colin thought.

Colin didn't answer either of them. He dropped his bag on the floor and looked around for Gina.

Paul lifted a bottle of Guinness from the coffee table, took a slug, opened a fresh pack of cigarettes, and bit one out of the pack. He lit the cigarette with a wooden match and also lit the cellophane from the pack, watching it crackle to flame on one of Jack's delft plates, which he was using as an ashtray. Colin stared silently. Paul Lynch giggled, gazing glassy-eyed into the flames like a swami into the sun. Colin remembered that the big Dublin cop had said that Paul was a pyro. Even Gina had admitted he was a fire freak.

"Hi, Colin," Peggy Johnson said, her eyes dreamy with cannabis, smacking Paul's hand as he cupped one of her breasts.

"Where's Gina?" Colin asked.

"Upstairs, gettin' ready to go out," Peggy said.

"Me and Peggy is baby-sittin'," Paul said.

Colin bounded up the stairs to his old bedroom, where he found Gina dressed in a black bra, matching thong panties, and a pair of knee-high boots, bent over at the waist blow-drying her hair.

"Nice," he said, startling Gina, and closing the bedroom door.

"Sweet Jaysus the Savior, you freckened the shite near outta me," she said, shutting off the hair dryer and shaking out her curls.

"Some fucking surprise," he said, trying to stay calm.

"Och, poor wee Paul, wha'?" she said. "The least we could do for him. The Fureys is like brothers to him. One brother, Derek, dead, and the other, Rory, on the run for the murder at the funeral. Feckin' 'el. There was killin's at the funeral, all right, just as Granda predicted. Good job we was on a plane outta alla dat, wha'?"

"Did I pay for that pyromaniac's ticket over here?"

She stood, turned, and walked to the bureau and leaned on it to look at her face in the vanity mirror, her mostly bare ass thrust out at him.

"Dead-on of Susan to fly over with poor Paul like that for a bit a company, as well," she said. "Such short notice and all."

"Considerate of her," Colin said.

"That feckin' sarcasm I hear?"

"No, I'm fucking thrilled she's here to mooch off me," Colin said. "And so Paul Lynch can teach the kids arson for dummies."

She didn't respond to the remark.

"The movers called," she said, applying lipstick to her mouth, bending farther over the bureau top toward the mirror.

She knows I probably have the highway hornies and so she's wiggling her moneymaker at me as a way of changing the subject. And, goddamn it, it's working. He became aroused. He knew that she knew she was getting him excited. "They said the furniture'll be delivered to the new house tomorrow morning."

"Where you going tonight?"

"Oh, Susan met a fella the other night who's loaded with lolly and drives a car as big as a Hollyhead ferry," she said. "He's coming to pick her up and she asked if I wanted to go because she's a bit nervous. He's a lovely-lookin' Mafia gangster, and he's only fit as an American footballer as well."

"A gangster?" Colin said. "Great. He told you this?"

"Cop on, for fuck sake, gangsters never call themselves gangsters, do dey?" she said. She spaced her feet farther apart as she bent over the bureau closer to the mirror to apply her mascara.

She's wiggling the lure, he thought. *Trying to hook me and reel me in. This time, I'll rob the bait and cut the fucking line.*

"How do you know he's a gangster, then?" Colin said.

"He's Eyetalian and wears a gold watch, gold chains, diamond rings, and shiny shoes. He has lots of cash and looks like he got his hair cut in a jeweler's. He said he'd find out what he can about me da."

"Where'd you meet this gangster?"

"I saw on the telly about a place in Ozone Park that the cops aren't allowed to eat in because it's an organized-crime hangout," she said, winking at him in the mirror as she teased darker lip liner around the soft red lipstick. *The old fellatio finish,* he thought.

"I think I know the place," Colin said.

"It sounded like a great place to me, so when Susan and Paul arrived I wanted to show them a good time. I called Peggy Johnson because I thought she might like Paul. A few young fellas at the bar were giving me and Susan the eye, so I goes up to them and I says that I'm spoken for, thank you very much, but me cousin is just on holliers from Dublin, as single as a bad penny, and not to be shy. The best-lookin' one sends over champagne and we drinks that. He sends over a second bottle of chambo and we drinks that. He brings the third bottle over hisself and I lets him slide in next to Susan and he even picks up the check for the whole dinner, so he did, paid in cash lolly, too, fair play."

"Where were the kids when all this was going on?" Colin asked.

"One thing about them Eyetalians," Gina said, "they always have high chairs."

"I thought we'd stay in tonight," Colin said.

"To do wha'?" she said with a mischievous eye.

Colin locked the bedroom door, took a condom from the night table, walked to her as she leaned over the bureau, opened his belt, dropped his pants, sheathed himself, pulled the thong strap aside, and entered her from behind. He pushed the thumb of his right hand into her mouth, smearing the lipstick. She sucked his thumb as they stared directly into each other's eyes in the mirror until he came in less than two minutes.

"Better now?" she said, her face smeared with lipstick.

"Not yet."

Colin hitched up his pants and marched straight downstairs.

Peggy was still on Paul Lynch's lap, sharing a joint.

"Colin, sham, where's the oul remote?" Paul said.

"Get the fuck out," Colin said.

"Wha'?" Paul said, startled.

"I got kids here," Colin said. "You play with matches and you're getting stoned. Get your nasty ass out of my brother's apartment before I give you a good fuckin' smack."

Colin raised his hand and bit his lip as if to backhand Paul.

"Colin, no!" Peggy shouted, standing quickly. Paul lept to his feet and backed away.

"C'mon, Paul, we'll go to my place," Peggy said.

"Pick up a bottle of A-2000 on the way, Peggy," Colin said. "And a fuckin' fire extinguisher."

Gina came down the first three steps, fastening a short skirt around her hips. "What's goin' on?" she said.

"A little housecleaning," Colin said.

Paul paused by the front door with Peggy. "Yer fella's in a bad humor," Paul said. "See yeh later, Grace, so."

Susan now joined Gina on the steps, a towel barely covering her otherwise naked body.

"New rules," Colin said. "No one gets stoned with kids around. No smoking in the house. No one robs or brings cops to my fuckin' door. This ain't fuckin' Ballytara."

Susan smirked at Colin. "Yer mon needs to be puppy-schooled,

Grace," she said, and climbed the stairs. Colin stared up at Susan, her privates visible under the short towel.

Tools of her fucking trade, he thought.

"This the way you think it's gonna be?" Gina said.

"I'm just getting started, baby," he said.

"Oh, and I."

The doorbell rang and Colin went to answer it. Standing on the welcome mat was an immense man, six-foot-four, 260 pounds. His muscles were barely contained by his sharkskin suit. He looked like an ape in a body condom. He also looked vaguely familiar.

"Yo," the guy said. "You're whosiz from the gym, no?"

Now Colin recognized him as one of the monster iron pumpers from the local gym. There was a group of Sicilians who were nicknamed the Steroid Siggies. They spent most of their waking hours in the gym, taking book on the pay phones, rapping to chicks, lifting weights. Waiting for loan-sharking and leg-breaking orders from the elderly capo named Louis.

"Colin Coyne," Colin said, extending a hand.

"Joe Monte," the muscle man said, shaking gently. "I seen you in the paper, too. *Queens Courier* had a write-up on ya. The movies, you're in, right? *Mingya,* but do I got a couple a movies I could tell you some day."

Joe Monte was an enforcer, a goon who maimed people for a living—and probably worse.

"Wanna come in?" Colin said.

"Nah," he said. "I better wait in the car before some Rican leaves it on milk boxes. No offense, but your sister-in-law, Susan, she's a knockout. I can't always understand her too good. So I just nod a lot. When I saw her, I sez to myself, if I didn't already have a wife, that's the girl I wanna marry. She's not one of these Queens, Brooklyn knuckleheads. She's refined, with an accent. *Mingya,* but her skin is whiter than pharmaceutical coke."

A real fucking bard, Colin thought.

"Good luck," Colin said.

"You too," Joe Monte said. "Tell her I'll be downstairs."

Colin closed the door and when he turned, Susan appeared, her tight, curvaceous body vacuum-packed into a black dress.

"Have fun, darlin'," Gina said. "Make him spend till he needs a calculator to count his losses."

"You sure you won't come, Grace?" Susan said, as if Colin weren't there.

"I'm grand, sure," she said.

Finally, Gina and Colin were alone.

"The leg-breaker she's going out with is married," Colin said.

"I'm sure that's the least of his legal problems."

"Yeah, he's also a fucking *killer*," Colin said.

"Who isn't?" said Gina as she climbed the stairs.

forty-eight

April 5

The move went smoothly.

Colin worked the night shift in the basement on both scripts, and slept most of the mornings.

Every afternoon, Colin took time to bring the two kids to Crocheron Park, put them on the swings and the slides, chatting with some of the neighborhood mothers he knew from high school or the divorced part-time fathers he knew. He realized that besides kids and the Mets, they didn't have many of the same interests anymore.

At night, he read bedtime stories to both kids, trying to get Seamus to be still while he told Brianna Sticky stories.

"Tickle," Seamus demanded, and Colin would have to tickle his son until the kid was out of breath.

It was the same routine every night: tickle Seamus until the kid passed out from exhaustion, then tell Brianna a Sticky story.

When they were asleep, Colin would retreat to the basement. He was actually happy that Gina had Susan to help her upstairs while he worked on *Middle America* and *Diamond in the Rough.*

He thought he could shoot *Middle America* dirt cheap. It only had two main characters, no special effects, no foreign locations, no child actors or animals, mostly daytime exteriors and nighttime interiors. If he could get the right mix of humor and pathos, it could become a sleeper hit.

He needed to get something going fast. His money was dwindling. The unforeseen costs of moving into a new house were astronomical. Plus there was car insurance, house insurance, water bills, property tax, telephone, gas, electric, cable TV deposits, landscaping, new drainpipes.

As Colin slaved in the basement, Joe Monte showered Susan with cash, jewelry, clothes, weekends in Atlantic City and Montauk and the Jersey shore, and dinners in the best wise-guy joints in the five boroughs. But Susan also started dating an Irish-American guy named Petey O'Toole from the west side of Manhattan, who said he was in banking. Colin feared the day Monte and O'Toole crossed paths.

With his bank balance sinking to less than three grand, Colin got tired of supporting Gina's freeloading family. She said Paul would be happy to work if he could find an off-the-books job, so Colin convinced Davey Grogan to give him a porter's job at Grogan's. He would be sweeping, mopping, cleaning out the back bar, scouring the toilets, and packing the urinals with ice.

"Who the fuck is gonna drink outta the jacks?" Paul asked Davey Grogan when told to put ice in the urinals. Davey Grogan had to explain to Paul that it was to cut down on the urine smell. The hundred dollars a week he received to clean the saloon every morning kept Paul in cigarette money.

Gina seemed to be adapting nicely to life in Bayside, with streets she could walk on, a mixture of rain and sun, and Irish saloons named Yeats's, Pearce's, Dempsey's, Donovan's, and Fitzgerald's, all of which sold Guinness on draft.

If he could only finish the script and get it set up he might finally have a very good life here with Gina and the kids.

April 15

Jack met Colin at his father's house in the afternoon to watch the Mets season opener. When he arrived, Jack passed Colin a message he had received from Linda Parks. She said she knew his movie fell through and wanted to know if he was interested in shooting a few videos.

"I hate music videos," Colin said. "They burglarize the listener's imagination."

"Hey, it's honest work," Jack said.

They drank mugs of tea and ate scrumptious seven-layer chocolate cake from Manetta's bakery. The Mets announcer was doing his best to keep the fires of baseball alive as the rain doused Shea Stadium and continued to delay the game.

"I might as well drive over to Park Slope and do some measurements for this brownstone rehab job I got," Jack said. "Me, when there's work, I take it."

"I'd rather shoot dog-food commercials than music videos," Colin said. Jack shrugged, said good-bye, and left.

Colin and his father were now alone.

"Just our luck it's a rainout, Dad," Colin said.

"I see less of you now than when you lived in California," his father said.

"I've been trying to work myself out of a hole."

"It's not too late for Ma Bell, I still have connections."

"It's just not for me, Dad," Colin said.

"With kids involved, you do what you have to do, not what you want to do."

Colin looked down at Linda Parks's phone number.

"You ever backed into a corner like mine, Dad?"

"I'm betting your mother told you about the son she gave up," his father said, looking Colin in the eye.

Colin looked at him as spring rain pelted the windows.

"You always knew, Dad?"

"Of course I knew," he said. "Just like I knew about all the money she gave you to make your films. I never let on I knew, but of course I knew."

"I can't believe it."

"I let her think she had her secrets," he said. "I knew she had the cancer before she did. When we were first married, I learned about the son she gave up for adoption. She didn't know I knew. I saw her paperwork, and tried my damnedest to locate him. I even hired a private investigator back then to try to track the wee lad down. Och, needle in a haystack. The search never got far."

"You didn't hold it against her?"

"Life's a small collection of right choices trapped between the mistakes, kid," the father said. "She'd already punished herself enough over it. It haunted her all her days. I'm proud you didn't do that with your son."

"Me, too."

"Mind if I give you my two cents' worth of philosophy?"

"Please."

"I won't say what I think about all the freeloaders you have hanging about, but taking care of your son and the other wee child is one of your right choices amid the mistakes. You have obligations now. So if there's work being offered, put your pride in your pocket and get the cabbage into the house for the kids."

Colin nodded, again looking at Linda Parks's phone number.

"Why did Mom stop looking for her son?" Colin asked.

"I think she stopped when she knew it would do the boy more harm than good to find him," he said. "When it stopped being about *him* and was only about *herself*. There wasn't a selfish bone in that woman."

"I swore to Mom I'd never abandon a kid of mine."

"I thought as much. She knew you were a skirt-chaser, not the marrying kind. She was afraid you'd leave a baby lying around somewhere. Do what you have to do for your son."

Colin finished his tea, stood, shook his father's hand, said good-bye, and walked out the door, his mother's silver bells ringing as he left.

That night, he left a message for Linda Parks.

April 25

When Colin awakened from his morning sleep, Gina asked him to go to dinner with Susan and Petey O'Toole.

"What happened to Mighty Joe Monte?" Colin asked, sitting on the couch in the living room while the kids played in the yard.

"Susan told him that if he wanted to keep seeing her he'd have to leave his wife," Gina said. "He kept promising he would but never did, so she ended that. He was full of shite anyway, he promised to look for me da and never lifted a finger."

"I can't say I'm sorry to see Susan ending that relationship."

"Nothin' wrong with gangsters," Gina said. "Not everyone has the connections to make a livin' jottin' down bits and pieces of this and tha', yeh know."

"That's what you think I do all night long, isn't it?" he said. "Jot down bits and pieces of this and that?"

"You don't mix feckin' cement," she said.

"Either do you, baby," Colin said, his voice rising. "Maybe it's time you got a fucking j-o-b. You and Susan the mooch and the belly-crawler, Paul."

"I made my own livin' afore I met you."

"You were a fucking thief!"

"And what the hell are you?"

"I work!"

"No, yer a feckin' robber! Yeh robbed my feckin' life for your story. Yeh stole all the things I did and said and put them in your script and sold it. Now some other arsehole stole it from you, serves yeh right, too. After yeh stole me life, yeh stole me out of Ireland. Yeh robbed the feckin' road from under me feet and dropped a house on me in America like the Wicked Witch. You are my ball and chain, Colin Coyne. Because I want a few family members around me yeh condemn me like I was something durty and worthless and lesser than what you are."

She went abruptly silent, closed her eyes, refused to shed the tears forming behind the eyelids. "Well, I'm not," she said softly. "I'm Gina Furey, the one and only, and I'm as good as you."

She turned from him and walked into the kitchen and took a bottle of Guinness from the fridge and carried it into the backyard and stood looking at the clouds in the spring sky.

Colin watched her from the living room, realizing she was partly right. *When I met her, she was just a petty thief,* he thought. *She was raising a kid on her own, and getting along. She robbed money from tourists, ruined a few vacations. But whose life did she really hurt? And all of a sudden I knock her up, take her to America, and try to make her fit in here. As much as she fucked up my life, I fucked up hers. She's a victim, too.*

At 7:30 P.M., they waited on the stoop for Petey O'Toole and Susan to pick them up. The high-school-age daughter of a local Bayside friend was baby-sitting.

Colin had avoided this guy O'Toole's invitations for as long as he could and knew that if he'd turned him down again for dinner it would be interpreted as a snub. He didn't need another mick with an attitude in his life, so he agreed to go to dinner.

"Gina, please, no static tonight, okay?" Colin said.

"What the hell could happen at dinner?" Gina asked.

"That's what Jesus thought at the Last Supper," Colin said. "He should have stayed home and ordered takeout. Something tells me I should, too."

O'Toole picked them up in a chauffeur-driven Cadillac limousine. He poured champagne for everyone while the two cousins talked about the kids.

"So you make movies," O'Toole said.

"Well, it's been a while," he said. "But I'm trying."

"I know a few guys who'd like to invest in movies," O'Toole said. "Hedge-fund guys."

Colin knew right away from the cut of his suit and the cocksureness in his voice that O'Toole was also at least a half a block on the wrong side of the law himself. *The Cousins find them like flies find shit,* Colin thought.

"It takes a lot of money these days," Colin said, trying to steer him away from the subject. "Movies are a bad investment. If they don't make money in the first weekend, they usually drown in red ink."

"That's good," O'Toole said, sipping some champagne.

"Yeah?" Colin said. "Why?"

"They're a tax write-off," he said.

"Except I want my movies to make money," Colin said.

"That's okay, too," O'Toole said. "Then my friends get to smoke cigars at big Hollywood parties and meet stars. It's a win-win situation."

Colin was intrigued. His movie could be shot for a couple of million bucks if done right. *Sling Blade* was done for about a million, *The Brothers McMullen* even less. *Maybe a few investment bankers looking for a tax shelter and a chance to meet chicks was one way to raise money for* Middle America, Colin thought.

"Maybe they'll meet with my agent some day," Colin said.

O'Toole smiled and said, "Long as he isn't a federal agent."

They arrived at Lupo's Italian restaurant in Ozone Park about ten minutes later. Colin watched as the chauffeur held the back door open. Colin helped Gina out while O'Toole guided Susan from the backseat. Colin watched Susan wrap an expensive red fox stole around her shoulders, noticing that she also dripped with jewelry.

This mooch moves from the dole to a fox stole inside two months, Colin thought. *A fucking genius.*

As they entered Lupo's, Colin heard O'Toole say, "I don't mind wop food, but I skeeve the idea of guineas preparing it."

Three muscle-bound guys sitting at the small bar turned when they heard O'Toole's remark.

"Yo, Petey, easy on the big mouth, huh?" Colin said. "You wanna commit suicide, swan dive off the roof. Alone."

O'Toole stared at every one of the muscle guys as if he were standing in the center of a boxing ring. No words were exchanged.

Finally, their party was led by a nervous maître d' into the dining room. As soon as they were all seated at a round table in the center, they began reading the menus. Then, over the top of his menu, Colin saw Joe Monte. The mobster had his back to them, sitting at a red leather booth with a woman in her late thirties wearing a huge diamond wedding ring.

Monte's wife was facing their table. Something caught her eye almost immediately. Joe Monte poured his wife another glass of chianti. Colin's heart started to pound when he noticed the woman staring at Susan, her eyes transfixed. Then Colin saw Monte's wife fumble in her Gucci handbag, pull out a pair of gold-rimmed glasses, and jam them on her nose, staring more intently at Susan. Monte's wife bit the knuckle of her right index finger so hard Colin thought she'd draw blood.

"Uh-oh," Colin whispered.

Colin saw her say something to Joe Monte and nod toward Susan, as he chewed some linguine and took a sip of red wine. Monte turned and a small spray of wine and pasta shot from his lips when he saw Susan sitting there, staring at him, dramatically flaunting the fox stole.

"It keeps me lovely and warm, Joe, thanks, luv," Susan said aloud, snuggling her face in the fur. Many of the other diners watched the exchange in confused silence.

Susan flicked the pearls and the earrings. "And the jewelry is also lovely," Susan said. "T'anks, macho man."

Joe Monte started to rise from the booth in anger but his wife got up even faster and smashed the bottle of red chianti against his face. Joe Monte fell back on the seat in a wet crimson crunch, the blood indistinguishable from the wine.

"You dirty fuckin' cuntrag," Joe Monte shouted, cowering.

"Who you callin' a cuntrag?" his wife screamed, brandishing a fork in her fist.

Joe Monte covered his face with his overdeveloped arms, lying across the seat of the booth.

"Not you, Mella," Joe Monte shouted. "Her . . . Susan . . ."

"You know her mudda-fuckin' naaaaammmeee!" Mella shouted, stamping her feet, stabbing madly at his crotch with the fork.

Colin popped to his feet.

"Let's go," he said, yanking and shoving Gina toward the front door. The three muscle goons from the bar appeared in the dining room in a startled flourish, dragging Mella off Joe Monte.

The smallest, most lethal-looking goon glared at Colin and O'Toole.

O'Toole was on his feet and Colin saw him remove a small handgun from a holster in the back of his pants and palm it in his right hand. *Fucking maniac,* Colin thought, lurching for the front door, pulling Gina behind him. A fearless, crooked smile split O'Toole's face. There was a crazed glint in his eyes, a man high on the excitement of near death. "Easy, Antipasto," O'Toole said, grinning, chomping a bread stick. "Ladies here."

"Yous better get the fuck atta here," the small goon said.

Colin opened the front door, shoving Gina out. But Gina grabbed the door frame. "I'm not leaving without Susan."

"That fuckin' *putan* stole my fuckin' stole," Mella screamed.

"Yer husband's after givin' it to me, sure," Susan said.

His wife lunged at Joe Monte again with the fork. The biggest goons finally wrestled it from her hand.

"He took it atta my cold storage, you little McGinty twat," Mella screamed as she fought to free herself from the goons.

"Maybe you should keep your husband's willie in cold storage, luv," Susan said.

Mella Monte writhed to get at Susan, but the goons restrained her. O'Toole herded Susan past Colin and Gina out the door, his handgun still palmed for all to see.

"I'll remember yous," the small Italian goon said.

"I got no beef with you *bacciagalupes,*" O'Toole said.

"Joe," Colin said. "I had nothing to do with all this . . ."

April 26

Colin never slept. He knew Joe Monte would be by in the morning looking for Susan. The night before, Colin had made her collect her son, Sammy, and go with Petey O'Toole to his apartment in Manhattan. There would be reprisals for what happened in the Italian restaurant.

Colin made a call to Davey Grogan to ask him to have one of

the cops who came into Grogan's run a background check on Petey O'Toole from Manhattan.

"Like the *Lawrence of Arabia* actor?"

"Yeah," Colin said.

Two hours later, Davey Grogan called back. "Petey O'Toole has done two stretches for bank robbery. He's a suspect in that armored car robbery in Buffalo three months ago. They stole three million dollars."

"Great," Colin said. "Fuckin' great."

Colin searched his wallet and took out the card the guy named Rocco had given him in the Vesuvius Soccer Club when Gina had wandered in there looking for her father. He dialed the beeper number and Colin punched in his own number. Ten minutes later, Rocco called him back.

Colin reminded him who he was and Rocco said he'd never forget. He asked if they could talk. Rocco said he was on a pay phone in a church basement and not to mention his last name. Colin then briefly told Rocco what had transpired in the Italian restaurant, and asked if there was any way to straighten it out.

"That's what I do," Rocco said. "By the way, I'm still lookin' for your wife's father. I think I might even have a lead."

Joe Monte arrived with the short goon at the house at 11:00 A.M. He had stitches in his head and face, and was walking with a slight limp. Colin assured him that Susan wasn't home.

Colin saw Lipinski and several of his new neighbors watching the two wise guys standing on his stoop, their Cadillac parked at the curb. With their tight suits, slicked-back hair, no sideburns, and lots of gold jewelry, they might as well have been wearing jumpsuits that said MAFIA across the back.

"Come on in," Colin said. "You can look for yourself."

"I believe you," Monte said, softly. "My people got a call from a friend of ours that you know. So what I have to say won't take only a minute. I was nice to this Susan broad. I took her out, I gave her stuff, jewelry, clothes, shit for her kid. I showed her the town, we got it on."

"Joe, I had no idea what she was gonna do last night."

"I treated her like a lady," Monte said, holding up a hand for Colin to be quiet. "I was up front about my wife, my kids, and my family. Then, alla sudden, she asks me to leave all that for her. I says I couldn't do that even if I wanted to. My wife, Carmela, she has a father, uncles, brothers, a family name, you understand?"

Colin nodded.

"Then Susan comes into the place where I hang out," Joe Monte said. "On a Tuesday night when she knows I'm always there with my wife. She proceeds to humiliate me, which I can live with, because I'm a man. But Susan, she humiliated my *wife*. In public. In front of other wives. This is cruel. This ain't right. My wife never did nothing to her. Alls I ever did was treat Susan nice. What she did is unforgivable. Now I gotta go repair my marriage. I gotta face my daughters. I gotta explain myself to my bosses, to my wife's father, uncles, brothers. The reason I'm here is to tell you to tell her that it's time she goes home. I can't say what my wife is gonna do even if I decide to do nothing. See? Tell Susan for me, go home."

Colin nodded and said, "I'll tell her, Joe."

"And tell her if she decides to hang around with that O'Toole, anything could happen," he said. "And you should find a new gym."

Joe Monte and the small goon walked back to their car and climbed in. Lipinski and the other neighbors all watched the Cadillac drive away.

When Colin closed the door, Gina was standing in the foyer, off to the side. She'd heard everything.

"Gina, our kids live in this house," Colin said. "Today there were gangsters at the door. Susan's running with a guy who did an armored car heist. The feds'll be here next. She could do time for aiding and abetting. Or be killed by Monte's wife."

"I'll tell Susan it's time for her to shift," Gina said.

Gina packed all of Susan's stuff that afternoon and she booked a flight to Dublin for Friday. As soon as Paul Lynch heard that Susan was going home, he also announced his desire to go home. Colin dipped into his last few grand to buy them one-way tickets to Dublin.

Some investments are sure winners, he thought.

On Thursday, Colin heard back from Linda Parks, who said she was back in town and asked him to come see her in her SoHo office on Friday morning. She said she had several music-video jobs and she could sure use a director of his caliber.

Colin was finished with a first draft of his *Middle America* script but was letting it "cool" for two weeks before rereading it and sending it to Bonnie Corbet to send out.

April 28

On Friday morning, Colin drove down Bell Boulevard on his way to Manhattan to see Linda Parks when he saw the twirling lights of fire engines outside Grogan's Tavern. When he got closer, he saw a swelling, bereaved-looking crowd on the boulevard.

Colin double-parked the car, clicked on his hazards, and hurried to the scene. Davey Grogan stood outside his saloon, haggard and unshaven, staring as firemen with hooks pulled smoldering sections of the bar out onto the sidewalk. A mud slide of black soot lapped out the back door of the bar, the twirling lights of the fire trucks licking the scorched windows.

"Davey, what the hell happened?"

He gaped at Colin. His eyes looked like shattered lenses, his face purple with anger. He pulled a charred strongbox from a crumpled paper bag and flipped it open. It was empty.

"They pulled this out of the fire," Davey Grogan said.

"Yeah?"

"It was locked with a padlock and a fucking key when I closed up last night," he said. "A fire don't pop a padlock, Col."

"What are you saying, Davey?"

"Last one here was the porter," Davey said. "The marshals are gonna want to have a talk with him. He won't have a tongue to talk with if I find him first."

"Paul . . . ?"

"Didn't you say he liked to play with matches, this little fuckin' wetback, ingrate, shanty, tinker prick?"

"Jesus Christ, Davey, I'm so sorry."

"I'm insured," he said, crunching and squishing through the incinerated rubble, picking up a section of the hand-etched mirror, the glass shattered, the ancient oak framing blistered and seared. "Between the fire and the smoke damage, I'll never replace the old wood and cut mirrors, tin ceilings and cracked tile."

He lifted some old framed sepia-tone photographs, now water-logged, buckled, and sooty. Under the grime, Colin could make out the familiar images of Davey Grogan's grandfather and great-grand-father, proud men dressed in white aprons and bow ties, posing behind the beer stick and with horse-drawn beer delivery wagons. The photos had been passed down to Davey as family heirlooms. Now they were destroyed, ruined.

"How the fuck do I replace history, Col, huh?" Davey asked, holding the photos in his hands, black water dripping from the blistered frames. "The history of my family up in smoke. The soul of the joint is gone. The magic, poof. Insurance companies don't replace magic."

Listening to Davey Grogan, a simple bar owner whose life was changed by a single selfish act, made Colin feel dirty and grubby and guilty.

"How much was in the strongbox?" Colin asked, lamely.

"The day's take," Davey Grogan said, shrugging. "Little less than a grand. He looted the place, this brain surgeon, and thought he could cover it up with a torch job. He robbed a family legacy from my kids, Colin. This hurts me."

The insurance would pay for a new bar, gleaming with modern machine-made mirrors and freshly milled wood. It would have the same name but it would never again be Grogan's.

"Davey, I just don't know what to say."

"Me neither," Davey Grogan said. "But the minute you find this sick fuck, promise you let me know where he is."

"Promise."

Paul Lynch had torched a neighborhood shrine and the dirty deed wouldn't be forgotten for many years. If ever.

He watched Davey Grogan step through the broken glass and lift a framed liquor license, issued right after prohibition was repealed. Black water dribbled from the seams. Colin started walking back toward his car when he ran into Peggy Johnson, who looked desiccated and distraught, her eyes puffy and red, her face pale. *Another lemon squeezed dry,* Colin thought. *Another Paul fucking Lynch victim.*

"Where's Paul?" Colin asked.

"I'm looking for him," Peggy said. "He never came home all night. He usually comes right home after he cleans Grogan's."

"He won't be cleaning it anymore," Colin said.

"I need to find him."

She looked ready to cry again.

"Peggy, what's wrong?"

"Nothing."

"Peggy, this asshole might not be coming back, so maybe you better tell me."

She fell back against Colin's car and put her hand to her head, trying to hold back the tears.

"He took all my cash, about three hundred dollars, and my jewelry," she said. "I'm sure he pawned it. I bought him a watch and he pawned it three days later down in Hagen's pawn shop."

"Did he tell you he was leaving for Dublin?"

"No," she said, shaking her head, sobbing. "He got pissed off when I told him I was pregnant and then later he robbed me."

"You let him knock you up? Jesus, Peggy, he's a fucking *bum.*"

"He was good-looking," she said. "He was Irish, like you. He was funny."

"No one's laughing now," Colin said.

forty-nine

Linda Parks said, "I have two videos that can be shot and edited in a month. The first one is in L.A., the second one is here."

"I'll take both," Colin said, without even negotiating a price. He sat on the edge of his chair, distracted and fidgety.

He looked at her oddly. Her nose stud was gone and so were the hoops going up her left ear. The rock-climbing outfit had been replaced by a blue wool pinstripe pantsuit. She wore dark heels and her full mane of hair had been frosted with blond highlights. Her makeup was subtly applied and small diamond studs dotted each earlobe.

"Don't you want to know who the bands are, or what the price is?" she asked.

"I need to work, I need to get the hell out of town for a while," Colin said. "I know you'll be fair. I'll do a good job. I promise."

"How broke are you?" she asked.

"Can you front me five grand?"

"Sure," she said. "Ten if you sign. I was gonna expect you to try to get fifteen grand each, anyway. I was going to lowball you to ten. If we met in the middle at twelve-five, plus airfare, hotel, car, and incidental per-diem expenses . . ."

"Deal," Colin said. "When do I leave?"

"Can we at least have lunch or dinner to talk out the storyboards, refine the concepts to your vision?"

"Can we do it now? Today?"

"Absolutely," she said, and changed the subject. "So, I hear you have a kid."

"Yes," he said. "Two kids. The mother of my kid already had one, and well, you come to love a kid fast."

"Not the mother?"

"It's a different kind of love," he said. "If it's love at all. I'm trying to figure it out and it's cost me."

"You seem frightened, Colin."

"I am."

"Who you afraid of?"

"Me. I look at you, at how great you're doing, and I ask myself how I made the choices I made. Like how did I ever let you go?"

"I don't bed married men," she said. "I hire them."

"I'm not married," he said. "And I didn't mean that as a come-on, Linda."

"I want your talent, not your body. You do a great job, and I'll look like a genius for hiring you."

"I'm sorry I didn't call you sooner."

"Like when you were single?"

"Yeah."

"Or when you were hot in the biz?"

"That, too," Colin said. "Hey, I'm an asshole. I'm guilty."

"Do a good job on these videos and you'll create a buzz for yourself again," she said. "They're hiring video directors like crazy to direct features in Hollywood these days."

"Let's get started," he said. "I haven't worked with film in so long I forget what it smells like."

Linda went into another office to get the material on the two bands whose videos Colin would be shooting. When she was gone, Colin called Gina and told her he would be tied up all day and part of the night and wouldn't be able to drive anyone to the airport.

"Susan said to say thanks for everything," Gina said. "She says sorry about the other night. Poor wee Paul had a grand trip and said to say thanks to yeh for everything, and so long."

"No problem," Colin said.

He never mentioned the fire in Grogan's or the farewell gift Paul had left in Peggy Johnson's womb.

Colin and Linda Parks spent the rest of the afternoon in her handsome loft on Mercer Street. She plugged in recent videos of the two groups he'd be shooting, playing the new songs that needed to be illustrated, going over concepts and storyboards. Colin came up with one idea after another. The fire in Grogan's weirdly inspired the video he'd shoot in L.A., for a group called the Girl Singers.

"Three firefighters dance out of a burning dance club, shooting water from a hose," Colin said, pacing the loft as he listened to a song called "Break the Devil's Dishes." "All the young people from the club mingle behind police barricades. Then the firefighters start doing a striptease with the fire regalia to reveal our three scantily dressed, soot-covered, hot girl singers doing their new single amid the smoke and the flames and the steaming water."

"You're getting me excited," Linda Parks said, her dazzling smile igniting her face. "I love it. Write a quick script and I think we can start filming in two weeks. I knew you'd be perfect, this could be the hottest video this summer."

She stood, pirouetted, and danced a few short steps.

The second group consisted of a bunch of Italian-American kids from Bensonhurst called the Du Wopps, who did "white rap" and had a new single called "Gangster Wrap."

Colin had an idea about using locations like Rocco's social club and an Italian restaurant, using the jealousy elements of the scene between Joe Monte, his wife, Susan, and Petey O'Toole, all ending in an operatic shootout while the Du Wopps sang the song.

"I like that, too," Linda said.

"I'll need a technical advisor written into the budget," Colin said. "I know just the guy to make this happen smoothly."

"Okay," she said. "Write the scripts. I like your energy."

"I like your new look," he said.

"When you start dealing in millions of dollars," she said. "You dress for the record company stockholders. I had a makeover."

"It suits you," he said.

"But I still have the tattoo," she said, looking him deep in the eye. Colin said nothing as Linda Parks wrote him a check for ten thousand dollars.

Colin stopped in a discount store on Houston Street and bought a black woolen ski mask. He drove east on Houston and took the FDR Drive north to the Midtown Tunnel, and then drove straight out on the Van Wyck Expressway to JFK airport. He parked his car in the short-term lot across from the Aer Lingus terminal.

He sat in the waiting area a few hundred feet from the busy bar at the Aer Lingus departure terminal, pretending to read a newspaper. Paul Lynch and Susan were already sitting at the bar, laughing, smoking, drinking. Young Sammy was asleep in his pram beside Susan. Colin watched Paul order his third round in fifteen minutes, reaching into his right jeans pocket and pulling out a thick wad of American cash. He peeled off a bill and handed it to the bartender. He watched Paul throw back the straight whiskey and then take a deep gulp of Guinness.

Paul lit a fresh cigarette, gazing into the flame of the match until it almost blistered his fingers. Then Colin saw Paul excuse himself as he walked quickly for the men's room.

Colin counted to ten Mississippi and then followed him in, pulling out the black wool ski mask as he entered the bathroom. One elderly man was pulling up his zipper and flushing the urinal. Colin watched him leave. He knew he had to act quickly. As the old gent passed him on the way out, Colin donned the ski mask and stole up behind Paul Lynch.

Colin exploded a fierce right hand off the back of Paul's skull, his face slamming with a dull thud into the shiny white tile wall. A small red smear streaked down the wall. Paul's eyes rolled back in his head, a crumpled, smoldering cigarette stuck in his lips. Colin heard a gurgle come from Paul's throat as the blood from his broken nose pooled in his trachea. He quickly dragged Paul by the collar across the floor to a toilet stall and sat him on the bowl. Paul's dick was still dangling through his zipper. He took the lit cigarette from his lips and balanced it on the toilet-paper holder.

Colin dug his hand into Paul's right jeans pocket and pulled out the wad of cash he'd robbed from Grogan's strongbox and Peggy Johnson's house. Colin jammed the cash into his own pants pocket and searched Paul's coat pockets. Amid a collection of matches, cigarettes, and used tissues, he found a receipt from Hagen's pawn shop. As Colin put the receipt in his jacket, Paul Lynch slowly began to stir.

Colin sat him up on the bowl and Paul's eyes opened momentarily, blinking in horror at the masked man. He opened his bloody mouth to shout but Colin hit his chin with a six-inch punch, thrown with the full engine of his shoulder and the whole weight of his body. Paul's head whipped around like a kewpie doll's and he went back to dreamland. In one ruthless motion, Colin yanked the zipper up on Paul's dick, making sure the metal teeth bit deeply into the soft flesh.

"For the baby you're running out on," Colin whispered.

He twisted Paul around and pulled the top of his pants down, revealing the crack of his ass. Colin picked up the lit cigarette, blew on the ember to make it hot, and shoved it down Paul's crack and let the elastic band of his underwear snap back in place.

"For the fucking fire in Grogan's," he whispered.

Colin closed the stall door after him as he heard Paul Lynch begin to moan in agony. He pulled off the ski mask and quickly exited the men's room.

In his car, Colin counted $1,770 in the wad he'd taken from Paul Lynch's pocket. On the way home, he stopped and bought a box of white envelopes from a corner candy store, put $770 into an envelope along with the Hagen's pawn shop receipt, and shoved it anonymously under Peggy Johnson's door.

Twenty-seven minutes after leaving Paul Lynch in the airport men's room, Colin was in his living room in Bayside when the phone rang. Gina answered. It was Susan reporting that Paul had been mugged in the men's room at the airport. Gina started sputtering in a combination of gammon and English, near hysterical, before finally hanging up.

"Every penny that poor lad earned scrubbin' toilets was nicked," Gina said. "Durty feckin' robbers in this city, wha'?" She didn't mention his mangled dick.

"Terrible," Colin said, and went downstairs to work on his music-video scripts.

Giddy with revenge, Colin wrote both four-page video scripts in about three hours, all the camera angles and bits of action, music cues and dance riffs. *This video racket was a license to print money,* he thought. Tingling with accomplishment, he bounded up the stairs to put the kids to sleep.

He tickled Seamus for ten minutes and then opened a *Pippi Longstocking* book to read to Brianna.

"Before I start reading, I want you to know that Daddy has to go away in a few weeks."

Brianna instantly began to cry and threw her arms around his neck. "No, Daddy," she said. "I don't want you to go away."

"Daddy has to work, honey, to get money to buy stuff."

"No," Brianna said. "I want you to work downstairs."

"Noooo," Seamus said, and he started to whinge. Gina came into the room carrying a glass of wine, looking distraught, and tipsy.

"I'm ready for tears meself," she said. "Me family is gone again. You'll be gone. I feel the cold hand of death inside me."

"Chrissakes, Gina, the kids don't wanna hear this."

"A miserable icy death that's goin' to happen soon," she said. "It's twistin' me guts. I'm afraid for me grannies."

Gina took a deep gulp of the wine, her eyes welling tears.

"I don't want Granny to die," Brianna said, sobbing.

Colin shoved her out of the bedroom, into the hall. "Gina, for chrissakes, stop upsetting the kids."

"I need to see them," Gina said. "Promise me in front of these childer you'll let me see me grannies. I want to go home."

"No!" Brianna shouted, standing at the door, growing hysterical, her breathing fitful and panicky. "I don't wanna go back to Ireland. I wanna stay here with Daddy!"

"Nooooo," Seamus said, crying more loudly. "Stay with Dada."

Tears dripped from Gina's eyes as she slugged the wine.

Christ, Colin thought. *Never one peaceful fucking night . . .*

"Gina, I won't discuss this in front of the kids," he said.

"No seep," Seamus shouted, rubbing his wet eyes.

"Promise me, Daddy, you won't let us go back to Ireland without you," Brianna said, her breathing fitful with worry.

"We could fly them over here," Gina said.

"Who?" Colin shouted, dread mounting. "Fly who over here?"

"Me grannies," she said, handing Colin a glass and wiping her teary eyes with the back of her hand. "Och, it would be great crack. Their last shift. They'd get to see America in their lifetimes. They could brag about that to the other oul travelers till the day they die."

"Gina, I can't work with your crazy relatives in the house," he said. "And the money . . ."

"Och, yer only after braggin' that yeh jotted a pair of wee video scripts in less than three hours for ten grand," she said.

"I'm not paying to fly anyone over, period."

Gina went into their bedroom and slammed the door.

Linda Parks loved both of Colin's video scripts. So did the record company executives. The artists had only a few suggested changes. Linda gave the go-ahead to hire Rocco as location scout for the New York shoot of the Du Wopps video. A production manager was scouting Colin's west coast video, finding a dance club and securing other locations.

May 10

After location scouting in lower Manhattan, Rocco told Colin he thought he finally tracked down some information he wanted.

"Owl Fulluh," Rocco said with a laugh. "They're still talking about Owl Fulluh down the club. Anyways, I was right about a guy in the old days name of Gino Barilla. He can't be your wife's father because he's too old. Plus he was whacked maybe twenty-five years ago and nobody remembers him ever going to Eye-land. But people I talked to said he had a grown son he sent to Europe to study in the seventies because there was a war between the families ready to explode. People were startin' to hit the mattresses, and Gino Barilla, he didn't want his son in the life, didn't want his only son around to get whacked, know what I mean?"

Colin nodded. "Junior wound up in Trinity College in Dublin?"

"I guess so, and after his father got whacked, the son, this Gino Barilla Junior, he changed his name to Gene Barr," Rocco said. "Today, this Gene Barr, he's a respected corporate lawyer. He lives in Long Island, Manhasset. Far as I'm concerned, this is the guy who twenny-and-change years ago had a fling-flang with your wife's mom. I got an address, but since the guy's legit, I don't want nothin' more to do with it. You asked me to find him. You kept your word and got me movie work, I'm keeping my word."

He gave Colin the name and the address.

fifty

May 13

On a bright, sunny Mother's Day, Colin parked at a curb across the street from the large red brick house in Manhasset. Gina stared at the small wooden sign hanging from the mailbox that read: THE BARRS. A new silver Mercedes 500 was parked in the driveway alongside a Porsche sports car and a Lexus GS 300 that had Yale and Princeton insignias on the back windows.

Colin told Gina about the news of her father right away, but Gina waited until Mother's Day to confront him. She liked the symbolism and she was certain the family would be home.

Colin had never known Gina to be so nervous. She'd bought black fabric and sewn herself a duplicate of the dress her mother wore in the dance-hall photo, the photo of Gino Barilla that Gina carried with her. She even speared a peacock feather into her hat, her red curls spilling down from under it. For more than fifteen minutes, she sat in the Lumina, fidgeting, looking at the house with its sprawling lawns, Olympic-size swimming pool, pool house, guest house, doghouse, tree house. She just sat, staring, blinking, her face a bag of anxious tics.

"Must be someone home," Colin said. "Three cars in the driveway."

"The rich sleeps late," Gina said.

"What're you gonna say to him?"

"I haven't a blind beggar's clue," she said. "I've been waitin' all me life to say what's on me mind, and now me mind's as blank as me bankbook. Desperate. What do yeh think I should say, Colin?"

Sitting there, wringing her hands, chewing the inside of her lip, she looked like a frightened little girl.

"Say, 'Hello, I'm Gina, I think I'm your daughter.'"

"Sometimes you're as useless as tits on a nun," she said.

Finally, a forest-green Lexus LX 450 rolled down the leafy street and turned right into the gravel driveway of the Barr house. Gina swallowed hard as the car came to a rest. Her eyes didn't blink. She watched as a dark-haired, athletically built man in his mid-forties stepped out of the driver's door, dressed in an expensive dark suit and tie. The back doors opened and two very attractive teenage girls, one maybe nineteen and the other about seventeen, and a teenage boy, about fourteen, climbed out. They were all dressed in Sunday churchgoing clothes. One of the girls wore long white gloves and carried a prayer book. The father hurried around and opened the front passenger door and a woman in her early forties stepped out, wearing a neat white dress pinned with a corsage and a matching bonnet decorated with flowers.

Gina's eyes were wide and staring, still unblinking, drinking in the family that, but for fortune, might have been hers. These were her half-sisters and half-brother and the father she had pursued for a quarter-century, through orphanage dreams and hotel lobbies, in the wallets of drunken men in tourist pubs, in her childish fantasies and even in a heartbreaking little song.

Yer daddy's in Americay
And yer mammy's in her grave . . .

"Gina . . ."

She held up a hand and whispered, "Please . . ."

She bit her lower lip and watched Gene Barr reach into the car, take out a camcorder, and make the kids pose with the mother—kissing her, hugging her, putting on dopey faces, striking comical stances. A good, solid, functional, affluent, happy American family on Mother's Day. The older girl took the camera from her father and shot footage of him kissing the mother as the other two applauded.

The teenage boy bounded up the stairs, unlocked the door, and opened it. A big Old English sheepdog came bounding out, barking, its tail wagging madly, jumping up on each member of the family, licking, panting, barking. The son disengaged a burglar alarm, disappeared inside for a few moments, and came back out, jacketless and tieless, and threw a perfect spiral football pass to his father.

The father caught the ball, pulled off his jacket, quickly shed his tie, and tossed them on the massive front lawn that was circled by a natural log fence. He threw a long pass to his son, who ran toward the rear of the house. The mother and the girls went chattering into the house together, the big panting dog tearing in after them.

"I can see the resemblance," Colin said.

"He married a redhead," Gina said in a soft, faraway voice. "Like me ma. Why couldn't it have been her?"

"There were probably a thousand reasons," Colin said, staring across at the father now entering the house, his arm draped over his son's shoulder. "Maybe because they were too young. Or because his father was killed and he had to go home for the funeral and lost contact. Your mother was a traveler, Gina, on the road, and maybe he couldn't find her."

"He knew where to send the letter that got her kilt," Gina said.

He had no response to that and kept staring at the house. *I wonder where my half-brother is,* Colin thought, knowing he'd never know. When he turned to Gina, she had quietly stepped out of the car, circled around the back bumper, and was walking across the street toward the house. Her floppy white hat lay on the passenger seat next to him. He watched Gina approach the big wide stoop, humble as hired help, the sun gleaming in her red hair.

The whole family was inside the house now as Gina stood between two Georgian columns. Colin swung out of the car, quickly crossed the quiet street, and bounded up the stoop. He wanted to be with her. *This is a real fucking movie moment,* he thought. *Besides, I don't want her to be alone.* Gina put her small right index finger on the bell and hesitated. She blinked several times. Took a breath. Finally, she pressed the doorbell button and a series of elaborate chimes, straight out of a Hollywood movie, rang from inside.

"I got it," came the father's deep voice from within and then Gene Barr pulled open the door. He wore a big smile as he appeared before them. He glanced at Colin quizzically and then looked at Gina. *He's a man confronted with an apparition,* Colin thought. The smile hardened on Gene Barr's face like a fossil. The color began to drain from his cheeks as the wheels behind the disbelieving eyes seemed to whir back in time.

He knows, Colin thought. *He fucking knows.*

"Yes?" he finally said, his voice a murmur.

"Who is it, Gene?" came the mother's vibrant voice.

"Is there an Anne Furey living here?" Gina asked.

The father shook his head and swallowed. "Sorry . . ."

"There should be," Gina said.

The mother now appeared at the door, drying her hands on a Easter bunny dish towel, her eyes sparkling. The two teenage girls appeared in the foyer behind her. Colin watched Gina evaluate them and then saw her look beyond them at the opulence of the million-dollar-plus home—the antique furnishings, the deep pile rugs, the framed art, the leather-bound books, the expensive lamps, the porcelain figurines. Colin tried to imagine Gina's mother raising her in a place like this and couldn't. *There'd be a fucking goat and a pony and a covered wagon on the lawn,* he thought.

Gina stared at her two half-sisters and her younger half-brother, who appeared behind them. She looked from one face to the other, mesmerized with curiosity and what appeared to be a genuine fondness forming in her eyes.

"Who are you looking for, honey?" the mother said.

"I'm sorry," Gina said. "I must have the wrong family."

Gina turned and hurried down the stoop. The curious wife studied her husband as he watched Gina walk away. As she crossed the street, Gina tilted her head to the clean blue sky. Colin stared at a nervously perspiring Gene Barr for a long moment, watching his face turn the color and texture of bean curd. Colin figured Gina was a missing piece in the puzzle of Gene Barr's life, and the rich lawyer and happy family man was clearly afraid that if he tried to fit her into the space where she belonged the whole picture would collapse.

"Gene, that girl look familiar to you?" the mother asked as

Colin followed Gina down the stoop. The father didn't answer. Colin turned and saw Gene Barr, formerly Gino Barilla, Jr., standing there, his wife and kids joining him in the doorway. He was still staring after Gina. Spooked and speechless.

Gina walked swiftly to the car. Colin followed her and climbed into the Lumina. The end of her search was now the start of a cold reality. *Gina is who she is,* Colin thought. *A bastard child from the misty past. That man, Gene Barr, no matter who he used to be, would never be her father.*

Right then, in that fragile moment, Colin felt what he thought might be genuine love for Gina Furey. *Don't confuse love with pity,* he thought.

"Are you okay?" Colin asked, putting his arm around her and trying to draw her near. She was rigid.

"Take me home," she said softly.

As they departed, Gina stared at the family still in the doorway of the big house in the plush American suburb.

Colin made a left turn off the street and the Barr's became a faded image. He drove slowly through the opulent, immaculate neighborhood toward Northern Boulevard. "Stop the car a wee minute," she said.

Colin pulled to the curb in front of another sprawling estate, rimmed with weeping willows. Gina got out, walked to a perfect spring-green lawn, and uprooted three clumps of grass. Colin watched, eyes squinting, as Gina carried the three sods and arranged them into an arrowhead formation in the center of the road. Then she climbed back into the car.

"Done," she said brushing the soil from her hands. Colin put the car in drive and slowly pulled away.

"What the hell was that all about?" he asked, as in the rearview mirror he saw a man appear on the damaged lawn of the house, waving a fist at his car.

"The three sods in the road," she said. "Father, Son, and the Holy Ghost. It means I've traveled past and left me blessing."

"Instead of leaving a goddamned *blessing,*" Colin said, "why don't you just go back and tell your father who you are?"

"I could never do that."

"Why?" Colin said. "Are you afraid of hurting him?"

"Not him," she said. "He's a pig for abandoning me ma. And me. He sent money for me just the once't and then wrote me off like money spent on a lame pony. I'm not afraid of hurting his pampered wife, neither. But those girls, that boy, they never did me no wrong. When I looked at them, I could see me own blood in them, and I suddenly realized I'm their big sister. I was never anyone's big sister before. They're happy. They don't need me messing up their happy little lives. I couldn't hurt them. You just don't do that to family."

fifty-one

May 21

On the way to the airport, Colin drove past Grogan's Tavern, where workmen were already starting to rebuild. Colin spotted Davey Grogan and stopped to give him the thousand dollars in cash that Paul Lynch had robbed from him.

"Jesus, Davey, I know this doesn't mean much, but it's what the mutt took. Again, I'm sorry."

"It's done," Davey said, pocketing the cash. "The place'll be opened in three weeks. More smoke and water damage than fire. Where you headed?"

"Airport," Colin said, too embarrassed to elaborate.

"Don't tell me you're importin' more of 'em?"

"Her grandparents," Colin said, taking a deep breath.

"I dunno," Davey said. "I'm probably talking out of place here, but I've known you since you were a little kid. I served you your first legal beer. Like everyone else around here, I'm proud of what you've accomplished, Col. I'm also worried about you. Your brothers and your old man are worried about you. Now I've been touched by these people, too, so I figure I can talk from firsthand experience. Hey, I can rebuild a fuckin' bar. It won't be the same, the magic is gone, but I can rebuild it. You better start thinking about how you rebuild your life after these people are through with you. You've got kids to think about. It's hard to rebuild a kid once he's in pieces."

Colin nodded; he knew Davey Grogan was right. It was just too difficult to explain the trap he was in. It would be worse for the kids to let Gina take them back to Ireland. He dreaded a custody battle. So he treaded water.

"I'll see ya around," Colin said, got in the car and drove down Bell Boulevard. When he turned left onto Northern Boulevard, he was confronted by an assortment of white trailers and the equipment trucks of a movie shoot. He knew it was his movie, *Across the Pond,* which was here on location. Colin stopped for a red light and looked over at the crew huddled around the camera. Frank Burston was wearing a Yankees hat, in Mets country, and was strutting around like a man in charge, smiling, pointing, giving orders to the crew. *It's like watching someone else fucking my woman in my own bed,* he thought.

He scanned the set for Melissa Thompson but she was nowhere to be seen. He felt a nauseating emptiness, a malaise of failure set loose in his blood. *Frank Burston is in my stomping ground, shooting my film, probably involved with Melissa Thompson, a normal and beautiful chick who cared about me and my work. And I'm on my way to the airport to pick up two mental cases before I travel to Los Angeles to shoot a cheapo music video to pay for their stay. Jack's right, I do need a fucking psychiatrist!*

His life was an incalculable mess. He gaped at Burston, who was blocking a scene with his cameraman, until the motorists behind Colin started honking their horns. Frank Burston turned toward the commotion and Colin quickly drove away.

When he arrived at the airport, the grannies were waiting. With Bridie and Philomena. And their kids. *A full six-pack of greenhorns,* he thought. *In my house. On my block. In my neighborhood. Where someone else is shooting a movie inspired by my fucked-up life.*

"We thought we'd surprise yeh," Bridie said.

"You got me, all right," Colin said.

"Granny wouldn't get on a plane with Granda alone," Philomena said. "She said she was afraid he'd throw her overboard. So she asked us to come. She bought our tickets from the allowance Gina and you have been sending every month, fair play to yiz."

Colin just nodded. This was the first he'd learned that he was sending a granny allowance to Ireland every month. *Very fucking generous of me,* he thought.

"This isn't New York," Granny said, looking around the airport. She was dressed in a heavy winter wool coat, a cigarette dangling from her lips. "Where's Andy Sipowicz, wha'? I want him to suss out this bit o' nasty business with wee Paul Lynch bein' robbed and near kilt. That was my money he had on him, and I want it back."

"She told the boss woman on the plane that if she couldn't smoke she was gettin' off right then and there," Granda said. "I told them to let her."

"Where's Gina?" Bridie asked.

"At home with the kids," Colin said. "Making dinner."

"Where's New York?" Granny asked as Colin led them toward the parking lot.

"This way," Colin said.

May 22

The house seemed to shrink in front of Colin's eyes. The grannies got Brianna's bedroom and the cousins and their kids appropriated Seamus's, while Brianna and Seamus slept with Colin and Gina.

I'm camping out in my own home, Colin thought as he lay awake at night in the crowded bed. *I'll have to rent a motel room to get laid. I'll have to read in the library. Forget work. I might as well join the phone company and climb a fucking pole—for privacy.*

Colin could never get into either of the two upstairs bathrooms. The toilet-paper rolls were always empty. The women even began using the small toilet downstairs in his writing room in the raw cellar. At night, Granda thought nothing of going out into the back-yard to "have a wee splash" against the blue spruce.

The kids ran through the house all day long and the TV and radio played simultaneously and incessantly. The kettle whistled every twenty minutes. Cigarette smoke hung in the air like an indoor fog. Cookies and breakfast cereal were mashed into the four-thousand-dollar Persian rug, which was beginning to look like an op-art canvas. Granny lit the jets of the gas fireplace every time Colin shut it off.

"Granny, it's eighty degrees," Colin said. "We don't need the fire."

"I feel like a Protestant in a house without a fire," she said, adding pages of the morning newspaper—which Colin had not yet read—to the flames. She also tossed her cigarettes and matches and odd debris onto the ersatz logs in the fireplace.

"Granny," Colin said. "It's a *gas* fire, you can't throw stuff in it to burn. It'll clog the jets."

"Aye, I flew here on a jet all right."

Granny stormed off toward Gina in the kitchen and heard her say, "That fella o' yers t'inks I'm a right thick. Bollocks is trying to tell me there's aero-planes in the fireplace, wha'?"

Colin was happy he would be going away to Los Angeles in less than a week.

May 23

Gina took the whole tribe to a bar named Mulligan's on Thirty-fifth Avenue for happy hour. Colin tagged along to make sure no one burned it down. Crocks of cheese and crackers were placed on the bar and a steam table of Swedish meatballs and Buffalo chicken wings was set up next to the jukebox.

Colin had just ordered a round of drinks when he noticed Granda spread cheese on a cracker, then lick the knife and stick it back into the crock of cheese. "Great how they treat visitors in this country," Granda said.

Several other patrons noticed and made revolted faces and whispered and laughed among themselves. The bartender, a neighborhood guy named Hanley, looked at the knife in the cheese crock and then at Colin. He called Colin over to the end of the bar.

"The Paddy factor?" he asked when they huddled alone.

"Pi squared," Colin said.

"The old lady, the one with the winter coat on when it's eighty-seven degrees out?" he said. "She just did a Ratso Rizzo on the steam table. She put about forty chicken wings south into her coat pockets. The Swedish meatballs are in her pocketbook. No offense, Col, but are they, like, mentally mongoloid or something?"

"Something," Colin assured him.

"They don't play with matches too, do they?"

The story about Paul Lynch torching Grogan's was everywhere. The scourge of Colin Coyne's "in-laws" were fast becoming part of neighborhood legend.

May 27

Colin watched from his second-story bedroom window as Granda walked the length of the backyard, measuring it with one foot behind the other, while wetting a finger and holding it up to the wind. He touched the branches of the blue spruce and the Chinese maple tree and pulled up a sod of the Kentucky bluegrass from the lawn, running the soil underneath it through his fingers. He even tasted it.

Colin was proud of the lawn. He had paid for the best bluegrass sod, watered it with a hose, watched it flourish under the April showers and the sunshine of May. It was his piece of land. He wanted a nice soft lawn on which to wrestle and play with the kids, a place to chase them with the hose and dunk them in the splash pool.

Colin narrowed his eyes as Granda pulled a chair from the picnic table up to the six-foot wooden slatted fence that separated his yard from Lipinski's. He was clearly a man on a mission. Granda climbed up on the chair and peered over the fence. Summer had arrived early and Lipinski was busy preparing his in-ground pool with fresh water and new chemicals.

He looked up at Granda, startled, and said, "Can I *help* you?"

"Nothing I can't handle meself," Granda said. "Thanks all the same."

Colin strode into the yard, where he found Granda measuring

off another section of the lawn, near the rear fence separating his yard from the backyards of the houses on the next street.

"What's up, Granda?" Colin asked.

"Does this wee site belong to yerself, sure?"

"Yeah," Colin said. "It's our backyard, mine and Gina's."

"I'll sort it out for yeh, then, so," he said. "For nuthin'."

"Thanks, but I kind of like it the way it is," Colin said.

"No problem atall," Granda said. "Say no more, then . . ."

Colin now watched Granny waddle out the back door, dressed in her overcoat and head scarf, with tourist postcards in her hand and a cigarette dangling from her lips, mumbling to herself. She walked directly to the unlit gas barbecue, lifted the lid, and placed the post cards on the cold grill. She slammed the lid shut.

"Granny," Colin said. "What the hell are you doing?"

"Postin' me cards," she said.

Colin nodded. "Oh."

"I'm goin' for a walk, *you,*" she said to Granda, defiantly jutting out her chin. "Are yeh comin' for a glass of porter?"

"Ask me feckin' arse, woman," Granda said. "Never disturb a man when he's workin'."

"I'm away, then," she said and hefted her three-hundred-pound frame into the house. "I hope yeh die shiverin'."

Colin walked to the barbecue and removed the cards. They were all addressed to herself at the Whiterock Road address. One was signed Cary Grant, one Jayne Mansfield, the other President Kennedy. There were Easter Seals where the postage stamps were supposed to be affixed.

May 28

Colin awoke in the predawn to a deafening motorized roar. It sounded as if a Cessena had overshot La Guardia and made an emergency landing in his living room. Gina sat up next to him in bewildered alarm. The whole house was vibrating.

"What the bloody hell . . ."

"I have no fucking idea," Colin said.

Colin jumped out of bed as Brianna and Seamus awakened. He

ran out of the bedroom in his gym shorts and raced down the stairs. He stopped abruptly on the third-to-last step. There was Granny, wearing her head scarf and a sweater and Wellington boots, a smoldering cigarette dangling from her lips, holding the high handles of the roaring Black and Decker lawn mower, like a biker doing a wheelie.

Colin blinked in disbelief. The air was filled with a blizzard of dried chopped grass. The acrid smell of a burning motor choked the room. An ear-piercing whine emitted from the lawn mower because his four-thousand-dollar Persian rug—that she had been *mowing*—was jammed in the powerful blades.

Colin walked down the last three steps and yanked the plug from the wall, the motor finally whirring to silence.

"Thank Jaysus for small miracles and healthy babbies," Granny said.

"Granny, what the hell do you think you're doing?" Colin asked, astonished.

"I'm Hooverin' for yeh," she said.

Colin angrily took the handles of the lawn mower from Granny and tilted the heavy machine onto its side. He slowly untangled the mangled rug from the blades.

Gina, Granda, the Cousins, and the children appeared on the stairs, yawning and laughing.

"Och, she was only tryin' to help," Gina said.

Colin glared up at Gina and then at Granny, who stood smoking her cigarette, as he finally detached the rug from the lawn-mower blades. The two-foot gouge in the rug was beyond repair.

"Put a rug over it and a gallopin' horse'll never notice, wha'?" said Granda.

"Put a rug over the rug?" Colin asked.

"Aye," Granda said. "Like a bicycle patch."

Colin said nothing as he carried the lawn mower out into the backyard. *How the fuck do you respond to a bicycle patch on a Persian rug?* he thought.

Then he wordlessly went upstairs to shower and dress for a final meeting with Linda Parks and the record company executives before leaving for Los Angeles to shoot the video on Monday morning.

• • •

A little more than a half-hour later, he left the house and ran into Lipinski.

"Everything okay, Coyne?" Lipinski asked. "Couldn't help hearing the commotion this morning."

"Yeah," Colin said. "My Irish in-laws are a little unfamiliar with how we do things."

"Yeah, your father-in-law keeps telling me not to worry, that he'll take care of the eyesore for me," Lipinski said. "You have any idea what eyesore he's talking about?"

"Your guess is as good as mine," Colin said.

"They always get up this early?" Lipinski asked, his eyes widening.

"Jet lag," Colin said.

"Oh, okay," Lipinski said. "It's just me and my wife like to sleep in late Saturday mornin's . . ."

"And it's a nice, quiet block," Colin said.

"Thanks," Lipinski said. "I better go drop the missus at the train and get to work myself."

"Same here," Colin said.

Colin had a four-and-a-half-hour meeting with Linda Parks and three record executives in her SoHo office. He was astonished that five adults could spend that much time discussing the story points of a five-minute video. Everyone wanted to leave with a thumbprint on the project. The Girl Singers were patched in from the west coast on a conference call. They loved the script but wanted to choreograph their own dance steps. Colin thought that would be fine.

The executives finally left and Linda gave Colin his plane tickets and rental car and hotel reservation vouchers.

Colin hesitated before leaving.

"Something bothering you?" Linda asked.

He needed to talk to a neutral party about what was going on in his life. And so he told her about the in-laws, about the unexpected cousins, the house full of kids, the fire in Grogan's, the knife in the cheese crock, the gas fireplace, the postcards in the barbecue, mowing the rug.

Halfway into the tale, he realized that Linda Parks was bent in half, laughing. He wasn't.

"You don't find it hilarious?" she said.

"You do?"

"I think it's priceless," she said, catching her breath. "You have to get it all into a script."

He didn't want to tell her that the script Frank Burston was already filming was inspired by some of Gina's antics.

"Living it isn't funny," he said. "Having my kids growing up thinking this kind of shit is normal terrifies me."

Linda Parks nodded and saw that he was serious. She said, "Then you have to do something about it."

"I'm afraid of Gina taking my kids back to Ireland again."

"Colin," she said, composing herself. "Do you love her?"

"I'm not sure what the hell I feel."

"I don't know this woman," she said. "But I will say this much for her—she moved you closer to admitting you might be in love than you ever were with me or anyone else I've known you to be involved with. Ever since that first chick broke your heart, it became a block of ice. This Gina has melted it at least a little. Before you dump her and move on, remember all the good stuff she's obviously done for you."

"What the hell good has she done for me?"

"She taught you responsibility," Linda Parks said. "She taught you how to be a father. Which might teach you a little more about being a man instead of a skirt-chasing boy. I gave you the opportunity to see the tattoo on my ass last week and you didn't take me up on it. It was a blow to my ego but it meant you care about this Gina. You let these people invade your house because you want to make her happy. She might be a little crazy, but you ain't wrapped too tight yourself, ya know. Look what she's doing right now. She's making you go back to work instead of moping and waiting for a big break. Don't knock her because she got knocked up. She also knocked some sense into you and helped you find your heart."

"Some of that might be true," he said. "But this is never gonna work. Even if what I feel for her is genuine, I know we can't stay together. But at the same time I'm afraid of her leaving."

"Look, I'm just an old girlfriend. But if you live your life in fear of the woman you love, it's not love anymore, it's a compromise or something even sicker—like penance. Bottom line, you have to do what's right for the kids—and *you*. Sooner is always better than later—for you, and her, and especially for the kids."

He nodded. There were a few scary truths he had to confront. When he got back from Los Angeles.

"Thanks, Linda."

"I still think mowing the Persian rug is a fucking classic," she said.

When Colin arrived home, a police car was parked on the sidewalk in front of Lipinski's house. "Oh, shit!" Colin shouted, pounding the steering wheel.

Neighbors stood on their stoops, up and down the block, gawking at the scene. Colin could hear voices shouting from the backyards. He ran into his house and walked slowly toward the backyard and stood in the doorway. Gina, the Cousins, and the kids stood on the lawn. Lipinski was in his yard with two uniformed cops, screaming at Granda, who was wearing Colin's bathrobe, his hair a bonnet of shampoo lather. A scum of soap suds covered the top of Lipinski's cloudy pool.

"You shanty old son of a bitch," Lipinski screamed.

"Calm down, Mr. Lipinski," a skinny cop said.

"I'll put an apple in your mouth and twist yeh on a spit," Gina screamed, a second cop and the Cousins restraining her.

It took several seconds for Colin to see the big picture, to realize that the six-foot wooden fence dividing his and Lipinski's yard had been ripped down and sawed into bundles of firewood. The blue spruce in the rear of his yard had also been chopped down and cut into logs. Granda had built a lean-to against the rear fence, covering it with pine branches. When Lipinski saw Colin, he began shouting.

"Coyne!" he screamed, pointing a finger. "I won't need a fence because I'm gonna own your goddamned house when I finish with you!"

He made a move toward Colin, but one of the cops restrained him. Brianna and Seamus ran to Colin, who instinctively picked them up in his arms, as if to protect them from the madness.

"Don't let that pig's melt talk to yeh like that, Colin," Gina said. "If I were a man I know what I'd do with him!"

Colin looked at Gina and the Cousins and their kids all standing in the remnants of his backyard. Ballytara had been transplanted to Bayside.

"Colin, son, I was just having a wee wash after workin' on that fence all afternoon," Granda explained. "I did all the work for him and he's doin' all the complainin'. Look how nice and lovely and big I made the garden. You could park a caravan back here now. Plus I made meself a nice wee squat to sleep in, sure."

"He tore down my fucking feeeence!" Lipinski screamed and picked up a bottle of Ivory liquid, brandishing it. "And then took a bath with Ivory liquid in my fucking poooool!"

"Watch your language," the restraining cop said.

"We'll get you *out!*" Lipinski shouted. "There's already a petition going around the block. You're a pack of undesirables! Gangsters, hooples, drunks, bimbos, shanties, and dirty, loud kids, banging in and out of the door day and night."

One of the cops approached Colin and raised his eyebrows and motioned him inside the house. Colin invited him into the kitchen, still holding the kids in his arms.

"I can't say I blame this guy for being ticked off," the cop said. "He wants us to arrest the old man for vandalism. I don't wanna haul an old man off in cuffs. So I told him it's a civil matter. In order to stop this from being a criminal vandalism case, you gotta tell me it's a dispute over a property line, which makes it a civil case, *capice?*"

"Thanks," Colin said. "It's a dispute over a property line."

The cop nodded and wrote this in his log book.

"My advice is to get everyone inside the house, let this Lipinski cool off," the cop said. "I'll give the old man a summons for trespassing in his pool and you wait for the lawsuit."

"Great," Colin said.

• • •

That night, Colin stayed home only long enough to get the kids to sleep. Brianna and Seamus cried because they knew Colin would be leaving for Los Angeles the next day.

"Don't go 'way, Daddy," Seamus said, his face twisting into sobs.

"Like when you weren't there in Ireland," Brianna said. "We want you home."

"I'll be back in no time," Colin said, tickling Seamus out of his tears, lying between them, telling them a Sticky story until they drifted off to sleep.

He went downstairs and found Granny standing alone in the kitchen, her coat and scarf on, smoking a cigarette and drinking a glass of Guinness. Granda was in the yard in his lean-to reading by candlelight. Gina and her cousins were sitting around the dining-room table drinking French wine. They were having a good laugh imitating Lipinski.

"I didn't get the chance to tell yeh," Gina said. "The reason I wasn't home to stop Granda today was that we was down at the high school signing up for the GED program."

"All of you?" Colin asked.

"Aye," said Bridie.

"You've been after me to sign up," Gina said.

"But isn't it a twelve-week course?"

"Aye," said Philomena. "I can't wait to show them'ns back home that I have a leavin' cert from an American school. Take them'ns down off their high horse, wha'?"

They're planning to stay for three months, Colin thought.

"I'll talk to you about it later," Colin said. "I'm going to see my father before I leave."

"Grand," Gina said, pouring another glass of wine.

Colin sat with his father for half an hour, drinking tea, watching the Mets lose a close game to the Pirates.

"The business with Grogan's is desperate," his father said. "I heard there was a bit of a row with your next-door neighbor today as well."

"Bad news moves faster than good people," Colin said.

"I'm glad your mother isn't alive for all this carry-on." Colin remained quiet. *At least Gina didn't put the kid up for adoption,* he thought.

"Your mother and I never let our families impose on our own little family," the father said. "So I don't want to impose on yours. If you don't put a stop to what's happening in your family, the kids'll be ruined. Your mother's philosophy worked. No matter how much I drank and went missing when I was acting the lig, she always kept one focus—you guys, her kids. She always said kids need stability, kids need structure, kids need example. When I was too drunk to provide any of that, she did. At least one parent has to take control. So I'll say this, and I'll say no more. Take control of the lives of those kids or they'll have no one. You're blessed with beautiful children. Don't let bad things happen to them."

Colin nodded. Everyone—Davey Grogan, Linda Parks, his father, Jack—told him the same thing. *Your life is out of control,* he thought. *Do something about it. For the sake of the kids.*

"When I come back from Los Angeles, I'm going to make some changes," he said.

He finished his tea, carried both cups into the kitchen, washed them out, placed them in the drainer, and said good-bye to his father.

"Tell Gina that if there's anything she needs while you're away, not to hesitate to come over," he said. "I'll watch the babies."

"That's nice, Dad, I'll tell her."

"Godspeed, son," his father said as Colin left, his mother's silver bells chiming in his wake.

May 29

In the morning, Gina drove Colin to the airport. She insisted on taking Brianna and Seamus with them.

"Gina, by the time I get back home, I want the house to be empty," Colin said.

"It will in my shite," she said. "Bridie and Philomena is only after enrollin' in the GED."

"I can't afford to support all these people anymore," he said.

"What about the money yer makin' on these videos?"

"I owe the IRS a bundle on the last money I got," he said, trying to remain calm. "Besides, it's plain wrong that I have to support all these freeloaders."

"Yer asking me to tell my family to shift?"

"Yes."

Gina fell silent for a long time as she ran a red light in the airport and pulled to an abrupt stop in front of American Airlines.

"It's well for yeh to be near yer family, but not for me to have a few of mine over for a bit o' crack?"

"Gina, mine don't live with us, eating us out of house and home, mowing the rug, chopping down the neighbor's fence, stealing a cop's badge, and burning down a neighborhood bar," he said.

"No one ever proved that Paul did that," she said. "I think durty Grogan did it himself for the insurance."

"Bullshit!"

Colin looked at his watch. It was 10:15 and he had a 10:30 flight. He had no more time to argue.

When Colin turned to the kids to say good-bye, Brianna started to scream at the top of her lungs. "No, Daddy, please, no, don't go away Daddy . . . I beg you . . ."

He cringed at the way the word "beg" sounded in his child's mouth. He thought of the beggar girl on O'Connell Bridge.

"No go 'way, Daddy," Seamus screamed, beginning to cry.

"It's okay, guys," Colin said, turning to them. "I won't be gone long. Daddy has to go to work to get money."

"Please, Daddy, please, no." Brianna was in hysterics now, her body convulsing with panic, pleading with her father not to go away and leave her.

Colin reached behind him, and unbuckled Brianna's seat belt, and lifted her into his arms. Seamus held out his arms. Colin popped him out of his car seat, scooped him up, and kissed them both.

"I have to go, but not for long," he said. "I'll bring you back presents. I'll call you every day. Twice a day, okay?"

"Nooooooo," Brianna said, her eyes pouring tears.

Colin checked his watch: 10:20.

"Just go, they'll be grand," Gina said.

He kissed them and placed them on the backseat. Brianna wouldn't let go of his sleeve as she cried uncontrollably. Gina had to disengage Brianna's hands from Colin. Seamus threw himself on the floor of the backseat screaming, kicking his feet.

"My Jaysus," Gina said.

Colin blew kisses at the hysterical kids and got out. He ran to the back of the car, yanked the suitcase from the trunk, and slammed the lid shut. As he hurried into the terminal, he turned and saw Seamus and Brianna's faces mashed against the back window, still crying.

The tear-stained, emotion-twisted faces of his kids stayed with him throughout the flight west. Theirs wasn't a normal reaction; the kids were traumatized by a life of upheaval. There were too many adults moving in and out of their lives. There were too many places they called home. There was too much madness for them. And for him.

He knew that the octopus of Gina's clan was strangling him financially and professionally. It had helped him lose his first movie. He was afraid of losing a second chance.

The stewardess came around handing out New York newspapers. He took the *Daily News,* and scanned through it, trying to get his mind off the faces of the kids. School construction scandals dominated the news, but a small news story caught his eyes. SUSPECT IN ARMORED CAR HEIST FOUND SLAIN. The story said that one Peter O'Toole, a suspect in a three-million-dollar Brinks armored car robbery in Buffalo, was found murdered and sexually mutilated in his car on Manhattan's west side. Police theorized that one of his heist partners whacked him out of greed. *Greed is one thing,* Colin thought. *But only Joe Monte would want to cut off his balls.*

This was what Gina's family had brought close to Colin's home. *The madness must end,* he thought. *When I get back home I must put my house in order.*

He looked out the window at the clouds and all he could see were the emotionally wrecked faces of his kids.

fifty-two

Colin had spent his first week in Los Angeles looking at locations, meeting with the Girl Singers, rehearsing, and familiarizing himself with the crew.

He stayed in the Standard Hotel on Sunset Boulevard, ate mostly from the room-service menu, made more notes on his new screenplay, and called the kids every day. Seamus made him tell him Sticky stories over the phone.

During one evening call, Brianna said, "Daddy, when are we gonna live together, just us, me, you, Mommy, and Seamus?"

In the background, Colin could hear a barrage of noise, voices of men and women, radios, TV, laughter. Before Colin could answer Brianna, Gina had obviously taken the phone from her hand. Colin could hear Gina reprimanding Brianna. "The cheek o' yeh, yeh little troublemaker," Gina said.

"Everybody's always in my room," Colin heard Brianna say.

Gina came on the line to Colin, a sharp tone in her voice, from one too many glasses of wine. "No time to talk now, Colin."

"What's all the commotion?" Colin asked. "Who's there?"

"So what if I have a bit of company over?" she snapped. "It's well for yeh to be a gallivantin' with rock stars a million miles away while I have to get these'ns to sleep. I have buckets to do here and no time for gab."

"Gina, don't yell at the kid for wanting privacy."

"Privacy me arse," Gina said. "I have a pain in me tits over children makin' demands. *Privacy!* When did I ever have feckin' privacy growin' up? Five in a flea-bitten bed or in a feckin' dormitory. The trouble is these'ns is becoming spoilt Americans like the ones they see on the telly. That's their problem. They have their own rooms, air conditionin', central heatin', portable phone, private feckin' schools. What they need is a good dose of the road, a cold, durty swally of hunger."

For the first time, Colin admitted to himself that Gina was clearly clinically insane. She was jealous of her own kids for daring to have the kind of childhood she never had.

"Gina, for chrissakes, they're just kids," Colin said. "I want them to have nice things."

"Why shouldn't my family have a few nice things, as well?"

"They should," he said, "Tell them to fucking *work*. I'm not Santa Claus."

"Take your sack of shitey toys and shove it up your chimney," she said and hung up.

Although Gina had tracked down her American father, she'd made the hard decision not to impose herself on his family. She had decided to leave that family alone. Colin thought there was something noble, even selfless, about that decision. But it had affected her deeply. She had grown more and more icy, more bitter, more distant, more self-absorbed, more unloving. Colin didn't like cheap pop psychobabble, but he firmly believed that because she would never have the love of her father, Gina Furey might never be able to love any other man.

The Girl Singers video was a pain in the ass to shoot. While the girls loved the scripted concept of wearing firefighter gear, once they felt the fifteen-pound weight of the outfits they started bitching. The coats and protective pants made them sweat and itch. The coats smelled like old smoke. The "burning building" location was a club in Compton and the steam and fog machines kept breaking down. The Girl Singers' bodyguards had to work overtime and were afraid some of the gang leaders would show up looking for a payoff. The locals, a lot of them malevolent street gangsters, demanded extras jobs and extra chicks.

Through it all, Colin maintained his focus. He kept reminding himself that this was easier than going to dinner with the Fureys. When Colin did finally have to pay off a local gang leader as a "community coordinator," or what Colin called the Executive in Charge of Bribes, it was an easy negotiation. It was nothing like dealing with Granny, who insisted on talking to Andy Sipowicz.

Colin felt good to be behind the camera again, shouting action, with klieg lights glaring, film slithering through the sprockets, and watching the players move through a scene the way he'd conceived and blocked it. He used imaginative crane shots, a lot of hand-held sequences, a cinema verité style for the street scenes, and more elegant Busby Berkeley shots in the studio for the elaborate dance routines. When it was all spliced together, it would have a startling, steamy, sweaty, hellish look that would beautifully illustrate the sexy song.

The artists, executives, and Linda Parks loved the dailies.

June 9

On the fourth and last day of shooting, as dawn broke over the Pacific Ocean, the Girl Singers, dressed in string bikinis, chased "the devil" along the Santa Monica Pier, smashing dishes at his feet before making him leap into the sea. Colin called a cut.

The crew applauded. After they stopped clapping, Colin heard one person continue to clap. He turned around and saw Melissa Thompson sitting on top of a bench back, dressed in jeans and a loose peasant blouse, the ocean wind tossing her long blond tresses. Colin called for a ten-minute break and nervously walked over to her.

"Great scene," Melissa said.

"I thought you'd be in Queens," Colin said.

"I don't chase men who dump me," she said.

"I meant with Burston."

"Frank Burston?" she said, her voice rising with incredulity.

"And I didn't dump you," he said. "I went to get my kids back. I admit I didn't handle it well."

"No, you didn't," she said. "My father was so pissed off."

"He took what happened between us personally."

"What?" she said, her voice rising again.

"We broke up," Colin said. "I got fired."

"No, Colin," she said. "You walked out in the middle of casting. My father got pissed. You got replaced. It had nothing to do with me."

"Then you and Burston . . ."

"Me and Burston what?"

"Aren't you . . . with him? Working on my film . . . his film . . . the two of you, *together*, like?"

"Where did you get that ass-backwards idea?" she said and laughed, half insulted, half amused.

"I dunno . . . we break up . . . I get fired . . . he gets hired . . ."

"Jesus Christ, you really have some low opinion of me," she said. "I can't *stand* Frank Burston. I think he's a pompous asshole. I tried to talk my father out of firing you, but he thought you had lost focus on your film, said you were distracted by your, shall we say, *complicated* personal life. Then I told him Frank Burston was absolutely the wrong person to make your picture. He didn't listen again. Between me and you and the good times we had, my father's not thrilled with Burston's dailies. Says they're pretentious."

"I called you from Dublin twice. You hung up on me."

"I was trying to get you out of my system. If I had run off to Paris with a guy and I called you, what would you have done?"

Now Colin felt like a complete asshole. He had needed someone to blame for his problems and chose Melissa. He'd painted her as some on-the-make, star-fucking slut who'd sabotaged him.

"Melissa, I'm truly sorry."

"Oh, Christ, me too," she said. "It would have been a terrific picture if you'd made it."

"I mean about us."

"Well, what the hell, these things happen for a reason."

She lifted her peasant blouse with her right hand and rubbed her slightly swollen belly with her left hand, which was decorated with a wedding ring.

"Some guys have all the luck," he said.

"He's a cinematographer," she said. "French Canadian. You probably never heard of him. He's doing his first feature now in Toronto. I'm flying up tonight. He'd kill me if he knew I was here talking to you, but I read that you were filming here and I just wanted to come see you. I wanted to tell you there were no hard feelings. I never did say good-bye that day."

"You went to the ladies' room . . ."

". . . and came back pregnant," she said and laughed.

"I feel better now," he said.

"How're the kids?"

"Great," he said. She never asked about Gina.

"Now that I'm having one of my own, I understand where you were coming from," she said. "You went to get your kids. You did what a father is supposed to do. I didn't get it then because I was too selfish. I wanted you for myself. But I admire you for it now."

"You'll be a good mother," he said, wishing he had a normal woman like her mothering his kids.

"Your crew is ready to do the coverage and I better go," she said. "You'll have another feature in no time. I know you will."

"Good luck," Colin said. "And . . . thanks."

She got up, nodded, and Colin watched her walk down the pier. Then he went back to work.

June 14

He finished the editing two days ahead of schedule and decided to surprise the kids by going home early. He called his father to tell him he would be home in the morning. He asked how Jack and Eddie were. "Fine," his father replied.

His father seemed remote and cold. Colin asked what was wrong. His father asked him to come by to see him as soon as he arrived in the morning. Colin asked if his health was okay.

"Just come by here to see me first thing," his father said.

Colin promised he would. He guessed it was more embarrassing neighborhood gossip about Gina and her grannies.

Everyone involved—record executives, artists, Linda Parks—was thrilled with the video. Colin was quietly proud of it himself. There would be a little more tweaking to do, some computer enhancing and lip-synching, some Foley sound effects to add, but his work was essentially finished. He itched to get started on the next Du Wopps video in New York.

He also ached to see his kids. His recent phone conversations with Gina in the last week all bordered on hostile. When he spoke with the kids, Gina stood over them, as if censoring what they said. Brianna seemed hushed and inhibited. Once, Brianna had broken down crying, and Colin heard Gina scolding her, telling her to stop being another actress auditioning for her father.

"What is the matter with her?" Colin asked Gina.

"As long as she's got me, don't yeh worry yer arse."

In the background, Colin could hear Seamus, saying, "Daddy, come home, Daddy, come home, Daddy, come home."

It was the mantra of a disturbed kid.

Without telling Gina, Colin caught the red-eye flight east. He didn't sleep; he didn't want to. He needed to think in the half-darkened plane. He had not touched a drop of alcohol in the three weeks in L.A. In that time, sober and away from the madness, he'd made the decision that when he got home he would have to finally make some changes.

Colin and Gina shared one biological child. He also loved Brianna. He and Gina had never tied the knot, but they were essentially married. But he had not just married a woman. He had married a clan, a family of a different lifestyle, denizens of a subculture. *They are a tribe that has contempt for the laws and mores of modern civilization,* he thought. Once, it had been a thrilling, dangerous ride on a wild rocket, sometimes comical in its absurd nonconformity. Life with Gina was an antidote for the mundane. It was fascinating.

Now, as his kids were forming their personalities, that fascinating lifestyle had become scary and unacceptable.

The so-called marriage is over, Colin thought, as he listened to the snores of the passengers in the plane cabin. *It is not just her fault; a lot of the blame is mine. I allowed it to go out of control for so long.*

Gina was not so much a wife as a roommate and a coparent. Colin felt like just another fellow traveler on Gina's cluttered road. He couldn't even call her a friend because she rarely shared her secrets, her fears, her hopes, her ambitions. She never bared her feelings unless they were in anger. The sex had always been great, but without mutual love it was just animal lust. That attraction had also begun to fade, for him and for her.

He'd fallen stupidly in love with a woman from another world. He'd had unprotected sex with her, which led to a child. He had to accept responsibility for his reckless passion.

Until now, he had avoided a final showdown with Gina because he was afraid of an ugly custody battle. *Fuck it,* he thought. *I've wasted good money on worse things. I have to fight for Seamus. I have to fight for Brianna. I'm the only father she has.*

As much as he understood that the Fureys and the Lynches were victims of circumstance, of bigotry, of dysfunctional families, poverty, rootlessness, and ignorance, he also knew they didn't desire to rise above that level. Gina was a gifted singer and musician but chose to squander those talents. *Gina willfully chooses not to change,* he thought. *She thinks the solution to life's problems is to pick another pocket or open another beer.*

He simply couldn't let Seamus and Brianna think that was normal. He had to stop the madness.

As the plane banked for landing at Kennedy Airport, he knew he had to confront Gina. He wasn't optimistic about the outcome, but it was time.

fifty-three

June 15

When he walked through his father's door, he immediately knew something was terribly wrong. There was something important missing.

"Dad, what happened to Mom's silver bells?" Colin asked, dropping his suitcase just inside the door, looking up at the barren hook where they'd hung since her death.

"That's what I want to know," his father said.

Colin took a deep breath, feeling sick and angry.

"Just tell me . . ."

"A bunch of them came over to borrow the tools again."

"Who? Which ones?"

"Some redheaded fella who looked like Elvis Presley," he said. "Another creep with the dirty glint of the mad dog in his eyes, never seen him before. Never said a word, either. The minute he walked in, he started looking around like he was at a flea market."

"Didn't give a name?"

"No. But there was another stringy-haired one. One of the women, a cousin or whatever. She's young and pretty. Gina called, said she needed to borrow some tools. I said fine. What was I supposed to say?"

"What did they borrow?"

"The lot, both toolboxes and the power tools."

"For what?"

"They never said."

"So what happened to the bells?" Colin asked.

"After they left, I realized they were gone as well."

Rage throbbed in Colin's temples, blood roasting his face. His brain pounded.

"Dad, I am so sorry."

Colin left his luggage and swung open the door. He was again startled by the silence of the missing bells. He looked at the empty hook and hurried out into the street.

Lipinski was leaving his house when Colin marched down the street. He saw Lipinski duck back into his house and reemerge, a paper in his hand. He approached Colin, waving the document.

"Lipinski, I'm in no fucking mood," Colin said, and then saw that the front lawn of his house was littered with scrap—car seats, old tires, a broken-down go-kart, car fenders, hubcaps, car doors, a big spool of cable, a section of rusting fencing. It looked like the front lawn of the house in Ballytara.

"I have the petition, Coyne," Lipinski said as Colin stared in disbelief at his lawn. "These people, Jesus Christ, they've destroyed our nice, quiet block. Turned your lawn into a goddamned junkyard. They climb in and out of windows all day and night, drunk, play music, argue and fight, cook meals on campfires in the yard. They roasted a *pig* like a tribe of savages! They piss in your backyard. The cops come every night. The fire department has been here, warning them about the fires. Sanitation has issued summonses. You people are a public menace, Coyne. This petition is signed by every home owner on the block."

"See me later and I might sign it myself," Colin said.

Lipinski looked perplexed as Colin put his key in the lock. It didn't fit. He looked at the key to make sure he had the right one. He did. He tried it again, realizing the lock had been changed. He took two steps back and stomped the door open, splintering the frame. Lipinski said, "Uh-oh . . ."

Colin entered his house.

Paul Lynch jumped up off the couch, startled. Luke Furey, the red-haired Elvis wannabe, sat in the reclining chair with a pair of headphones on his ears, his eyes closed, bobbing to the music. The room smelled like feet, farts, stale sweat, hashish, and old beer. Granda, his face collapsed into an asterisk of wrinkles without his false teeth, sat at the kitchen table and nodded, gumming a banana. Granny, wearing her overcoat and head scarf, stirred a steaming pot on the stove. Bridie and Philomena hurried down the stairs, followed by their kids. Susan came out of the bathroom with her son, Sammy. Now the door leading from the cellar opened and Rory Lynch and a stringy-haired guy whom Colin had never seen before stepped out, yawning and scratching. Both of them were wearing Colin's clothes.

"What's the ruckus?" Rory said. "What time is it, anyways?"

"It's time to get the fuck out of my house," Colin said. "Every last fucking one of you."

A long moment of silence befell the house as all the Lynches and Fureys stared at Colin in disbelief.

"Och, lighten up, man," Paul said.

"After torching and looting Grogan's," Colin said. "You have some balls coming back here, asshole."

Luke took off his headphones and smiled brightly, "What about yeh, Colin, lad?"

"Daddy!" Brianna screamed from the stairs, running to him.

"Dada!" shouted Seamus, thumping down the stairs one at a time, holding onto the railing.

Gina appeared behind them, wearing a bathrobe, eyes lit with anger, and said, "Just who the feck do yeh t'ink y'are, talking to me family like tha'?"

"Where are my mother's silver bells?" Colin said as he lifted Brianna in one arm and Seamus in the other.

"What're yeh talkin' about?" Gina said.

"Your skanky, shit-heel, bum relatives were over borrowing tools from my father," Colin said. "And when they left, the bells were gone with them."

"That's not on," Granda said, sprinkling salt on his banana, taking a bite. "Stealin' from the dead will get yeh in yer sleep."

"Yer blaming us, like?" Rory said.

"That's right, lowlife," Colin said. "You were there."

"Very brave mon sayin' that while holdin' those childer," Rory said.

"Especially since one of them is mine, like," said the stringy-haired guy.

Colin looked at Gina and then he looked at the stringy-haired man. He was in his early thirties but had a face with the wrinkles of an old man. His arms and chest bulged with muscle. *Jail muscle,* Colin thought. *Body by Mountjoy. The "other fella."*

Colin looked from the man to Gina again for explanation.

"Colin, meet me husband, Barry," Gina said. "Barry Powers."

Colin looked at him.

"Barry's only out of nick a month ago and he tracked us down. Says he wants me back, so he does, and I told him he'd have to have a wee chat with yeh first, man-to-man, like."

Gina seemed to cherish the idea that two men might battle over rights to her. Colin placed both kids on the ground.

"He's not my daddy," Brianna said, pointing to Barry. "You're my daddy, right, Daddy?"

"You bet, angel face," Colin said. "Brianna, take Seamus upstairs, get dressed, and I'll take you two out for breakfast, okay?"

"Okeydokey," Brianna said.

"Okeydokey," Seamus said as Brianna took his hand.

"Pleased to meet yeh, sham," Barry Powers said, holding out his hand. Colin looked at it, stared deep into Powers's eyes, and walked past him. He saw that a big stone campfire had been built in the center of his backyard. Two sleeping bags occupied Granda's lean-to. Lipinski had erected a seven-foot cinder-block fence.

"Did yeh get milk for tay when you were out, Kevin?" Granny asked Colin, as if he'd just returned from a three-week trip to the grocer.

"Sorry, the cash cow just died," Colin said.

He approached Granda: "Where are my father's tools?"

"I told them'ns you'd be better messin' with a man's horse or his missus before his tools," he said. "But they'd pawn a child's leg if they needed drink or money for the French dry cleaners."

Colin nodded, strode across the room, looking directly into Rory's face. "If you don't get the fuck out of my house by tomorrow night, I'll break your fucking spine," Colin said. "And drag that piece of dog shit you call a brother with you."

Rory looked him in the eyes, but Colin took a step closer until the breath from his nostrils blew in Rory's face. Rory turned and walked through the kitchen into the backyard.

Colin went down to the cellar and found his desk shoved against a wall. He rummaged in the top drawer and found Seamus's passport and shoved it in his pocket. He looked around; his work area had been transformed into a messy living quarters with musty blankets, dirty pillows, and soiled clothes scattered on the floor. Overflowing ashtrays and empty Guinness bottles covered the top of his desk. The cellar stunk of cigarettes, cannabis, and sour socks. *They've turned my fucking office into a slum,* he thought.

He searched in the bags belonging to Rory Furey and Barry Powers, dumping their contents on the floor, looking for the silver bells. He didn't find them. He did find a Hagen's pawn ticket. He emptied the ashtrays into Rory's kit bag and tossed in the empty Guinness bottles and zipped it up. He picked up his own laptop computer, his new script, and some disks and went back upstairs.

Most of the clan was in the backyard, powwowing.

Gina stood in the living room, alone, looking pensive. "Barry's out front," she said. "He'd like a wee word with yeh."

"I want my mother's bells."

"Is that all you're worried about?"

"I'm taking the kids out of here until we make a final arrangement."

"Well, yeh have to talk to Barry if yeh want me," she said. "I didn't know if he'd want me back after me having a child with yeh, see. But I am still married to him, legal like."

"He can feckin' have you."

Gina stood looking at him oddly. "That's it?"

"Bet your pretty ass."

Brianna and Seamus came down the stairs, dressed and combed. Colin led them out of the house past Barry, who sat on the stoop, smoking, his hair uncombed. Colin walked to his Lumina, saw several new dents, shook his head, and buckled both kids into the backseat. He told them he'd be back in a minute.

He approached Barry Powers and said, "Let's talk over here, where the kids can't see."

Powers got up and followed Colin to the far side of the stoop, out of view of the car. He stretched, consciously flexing his muscles and assessing the house. "Nice piece of property," Powers said.

"Was once," Colin said.

"Worth a few bob, I'd say."

"Get to the point," Colin said. "You smell like shit, you ain't easy to look at, and my IQ drops ten points every time you open your fucking mouth."

"That's my daughter in that car, sham," he said.

"She disagrees. To be a father you have to act like one."

"Tell yeh what," Powers said. "I just got out. I'm trying to get me act together, like. I came into this country on my brother's passport when I heard Gina and Brianna was here. I don't want no trouble. But I'm a little skint at the moment, wha'? I see that Gina and Brianna are doing okay here. Lots of water under the bridge. A whole bleedin' ocean, in fact. These things happen in life."

"What the fuck do you want, pal?"

"Okay, I don't have much, but I got a pretty wife inside whose tight little bum I thought a lot about over the last four year, and a little girl over there who could be some earner back home," he said. "But, tell yeh what, I'll shift and let yeh have the lot if you help me get back on me feet, like. I only need about twenty-five grand, sham, and that's me away outta here. For good, like."

"Twenty-five grand," Colin said. "For your wife and daughter?"

Barry Powers shrugged and nodded. Colin dropped him with a straight right hand and watched his head slam onto the fourth step of the stoop. Powers never stirred as Colin walked to his Lumina, got in, and drove off with his kids.

fifty-four

Colin took the kids to an indoor playground and put them on all the kiddie rides. He took them shopping and bought them a bunch of new clothes. In the afternoon, he took them to the neighborhood pediatrician for checkups. They were both in remarkably good health.

On his way to Jack's house, he popped into the refurbished Grogan's and nodded for Davey Grogan to come outside the bar.

"What's up?" Davey Grogan asked, strolling out the back door.

"Your old porter is back in town," Colin said.

Grogan said nothing, just stared, rivers of anger flooding under his skin.

"Freeloading at my place with some dueling-banjos male kin," Colin said. "Volunteer exterminators are welcome."

Davey Grogan just nodded and walked back into his bar.

June 16

Colin spent the night in Jack's house with his kids.

In the morning, he went to Hagen's pawn shop and paid three hundred fifty dollars to retrieve his father's tools. Old man Hagen said no one pawned any silver bells. He left the kids with his father and told him not to let Gina or any of the clan in the house.

He called the telephone company and put a block on all long-distance and collect calls.

Colin saw his lawyer, Brendan O'Dowd, just before the lunch hour. He told O'Dowd that he wanted full custody of Seamus and Brianna. The lawyer said it was going to be a difficult and expensive custody case.

Colin said he was willing to let Gina live in the house with the kids—for now—so long as she threw the clan out, agreed to stay in the country, and didn't expose the kids to those of her relatives who were arsonists, shoplifters, pickpockets, or wanted killers. Colin gave O'Dowd a five-thousand-dollar retainer. O'Dowd told him to keep Seamus's passport in a safe place.

The lawyer called in a secretary and she took notes as Colin detailed the story of his last two and a half years with Gina. The lawyer told the secretary to track down that security-camera video-tape of the shoplifting episode on Rodeo Drive in Los Angeles. He also told her to get a copy of Gina's shoplifting report from Bloomingdale's and a copy of Interpol's fugitive murder warrant on Rory Lynch. He told her to get a statement about the pawned tools from Hagen's.

"We'll want to show a pattern of criminal behavior," the lawyer said. "It will show that she poses a danger to the children. I think that a judge will give you immediate visitation of both kids. No one will give you custody until there is a full investigation, child psychologists, depositions, the whole shooting match. Meanwhile, she is an illegal, so we could get the INS involved."

"I don't want her deported," Colin said. "Let's save that for later. I want the kids to have their mother and I want them to have me, too, which means I want them to live here, not in some covered wagon in a slum three thousand miles away."

"It's going to take time," the lawyer said. "In the meantime, I'm going to ask the judge to clear everyone out of the house but Gina, the kids, and the grandparents. He won't make the grandparents leave."

"They won't stay, anyway," Colin said.

"You're sure you want to do this?" O'Dowd said. "You won't have a change of heart in the morning? You want me to file the custody papers?"

"Absolutely," Colin said.

June 17

Gina was served her custody-hearing papers by a process server at 10:00 A.M. and by 10:30 she was ranting on the sidewalk in front of Jack's apartment building, with Brianna and Seamus at her side.

"You'll never get custody of my kids," she shouted. "Never. I'm gettin' outta this god-forsaken country. I have something very nasty planned for yeh."

Colin peered out the window at her as she ranted, clutching both kids as props.

Colin shot and edited the Du Wopps video in Manhattan over the next week as he waited for a custody hearing. Rocco, true to his word, helped make the shoot go smoothly in the streets of mobland.

Colin gave O'Dowd another five-thousand-dollar retainer and stayed in his old room at Jack's house.

June 25

The Queens County judge gave Colin custody of Seamus's American passport and forbade Gina from taking the child out of the country until he made a final custody ruling. He looked at Colin's charges about the criminal cousins and ordered Gina to remove everyone from the family residence with the exception of the grandparents.

He ordered that all the summonses issued by the police, fire, and sanitation departments be paid and that the lawn be cleaned up. He ordered Gina to behave in a quiet, civilized manner for the sake of the children.

"I want everyone out of that house by the end of the July Fourth holiday weekend," the judge said, looking at Gina. "Are you willing to abide by these stipulations?"

"I will in me arse," Gina said.

The judge leaned forward, glared at Gina, and said, "You will in my jail cell lady, where you won't see your kids at all."

Gina remained quiet, her lips quivering.

The judge also ordered that Colin be allowed to visit with both kids every weekend. Colin agreed to pay the mortgage, utilities, school, and medical bills for both kids in the interim. The judge also ordered Colin to give Gina child support of five hundred dollars every month.

The judge ordered a child psychologist to examine the kids.

O'Dowd, through a friend at Aer Lingus, put an alert on the computer file at JFK airport in case Gina tried to flee the country with a fake passport for Seamus. He sent over pictures of Gina and the kids to be distributed to clerks all over the airport.

"How long is this going to take?" Colin asked O'Dowd.

"If Gina wants a trial, it could take a year to get a date on the calendar," the lawyer said.

June 30

Brianna had a hard time accepting that Colin wouldn't be living with them anymore.

"Why do you and Mommy fight?" she asked Colin as they fed the ducks in Bowne Park, while Seamus slept in his stroller.

"I want you to stay here in New York," he said. "She wants you to live in Ireland."

"I want you to live with me and Seamus and Mommy in our house," Brianna said. "Nobody else. I like when me and Seamus pull your boots off at night, when you tickle us, when you tell us Sticky stories."

"I know, angel face," Colin said.

"I don't want to go to Ireland again," she said.

"You won't have to. I promise."

Colin watched Brianna feed the ducks and hoped he could keep the promise.

As expected, with no money coming into the house, the grannies went home to Dublin that night.

July 1

Jack called Colin to invite him down to Grogan's for a noon beer. Jack was half stewed at the bar watching the Mets when Colin arrived.

An effervescent Davey Grogan pulled a frosted mug of beer, and placed it in front of Colin, and rapped his knuckles on the bar top.

"On the house," he said.

"*Slainte,*" Colin said and took a deep drink, the bubbles chilling his nose. He hadn't seen Davey so cheerful since before the fire. There were a half-dozen other half-bombed regulars at the bar, wearing Grogan's softball shirts and the out-all-night look on their faces.

"Speaking of micks," Jack said, "word is on the wind that a gang of your esteemed houseguests ran into a vanload of neighborhood chaps last night."

"That a fact?" Colin said.

"Yeah," Grogan said. "Four of them were given a lift. They never knew it was such a long and bumpy fucking ride to the airport."

"Alive, I hope," Colin said.

"Yeah, but didn't look much like their passport pictures," Grogan said. "Especially the guy who likes to play with matches."

"Put it this way," Jack said. "They won't be fucking back."

That afternoon, Colin received a call from Linda Parks.

"You're back, baby," she said.

"Whadda you mean?"

"I'm ready to sign you for five more videos today," she said.

"What's going on?"

She told him that his Girl Singers video was rushed into MTV release and was a smash. The record was rising with a bullet on the Billboard charts. His second video was already causing a buzz.

Then he received a call from Bonnie Corbet.

"I have some very good news," she said.

"You got *Middle America* set up?" he asked eagerly.

"No, but your first script, *Death Dunes,* is finally going before the cameras August fifteenth, with a thirty-five-million-dollar budget," she said. "You get one percent of the budget, which means three hundred and fifty thou on the first day of principal photography."

"You're kidding me, right?" Colin said.

"My advice?" Bonnie said. "Don't go to Ireland to meet chicks with it."

July 2

Colin rang the doorbell of his house to pick up the kids. *There's something wrong about having to ring my own bell,* he thought. *I feel like a goddamn Jehovah's Witness.*

He heard Susan flip-flopping down the hallway to answer the door, talking loudly on a cell phone.

"We'll be at this place called the Water Club to watch the fireworks on July the fourth," she said into a phone. "All the arseways Yanks shows up along the river to watch the show. Tourists and stinkin' rich bastards, loaded with lolly, on yachts and in limousines. And the crowds is only supposed to be unbelievable. Lolly only beggin' to be took, wha'?"

It's pickpocket's heaven, Colin thought. *They're still at it.*

Susan stepped into the vestibule, saw Colin, and smirked.

"Grace," she shouted. "It's himself."

Then she started talking into the cell phone again. "So how's it down there? I bet the oul hillbilly music is grand. Be seeing you soon enough, Paul, love. Be patient. We need money for tickets, sure. Everyone here is skint."

Susan's voice trailed off. Colin figured she must be talking to Paul Lynch, who was somewhere in the American south. Colin waited a minute, and finally Gina came to the door, dressed in skin tight faded blue jeans, new high top white sneakers, and a little halter top. Her olive complexion was deeper and glowed with an early summer tan.

She carried two glasses of white wine, and she walked past Colin and sat on the stoop.

"Can we talk civilized, like?" she asked.

"Sure,"Colin said.

"Here, I poured you one," she said, offering him a glass of wine.

"Not when I'm with the kids," he said.

Gina put the second glass of wine down on the stoop. Her smile vanished and she looked at him, and her eyes gelled with emotion, her lips quivering. "I want yeh to know, because there's nothing left to lose anyway, that when I was with yeh, there was never anyone else," she said.

"Even if I believed that," he said, "it doesn't matter anymore."

"Suit yerself," she said. "The only reason I wouldn't marry yeh was because of the other fella, Barry. Because I spent most of me life searchin' for my father, I never wanted to shut that door on Brianna. Turns out all Barry wanted to see her for was to see how much money was in it for him, and for a bit of ghee from me, which he did not get, I swear to yeh. Besides, yer the best daddy that little girl could ever ask for. The only one she'll ever want. Thanks for that. I found yeh for her so I guess I still do some things right. And thanks for clobberin' Barry for tryin' to sell us to yeh."

Colin looked at her. She looked dangerously beautiful, so he looked quickly away. "Are the kids ready?"

"Colin, me cousins have to leave by the fifth," she said. "I have no money, I sold all me jewelry long ago, and I want to go home."

"I can't let that happen to the kids, Gina."

"Sell this house and buy us a nice place in Ireland," she said.

"Not a good idea," he said.

"Yer afraid I'll have all the family around me," she said. "But I won't. I don't want those kids raised as knackers. I want them to have schoolin', a fine house, a future."

"I can't live that far away from them," he said. "They don't want to be that far away from me. You can live here until the judge's final ruling."

"Pox on the judge. Come inside, gra, we'll talk. Alone."

She leaned forward, touched his hand. He didn't respond.

"Please, Gina, send out the kids," he said.

"Listen, please, I'll change," she said, urgently. "Things'll be different. I'll raise them right, with books and structure and discipline. Yeh can come and visit us anytime yeh want. I'll take proper care of yeh. For God's sake, yeh know Gina Furey will never beg, but I'm askin' yeh, as the mother of our kids to their father, please let me go home, where I belong."

He took a deep breath.

"Gina, I'm sorry," he said. "I don't want to see you unhappy. But I owe the kids the best life they can have. I'd like to have the kids now."

"I won't be kept a prisoner here forever," Gina said, softly patting his hand. "You have to know, one way or the other, I'll soon have the road back under me feet."

Gina called the kids and they ran from inside the house.

"Don't use'ns give yer Daddy any trouble, hear?" she said, kissing each kid on the lips.

Brianna grabbed Seamus's hand and led him to the car parked at the curb. She dragged her backpack with her overnight clothes and tossed it into the backseat.

Colin looked at Gina and nodded. "Take care of yourself, Gina."

"Just have them'ns back here tomorrow evening at six sharp like the bollocksin' judge says," she said.

Colin didn't reply.

He took the kids out to Eddie's house for a swim and a pre-Fouth of July barbecue.

Jack and his father arrived in Jack's car and the Coyne family sat around a picnic table in the shade of a big umbrella. Eddie grilled chicken, hot dogs, and hamburgers on the gas barbecue. His wife laid out a big spread of salads.

Brianna and Seamus played with Eddie's kids in the pool.

Colin looked around at the idyllic suburban setting. *This is normal,* he thought. *Laughing kids, food, family, blue sunny sky. Firecrackers popping in the distance.*

"It seems to me the judge should have let you have the kids for the Fourth, since you're the American," Eddie said.

"Yeah, but he said this year she could have them on the Fourth so the kids could say good-bye to her family. He's ordered them out of the house by the fifth," Colin said. "Fair enough and not worth fighting over. I'll bring 'em back tomorrow. There will be other July Fourths."

"You beat the traffic on the LIE today anyways," Eddie said.

"I just feel lousy dragging these kids through a custody battle," Colin said, staring at them splashing in the pool.

"You have no choice," Jack said, chewing a bite of a cheeseburger.

"Look at those two amazing kids," the father said. "Whenever you feel like you're cursed, remember that you're blessed."

"She'll crack up living in that house alone," Colin said. "Her so-called husband went back to Ireland. The guy cousins are down in Georgia with a clan of American travelers. She'll try to hook up with them again. I worry about Gina. No matter what, the kids still love her. It's a mess."

"You can't worry about what's beyond your control," the father said, putting forth his sage AA advice. "This too shall pass."

Brianna came running from the pool, giggling and dripping across the lawn. She rummaged in her overnight bag, searching for her favorite Barbie beach towel. She pulled out the wrapped towel, and when it unfurled Colin could hear the tinkling of bells.

He watched as his mother's silver bells tumbled onto the lawn, the sun glinting off them. His father and brothers stared in silent amazement as Brianna picked them up and carried them to Colin.

"Look, Daddy, Grandma's bells."

Colin held them gingerly, listening to them tinkle in the summer breeze. The Coyne family sat silent, staring at the bells.

July 3

After spending the night at Eddie's house, Colin returned the children to Gina the next evening. She answered the door, dressed in a robe, looking slightly hungover and rumpled.

"Care for a wee cup?"

"No thanks."

"Happy Independence Day, Colin," she said.

"You too, Gina," he said. "Thanks for my mother's bells."

"I found them in the cellar, behind yer desk," she said. "I knew they were important to yeh."

"Yeah," he said. "They are."

"Kiss your father good-bye," Gina said to Brianna and Seamus. He didn't like the finality in her tone.

The kids kissed Colin.

"Don't want you go away, Daddy," Seamus said. Brianna was silent, her eyes watering.

"Hey, stop it, guys," he said, bending down to the kids, kissing and hugging each one. "I'll pick you up next weekend. And I'll have you for a week, then we'll go wherever you want."

"Can we go to Disneyland?" Brianna said.

"You got it," Colin said.

"Disneyland," said Seamus.

"Yaaaay," said Brianna.

Colin stood and looked at Gina, who had a faraway look in her eyes.

"Have a good one," Colin said.

"I intend to," she said.

The kids ran into the house as Colin hesitated, something unsettling hovering in the air between them.

"Tell yeh somethin' fer nuthin'," she said. "There was a time there when I t'ink I was actually in love with yeh. Anyway, not to worry."

Colin looked at her, a smug glint in her eye, as she gently closed the door.

fifty-five

July 4

Like those early days in Dublin, he thinks, *this July Fourth will always be happening now, in the present tense, right now, before my eyes, like in a movie.*

Fade in, he thinks.
INTERIOR. GROGAN'S TAVERN. EARLY EVENING.

It's Independence Day. Ninety-eight degrees and humid. I'm having a cold holiday beer with Davey. The place is packed, three deep at the bar. The Mets are losing up there on the tube.

Jack rushes in, looking concerned.

COLIN: What the fuck's a matter?

JACK: She was in the apartment.

COLIN: Who?

JACK: Gina. I met her on the stairs. I was goin' up, she was coming down. She said she'd been upstairs knocking, looking for you.

COLIN: So?

JACK: So when I went in, the apartment smelled like cigarette smoke. She was in there. The door to your room was opened.

COLIN: Bitch probably kept her key from when we stayed there. Is anything missing?

JACK: I never keep money in the house. What about you?

COLIN: A few valuables. Laptop, printer, and video camera. And Seamus's passport.

The two brothers run out the door.

AT JACK'S APARTMENT.

Colin sees that Seamus's passport is missing from his top bureau drawer. He calls Aer Lingus to see if Gina booked a flight but there's no one named Furey or Coyne booked on any of this evening's flights, or any of the flights leaving the United States in the next week. He calls British Airways, in case she has decided to go through England. She isn't registered on any of their flights, either. Colin still thinks she's planning to leave the country tonight.

JACK: How would she get out?

COLIN: Same way I got her in the first time, Mexico. They could meet the cousins down south, go to Mexico, and grab a plane to Europe. I'll never see those kids again, Jack.

JACK: We better check the house.

AT THE HOUSE.

Colin rings the bell. There's no answer. The shades are down. Colin circles to the back door and uses the skeleton key to get in. The brothers enter and the house is eerily quiet.

Colin bounds up the stairs and enters Brianna's room. He looks in her closet. All the kid's clothes are gone, her bureau is empty. He sees the same thing in Gina's room. Almost all her clothes are missing; only the maternity clothes still dangle on hangers.

There isn't a suitcase in the house.

JACK: She hit the road, Col.

Colin paces and runs his fingers through his hair.

JACK: Does she have any dough?

COLIN: She said she was broke. Her sister Susan even told Paul the pyro that everyone was broke. It sounded like she was planning to get some money picking fucking pockets again.

JACK: Where the fuck would they go to do that?

The Water Club is mobbed.

Colin and Jack run down Thirty-fourth Street from Penn Station.

A quarter of a million people have jammed the FDR Drive and the street below to see the East River fireworks extravaganza.

The magenta sun is sinking. There are cops everywhere. Tourists and hawkers sell American flags, Uncle Sam T-shirts, and red, white, and blue phosphorescent neck hoops.

Colin and Jack push through the crowd under the FDR, trying to reach the Water Club.

Colin searches the New York crowd for Gina and the kids.

JACK: It's like looking for a needle in a needle factory.

COLIN: Listen for Irish accents.

JACK: We gotta find them before sundown, or forget it.

As they crush closer to the Water Club, the crowd surges forward to get a better view of the coming fireworks. Young guys drinking beer, passing a blunt, and swapping spits with hot chicks.

YOUNG GUY: Yo, push me once more, motherfucker, you'll see real fuckin' fireworks.

SECOND YOUNG GUY: You threatening me, man?

COP: Move along, assholes.

Colin watches everyone. His eyes slowly pan the crowd as he approaches Thirty-first Street. Faces pop out of the crowd—young and pretty, old and haggard, bald, hairy, black and brown, yellow and white. There are kids speaking Spanish, kids speaking Arabic, kids speaking Russian. Then he hears a familiar little boy's voice in the crowd.

BOY'S VOICE: I want my mammy.

Colin turns, but can't see where the voice is coming from.

JACK: That sounded like your Seamus.

COLIN: I know.

As he searches the crowd, the sky purples. Then he sees a hat, a yellow floppy hat, like the one Gina wore at the Saint Patrick's Day parade two years before. It pops out of the sea of heads like a flower in a desert. The hat bobs through the crowd up near the entrance to the parking area of the Water Club.

Then Colin hears a girl's voice from the side.

LITTLE GIRL'S VOICE: Hold my hand, Seamus. And hold Auntie Susan's hand as well. Mammy will be right back.

Colin's eyes pan the crowd until he zooms in on Susan in the crush. She's leaning against a support column under the highway. The kids are at her side, they don't see him.

Colin points them out to Jack.

COLIN: I think I see Gina, too. I'll grab the kids.

He points and Jack nods.

JACK: No! I'll keep an eye on the kids. Go get the goddamned passport, Col. Without it, she can't leave with Seamus.

Colin hesitates.

JACK: Go ahead, I got the kids covered.

Colin shoulders through the wall of bodies, people shoving him, startled by him, pushing back as he trails the bobbing yellow hat in the crowd no more than thirty feet ahead of him. Colin sees a crew-cut blond guy, five-foot-five, wearing pounds of gold chains, approach a hawker who sells phosphorescent hoops for ten dollars a pop.

The sky is growing black.

The guy with the gold chains takes a hundred-dollar bill from a wallet thick with cash and pays the hawker. He puts a phosphorescent hoop around his girlfriend's neck and one around his own neck. He puts hoops around the necks of the four other couples he's traveling with.

YOUNG GUY: We are the American Revolution, motherfuckahs.

The guy starts high-fiving his crew of white twentysomethings. All of them are drinking beer. The guys are dressed in designer jeans and tight T-shirts, the girls in hot pants, midriff tank tops, high-heeled sandals.

Suddenly, Gina slams into the guy with the gold chains, almost knocks him down.

YOUNG GUY: Yo, bitch, watch where you're bumpin' or I fuckin bump you into the fuckin' river.

GINA: Who're yeh callin a bitch yeh filthy wanker, yeh?

YOUNG GUY: What the fuck she call me? A wankuh? What the fuck's that mean?

YOUNG CHICK: Whad'ju call my boyfriend, donkey bitch?

Colin wedges and scrambles closer, can see Gina locked in the middle of the sweaty crew.

The first rocket whistles into the coal-black sky and pops into a red-and-gold asterisk. All eyes tilt upward as the crowd ooohs and ahh-hhhs.

The young guy shoves Gina and almost knocks her down.

YOUNG GUY: The bitch likes to push and mouth off.

Then he pats his back pocket and Colin sees the young guy's eyes blaze as he frisks himself.

YOUNG GUY: Hey, bitch, where's my motherfuckin' wallet?

Gina looks both ways. She's in the middle, like a roach trapped in a sink with the lights switched on.

YOUNG CHICK: Yo, bitch, you got my man's wallet?

She's chewing gum in felonious chomps.

YOUNG GUY: Get me my wallet, baby.

His chick moves closer to Gina.

YOUNG CHICK: Up with the wallet, ho.

GINA: Feck off, the lotta yiz, afore I calls yer mammies.

She turns to walk away. Fireworks explode brightly and loudly above New York. The crowd gasps and applauds.

Colin sees the young chick racing up behind Gina.

COLIN: Gina, watch!

Colin sees a switchblade flashing open, downward, in the young chick's hand at her side. The shiny blade reflects the dripping shower of light. He cups his hands, screaming.

COLIN: No! GIIIINA!

Colin shouts again as he knocks three people to the ground, barreling toward her through the crowd.

Gina's surprised eyes search the crowd for Colin.

GINA: Colin?

Colin sees the young chick bury the knife deep between Gina's shoulder blades. The light from the bursting fireworks illumates Gina's astonished face as she stumbles, turns, and takes another stab of the knife in her belly. Blood spreads through Gina's yellow dress like a fast-moving oil slick. She takes another step and collapses to the gutter. Colin, his face twisted in horror, pushes and shoves through the crowd.

COLIN: Please, God, no . . .

The crowd parts. Suddenly, cops stampede into the human thicket. Batons are swinging and hands grabbing. Colin reaches Gina, skidding to his knees. He touches her face as she struggles to speak.

GINA: Kiss me, yeh big bollocks.

Colin kisses her trembling lips.

Gina's body is jerking, bucking, and pumping blood from front and back. Her eyes are rolling in her head. She gasps for breath. Once, twice, three times. Then four. The fifth breath doesn't come.

COLIN: Gina?

A cop grabs Colin. Colin looks up. The fireworks explode.

FADE TO BLACK.

epilogue

That night, Colin gave his statement to the police, identified the stabber, and then was allowed to take the children home.

The next day, Susan Lynch had a local lawyer file a custody claim for Brianna on behalf of her great-grandparents in Dublin.

There was no way Colin was going to let the grannies raise Brianna.

Colin's lawyer, Brendan O'Dowd, said that they had a legitimate blood-relative claim. Colin asked if an American blood relative would supersede the claim of the grannies. O'Dowd said he thought the court would give preference to an American blood relative.

"Have you ever heard of a lawyer named Gene Barr?" asked Colin.

"I know of him," O'Dowd said. "He's a big Wall Street attorney."

"I think a DNA test would prove he's Brianna's biological grandfather," Colin said.

"Let's give Gene Barr a call," O'Dowd said.

When they met later that day, Barr clearly remembered Gina's visit to his house. He also remembered his fling with her mother all those years ago in Dublin. Colin described the life Brianna faced if she was sent back to the grannies in Ballytara.

"You'll raise her?" Barr asked.

"If you let me adopt her."

"It's the least I can do," Barr said.

The court gave immediate custody of Brianna to Gene Barr, who signed preliminary papers to award adoption to Colin.

The girl who killed Gina was from Staten Island. She was

charged with murder two but was already considering a plea to a negligent homicide charge, carrying seven to fifteen years.

During the week the authorities held Gina's body, Colin received his money from his *Death Dunes* script. With two kids to raise, Colin signed a quick contract with Linda Parks to do a half-dozen new music videos.

After the coroner's office released the body, Colin held a one-night wake in Lloyd's in Bayside before her body was returned to Dublin. Aside from Gene Barr, the Coynes, and Peggy Johnson, no one else attended.

The kids were home with Colin's father. Seamus had no conception of death, but Brianna kept asking if she could write letters to her mammy in heaven.

Just before 9:00 P.M., Colin knelt before Gina, who was dressed in the outfit she wore when she went to visit her father. Her fingers were covered in rings, and gold necklaces gleamed around her neck. *Her final shift,* Colin thought.

Colin looked down at her and touched her right hand, the one he'd grabbed that day when she'd picked his pocket in the Shelbourne hotel. The hand was cold and stiff but he lifted it and slipped his wallet underneath it.

"Time to shift," he said. "Crush on, a gra."

He stood, the undertaker closed the coffin, and Colin Coyne went home to his kids.

acknowledgments

Too little has been written about the world of Irish travelers but I'd like to acknowledge the invaluable research and information I gleaned from the following books: *Nan: The Life of an Irish Traveling Woman,* by Sharon Gmelch; *Traveller,* by Nan Joyce; *Irish Travellers: Culture and Ethnicity,* edited by May McCann, Seamus O'Siochain, and Joseph Ruane; and *The Irish: Portrait of a People,* by Richard O'Connor.

I'd also like to thank Patrick Farrelly and Liam Tiernan for their keen observations and Kate O'Callaghan for helping me locate some of the research.

Thanks to my editor, Mitchell Ivers, who traveled with me every inch of the way through the manuscript, steering me away from roadblocks, detours, and dead ends.

And, as always, thanks to my friend and agent, Esther Newberg, who made it happen.